THE KEY TO KELLS

A KEY MURPHY THRILLER
BOOK 1

KEVIN BARRY O'CONNOR

D1572460

First paperback edition October 2022

Title Production by The Book Whisperer

ISBN 979-8-9867131-1-3 (paperback)
ISBN 979-8-9867131-0-6 (ebook)

www.kevinbarryoconnor.com

For Lee Tracy

FOREWORD

The *Book of Kells* sits on display at Trinity College in Dublin, attracting over one million visitors per year to witness its beauty. Scholars consider it a medieval masterpiece and one of Ireland's greatest national treasures. Irish monks created "the *Book*" at the Columban monastery in Iona, Scotland in celebration of the Irish saint Columba, known in Ireland as Columbkille. This unfinished illustrated bible was moved to Kells, Ireland, for completion and to save it from Viking raiders. Vikings sacked the Iona monastery in 806. Two hundred years later, in 1006, this sacred artefact was stolen from the Kells monastery. The thieves removed the cover and several pages and later returned the *Book* by hiding it near the monastery. The cover and the pages have remained unfound, making it a dream of treasure seekers and those who would put their fingerprint on history by reuniting it with Ireland.

CHAPTER 1

November 6, 2019
Philadelphia

Dying tonight was not an option. Tomorrow, maybe, or the next day, who knows. But not tonight. The two guys that took me didn't know this yet. The one behind me in the van, his massive hand was around my throat. Each nervous movement of his fingers, the quickening beat of his pulse, the gathering of sweat on his palm, sent information to my brain. I could sense the drugs running through his fingers, him wanting desperately to squeeze the life out of me but urging himself to wait a few minutes so that he could properly beat me to death.

The driver was calm. Not a good sign since he was driving a stolen police vehicle. His gun rested in his left hand; his right was on the steering wheel. No drugs clouded his brain. The planner. The dangerous one. He was assessing me, figuring me out, calculating his options, deciding if he would kill me fast and get out of town or make it a more tasty and memorable meal.

They didn't know that they were part of the web that killed my best friend.

And they didn't care. But I knew, and I freaking made tonight happen.

The police had scouted the house for the past three days. They had fed me the photos of who was coming and going. Behind those doors sat the modern-day masters of bondage. They had started in Queens and cut a blood trail to Philly, their money flowing from fentanyl, heroin, and human trafficking.

Three squad cars pulled up behind us, a good thirty yards from the house. Even though I couldn't go in, I was instructed to wear a bullet-proof vest. I reached into the van for mine and handed one to Buck.

"I'm sorry, Key," Buck said to me while checking the clip on his Glock.

"It sucks, man. I need to see it for your little sister, our little sister."

Buck McCoy had been like my big brother my entire life. His Black family, my white family, inseparable. He was also the commanding officer.

"Become a low-paid grunt like me and you could go in and get your ass shot at. Until then …" Buck pointed to the passenger door and watched as I got in. He scanned the scene while the other detectives and cops readied themselves. He reached in and tapped my shoulder. "You made this happen. Thanks, little brother."

Buck had come to me the day before Tanya's funeral. He had found a newspaper in her room with a circle around an apartment listing. He asked if I knew she was planning to move. I hadn't.

I looked at that paper for hours, as if it was Tanya calling to me, her memory calling to me. And it was.

I had raced to the listed street, but the house number wasn't there. It didn't exist. An online search, same street number, same street name, gave me hundreds of locations, all across the country—all in classified newspaper ads. I built search parameters, and soon it was clear—the last four digits of the listed phone numbers were the keys to locations. An entire dealer network had gone offline and used Cold War-era communication tactics to schedule deliveries. It also provided places for users like Tanya to purchase drugs.

After I showed Buck, he brought me into the narcotics task force. I wasn't even a real cop, just a consultant, an advisor on loan from my family's business. I didn't carry a gun or a badge. But I did carry the ability to look at A and follow a path to Z. I was able to map out the locations of their operations and put them under surveillance.

Tonight's raid was one of six, plus two in Queens. I had found them. All of them. I was the quarterback, had the team on the one-yard line, sixty seconds to go, and I was benched.

I watched as the front door swung open against the battering ram. Shouting filled the air, but not gunfire. A good sign. The row houses on this block were in various stages of disrepair. A fresh can of paint probably hadn't been used on these homes in the last thirty years. This was the Badlands. Kensington. The working poor barely coexisting among dealers and addicts. Neighbors didn't look out of windows. They knew better.

I focused every fiber of my being on that house as I sat in the van. Movement caught my eye: two men running out of the alley toward the van. The driver's door flew open. My head snapped to the sound as a gun was pressed to my temple. A second man slid into the seat behind me. His massive hand jerked my head back. The key was in the ignition; the engine came to life. The jolt of tires screamed against the asphalt. They must have escaped the house in the confusion. Or they weren't in the house when it started? Didn't matter. I was going to die. Or I was going to live and make these assholes pay for what they did to Tanya.

As the van sped up, I slowed down and controlled my breathing, allowing my senses to take over.

Graffitied walls and trash-strewn streets slid into view before the van came to a hard stop in an empty lot. The neon lights of the River Casino and a few abandoned cars dotting the asphalt plain reminded me I was alone. The passenger door opened, and the giant from the back seat reached in and tossed me to the gravel. He smiled in joyous anticipation.

The driver circled the vehicle, his gun rising, pointing to my head, his finger closing on the trigger. He shook his dreadlocks and wiped the rain from his eyes.

"Yuh want this?" He looked at his friend.

Some men must be given birth by a bear. Nothing else could explain their size. He nodded to Dreadlocks, then motioned for me to get up. At six-three, I had around five inches on him. He had one hundred pounds of prison muscle on me. His fat was nothing but an outer moat, there to absorb any kinetic energy I could deliver. If I dropped him, I got shot. If I didn't drop him, I got beaten to death.

I rose and slowly backed away from him, my hands in a fist, egging him on, drawing him to me. Just enough for him to step between me and Dreadlocks. He pounded his right fist into his left palm and grinned, a one-toothed caricature of a jack-o'-lantern. And completely predictable.

"I hate cops," the giant slurred. White, with a greasy ponytail and New York accent, he moved quicker than someone his size should be able to. His right arm took a full swing. I dropped well below his punch, my left fist pile-driving into his nuts. His nostrils flared. His open mouth took big gulps of air. He reached for me with his right hand, his fingers extended, trying to take hold of my shirt, his left hand ready to pulverize my face. I grabbed his fingers and bent them toward his wrist, my left palm striking at the joint where the wrist met the arm. I could hear the snap.

His eyes rolled up as I yanked his broken arm, forcing his back to me. Now my shield from Dreadlock Man.

"I never liked dat fat piece a shit." Dreadlocks raised the gun and fired two shots into the giant.

The giant turned into dead weight, slipping from my grip. Dreadlocks' eyes danced over the dead man as a grin spread over his face.

"What you do now, bwoy?" He cocked his head to the right, his locks following. "Ya think you know me." He tapped his chest with his free hand. "I see it in your eyes."

The weight of the giant pressed against me, the smell of him seeped from my nose to my throat, my hands becoming slick with his blood. I fought to hold him up, my shield, but Dreadlocks' shoulder exploded. Cars and footsteps raced toward me. I got out from the tangle of the giant and moved toward the gunman as he fell to his knees.

A swirl of images ran through my brain.

I forced my eyes closed, then opened them. *A blade swept fast, inches from my throat.* I fell against the van to avoid it, the cold wet metal of the rear door pressing against my back. That blade was the same image I'd seen repeating over the last few months, fragmented pieces of something. I had pushed it away. I took a deep breath and tried to focus. It wasn't real. Then I heard agonizing screams. *People were running, falling, flailing, metal weapons flashing, impaling. Blood, lots of blood.* It was part vivid, part cloudy, but undeniably real.

This was not a daydream. I was viewing a memory. It was not one of mine. I didn't know how or why I knew this. I just knew. My legs began to give out. Something held me up.

A voice repeated, "I gotcha, Key. I gotcha."

"What the hell is happening?"

Buck's jaw pulled tight. His eyes were red. He gestured to Dreadlocks. "That asshole was about to shoot you. That's what's happening."

I looked at the dead hulking giant lying in his blood, then at the man who shot him. "How'd you find me?"

"GPS in every vehicle." Buck tapped the van then glanced around at the scene, another police car arriving. "We did a headcount in the house. There were supposed to be seven, but there were only five. I flew out the door." Buck cupped his hands on my shoulders. "You scared me, little brother. You okay?"

Two officers pulled the handcuffed gunman to his feet. He glared at me.

"I'll be coming for yuh, bwoy."

I had a fleeting impulse to hurt him, but my feet felt anchored to the ground. Buck walked to him and leaned into his face.

"I want you rotting." Buck's right hand formed a fist which he clenched so hard it shook. "That's the only reason you're still alive."

"Not afraid of yuh or the white boy. Nuh sleep well, nuh rest well," his eyes fixed on me as if he was in a shamanic trance. "When we want you dead, you'll be dead."

Raindrops slowly trickled, falling from his brow. The blood on his shoulder screamed loud and painful, yet he did not falter, his gaze on me as if the trajectory of my days lay clear in his vision.

Buck turned his attention back on me. "You did good. It's finished. Tanya can rest in peace."

The roar of cars and trucks raced up the nearby I-95. *The smell of cinnamon mixed with a heady scent of peat moss. The flavor of tangy grapes swirled my tongue. I closed my eyes and saw faces that lurked in the shadows.*

Tanya wasn't resting in peace, not yet. Neither would I.

Nothing felt finished.

CHAPTER 2

I 've heard it said that there is nothing like a near-death experience to clarify things, to bring your life's purpose into focus. Not for me. Since the raid two weeks ago, everything in my brain was jumbled. Faces appeared. Unfamiliar accents bounced around in my head. The worst part was the screaming and the haunting smell of burning wood and flesh. It might last for three seconds, twenty seconds, two minutes. I had no control over any of it. Not a great way to go about your day.

I was on a one-year consulting contract with the police. Buck had told me that I was being considered for a permanent hire. As a result, they wanted to make sure I wasn't damaged goods, so I sat through debriefs with detectives and sessions with psychologists.

I hadn't wanted to be a cop; it wasn't my desire. I had lived vicariously through Buck's crazy-assed life. But damn, when we busted the drug ring, it lit me up. I wasn't just good at it. I was great. Being great was an addiction that just being good could never cure. When that piece of you goes away, the cravings hit you hard.

And everything I'd ever been great at eventually disappeared.

The department shrink diagnosed me with mild PTSD. He told me that almost being shot can have that effect. I wanted to tell him that he didn't know the half of it. I didn't need the job and wasn't sure I wanted it, but I kept my lips from moving. He told me to take two weeks off. This was day one.

I booked an afternoon session at the martial arts studio owned by my friend Enrico Fuentes. He'd trained some of the best MMA fighters in the world. I taught the Israeli martial art Krav Maga to his students once a month. In exchange, he punished me.

"Rico, I'm full of piss and vinegar, toxins and testosterone. Take no mercy on me."

He gave me a sideways glance. "Careful what you wish for, hermano."

Rico was the master of endurance training. He shoved a jump rope into my hands. "What the hell are you standing there for? You know the fucking drill." He hit the timer. "So drill."

The drill was three minutes of jump rope, followed by bag kicks, then punch drills with ten-pound dumbbells in my hands, thirty seconds of recovery, then repeat six times. When the clock hit seven minutes, I put my hands on my knees and sucked in air.

"No breaks. Repeat the drill, five more to go, punk ass." He folded his arms. When I picked up the dumbbells for the punch drills, he stood an inch from my fists. "By the way, you punch like a sissy. Put some power behind it."

By round six I was ready to puke. And then the hard work began. I put on my gloves, footpads, and headgear, then Rico launched all-out assaults until I considered that death might have been a better alternative. He took out my legs with a sweep so low and fast I didn't see it coming. The timer rang. I pushed up on my elbows. "That's it? That's all you got?"

Rico smiled and reached down to help me to my feet. "You should quit this and take up knitting. You'd be better at that, amigo."

I threw my arm around his neck in a pretend headlock. "Maybe you should teach me how to knit. You'd be better at that."

I headed into the locker room. Got in the shower, turned up the heat as hot as I could stand it. The quivering in my muscles calmed. Then I made it as cold as possible.

Exhilarated, I walked on sore legs to McGillin's Ale House to watch the Sixers game with Buck and some cop friends. Unsurprisingly, they greeted me with Philly cop charm.

"Here comes Catatonic Key."

"Here's the Key to the nuthouse."

"Ginger snapped." My reddish hair, making a star turn in the cop comment section.

I gave them the finger.

"Just call me Defective Murphy," I said while pulling the chair out.

Before I could sit, Buck took me by the arm to a quiet corner of the bar.

"I'm worried about you. Talk to me." At thirty-six, Buck was six years older and a million times more experienced than me.

"I really don't know. It's like I slipped into a real-life daydream. It keeps happening, and it's messing me up." I had told Buck that this had started before the night of the raid.

"Let me guess: shrink said PTSD?" Buck shook his head. "That's his answer to everything. I don't want to ask you this, but I have to." A Dropkick Murphys song came on. The crowd responded by drumming their tables to the beat. Buck ignored the interruption. "We're around some crazy-ass drugs. Have you used any?"

I had one inch on him. He looked up with that Buck stare, like he could search your soul and mind, giving you nowhere to hide. I felt myself flinch.

"Damn, Buck, you know better than that."

He rocked back like he'd taken his best shot but had missed. Buck had been in my life since I could remember life. Our dads served in 'Nam together. Buck's dad saved my father's life there. Both were Philly boys. My dad, Shaun Murphy, was first-generation Irish. Buck's dad, Brian McCoy, came from a line of military men since the Civil War, escaped slaves aching to fight back. To me, Buck's dad had always been Uncle Brian, which garnered strange looks when I introduced him that way.

We turned as someone came down the stairs, and moved off the landing to let them by.

"You sure are acting like it. You know I have experience with bipolar disorder. It messed up Tanya. Just saying, you've had all these times when you go all Einstein, you get the prodigy thing going and then boom, gone. Can mess you up."

I steadied myself against the wall at his words. "It can. But I'm fine."

"You're not. Could be the shrink is right. You almost got killed that night." Buck tapped his knuckles on his chin and drew in a deep breath. Photos from Philly and Ireland lined the walls, sports figures next to revolutionaries, an homage to the weird and wonderful.

Buck put his hand on my shoulder.

"The other day, you were looking right at me and saying *Thomas*, or *Tomash*, or some damn thing, over and over. Do you remember that?"

It was like a punch to the solar plexus, knocking the wind out of me. Pieces of the memory rushed in. I saw a distorted face, young, familiar, staring into my eyes, daring me to reach out and touch him. I heard him say his name. Tomás.

"I gotta go, need to deal with this."

As I turned to leave, he pulled me back. There was sadness in his face, a loneliness.

"It's scaring me." I gave him a brotherly love-tap to his chest. Just something we do. "Let me go deal with this. I'll call you."

Buck held on to my shoulder a moment longer.

"You don't do this by yourself. Twenty-four seven, whatever you need."

The bar erupted with cheers and claps, everyone staring at the TV as the Sixers landed a three-pointer.

"What I need is time." I tilted in toward Buck, the name Tomás roiling through me. "This is freaking me out, but I'm not crazy. I'm going to do what I do best and figure it out."

"You do that. But hurry the hell up. We need your white Irish ass at the station. I don't want to put all the bad guys away by myself." He smiled.

————

I lived three blocks away. Walking fast, wanting to be alone with my thoughts, I turned right on Thirteenth Street. This was the heart of Midtown Village, one of the busiest restaurant districts in the city. Most of the narrow sidewalks were bustling with outdoor diners huddling under heat lamps. I brushed past them, unlocked the street-level door, took the stairs three at a time to my third-floor apartment, and dropped onto the couch.

I closed my eyes as the face I had seen earlier floated into murky view. Red hair, twenty, twenty-five years old. He faded, his hand reaching out to me as he did. The other images I had seen for the past weeks replaced him. They increased in speed as if someone tossed black and white photos in front of me so fast that no image was clear. The photos disappeared. A man stood before me, clothed in a brown cassock. He turned to me as I approached.

"Brendan, be on alert. There has been word of sightings," I said.

"And you must relax. We are in God's hands," Brendan replied with his usual smile. "You burden yourself too much. Go to the village and enjoy the view of the redheads and blondes. That's how God makes you smile—just keep your robes on." He winked and waved me on.

I was envious of his ease. Most of the monks seemed to have it. I wore the same garb, my head was shaved at the top as was theirs, but I had none of their easy spirit. They were at this monastery to pray. I was here to protect. And yes, a walk to the village and the sighting of one particular blonde, Siobhán, was my preferred form of prayer.

I thought about her as I walked through the farm toward the village. I waved at Brother Patrick as he and his mule plowed the earth. Grains for our bread were his calling. Children played on the hillside, chasing the sheep and laughing. I walked on, the breeze gentle, the smell of the ocean carried with it.

A scream caused me to stop. The children had frozen on the hillside, one pointing frantically toward the village. A barbarian leaped the stone wall and took an axe to the head of Brother Gregory. Every muscle in my body screamed to have my sword in my hand and to slam it into this heathen's heart. But I was here for one reason. I ran to the monastery. The screams of women and children reached my ears, and the smell of smoke penetrated my nose.

I needed to get to the tunnel.

Racing across the courtyard to the scriptorium, I found my accomplices preparing the escape. They looked at me and nodded. Donal folded his hands together for a brief prayer.

"The Book?"

Tomás nodded to the wooden box on the table. He slid it into a satchel and secured it around his shoulder.

Kneeling on the floor in front of the wooden inlaid cross, the width of a man, I inserted the slim key into the bottom edge. I had created an intricate design in the flooring to make the slot invisible. As the key took, I lifted the panel to reveal the ladder. The four of us descended and lit a torch that awaited us, just as we had practiced dozens of times. I secured the floor in place above me and joined them.

I stepped behind the ladder to the earthen wall and, with practiced fingers, applied pressure until the hinges took over, and the four of us entered the escape tunnel. Tomás went first with the torch. We uttered no words. We made no sound. I knew this day would come. I was a warrior from a long line of warriors. My brother monks loved God. It was my job to make certain they did not meet him too soon.

There was a vital task to complete. I pledged to my God and my King that we would complete it. Rumors that the barbaric Norsemen would soon return had traveled to this remote monastic village. They had been here before, leaving only death and destruction behind.

As I secured the wall in place, the bloodlust cries of men above us and the crashing of axes against wood rang in my ears. The scriptorium was nothing but loot to them. When they finished, it would burn.

I viewed in my mind every step of our escape. The Book was God's work. His words and years of the monks' painstaking devotion lay on these pages. It would take more years to complete. I knew that I might not live to see that day, but now God had entrusted us to safeguard it on its perilous journey from our monastery in Scotland to our brothers awaiting us in Ireland. With our guidance, they would finish The Book at the new monastery in Kells, far from the reaches of the Norsemen.

If the barbarians don't kill us first.

• • •

I pushed off the couch as the movie in my mind played on. I couldn't stop it. I was growing used to the fragments, but this was as real and visceral as any other experience in my life.

I grabbed my pen and found my notebook next to the coffeemaker. I read my notes. Not much there: axes, swords, a face, smells, accents. I added the *Book*, Brendan, Siobhán, monastery, tunnel. And I shook at the memory of a monk being bludgeoned by an axe.

My cell phone rang.

"Shit."

My dad had left several messages I hadn't returned. He was probably pissed or worried, or both.

"Dad," I said into the phone.

"Key, we've been trying to reach you."

"Sorry, I've been—"

"I talked to Buck. I called him when I couldn't reach you. He told me what's going on."

"Buck doesn't know what's going on. Hell, I don't know what's going on." I looked at my notes, and the image of that face swept before my eyes. "Dad, are you there?"

"I know what's happening to you." His labored breathing unsettled me. "I can explain it to you," he finished.

"What?" I dropped my pen on the table and stood. "What do you mean?"

My heart raced at his silence.

"Dad?"

"I know this will sound crazy. I can tell you about Tomás."

CHAPTER 3

November 20, 2019
Delancey Place, Philadelphia

Mom greeted me with her trademark enthusiastic hug. At fifty-nine, she remained a natural blonde with only a hint of gray, barely a wrinkle, and a young woman's figure. Dad entered the foyer looking like he carried the weight of the world. Four years older than my mom, his gray was winning the battle. He looked at me and turned to the living room without a word. I followed.

"You have succeeded in completely freaking me out. What were you talking about?"

My eyes caught several framed photos that I didn't remember seeing before. One was of me, maybe age nine or ten, at an archeological site with my mother. She was a music archaeologist.

"I just hung them around a week ago," she said, responding to my gaze.

Dad sat in the chair, and I took the couch where Mom joined me. My father fidgeted, his fingers rubbing the arms of his chair. My mom was on the edge of her seat.

"What I am about to tell you will sound impossible, I know. But I've been through this," my father said.

"Through what? What are you talking about?"

He looked away, rubbed his knees, and turned back to me.

"When I was seventeen, I experienced the memories of another person. I thought I was having a mental breakdown. My grandfather recognized what was happening and explained that, although he did not understand how, several generations of our family had experienced memories. I've since learned that we have a genetic mutation that somehow allows us to experience the memories of an ancestor."

I laughed nervously. "You are kidding, right?"

Dad picked up a remote from the armrest and clicked a button. I appeared on the screen—my fifth birthday party. I was jumping around like a little madman. Mom must have been holding the video camera, and I said to her, "Mommy, is Tomás coming to my party?"

"Who is Tomás, honey?" she asked.

"My friend, Mommy. You know, the one with the funny clothes and the funny hair."

On the couch next to me, Mom took my hand, seeming to sense I was ready to burst.

"Someone better explain this to me, fast."

"First, you aren't crazy," Dad said as he paused the video.

"There was no need to tell you about this. You were just a kid. After you turned six, you never asked about Tomás again. It wasn't until Buck told us that we realized the memories were back," Mom added.

"Wait, hold on. Are you telling me I'm experiencing the memory of an actual ancestor?"

"Yes." My father let that settle. "But it's not actually happening to you. You're a passive observer."

He leaned forward, reached across to me, and put his hand on mine.

"I have much more to tell you, but now I need you to tell me what you experienced."

I didn't move or say a word. The voices of people, laughing and talking, sifted through the windows as they walked past the house. The heat kicked on as the November chill settled on the night. My five-year-old self was frozen on the screen. The old photo hung so perfectly straight on the wall.

My eyes grew heavy as I tasted the ocean air, felt the longing for the blonde woman, and braced at the horror of an axe crushing the monk's skull. I recounted every moment to my parents.

The deep relief I felt almost stole my breath. Maybe I wasn't falling apart.

CHAPTER 4

Padraig Collins would never be happy with the way he looked. He couldn't be. His was the curse of an unsettled soul.

From the House of Caraceni in Milan, his bespoke suit draped his trim body, forged hard by a fire inside that demanded discipline. His handmade Italian leather shoes accentuated the gray suit. By any measure, he looked the pinnacle of elegance and power.

At sixty-one, he was a long way from his days of poverty in Derry. A long way from the sixteen-year-old who worked his way up in the Irish Republican Army to become one of its fiercest commanders. Now, Padraig Collins was one of the wealthiest men in Europe.

He stood over his desk. Under the glass protector lay a shard of paper. The paper was enveloped in a special laminate to protect the fifteen-hundred-year-old vellum. It read, "adoremus sanctum nomen eius," and was written by the hand of his patron saint, Columba. He kissed his fingers, placed them over the paper, closed his eyes, and quietly prayed.

"The time of my absolution is at hand. Lift me so that I may not fail."

Collins's eyes opened as his secretary opened the door to his office and stepped aside so his guest could enter.

"Joseph, it's good to see you again."

Padraig Collins and Joseph Murphy had met one week prior at a private dinner that Joseph hosted for potential investors. From one of the wealthiest families in Jamaica, the company he chaired, Futuro Biologics, was shaking up the world of genetic testing and gene editing. Still, Joseph, twenty-one years younger and five inches taller, held his tension in his jaw and shoulders as if approaching a feral cat that might bite or claw.

"Padraig, thanks for inviting me." They shook hands, and Joseph seemed relieved to remove it from Padraig's vigorous grip. "Are you in New York for long?"

"No, I leave for Dublin on Wednesday. And you?"

"I have several meetings in California, then back home to Jamaica."

Collins sat and gestured to the chair across from him. Joseph followed.

"To what do I owe this invitation?"

"We are both busy men. I'll get right to the point. I understand that Mack Murphy is your great-great-grandfather?"

Joseph was leaning forward but sat back; his jaw tightened further.

"I did not see that coming. Why do you ask?"

"Mack remains a legend in Irish patriotic circles. There is a rumor that he left clues for your family where to find the missing part of the *Book of Kells*."

His fingers splayed. His lips pulled tight against his mouth. "I'm confused. You said you wanted to see me about a business proposition. I don't understand why you're asking me about these things. They're private family matters."

Collins leaned forward.

"This is about business. If the rumors are true, then you have what I want. And I have what you want."

"What is it you presume I want?" Murphy asked with an edge.

Collins spread his hands toward his guest, like a father addressing his wayward child. "I don't presume anything, Joseph. I know what you want."

Murphy shook his head before gesturing to continue.

"You want to control your own empire, not just manage your family's wealth. You are a man of means, but you're far more ambitious than the others in your family. You dream of your empire. I can help you get it."

Joseph stood and walked to the window. Central Park stretched out below on an early Spring Day. "What do I have that you want?" he asked firmly.

Collins responded softly, reverentially. "If your family found The Book, is it true that you would return it to Ireland?"

Joseph continued to stare quietly at Central Park, where Collins knew the John Lennon memorial was likely visible.

"I don't know what you think you know, but it's all fantasy. Why are you wasting your time with this?"

"Humor me. If your family found it?"

"Yes, it was my father's dream."

"Good. You cannot imagine what that would mean to Ireland." He gently cleared his throat. "It's also rumored that on one of the pages there are clues to finding a hidden treasure. I want the treasure. And for that, I will help you build your empire."

Murphy intertwined his fingers and rested them under his chin for a moment. "My father wasted years of his life on this bullshit. Are you telling me you believe it exists?"

"It doesn't matter what I believe. It only matters that you find it." Collins put his hands on his knees. "We know the *Book of Kells* was stolen and returned with the cover and some pages removed. That's a historical fact. I know Mack took it from Ireland to the US. If you can find it, and if there are clues as to where the treasure was hidden, then it's possible. All I want right now is the possibility."

Joseph folded his arms and looked straight into Collins's eyes.

"How do you know these things? Mack's information has been a family secret for generations."

"Joseph, I own several IT data mining companies. I assure you that there are no secrets anymore." Collins let the words permeate. He measured the discomfort they brought, the accusations implied. "What do you know about me?"

Joseph swallowed hard. He took his time answering, his hands uneasy, fingers interlacing and flexing. "I know what's published about your wealth. A billionaire—congratulations. And that you have a vast real estate and IT empire. I know very few details, so I'm at a disadvantage."

Collins got to his feet and walked to his office door. Joseph watched his every step. Without malice or anger, Collins said, "You should leave."

"Excuse me?"

"You heard me."

Joseph Murphy felt glued to his seat; no one ever told him to leave.

Collins stood firm. "I've had my team analyze your offer and look into every corner of Futuro, but you walk in here without having done your homework. How dare you disrespect me or your own business."

Joseph's neck strained, his jaw jutting outward. "With all due respect, you are talking to me as if I am a child. I meant no disrespect. None."

Collins kept his eyes squarely on Joseph. "Before you were

born, I was a commander in the Irish Republican Army. By the time you were a one-year-old, I had executed two people personally. Have you ever killed someone?"

Joseph's lip trembled at this, but he looked away. Collins regained a fatherly demeanor.

"I've never held a gun," he finally responded.

"Good. It's a terrible burden. It eats at my soul." Collins stepped to a liquor trolley. He poured two drinks. "No matter how much I justified it as being the cost of war, I couldn't see continuing that way." He handed a glass to Murphy. "This is a twenty-year-old single malt. I shouldn't admit this. I like Scotch better than Irish whiskey."

They both sipped the drink, Joseph's lips puckering.

"I found another way to exact an even more terrible cost on the Brits and the Unionists," Collins continued after swallowing. "We damaged their economic lifeline. We hijacked delivery trucks to their butchers' shops; we stole their shoes, clothes, toilet paper, laundry detergent—the basics that most Catholics could not enjoy. That's where we hit them."

Collins walked to his desk and ran his fingers over the relic of his saint. "To do that," he continued, "I needed to know when shipments were happening, where they were going. I developed a network of informants. We watched the ports, infiltrated the warehouses, moms pushing baby carriages past stores, noting the times of delivery. I wasn't just good at it; I was the best. We put away the bombs and killed them with information."

He returned to the cart to refill his glass and held up the bottle as an offer. Joseph shook his head. Collins poured his own, then raised his glass.

"You have an MBA from Harvard. I don't have a high school degree. What I do have is a degree in guerilla and information warfare. I can tell you things about you that you believe to be secret."

Joseph looked like his world fell away, as if he sensed and

smelled and tasted the fear of something bitter and buried rising to the surface. He drank the remaining Scotch, recoiled a bit, and, changing his mind, held it out for another pour.

"I have made myself extremely familiar with Dr. Garcia's research and the patents you are filing. Do you believe you'll be ready for an IPO in a year?" Collins refilled Joseph's glass, the amber liquid as brilliant as gold.

"Approximately."

"I disagree. You need two years, minimum, to raise the value." Collins returned the bottle to the cart. Joseph started to respond, but his host held up his hand.

Collins took his seat and leaned toward Joseph. "You believe the IPO would start at fifteen dollars per share. Follow my plan and we push it to thirty or forty. I will provide the resources that you'll need to become fabulously wealthy." Collins tilted his glass toward Murphy. "I'll own a fair share of the company. If you bring me the treasure, I will take less. Don't, and you'll own less."

"What the hell? Why would I do that?" Joseph stood abruptly.

"You're trying to raise one hundred and twenty-five-million. It's not enough. You need two hundred million. I'll provide the entire investment and the governmental influence that you need to fast track patents and FDA approvals."

Joseph Murphy looked at the older man, waiting for more.

Collins moved to within inches of his guest. He had to look up. His neck was all sinew and muscle, his face taut and fierce.

"And just so we're clear, I grew up in poverty. You, Joseph, never had to fight for a penny. With one exception. On your eighteenth birthday, at a party with friends in the Blue Mountains of Jamaica, you got into a drunken brawl. There were three of you. You had gone into the woods, drinking some very strong rum when the fight broke out. You were carrying a gun, and when the other guy got the best of you, you shot him. You and your other friend framed a local man. The boy you killed, his father became Prime Minister. He would be very unhappy with you, Joseph Murphy, who never held a gun."

Collins locked eyes with Joseph, who turned away. "Hopefully, you realize that you should never lie to me again. Am I clear?"

Joseph nodded. His shoulders sank into his body as he sat and looked toward the door.

"Good." Collins smiled, putting his hand on Joseph's shoulder." Now, let's discuss Futuro's genetic discovery."

CHAPTER 5

November 20, 2019

Delancey Place, Philadelphia

As I finished recounting the memory, my father's hands trembled. He stood, stepped to the liquor cabinet, and poured two glasses of Young Dubs Irish Whiskey, a brand he helped bring to the States. He handed me one.

"Did you hear anyone say his name?"

"Whose name?"

"The one from whom you see the memories." He tilted the glass and swallowed his remaining whiskey.

"No, I don't think so. Why?"

"His name is Aedan."

"How can you possibly know that?" I downed my whiskey in one shot and got a refill. I filled Dad's empty glass too.

"I see through the eyes of Conall, one of his line. Conall tells the tale of Aedan, the great warrior monk who saved the *Book of Kells*."

I put both hands up and shook my head.

Mom put her hand on my shoulder. "I know this is overwhelming. Let's take a break. I'm going to put some food out. Fifteen minutes."

I stood. My five-year-old self was staring at me from the TV screen. I felt frozen in place but needed to get out of there.

"I'm taking a walk, back soon."

When I opened the door, I half expected to enter a tunnel with Tomás in front of me. He wasn't there. I wished he was. I had so many questions for him.

I forced my feet forward and walked around the corner into Rittenhouse Square, an oasis in the city, shared by the well-off, the pot smokers that harmlessly dotted the park, and an alarming number of people in an opioid stupor. Enormously expensive high-rise apartment buildings surrounded the square, like sentinels for the wealthy. Oddballs and CEOs walked their dogs. It remained one of my favorite places in the city to people-watch.

The night was cool but not cold; Thanksgiving only eight days away. I strolled for a few minutes, thinking of the many times Tanya and I had hung out here. Our families took us here for the Christmas tree lighting when we were kids. I missed her tremendously. She had saved me when I was going down into a dark place. She wouldn't let me save her, though. I still wanted to scream at her.

An empty bench faced northeast. I sat and stared at the lights of the Philly skyline in full glory. The park was buzzing with people, buskers singing for tips, strings of bright snowflakes lit the walkways throughout. I had lost my balance on a thousand-foot-high cliff and the only thing to grab onto was my parents. They'd guided me through all of those episodes I had as a kid. I was a freak of nature, lauded as a genius one year, learning-challenged the next, then a genius again. I learned to expect it, navigate it, even look forward to what strange skill I might have the next time. But this was different.

Whatever this was, I knew I had crossed a line and there

was no return. Nothing would be the same. Living in my own head was difficult enough sometimes. And now someone else was there.

An autumn breeze blew as a Starbucks cup brushed against my shoe. Two dogs greeted each other by nose as their owners chatted. A woman walked through the park, conversing loudly with no one, but I knew that it all made sense to her. Ordinary life surrounded me, smacking up against the reality that my father had also been a freak of nature. Yet he'd never told me.

I needed to hear his story.

As I returned to the house, Van Morrison sang the opening lines of "Astral Weeks". I found my parents sitting at the dining-room table, and I walked behind Dad, put my hands on his shoulders and gave a light squeeze like he'd done to me a million times.

"Tell me."

Mom patted the chair next to her.

She waved her hands over the kebabs and salads she'd prepared. "Sit, eat. It's time for your father to do the talking. Do you want a beer, wine?"

"What beers do you have?" I asked.

"We have Guinness and Yards." Dad started to get up, but Mom gestured for him to sit. "I'll get it. Start talking, Shaun."

"Thanks, Mom. I'll have Yards."

I filled my plate and took a bite of the kebab wrapped in warm pita bread. Some of the juice settled on my chin. Dad's demeanor changed from pensive to excited. Van still played softly in the background as my dad took a long pull of Guinness and began.

"The first part will be strange, talking to my narc cop son. I was experimenting with pot for the first time. That night, I'd smoked something powerful." He gave me an embarrassed look.

"I wish you hadn't confessed. Now I have to bust you." He laughed and looked relieved by my sarcasm.

"That night, I had these intense visions of Conall and his brother," he continued. "I thought it was the pot, so I stopped smoking. But it continued, just three-second images flashing in my brain. Is that how it started with you?"

I nodded.

"Before long, it became crystal clear: I was seeing the world through Conall, and I was certain I was losing my mind. One day at Mass with my parents and grandfather, all hell broke loose. The priest was giving his sermon and my thoughts drifted off. I started breathing heavily. I, meaning Conall, was with Deaglan, who I soon realized was his brother, and we were running for our lives. Their lives. A man with a sword was hunting them down. The large, bearded man closed the gap and readied his weapon, screaming, 'It is time for you go to hell for what you have done.'"

He closed his eyes and took a deep breath before continuing.

"The sword rose and aimed for Conall. Deaglan pulled a knife from his belt and spun quickly behind the giant. He slashed the hamstring on his left leg. Conall quickly leaped to the side as the swordsman dropped to his knees. Deaglan grabbed his hair, yanked his head back, placed the sharp blade against his throat. Conall yelled, 'No, don't kill him.'"

"I remember the answer so clearly," my father recounted. "'Brother, he's the only one who knows it was us.'"

"I watched as Deaglan sliced and blood spouted from his throat. I started coming out of this trance, shaking, mumbling, my mother asking me what was wrong. I couldn't sit there. I ran from the church and kept going for several blocks. My father finally caught up with me and hugged me tightly. As far as I was concerned, I had just witnessed a murder. That's how my nervous system was responding."

If anyone else told me this story, I would think they were bat-shit crazy.

"Who is the one I'm experiencing? Aedan? Who is he? When did this take place?"

Mom added some salad to her plate and speared a kebab chunk. "The historical record shows that Vikings raided the abbey in Iona, Scotland in 806. Sixty-eight monks were slaughtered. According to your account, Aedan moved The Book the day of the raid."

I shook my head, clearing the memory of the claustrophobic feeling in the narrow tunnel and the thick smell of dung and dirt. "I don't know what to say. It makes no sense."

"It's challenging to accept, I know," my father added.

I forced a smile and rubbed the back of my neck, trying to work the kinks out.

"Conall and Deaglan, who are they again?"

"They are brothers, descendants of Aedan," Mom answered.

"The reason they were running," Dad offered, "they had stolen the *Book* and several pages. They believed Aedan made clues on those pages."

I pushed the salad around on my plate.

"Clues to what?"

" He'd hidden a treasure that he'd brought with him to Ireland from the monastery in Scotland," Mom joined in. "To protect it from the Vikings."

"As far as I can tell, they were never able to decipher the clues." Dad leaned across the table, his eyes looking toward me, unfocused. I sensed his mind was seeing something else. "It's possible that you will witness him writing the clues."

I felt disconcerted by his hopeful stare.

"Okay, so what?" I asked.

"It's believed that what he hid contains precious artefacts. The value to Ireland would be immeasurable."

"You are messing with me, right? I go from telling you

about this—what? 'episode'—to finding out that we have some time-travel freaking gene, and now you think we might go treasure hunting?"

"You're right, Key," Mom added. "Too much, too fast. Shaun. You've had forty-plus years to deal with this." She turned to Dad then back to me. "Honey, this is real. You need some time to absorb it."

I put my hands up in surrender.

"I'm going home."

I turned to my mother for a hug. You couldn't leave her house without one. It simply was not possible.

"Come back in the morning," she said, not quick to let go. "I have letters from your great-grandfather. They'll shed a lot of light." She kissed my cheek and brushed my hair, welcoming me back into her little circle of genetic conspirators.

As I turned to my father to say goodnight, he pulled me in for a long embrace, not our typical goodbye. When finished, he moved back a bit, his hands still on my shoulders, his eyes moist with a thousand questions in them.

———

My mind swirled with thoughts of Aedan, Conall, and Deaglan. I walked on autopilot, trying to make some sense of today's revelations. When I heard my name, my adrenaline hit my insides like a firehose and I spun around defensively, ready to kick the shit out of someone. Buck stepped out of the shadows.

"What the hell." I put my hand over my pounding heart. "What are you doing here?"

"When you were at the park earlier, Kelsey was shadowing a few perps there. She saw you and suspected that two guys were watching you. When you left, they pursued. She called me."

"Did you approach them?"

"They were gone by the time I got here. I want you to walk home on Walnut and turn right on Thirteenth Street. I have the team in place to follow you. Text me when you get home. Go," answered Buck.

I turned toward Walnut and said out loud, "What a fucking day!"

CHAPTER 6

Buck texted me: *Same two from the park are following. Go to Pine and wait for my text. I don't want them to see where you live.*

After I made it home, I unlocked my gun safe and put my pistol on my desk. I don't carry a police service revolver, but I am licensed. And I'm a good shot. Buck would deal with the people following me, so I pushed them out of my mind. I sat at my computer and looked up the *Book of Kells*. I knew a bit about it and had seen it in Dublin when I was around fifteen.

But I took a quick refresher course on Wikipedia:

The *Book of Kells*, sometimes known as the *Book of Columba*, was an illuminated manuscript Gospel book in Latin, containing the four Gospels of the New Testament together with various prefatory texts and tables. It was created in a Columban monastery around c. 800 AD, a masterwork of Western calligraphy, representing the pinnacle of Insular illumination. It was also widely regarded as Ireland's finest national treasure.

I scanned the pages and found what I was looking for:

Kells Abbey was plundered and pillaged by Vikings many times in the ninth century, and how the *Book* survived is not known. The earliest historical reference to the *Book*, and to the *Book*'s presence at Kells, could be found in a 1007 entry in the *Annals of Ulster*, which recorded that "the great Gospel of Columbkille, (Columba) the chief relic of the Western World, was wickedly stolen during the night from the western sacristy of the great stone church at Cenannas on account of its wrought shrine." The manuscript was recovered a few months later—minus its golden and bejeweled cover, "under a sod".

Conall and Deaglan, my ancestors: thieves and murderers. Nice. I tried to remember the details of what I had viewed in the memory of Aedan. He'd asked about *The Book*, and Tomás had gestured to it. I recalled that it was in a wooden box with no markings on it. Everything happened so fast in their escape. I pictured a tunnel so small and narrow that my muscles tightened thinking about it. I note three people ahead of Aedan, moving slowly but purposefully through the tunnel. That was where the memory ended.

I read some more, but the words bounced from here to there; the chill of wet, cold earth made me shiver. Odors of sea and clay penetrated my nostrils. I felt light-headed and images churned: the giant pounding his fist while the dreadlocked gunman sneered; the pleasure of watching me die was alive in his eyes as he chased me through the tunnel. I dropped to my knees and looked at Tomás.

"Aedan," Tomás said, "I will carry the Book.*" He moved so that I could get around him.*

"Brendan, Tomás, gather the supplies. Donal and I will ready the boat. I will check to make certain there is no one to see us."

I take my sword in hand. "Donal, wait at the entrance. I will signal you."

I had designed the tunnel to open at this small alcove. Rock walls cradled the tiny beach, all but hiding the tunnel. Stunted trees bowed toward the water and the sun. A natural shelf on the eastern wall was just large enough to conceal the currach. Fighting and screaming echoed in the distance, but there was no sign of the savages near us. I wished there was at least one stray for me to kill.

Donal emerged at the signal, and we pulled the currach to the water. Brendan and Tomás loaded the supplies. Tomás went back into the tunnel and returned with the satchel containing the wooden box, held protectively to his chest. Without a sound, we took up oars and, with practiced arms, rowed silently across the channel, the ocean spray on my face reminding me of the long journey that lay ahead.

We were exposed to the enemy on open water for the twenty-minute crossing to Mull. I had hidden the larger seafaring vessel there. Please, God, that it will take us safely to Ireland.

Tomás and Donal moved the supplies from our small craft to the larger boat. The moon was but a few days old, yet we dared not light a torch. We moved slowly and carefully, noting that the beach and the water seemed as one on the almost moonless night.

Brendan followed me along the dark path. A tall tree stood against the night sky. Its needle-covered branches pointed upward as if to say, "Behold the stars." I felt for the tree trunk, its sap sticky on my hands. When I stepped behind it, my foot searched for the pit in the dark. Finding it, I flung away the branches.

"Brendan, here." We leaned over the pit. "It's not heavy. But blinded by the dark, it is safer if the two of us carry it."

Joining the others at the beach, I opened the chest. We dropped to our knees.

"Tomás, lead us in prayer that God would protect the treasure of Saint Columba."

My brothers in Christ secured the treasure on the boat. I stood at the water's edge, looking across the channel to Iona, the sky red with *the remains of the fire. The faces of the monks, most certainly dead, danced ghost-like across my eyes. I had failed them, my shame everlasting. But my King, my kinsman, demanded only one thing; protect the treasure.*

I demanded one other. "Siobhán, please have followed my plan, every step as I instructed," I whispered. "If you have, I will see you before first light."

I returned to the currach and viewed the shapes of my fellow travelers, wrapping blankets around themselves, protection from the cruelty of our witness today, prayerful for lost souls. "Rest well," I offered, "we will need our strength for the crossing."

My eyes opened. It was already morning. I scrambled for a pen and paper to take notes. My mother had said she had information from my great-grandfather, but I strained to remember his name as I put on the coffee and took a shower.

My phone buzzed with a text from my mother. *Bring your passport, I want to check an entry date.* Strange request.

I finally raced down the steps, eager to get to my parents' house twelve minutes away. I froze when I hit the sidewalk, remembering the possibility of being followed.

I headed up Drury Street, a one-block stretch that looked more like a back alley. Dumpsters dotted most of the small street, McGillin's Ale House on the corner. It would expose anyone trying to follow. Nothing. I hurried up Locust Street, lost in my revelations. As I passed the display window of the violin repair shop, I stopped short. There, in clear reflection, was a familiar face. I tried to remain calm. He drew closer, and I turned to confront him. But Tomás vanished.

I attributed my delusion to stress and found I wanted the comfort of more coffee and my parents' knowledge. Getting to their house, I found them sitting at the kitchen counter, not so different from how I left them, though now they had coffee in hand. The aroma of coffee and the smell of scones baking in the oven stirred a feeling of warmth. I poured one for myself and relayed the memory from Aedan.

"Who is Siobhán?" I asked, another Irish name difficult to pronounce. It's pronounced Shiv-awn. My name, Cián, is pronounced Kee-an, but everyone just called me Key in grade school, and it stuck.

"Everything I know is based on what I experience from Conall. Siobhán is either Aedan's wife or lover."

"He was a monk, right? They were allowed to get married?"

"It's unlikely he ever took the vows," Mom answered. "There are references in ninth- and tenth-century writings of protectors like Aedan. They adopted the monk's lifestyle to blend in. Think of them as being the head of security."

"What else do we know about him?"

"I can tell you from my experiences that Conall and Deaglan saw Aedan as a hero," Dad answered. "The Warrior Monk, that's what they called him. He obviously had children. Aedan would have come from a royal family or at least a prominent family. My guess is that he was either a nephew or a son of an Irish king."

"Why do you think that?"

Mom had reached for the carafe and topped off the coffees. "Wealthy families were expected to be patrons of the Church," she said as she poured. "Their youngest sons were to become priests or monks. And the wealthiest increased their power by sponsoring art, jeweled chalices, church buildings, monasteries—the grander the gift, the more elevated a family became."

I grabbed a handful of blueberries from a ceramic bowl. I recognized it from a family trip to France when Mom had led an excavation in Normandy. Fond memories.

"Da Vinci; Michelangelo," Mom continued, "all of the great artists, their money came from benefactors, the rich and powerful. The same was true in medieval times."

Mom opened the oven and removed the scones. "Think about it like this: Columba's fame grew after his death. He was a legend. Revered. It was a cult-like following. Pilgrims traveled in their thousands to Iona to walk in his footsteps. He made prophecies. Debates and sermons about their meanings were discussed throughout Ireland and Scotland." She put three scones on a plate and laid them in front of Dad and me. "The king puts up the money for the creation of the *Book* to celebrate Columba's life. Do you think he would leave it in the hands of a bunch of peaceful monks?"

"I guess not."

"No way. And there's no chance he would choose a half-arsed family member to guard it. Aedan would have been an elite warrior."

She nodded to the warm scones. The raspberry and buttery smells were making me hungry. My mom was born in Ireland and was an archeologist specializing in ancient Celtic music and lyrics. And a great baker. At least, of Irish stuff.

Dad walked to the side table and returned with a yellowing 1969 Michelin map of the British Isles.

"Here's Iona." He put his finger over Glasgow and ran it northwest to the ocean. "It's a minuscule rock in the sea, one mile wide, four miles long. Across from it is Mull, a much bigger island."

"There were large villages on Mull to accommodate the thousands of pilgrims," Mom added. "Dad and I did a camping trip there before you were born."

Dad pointed to an enlarged map of Iona on the adjoining page. "The monastery was founded in 563 by Columba and became the most important site for the faithful of the Celtic Christian world."

I followed his finger as it traveled from Scotland to Ireland. "This is Belfast. On a clear day, you can see Scotland from the north coast. In the Celtic world, the northeast of Ireland and the west of Scotland were the same place, with water in the way, which they had traveled for centuries on well-established sea lanes."

"We've researched that period extensively," Dad continued. "There was a king of the Murphy Clan. He ruled the Northwest. St. Columba was born there, so it makes sense that he would have been a patron of the *Book* and the monastery."

He then traced his finger south from Belfast. "And this is Kells, where the monks will complete the *Book*, thanks to Aedan." He looked at me expectantly.

I put my finger on the map at Iona and drifted back for a moment: Aedan on the shore, fearful for Siobhán's safety. I could feel his heart pound for her in my chest.

"Look at the photo behind you." My mom pointed to the wall over my shoulder. I turned to see her and four others, smiling and exuberant. "That was one of the first digs I led. We found a fifth-century book of hymns that St. Benedict had commissioned. I'll never forget the feeling, like I'd found a missing child and took her home to her parents. It was a small act, mostly unnoticed."

I turned back to her, sensing there was more.

"Finding the missing pages," she paused, placing her hands on mine, "would not be small or unnoticed. Your memories may be the only way to find the treasure that Aedan hid. Then we, our little family, could return it to Ireland. That, Cián Murphy, would be a brilliant use of your amazing brain, and the accomplishment of a lifetime."

I poured some cream into my black coffee and watched it swirl and cascade. I took a sip, followed by a deep breath.

"I know this is important to you. I'd do anything for you, but I don't know about this. Not yet anyway." The hurt on my father's face made me cringe. My stomach tightened. "I didn't want to burden you." I stirred the cream with my spoon, still trying to wrap my brain around my genetic inheritance.

"With what?" Mom asked.

I fought the visceral, dizzying feeling. "The night of the raid. I was taken at gunpoint. Two of the gang, they got me in the van, drove to an empty lot. I was around five seconds from being shot. Buck saved me."

Mom squeezed my hand. Dad's body snapped to attention, his lips trembling.

"Between that and now this memory stuff," I tapped my head, "I'm …" I threw my hands up. "I don't know what the hell I am right now, to be honest with you."

My father stood and leaned his elbows on the counter, his eyes meeting mine. "Buck's father saved me. Buck saved you. If we died, the memories would die with us. Think about that, son. There is a purpose to it."

I found my throat dry, my eyes blinking. I broke eye contact and stared at the floor.

"Others are searching," he continued.

I looked up, surprised to learn this.

"Some believe the clues lead to the Holy Grail." He tapped his fingers on the map. "They don't. But they think so. Therefore, it's believed to be worth hundreds of millions. Someone may be willing to kill for it."

My father appeared to get taller, stronger. "The search is intensifying. But the memories were given to us so that we can return the treasures to Ireland. It's our privilege and our burden."

"I think you mean my burden." I felt a chill run through my body.

CHAPTER 7

November 21, 2019
Philadelphia

"We're leaving for a few hours," my mom said, standing up. She took my hand. "There are three things I want you to do today. Do them, please, then decide."

"Of course," I responded. "What are they?"

"Follow me, I want to show you something."

We strolled into her study. She gestured to her desk chair, and I sat. She opened a drawer and lifted out a large leather-bound book. The cover was embossed: a lion standing on each side of a shield, upon which an armored helmet sat atop four smaller lions, each in their own square. I recognized it as the Murphy coat of arms.

"These are the notes of your father's and great-grandfather's experiences. You'll find a few surprises." She kissed the top of my head and left.

I'd never spent much time in this room. I felt calmed by its peacefulness. Natural light streamed in, casting shadows. Photos dominated the walls, a monument to my mother's work and family. I spotted a few that I'd seen before: Mom at sixteen in front of the Abbey Theatre in Dublin with her parents, and one of me with Mom and Dad at the *Book of Kells* exhibit at Trinity College. We were about the same age in those two photos.

I smiled at the photo of her on stage with Bruce Springsteen at Slane Castle, a reminder that she was a fantastic Irish Fiddle player. It read June 1, 1985. She was twenty-five and beautiful.

My hand played over the embossed seal of the leather cover. I opened the book, and the first page held a photo of Eamon and Fiona Murphy, my great-grandparents. A copy of it hung on the wall upstairs.

I turned the page. My dad, Shaun Murphy, wrote the overview, with research notes compiled by my mom, Megan Fitzpatrick Murphy. Their names stood side by side on the paper, united like they'd been every day of their married life.

I thought of my father's tales of Conall and wondered what mysteries this journal would unveil. The book felt cared for, loved. An archeologist's reverent preservation of history; a wife and mother's care for her family. I let the pages fall open where they would, like a tarot-card reader allowing the spirits to reveal meaning.

A page opened, and there stood two words in large block letters:

THE GHOST

Eamon Murphy was a lawyer in Dublin and a leader in the Irish independence movement for autonomy from Britain. In 1915, aware that violence was brewing, he sent his son James to the U.S. to prepare a home for the family.

James carried a written testimonial from his father, which was to be closely guarded, for family only. It read:

The following is my testimony. I, Eamon Murphy, wrote

this in Dublin, September 1915, and entrusted it to my son James for safekeeping.

On September 14, 1915, at 10:00 a.m., a courier brought a sealed message to my desk, telling me to enter the stage door at the Empire Palace Theatre, 72 Dame Street, at precisely noon, with additional instructions to ensure that I would not be followed. If it was safe to enter, I was to look to the north-east corner of the alley, where a man I would recognize would put the newspaper he was reading in his left pocket, or if not safe, he would put it in his right.

I had been called to clandestine meetings before but rarely on such short notice. I entered the alley and saw one of our soldiers, a banker in a dark gray pinstripe suit, a white shirt with a black tie. His black fedora held a dark gray band, matching his suit. Without giving me a glance, he placed the newspaper in his left pocket. With that, I entered. A broad-shouldered lad regarded me with suspicion. I believe he could have laid a prizefighter to waste with one hand. He lifted my arms and searched my body for a weapon. Without a word, he turned, nodding for me to follow. He opened a dressing-room door. There sat a tall, lanky, bearded man, late in his years. He seemed burdened, yet simultaneously exuded power and optimism.

He stood and extended his hand.

"My name is Mack Murphy. You know me as The Ghost."

The Ghost was a legend in the movement, the main conduit for raising money and weapons from American Irish. No one saw him. We only heard the whispers and the rumors. He was the most wanted man in Ireland, a top prize for the Brits. I was aware that I was staring, but I couldn't break my gaze.

"You're wondering why this meeting." I heard a little Irish in his accent but mostly something unfamiliar. "It seems we have more in common than our surname. Is it true that you have experienced day visions, memories from someone long ago?"

I almost retched. I had only told a few trusted friends of these experiences. I nodded.

"Am I correct that these visions are from a young man named Fergus? Cromwell's police stole him and sent him to Jamaica. That Fergus?"

I had no words. I simply nodded. I recognized Mack's accent as one from the West Indies.

Mack took a handkerchief from his workman's coat and rubbed his nose. He was dressed like a dock worker, in his nondescript corduroy coat, tattered blue work shirt, and ill-fitting brown work pants. Part of the invisible masses. A cop would more likely toss him a penny than a glance.

"You see, Eamon, we do have more in common. I am one of his great-great-grandchildren, as apparently are you. By some freak accident of nature, I too have visions—so real at times that I shake and sweat and have found myself hollering aloud. My visions come from one of our ancient ancestors. He hid something of great value hundreds of years ago. It is priceless to Ireland and needs to be in her possession, but not until we are free."

Until that moment, I had no idea that anyone else had ever had this experience. I'd told my confidants of my visions only to keep my sanity. I saw my ancestor Fergus arrested. I saw him on the prison ship. I saw him in the fields toiling under the punishing sun, crying himself to sleep, desperate for his pregnant wife left behind, seeking comfort in his fellow Irish captives. And I had no idea why this was happening to me. But I did know that it fueled my passion for making the British oppressor pay.

I finally found words. They came out shaky. "How do I fit in?"

"I know you are a trusted brother in the cause. I learned of your experiences with the visions because I shared my own with a few of my lieutenants. One of them told me of yours. That led me to you. Now I need your help."

I closed my eyes for a brief moment. I heard the breath expelling from my nostrils, my lungs refilling with air, surprised that I could breathe at all. "It's through Fergus that I see. Please, tell me about him."

He went on to tell me that Fergus Murphy had become a legend among the Irish in Jamaica, of his hard life, and his dedication to free his people from the British in Jamaica. He wrote of the waves of African slaves brought to the island and the horrific conditions in which they toiled. Our ancestor was one of the few who could write in English. He wrote of the Irish suffering in Ireland and Jamaica. He told of the hellish life of the Africans. Fergus documented the growing confederacy of desperate Irish and Africans, the intermarriages, and the violence sometimes between the two groups.

Mack Murphy dropped his head as a harsh cough escaped his lungs. He wiped his lips with his sleeve.

"But Fergus wrote one important piece of history for family only. He knew, either from family legend or perhaps from visions, the approximate location of a hidden artefact. One that would be priceless in pounds but even more priceless to the pride and heart of the Irish people. I have made it my life's mission to find my way back to Ireland and search till I found it. I have, and it is not safe here."

"May I ask what it is?"

"I trust that you know what it is since you see through his eyes. Think, Eamon."

I tried to think of all that I knew from Fergus but was at a loss. I shook my head.

"It was his great fear that he would die before having children whom he could pass the knowledge to," said Mack.

The memories washed over me. This is not possible.

"Jesus, Mary, and Joseph, and all the saints in heaven. Is it the missing pages from the Kells scriptorium?"

Mack smiled and nodded.

My hands shook. My voice sounded far away to me.

"I thought it all a fancy of my imagination. You have it?"

"Yes. And I must leave Ireland for the U.S., where I can continue my work for the cause and secure a safe place for the artefact. It will come back to Irish soil when we win independence, God willing, soon."

Mack's brow creased. His jaw pushed forward. His right hand clenched into a fist. I pulled back a few inches.

"I have reason to believe that there is a traitor in my inner circle," he continued. "I need you to make secure arrangements for my travel. I know that you have contacts in the U.S. Have your most trusted person meet me wherever you determine I may safely land. I must remain a ghost. England's long arm can reach 'cross the oceans."

"I will gladly help. How soon do you want to leave?"

"No more than two weeks. Two days is better."

"It won't be two days, but I'll do my best."

Mack nodded.

"I'll contact my friends in Cork Town," I told him.

Mack Murphy put his hand on my shoulder.

"That's not the only reason I sought you out. Fergus made it clear that what I found, and the story of our memories, must only be entrusted to family. Eamon, by the mystery of God, our ancient family tree has swept through a thousand years of Irish history and led me to you. I have followed Fergus's will. You are family."

I watched as his eyes moistened with the thought of it.

"I will send you the location of where I have hidden the artefact when I choose a place. There is no guarantee I will live to see the day of Irish Nationhood. If so, you must pledge to retrieve it and bring it to Ireland. On the pages exist clues as to the hiding place of a chest that contains the relics of St. Columba. When Ireland is free, trusted family members must find it. God willing."

I looked into the eyes of Mack Murphy, took his hand firmly in mine, and swore on the sacred graves of our ancestors that I would do as he wished.

With that, he told me that I would not see him again, that the young man in the hall would be the conduit.

"You would think I would want to come back and lay to rest here, but I do not," he added before taking his leave. "My home is Jamaica. I left behind the only woman I have ever truly loved, and my heart has been broken since. But my soul could never rest until I complete Fergus's mission."

Mack knocked on the door to alert his colleague in the hall that he was ready to leave. A minute later, the door opened. The Ghost departed. I was told to wait five minutes. I wanted to run home and spin my wife in the air. The visions were not a sickness of my brain. They were a hand reaching across the ages, and I was chosen to be touched by The Ghost.

The letter was signed by Eamon Murphy. I touched my great-grandfather's signature, the tall bold E and M, a calligrapher's stroke. He had no one to explain to him what was happening with these visions until Mack Murphy arrived. Now I was the inheritor from a long line of seers.

I closed the book and looked to the photo with my parents at the *Kells* exhibit. I moved to it and placed my hand on the frame. My parents had been thinking about this treasure since the day my father told my mother about his visions.

Mack crossed the sea to hide it in America.

"Where did you put it, Mack?" I said aloud, to no one.

A glint of red crossed my eyes. I looked up to the source, a framed stained glass rendering of a cloaked woman, her hair long and flowing over her garment, her back to me. She seemed fixed on a distant horizon. The southern exposure reached over the cityscape and lit her, refracting the prism of the glass, dancing the magnificent colors about the room. I stood transfixed as her garment fell; an astonishingly beautiful blonde, naked, turned to me, her breasts firm and alluring. She wrapped her arms around me and pulled me close.

"Aedan, my love," she whispered over and over, her voice a Siren's call. Her musk overwhelmed me with passion. I squeezed her bottom as she rode up and down. I strained not to release. I didn't want this to end. My fingers found her nipples. She sighed at my caress. I pulled her to me, her lips meeting mine, her tongue exploring my mouth. I thrust and thrust as she shuddered in pleasure. Minutes passed in this ecstasy until there was no holding back.

"Siobhán!" Oh, the sweet relief.

"What the hell," I hollered, incredibly aroused from the experience, letting the image of a naked Siobhán play in my head. Dad said things might get weirder, but I wasn't expecting anything like this.

CHAPTER 8

1977
DERRY, NORTHERN IRELAND

"Jesus Christ, Padraig. You know I didn't do it. Some fecker set me up. Tell them, Padraig. Just fecking tell them."

Jimmy Riley knelt in the corner of the abandoned barn, with a gun aimed at him. One of his childhood friends, Padraig Collins, was the one holding it.

"How can you even think of it, Paddy? Did they send you to test your manhood?"

"It doesn't pain me to kill you, Jimmy. It pains me that you betrayed us. Ya coulda got me and the boys killed, so I asked for the assignment. Take a moment and pray, Jimmy."

Riley began to cry. Collins looked at his friend in disgust. Three IRA soldiers had been killed by the Royal Ulster Constabulary because of Riley's betrayal. The retribution began tonight. Padraig closed the distance and placed one shot to the head. Jimmy Riley ceased to exist.

Collins looked at his friend and wondered if he would feel something. He didn't, and that scared the nineteen-year-old.

His first kill. He left the barn and traversed the field to Lough Foyle, where a boat awaited him. As he approached the shore, he dropped to his knees and threw up. He felt the release of tears. He placed a metal cage around those feelings, wiped his mouth from the foul puke, and walked to the boat. He rowed the eleven hundred meters hard, pushing away the image of the friend he had just killed, his muscles aching from the hard row. Traveling the water by moonlight, he aimed for his destination. He sat on the bank of the lake, sweaty and exhausted, and felt the calming hand of St. Columba brush his face. Columba was born near here and sailed these waters. The saint often visited Collins in his prayers. Columba was known as the Warrior Saint. He had killed men in battle. If a warrior could be a saint, maybe there was salvation for him.

But salvation would wait. There was more killing to be done, a war to win.

CHAPTER 9

The front door opened, dragging me out of the swirl of a naked Siobhán playing in my brain. I missed her, as if somehow it was me she was in love with. Intellectually, it made no sense, but I was having a hard time shaking her.

It took me several minutes to pull myself together. I joined my folks in the kitchen and forced myself to focus.

Mom placed a *Time Magazine* in front of me. The cover showed a woman in a lab coat and a rendering of a double helix DNA strand. At the base of the strand, artistically blended with the DNA, was a person in modern dress, and at the top was someone in old-world clothing. The caption read:

DISCOVERY UPENDS EVERYTHING WE KNOW ABOUT
MEMORY AND GENETICS

"This gets released tomorrow." Mom pointed to the cover, her finger resting next to the woman. "She's the scientist who discovered the genetic mutation, and we've become friends over the past year. Dad and I have invested in her company. She wants to meet you, so I invited her to stop by. She'll be here in a few minutes."

I looked at the cover once more, then at my parents. "I assume that this is thing number two. Why is she coming here?"

Something was off in the way they were acting. "Does she know about your search for the *Book*?" I asked.

"Aye, a wee bit, enough to guide us. She found a DNA match in our family tree and believes this person has the information we want," Mom answered while slicing some brown bread and cheddar. "She also wants to discuss the results from the ancestry DNA test you did a few weeks ago."

I ran my fingers over the DNA strand on the cover of the magazine. "You had me take the test to be certain I had the gene, right?"

"Guilty as charged," Dad answered.

"Do you trust her?" I asked, joining a slice of cheddar to the bread.

Mom looked a bit unsettled.

"I do, but we must limit the number of people who know the details. As your father said, there may be people willing to kill for it."

"I don't get it." I broke off a piece of cheddar, its tangy sharpness reaching my nose. "Why?"

"The cover is priceless. The *Book of Kells* is considered a medieval masterpiece. It's Ireland's *Mona Lisa*. That said, there is only so much the government or Trinity College could pay, probably in the forty to fifty million range. But the treasure, if it is what we think it is, could command hundreds of millions in the antiquities market."

"Seriously?" I looked at Dad then back at her. "It must be full of gold."

"Far more valuable than gold," Mom quickly responded. "It's long been believed that sacred relics of Columba were moved from Iona to Ireland at the same time as the *Book of Kells*. Several antiquities collectors, powerful, wealthy people, believe it contains the Holy Grail, the last supper chalice of Jesus."

I nod to my father. "You said it's not the Holy Grail. How do you know?"

"I don't for sure, but I'm ninety-nine percent. The king, the bishops, they would have known. They wouldn't bury it. Nah, they would have used it to increase their power." I detected a touch of fear in his voice. "I don't doubt that the treasure contains something vital, but not the Holy Grail."

Dad lifted the magazine from the counter, opened to the cover story, and handed it to me.

MUTANT GENE UNLOCKS ANCESTRAL MEMORIES

Molecular biologist Dr. Sylvia Garcia might need to book her ticket to Stockholm for a Nobel Prize. Her breakthrough work on genetic mutations has led to the discovery of a gene that passes memories from someone in their ancestral tree. It sounds like a script from Star Trek, but more than two thousand individuals have been tested with the gene and some four hundred have confirmed that they have experienced memories not of their own. We have been permitted to speak to several individuals who have agreed to be interviewed for this article.

I read a few more lines out loud.

"Mary Stewart summed up the experience of most of the people we interviewed for the article. A high school teacher in Wisconsin, Stewart lost her job due to frequent episodes of memories rendering her in what seemed like a catatonic state that could last for minutes.

"'One moment I was teaching math, the next I was wandering the cliffs and beaches of Brittany.' After a friend bought her a DNA kit, she learned that she had the gene. 'In an instant, I went from dread to hope. I am getting my life back and now enjoy the memories of my Ancestor.'"

I looked at my parents and realized how lucky I was to have them guide me through this.

"Dr. Garcia calculates that at least two percent of the world's population has this mutation," my father said. "Think of the history and knowledge that can be learned."

I scanned a few more of the interviews.

My new reality was setting in. I was in a small fraternity. Our line of Murphy's was cursed or blessed, inheritors of a cosmic joke or a genetic wonder; I wasn't sure which.

"At least we're out of the closet. People might not think we've lost our minds."

The doorbell rang. A moment later Mom returned with our guest.

Dr. Garcia looked like Ruth Bader Ginsburg's twin. I guessed she was in her seventies, all of four-foot-ten and a ball of kinetic, intelligent energy.

She took one look at me, turned to my mother, and said, "I thought you told me he was handsome." She burst out laughing. How could you not love that? She would fit right in at the police station.

"Okay, Mister Big Shot Detective. It sounds like you've had a hell of a ride these past few weeks." Her Spanish accent hung in the air, with its lispy S's. "I'm all ears. Well, actually, I'm not all ears. I have two eyes, a nose, and a big, big mouth. But now I shut up and listen to you. Just give me your two-minute overview."

She took a seat next to me and waited for my response.

Her eyes fixed on me, concentrated yet inviting. I felt like I was about to confess my insanity. To a stranger.

"For several months I've had the image of a blade of some kind swinging toward me. Around two and a half weeks ago I started having images popping into my head. Some were violent, none were familiar. Most were disturbing. Swords thrust into bodies, throats sliced, blood everywhere. I was also saying names. Last night, it changed from still images to a vivid memory, more like a movie."

"I'm very familiar with this phenomenon," she said.

"You're the expert. I'm hoping that you can shed some light."

"Some light, but there is a lot we don't fully understand. Yet." She turned to my parents then back at me. "If you interview ten witnesses to the same crime, how many answers will you get?"

"Probably ten," I replied.

"If you ask ten geneticists to explain this phenomenon, you'll get at least twenty theories. Genetic mutations are normal. They occur throughout human history. With millions of people taking DNA tests, we're starting to see this mutation show up worldwide."

Dad had prepared an espresso for her, which she sipped.

"Not everyone who has the gene experiences the memories. Why?" She let this hang in the air for a moment. "We don't know yet. Let's take you, for example. Your mother tells me that you had some minor episodes between ages five and six. Then nothing. Right?"

"I guess," I answered, shrugging my shoulders.

"All of a sudden," Dr. Garcia clapped her hands together, "at thirty, it begins again. Your father had them at seventeen for a few years, then they stop. We don't know for certain what activates or deactivates the gene, but we are making progress." She left her seat and paced between me and my parents, a professor addressing her students. "And now to the big question: how is it even possible that you can experience the memory of someone else, never mind someone from a thousand years ago?" She threw her hands up in question and gave a little laugh.

"This is where, if you ask ten geneticists, you get *forty* answers," she continued. "We are narrowing it down to two main theories. One, borrowed from modern neuroscience: the person whose memories you have also had the mutated gene. Their memories, like all memory, are embedded in the neurons in the brain. Somehow, the theory goes, a copy is made and encoded in this mutated gene and, through some random lottery, passed to a future generation."

"I think I follow," I told her.

She took on the wide grin of a comic conspirator, the owner of an inside joke. A look that told me that the crazier idea was coming.

"The next theory borrows from quantum physics. It states that all memory actually exists in a cloud storage system or quantum field. The mutated gene is your passcode. When it activates, it accesses the file."

I must have had the "Are you crazy?" look on my face. She called me on it.

"There you go, Detective Murphy. You are violating the fundamental law of investigation. Because your brain is unfamiliar with this information, you shut it out and potentially miss solving the problem. In fact, this theory is becoming the predominant one. Some of the top molecular biologists in the world are testing it."

"Okay, you got me. My mind is wide open." I high-fived her. She seemed to be delighted as her tiny hand smacked hard against my own. "But just to be clear, I'm not a detective. Not yet anyway."

She nodded then spread her hands toward me. "Your

parents have told me that several times in your life you have experienced prodigy-like mastery over a subject, and then, *poof*, it disappears."

My stomach tightened. The feeling of dread that came with thinking about this subject turned my curiosity to unease.

"It was difficult, right?" She put her small hand over mine and patted it reassuringly. "The gene expanded your neural pathways."

I shook my head. "I don't know what that means."

She was about to explain, but Mom had put a plate with her homemade bread, along with butter and strawberry jam, in front of her. She eyed it with pleasure, added a generous slab of butter and a thick gob of jam, smiled, and bit in. She winked at Mom. "Your mother knows my weakness."

They had obviously done this before.

"Did you see the movie *Rain Man*?"

"Yes," I answered.

"Do you remember the scene where the waitress spills the box of toothpicks? Dustin Hoffman takes one glance at them on the floor and said, 'Two hundred and forty-six total.'"

I nod, wondering what this has to do with anything. I was surprised to see this scientist eye a bit of jam on the plate, dab her finger into it and lick it. I smiled my approval.

"Hoffman's character was autistic, non-functional in many regards but a genius in others. His neural pathways were highly developed and focused in one arena. We see these phenomena of a focused talent in approximately fourteen percent of those with the mutation. It eventually expresses itself in the memories."

This revelation took my breath away. I didn't know whether to be relieved about the past or fearful of the future.

She put both palms toward me, like a preacher delivering the good news. "You are a freak of nature, Key Murphy. The idea that someone could observe the memory of another person is beyond what any scientist could have predicted, but here you are, the alien walking off the spaceship and showing us that there's another world out there. This is the stuff of historic breakthroughs that shatters the constraints of our thinking."

"You make it sound all positive, but it's disconcerting." I became aware that I was still breathing shallowly, and drumming my fingers on my right leg.

"That's because your nervous system responds as if it's happening to you. After you witness the event, it will embed in your memory like any other experience. For that reason alone, you must take detailed notes so that you can keep Aedan's events as a separate memory from your own."

That explained my feelings for Siobhán. "Okay, I've been taking notes."

"Excellent. As you know, some people that have the gene for memory do not experience any memories—like your grandfather. We're testing some of them to see if we can stimulate or activate the memories."

"And?" I asked.

"We have thirty people in a preliminary trial. Ten are on a regimen of mild electrical stimulation, ten are using a pharmacological approach, ten are using a placebo. It's early in the trial, but so far we have two subjects that are responding to the electrical stimulation, five responding to the pharmacology, zero from the placebo group."

"And will this tell you anything about the two theories?" my mom asked.

Dr. Garcia shook her head slightly, started to say something, then hesitated. "I don't know yet." She looked around the room, her eyes landing on a photo of me catching a pass during a high school game. She continued, "It's going to take some time to determine the mechanisms that cause people to have the experience."

I asked, "If you can stimulate the people who aren't

having memories, can you accelerate or enhance the experience for people like me who do?"

"That," she said with a big grin, "is the million-dollar question. We recently received FDA approval to begin clinical trials to test that. It would take me hours to explain, but we're making progress." Dr. Garcia folded her arms and gazed at me warmly. "This is happening to you whether you like it or not. If I were lucky enough to be you, I'd take it for everything it's worth."

I let her words play in my brain. "I can do that," I finally said. To my surprise, she responded with another high-five.

"Key, I need you to do two things."

"Uh-oh," I responded with a smile.

"When you submitted your DNA, I was not able to get a clean reading on the mutated gene. It's important that I compare the sequence with your father's sample. Sometimes we see variations in family members. I need to re-do it if it's okay with you." She opened her purse and took out a DNA swab kit. "Please rinse your mouth."

I did. She swabbed.

"The other thing?" I asked.

"I need you to meet someone today. Her name is Arin Murphy. She is a very distant member of your family tree. She can help you find what you and your parents are looking for."

"Okay, no problem. Where's the meeting?"

Dr. Garcia smiled and looked at my Mom, who answered. "Kingston, Jamaica."

My double-take must have been amusing. "Is this a joke?"

"She's the grandchild of Mack Murphy, three times removed," my mom continued. "I've made the flight and hotel arrangements. You keep enough clothes here, so I packed a carry-on for you. You'll be back in two days."

I tapped my pocket, finding the passport there. "You

should have told me this morning," I said to my mother with more of an edge than I intended.

Dr. Garcia tugged on my arm. I looked down at her. "You just told me that you would take this experience for everything it's worth. Go find out what it's worth, Mr. Big Shot Detective. You might find what you've been looking for."

With that, she said goodbye.

CHAPTER 10

Padraig Collins peered out of the window of his private jet. His mind focused on the points of his upcoming meeting. He had long lived by his favorite American saying: "Money talks, bullshit walks."

Money bought informers. Money bought loyalty.

Money overcame sectarian division in Ireland, his most important lesson. A lesson that made him wealthy.

When Ireland prospered and became the Celtic Tiger in the mid-90s, Northern Ireland wanted a piece of the pie. To get it, the borders had to go. They did—the economic ties made for a more peaceful and relatively united Ireland. And now the idiots in London were ready to destroy the peace and erect borders once again. If managed correctly, Catholics and Protestants would unite in opposition. And Collins was making sure of it. His social media troll farms in Ireland, Bulgaria, and Hungary had pushed for Brexit, influencing enough of the public to vote how he'd wished.

When Brexit won the vote, his investment and logistics

firms reached out to every global company headquartered in the U.K. The message: English-speaking Ireland was open for business and would forever be in the E.U. The response was slow for a few months, but as the business world watched Theresa May get her ass kicked, Padraig Collins witnessed something he could never achieve as an IRA soldier: Ireland was draining an abundance of England's money, and much of it was coming to him, one way or another.

The Cessna 680 taxied toward him. Unlike its busier cousins closer to Manhattan, the Farmingdale Executive Airport on Long Island was away from the eyes of the press and the paparazzi. Collins's larger Gulfstream Four already had its steps lowered and in place. His security chief climbed the newcomer's stairs to inspect the interior, and after a few minutes Collins was given the all-clear sign and exited his plane. He had agreed to board Joseph Murphy's Cessna to meet with the young man and his partner.

Collins wore a tailored sports coat, silk T-shirt, and jeans. Murphy was dressed in the clothes he put on in Kingston that morning, a blue linen short-sleeve with white linen pants. Dr. Garcia wore a black dress and jacket, accented by a diamond necklace and matching earrings. Joseph Murphy and Dr. Garcia reviewed documents at the conference table, and Joseph stood to shake hands with Collins before turning to his partner.

"Padraig Collins, meet Dr. Sylvia Garcia."

Padraig's hand outstretched in greeting. Garcia didn't take it.

"I don't like you. Let's just get this over with."

Collins shot a glance at Joseph, who looked aghast, then back at Dr. Garcia, before he started laughing.

"I, on the other hand, like you. My kind of person: just gets right to it. You and I will get along very well."

"Mr. Collins, I sincerely doubt it," responded Garcia. "I don't trust someone who thinks they can muscle in on our business."

"Muscle?" Collins shrugged. "I'm offering a two hundred million investment and the leverage you need to receive your patents."

"You blackmailed Joseph, which means you blackmailed me." She rubbed her hands together as if washing away germs.

Collins sat, resting his hands on the table.

"I haven't blackmailed you, at least not yet."

Dr. Garcia put down the pen she was holding and stared Collins down.

"What is that supposed to mean?"

"There are no saints at this table. Are you sure you want me to answer that question?" Collins could see some bluster leaving Garcia as she slowly exhaled and sat back in her chair ever so slightly.

Collins examined the inlay of a hummingbird on the table and drummed his fingers on its long bill.

"One of the first things we need to do is fix your firewalls. Your company is an open book to hackers. My team entered rather easily, and you have a tremendous amount of sensitive information you would not want competitors to see. By the time we get done, no one will get through."

"Okay, you've seen sensitive information. There is nothing illegal there," Garcia responded defensively.

"I want to be very clear about this. I am here to help. The work you are doing will have an enormous benefit to humanity." Collins leaned forward, his eyes intently focused on hers. "Dr. Garcia, your company is on the doorstep of some of the greatest biomedical breakthroughs in history. In twenty years, the largest companies won't be in IT. They will be in genetic engineering and biomedicine. With my help, you'll be the Steve Jobs of that world."

"I don't need you for that," Garcia spat, her eyes narrowed.

"That's where you're wrong. We both know that your colleague Dr. Ambati made the discoveries, not you. Don't misunderstand me. You are brilliant, but when he died unexpectedly from a heart attack, you inherited his research and eventually published it in your name, with no mention of him. He'll be forgotten, and you will likely have a Nobel Prize, your name living forever." Collins tilted toward Murphy. "Did you know that, Joseph?"

Dr. Garcia slapped Collins in the face. Collins didn't flinch, but smiled.

"A fighter, that's good. We will do great things together."

"Mr. Collins, what is it you actually want?" After slapping this enormously powerful man she sat back to observe him.

"First, I want you to call me Padraig."

"That will never happen, Mr. Collins. People might get the idea that we're friends. Please continue."

Collins took his time. His eyes roamed the cabin, the splashes of green, yellow, and black in the décor reflecting the Jamaican flag.

"I made it clear to Joseph. I want him to find the missing part of the *Book of Kells.*"

Dr. Garcia tilted her head.

"Why? What's in it for you?"

Collins was used to directing the questions. Now this woman, the size of a leprechaun, was trying to exercise control. She was good. He let her play her game.

"It would be home, where it belongs. The Irish world will be astonished and grateful, and you'll be even more famous. Most importantly, if it leads to the treasure of Saint Columba, then Ireland will rejoice even more. With it, I will help unite Northern Ireland with the Republic. We'll be one nation again, no violence."

Garcia leaned forward, her voice gentler.

"What do you think is in there that will accomplish this?"

"You're a treasure hunter, Dr. Garcia. Am I right?" Collins held his thumb and forefinger together. "You look in infinitesimally small places for genetic clues. The chances of finding something are slim. Yet you persist. Why?" Collins folded his hands in prayer-like fashion, emphasizing the question. "Because you believe something is there, and that it might change some part of the world."

Collins leaned back, causing his hosts to lean a little closer to him. He spoke reverentially. "I believe there are relics from Saint Columba. Even a small relic, his writing, his bible, a chalice, anything from him, will help heal the final divide. In Ireland he's known as Columbkille, and he's revered by Catholics and Protestants alike. The economics of Brexit is pushing them together. Something from Columbkille can bind them in spirit."

"How do you know there's a map?" Joseph Murphy asked.

"Not a map, just clues. I am an antiquities collector. The rumors about Columba's treasures have been around forever. Approximately six months ago, I purchased the personal journal of one of Mack Murphy's closest confidants. An antiquities hunter knew I was seeking any information about Mack. He found the journal in a trunk that the friend had owned. The great-great-grandchild was happy to part with it for a thousand euros."

Collins rested his elbows on the table.

"Mack's confidant wrote of Mack's memories, of an ancestor stolen from Ireland and sent to Jamaica. He wrote that in the *Kells* artefact were clues about the treasure. Mack's team in Ireland never heard from him again, but there were rumors that he was writing home to his wife in Jamaica and likely left clues in his letters." He gestured toward Joseph. "It was a simple matter of finding Murphy descendants in Jamaica that have been there for many generations."

Collins regarded Joseph, his smile broad, his eyes wide. "You are a lucky man to descend from one so brave and focused. Mack Murphy is a hero."

Joseph turned in his chair to Dr. Garcia.

"I always thought this was nonsense. Perhaps I'm wrong."

Dr. Garcia did not respond to her partner.

"You will invest two hundred million into the company, treasure or no treasure?" she asked Collins.

He nodded.

Her chest heaved as she drew in a deep breath. "If we find the treasure and turn it over to you, you'll reduce your holdings by half?" Garcia clarified.

Again, Collins nodded.

"It's all in the agreement."

Dr. Garcia shifted in her seat and put her right elbow on the plush armrest. Her eyes narrowed. "You have leverage over both of us. You are putting in two hundred million and taking a fair stake. You could try to screw us over. It makes me nervous that you're being fair."

"I told you there are no saints at this table. But I am the biggest sinner here." Collins sat quietly for a moment, his confession hanging in the air. "Uniting Ireland is the penance for my sins and the path to reclaiming my soul. And by helping your company help people, I see that as a further act of contrition."

Her face softened, as did her voice. "This makes you seem like a good guy, like a hero."

"I'm not. If someone gets in our way, I'll kill them and add them to the long list of things for which I need forgiveness." Collins watched as horror crossed their faces. "Just kidding," he added, without the slightest hint of assurance in his voice.

He patted the folder with the agreements. "Have your lawyers review it and get back to me with your plan. Soon."

He got up, nodded to his hosts, and left the plane.

CHAPTER 11

November 21, 2019
Kingston, Jamaica

The last time I jumped on a flight to Kingston with a two-hour notice was never. I've grown used to living life in a vortex, losing one skill, gaining another. It can mess you up, but there is also an excitement to it. I just wanted to slow things down, catch my breath, and understand what was happening to me. Maybe I'd extend my stay for a few days, count this surprise trip as a gift from the gods of tranquility. Unless I see details in a memory, there isn't much I can do. Luckily, I was in business class and had a decent lunch.

The words of Dr. Garcia and thoughts of Tanya kept playing in my mind. Dr. Garcia had explained that the mutation had created neural pathways that gave me some extraordinary abilities. Then, *boom*, gone after a year or three. It didn't bother me when I was younger; it just seemed normal. It wasn't until my early twenties that it tore me up. I recalled the dark thoughts, the clawing urge to end it all. I had hidden away in my bedroom at my parents' house, sitting in the dark, talking to no one. My parents, frantic. Me, a twenty-year-old football phenom. And in a flash, a twenty-one-year-old loser.

I think it was the third day when Tanya walked in, grabbed a pillow off the bed, and sat next to me. She didn't say a word, just held my hand. I fell asleep in her lap, and she fell asleep in mine. She did that for three days. She had left the room to get some food and water and came back a few minutes later, stood next to me, and finally spoke. "You stink. Go get a shower."

I found that hilarious. I laughed uncontrollably for a good twenty minutes, then got in the shower. I came back into the room and said, "I'm starving. Let's get some pizza."

We sat in the pizza shop. Oil, oregano, garlic, all sliding gloriously over my tongue. The heavenly mix of parm and pepperoni, as if I had never tasted this before. Then Tanya, reaching in, arresting my soul. "You are different, Key. There is no one like you. If you don't accept it, it will kill you."

She saved me. She didn't let me save her.

God, I missed my little sister.

My thoughts shifted as the wheels went down. A shot of excitement prickled my skin at the prospect of a new adventure and meeting a long-lost member of the Murphy tribe.

I exited the air-conditioned comfort of the customs area and stepped outside into the tropics. The wind and heat hit me like a fastball. Sweat formed. Palm trees waved in the breeze. Beer vendors and taxi pimps vied for my attention. The smell of fresh pineapple and coconut made its way from a market stall. A young woman with glasses and a navy-blue pantsuit held a chalkboard with my name on it. I waved to her, and as I got closer, she gave a broad smile.

"Welcome to Jamaica." It sounded like poetry, with her singsong accent. "Mr. Murphy, my name is Kenise."

"Please call me Key," I said with my flat Philly accent, knowing I sounded like a brick hitting the floor.

She turned to walk toward the car park.

"First time here?"

"Yes, and I'm a little embarrassed to admit that I don't know where we're going."

"Dr. Murphy asked me to bring you to her office."

"Dr. Murphy?"

"You don't know where you're going, do you?"

"I only learned today that I was coming here to meet her. I didn't know she was a doctor."

"She's not a medical doctor. She's a professor with a doctorate. Social Anthropology," Kenise clarified. "You are a trusting person to come all this way."

"Not really. I work with the police. Trust doesn't come with the job description, but we have a mutual friend who asked me to meet her. Here I am."

Kenise drove over a long causeway, maybe twenty yards wide, eight-foot-high boulders provide the breakwater. Palm trees and the city to my left and ocean to my right. We exited the causeway into the city. Slums went in and out of view along with beautiful gated apartment complexes. Kentucky Fried Chicken, Burger King, and Subway mixed with street carts of jerk pork, jerk chicken, curried goat, and coolers full of Ting, Red Stripe, and Guinness. The scent of curry and exotic spices made me hungry as we passed the street vendors. I felt like grabbing an ice-cold Red Stripe. Before I could make it happen, though, we turned onto the campus. She parked, and I followed her to an office building.

Kenise opened a door and beckoned me in.

"Dr. Murphy is finishing a lecture. She asked for you to wait here in her office. She should be here any moment."

"Thanks, Kenise. It was nice meeting you." When the door closed, my eyes immediately fell on a signed Philadelphia Eagles jersey hanging on the wall. Jerome Pinter, tight end.

I never heard the door open, only a voice.

"Dated him for a few months when I was a visiting professor at Temple."

I turned and was overwhelmed by her smile and surprised by the electrical charge I felt. The first thing I noticed was the slight gap in her teeth and the freckles that dotted her light brown skin. Her green eyes drew me in, her black ringlets framing her rounded cheekbones. She wore a plain black pantsuit with a T-shirt underneath it that read: *I love forensic anthropology, no bones about it.*

"Pinter was good," I said lamely.

She stared at me as well. "You look just like him."

"Pinter? I don't think so."

"No, Mack Murphy. We have a portrait of him at my mother's house. I'm sorry, it took me by surprise." She walked the few steps and held out her hand. "I'm Arin."

We shook hands.

"I'm Key."

"I thought your name is Cián?"

"Everyone just called me Key, and it stuck." My heart was racing a bit. My eyes landed on a photo on the wall just over her shoulder. "That's very cool," I said, nodding to the picture. "I'm a fan."

Arin turned to the photo of her and Usain Bolt. She smiled, then looked more serious.

"Key, I'm embarrassed to tell you after you came all this way, I have a faculty meeting that I tried to get out of but the Dean insists I be there. You are welcome to wait here, but I thought you'd be more comfortable at the hotel. I can be there in about two hours, and we can have dinner. Kenise will drive you."

"That sounds great. I would like to freshen up."

"Thanks, I have a lot to tell you." Arin smiled, a little devilish, a little shy. "Walk with me to my meeting. Kenise will meet us there."

Arin took a notepad from her desk and opened the office door. I grabbed my suitcase and followed.

"I was surprised to see an Eagles jersey. How did you like Philly?"

A breeze washed over us as we stepped out of the building, her alluring scent in the air.

"I loved Philly. Too bad you won't be here long. You would enjoy going to a football match. Sorry, soccer. You'd find Jamaicans are just as crazy as Eagles fans."

Arin stopped walking for a moment. Mango trees hung overhead, ripe fruit about to fall.

"Key, so that you know, Mack Murphy has been a family obsession for close to one hundred-fifty years. He was eighteen when he left Jamaica to fight in the American Civil War. He was a ghost that haunted my father."

"Did you know that he was known as 'The Ghost' in Ireland?" I asked.

"We can compare notes." Arin turned to the right. "We have letters that he wrote. I'll show you them tomorrow." Kenise came out of the building as Arin entered, and stopped with the door open. "Dr. Garcia sent me your cell number. I'll text you when I'm on my way. See you soon."

I watched her walk down the hall, as Aedan had observed Tomás wend through the tunnel, satchel over his shoulder. I was startled by a voice from behind me. I turned. Kenise. "Mr. Murphy, are you okay?"

CHAPTER 12

November 21, 2019
Pegasus Hotel, Kingston Jamaica

After checking in at the Pegasus Hotel, I grabbed a quick shower, hit the pool deck, and just about melted. It had to be eighty percent humidity. The water had an invigorating chill, and I loved it. Fifteen minutes of hard pounding laps and I was ready to work out my arm by lifting a Red Stripe to my lips. I'd had Red Stripe before, but never in its home, Jamaica. It's like the first time having a Guinness in Ireland, a bit of magic to it. The bartender fished out the coldest one he could find while telling me that Guinness was also brewed in Jamaica. Welcome to Paradise.

I casually glanced around and spotted a guy looking at me. He saw me and turned away. I gave it two minutes and looked again, and again he turned away. But a moment later, he stood beside me at the bar.

"Sorry, you look very familiar." He extended his hand. "Jimmy Downey. Have we met?"

"Key Murphy—not that I recall. Where in Ireland are you from, Jimmy?" His accent was a dead giveaway. He wore a white Tommy Bahama polo, black Tommy Bahama swim trunks, and sandals. Odd. You can't buy Tommy Bahama clothing in Ireland. It's not an Irish look. Most Irish wouldn't be caught dead in it.

"Cork. And you?"

"Philadelphia. What brings you to Jamaica?"

"Besides an Irishman's need for the sun? I do IT consulting. It's a growing sector here. Some excellent opportunities." He took a sip of what I assumed was a pina colada. "What about you?"

"Just a quick visit with some family."

He held his glass toward my bottle and clinked it. "Enjoy your stay. Sláinte."

That was what I would have done: walk right up to deflect suspicion. It was probably nothing, but his nonchalance seemed practiced. This guy was coiled. Guessing he's five-eleven, one eighty-five, wiry muscles. He had an Irishman's disarming smile but something behind the eyes. Like he could pour you a whiskey, chat about your day, then smash your head with the whiskey bottle, cursing you to the end of time if a drop escaped.

My phone pinged with a text. *Soon come, 20 minutes.* I headed to my room to get dressed for dinner.

―――――

When Arin walked into the lobby, deference was definitely being paid, with the doorman to the concierge and a man I assumed was the manager scurrying to welcome her. This was not just a professor entering. She was closer to royalty in their response to her, but she had no air of entitlement. If anything, she seemed eager to get away from the fawning attention.

She had changed from her earlier outfit to black jeans, a black scoop neck Beatles Abbey Road T-shirt, a black blazer and white low-cut Converse sneakers. To say that she looked amazingly cute was an understatement.

"I apologize again for abandoning you," she said. "I got here as soon as I could."

"I needed the break. Gave me a chance to recharge. It's been a crazy few days," I said, watching her wave hello to a few people in the lobby coffee shop—all eyes on her. I could tell people wanted to approach, but they seemed to be warded off. I was curious.

"It's a little early for dinner," Arin said. "Let's sit by the pool and talk."

She led the way, past the tropical floral centerpiece, down the steps to the pool level. A staff member saw us coming and rushed to open the door. Arin looked over to the bar and waved at the bartender. He smiled back and nodded, hands occupied by a shaker of some Jamaican rum drink, I assumed.

The pool deck had filled since I was here thirty minutes ago. A conference at the hotel must have let out for the day. Waiters moved in and out of the groupings, offering hors d'oeuvres and drinks.

Two women turned at the sight of Arin, waved to her, one blowing a kiss, then turned back to their discussion.

"It's a Caribbean bankers' event," Arin said as I noted Jimmy Downey across the pool. "My mother is the keynote speaker at their dinner tonight. You'll meet her tomorrow."

A waiter pulled the chair back for her as we sat at a poolside table. A moment later he returned with two glasses. I wondered about the Jamaican Murphys and why her mother was a keynote speaker.

"It's Prosecco. He knows I like it," Arin said, tilting her glass to the bartender. "Would you prefer something else?"

I was more of a beer guy, but I gave it a try. I didn't love it, but it was cold and refreshing.

"This works," I said.

Arin sipped her drink then spun the stem in her fingers for a moment. "I understand that you met Dr. Garcia."

"Yes." I smiled, recalling her. "Impressive woman."

Arin's eyes lit up. "You have no idea. She's brilliant, one of my mentors in college. She's a close family friend," she said, batting a fly away. "And it's brave of you to jump on a plane on zero notice. I'm excited you're here."

"Thanks." I let out a little laugh.

"What?" The corners of her mouth rose. "Why are you laughing?"

I hunched my shoulders up and raised my palms.

"I'm not sure why I'm here."

Arin had taken a sip of Prosecco and almost spat it out.

"What did she tell you?" She leaned closer.

"That I'm meeting with the great-great-granddaughter of Mack Murphy, that we share the family tree separated by centuries, and that she has information that might help find the *Book*."

"That's all?" asked Arin, her eyes widening. "Here's to you, Key Murphy, a trusting man."

"Isn't 'go with the flow' kind of a Jamaican thing?"

"True, that." She raised her glass. I met hers with my own.

"Besides, I learned today that you have a doctorate in social anthropology, taught at Temple, and dated Jerome Pinter. And you are friends with Usain, can't leave that out. What I don't know is if you experience memories."

Arin sank back in her chair, a slight twitch crossed her cheek, and she allowed an almost imperceptible moan in her exhale.

"I wish," she answered. "But you give me hope. We are around the same age, so it's possible they will kick in. All I have experienced are occasional pictures, like stills, that are not of anything I know."

"Why do you want them?"

"Are you serious?" Her brows arched; her green eyes narrowed. "I am completely envious."

I shook my head as the terror of the Viking attack at the monastery raced through my veins, the blade cutting the air toward my throat.

"Be careful what you wish for. I know my life will be changed forever. I just don't know how."

"That's the point," she answered, her eyes alive, beaming. "It will be changed. Who gets to do that? Do you have any idea how special you are?"

I said nothing but felt my heart race at her words.

"I study tribes and clans from the past and their migrations." She swept her hands toward the bankers. "What do you see?"

I looked at them closely. They appeared to be middle-aged, well-dressed businesspeople, mostly various shades of dark skin. Thankfully, she didn't wait for an answer.

"The woman in the blue dress, with the purple sash," she gestured toward her, "Black Trinidadian mixed with East Indian heritage. The man she's talking to, you probably think he's white. I'm guessing German Irish, from Barbados, with a healthy sprinkling of West African. I can give you fairly accurate detail about most of these people by observing their skin tone and bone structure."

She leaned close as if to share a secret. She blinked, her breath cool against my skin.

"Do you know what I *don't* get to do? I don't get to see through their eyes." She put her hand on my forearm. A charge ran through me. "Tell me everything you can about the memories—what you learned, what it felt like."

She rested her arms on the table, her fingers laid a matchstick away from my right hand. Her body leaned forward, eager to enter some secret world.

I started with the scriptorium, Tomás securing the *Book*,

the escape from Iona, and ended with Aedan and Siobhán making love.

As I finished, Jimmy Downey was walking our way. As he passed our table he nodded and kept going, like he didn't have a care in the world.

I still wasn't buying it.

CHAPTER 13

November 21, 2019

The Blue Window Restaurant, Pegasus Hotel

"That's extraordinary, Key. You actually saw the *Book*?"

"I saw the box it was in, not the *Book*. Not yet." I noticed it was getting dark and that her eyes had closed. Better to conjure the images, I assumed.

The manager approached our table.

"Dr. Murphy, the chef awaits you."

We followed him into the restaurant, past white and red poinsettias, large and small. Christmas lights and candle displays created a festive ambiance while Bing Crosby promised a white Christmas. With seventy-nine-degree night-time temperatures, it was hard to imagine Christmas just four weeks away.

He seated us by the window overlooking the pool. The outdoor lights came on, reflecting upwards onto palm trees. The pool, lit up, blue and rippling in the soft breeze, created a romantic mood. I had to remind myself that I was not on a date. I hadn't been on a date in a while.

I scanned the menu.

"So many great choices, but you know the menu. Would you order for me?" I checked to make sure I was reading it correctly. "Anything but goat and oxtail."

Arin beckoned the waiter and ordered in words beyond me, in a thick Jamaican accent. I knew there was a dialect here that contained English, but I was lost.

"I told him to do the chef's table, several small plates so that you can get a taste of Jamaica. No goat, no oxtail, but I hope you are okay with the curried snake. It's an island delicacy."

She must have seen a flash of my discomfort, and laughed. "Don't worry, I told him the snake is for me, but I'll share if you want." I couldn't tell if she was joking.

Moments later, two wineglasses and a bottle of cabernet sauvignon arrived with the manager. "We've been holding this for you. May I open it?"

Arin nodded.

She sipped the wine and offered her approval. This college professor was being treated like the Queen. While she was involved with the wine ritual, I observed her: confident, passionate, playful. She brushed back a few stray ringlets and glanced over at me.

"Your turn," I said quickly, to distract myself from my staring. "Tell me about Mack."

"Does your family have an obsession?" She answered my question with a question.

I chuckled.

"Absolutely, my parents are obsessed with Ireland."

"So were Mack and my father. As I told you earlier," Arin continued, "Mack has been an obsession in my family for over one hundred and fifty years. As you've probably figured out, my dad is white, my mother is Black. Even though she's not a descendant of Mack, her obsession might exceed my father's. He died a few years ago."

"That's rough," I said, thinking what it would be like losing my father.

"It was." Arin looked past me, her eyes far away for a moment. "Not was, is."

"We have something in common regarding our parents. Mine have been praying that the memories awaken in me and that it might lead to finding the *Book*." I lifted my wineglass, and she joined me. "To our ancestors."

Arin's eyes brightened, both of us sipped the wine.

"Your great-grandfather met my great-great-grandfather, Mack. That's just amazing."

The enthusiasm in her voice excited me.

"And here we are, you and me. Fate? Divine providence? The cosmic roulette wheel?" She leaned in close, waiting on my answer. I had no idea what to say.

"I just found out today that they met. Tell me about Mack. I know that he descends from Fergus Murphy and that Fergus was taken from Ireland around 1690 and sent as a convict to Jamaica."

Arin reacted quickly, fire in her eyes.

"He wasn't a convict. That was England's attempt to give it some legitimacy. He was stolen. There were thousands of Irish sent to British plantations all over the Indies. Some were indentured. Most were arrested on whatever false charge they cooked up. It did not matter. They couldn't fight it. They were British property to do whatever the Brits wanted them to do. Do you know about the Cromwell period?"

"I'm embarrassed to say that I know very little," I said contritely.

"Oliver Cromwell was sent to subjugate the Irish people and ensure it was a defenseless colony that offered no resistance. He tried to destroy their language and religion." Arin shook her head, interlaced her fingers, and drew in a deep breath. "He settled Scots loyal to the crown to populate the country, particularly in the north. His aim was to eradicate

Irish culture and identity, to make it a wholly owned subsidiary of England. Just like they did to Jamaica. Just like they did to African slaves. But the Irish had something the slaves didn't. Do you know what that was?"

I shrugged my shoulders and kept my attention on her. A look that flirted between pain and anger played on her face.

"They had a name. They had a place they dreamed of called Ireland. The Africans were stripped of their names and made to forget where they came from. They had no country to call home. They were simply property. Imagine having no name. Imagine having no identity. Imagine having to use the surname of your owner. Imagine being owned. They had to create their own identity out of the little bits and pieces that elders could remember."

All I could think of was Tanya and Buck. Their surname was McCoy. Was that their slave name? Did Irish people own their ancestors? Marry them?

Arin turned her eyes to the pool deck and kept them there for a moment.

"Fergus Murphy was ripped from Ireland as a young man. As miserable as his life was, he was still indentured and would work his way to some semblance of freedom. And he could read and write. He wrote about Ireland and the Africans whom he lived among. He wrote about the Irish warriors of the past, the horrors of slavery and the treatment of Africans. His legend and writings were passed down in the family, and it found life in Mack Murphy."

A waiter placed a cedar plank on the table. Curry shrimp lined it. Swirls of colorful sauces were artfully displayed on the board. The waiter explained that the golden-colored sauce was mango-coconut; the green was Scotch bonnet-guava-pesto. The smell teased my senses.

"True confession: there is no curried snake. The shrimp

will have to do." Arin took a shrimp, lightly touching it to the green sauce. "This is very spicy. Go lightly at first."

I eagerly dipped a shrimp into the mango sauce and nodded for her to continue while the spices lit up my taste buds.

"Slavery ended in Jamaica before Mack was born, but he had a fire in him and a hatred of injustice and England. Mack Murphy knew that his destiny was written by Fergus. He was to find his way to Ireland. But first he had to fight slavery where it still existed. America."

"I wish I could have met him," I said. "He sounds amazing."

Arin smiled and put her hand on mine for a brief moment.

"Your great-grandfather met him. He helped Mack. He was part of the story, and now so are you." She paused to sip her wine. "Sorry."

"For what?

"Talking too much," she said, toying with her earing.

"I want to hear more." I nodded my wineglass to her. "Please."

"Think about it. Mack was eighteen. White. He could have left Jamaica and made an easier life in America. But he chose to fight."

Arin speared another shrimp. I followed, the sweetness of mango and the savory spices of the curry making my stomach rumble.

A soft smile played on her lips.

"I'm glad you are enjoying the food."

"Ya mon," I said, sounding stupid, but happy to get a little laugh from her.

"Please finish the story."

Arin played her fork absently in the sauces, quiet, seeming to contemplate.

"Most people don't know this, but many of the slaves in the American South were the daughters and sons of Jamaican slaves, sold to the Southern plantation owners. He could not let that stand. He fought with the Irish Brigade in the Union Army and made the connections that would eventually lead him to Ireland. He married before leaving Jamaica with the full intent of being back in two to three years, but he never made it. He didn't know at the time that his wife was pregnant with his child that he never met. And generations later, here I am."

I sat back in my chair, feeling the impact of this last sentence. I had never given thought to the idea that several generations later, here *I* was. I tried to be a typical American kid. Not easy, with all this prodigy stuff happening. But I longed for it: baseball, football, summers in Wildwood, girls. Nothing wrong with that, but I felt like I'd missed something important, though it wasn't from my parents' lack of trying. Growing up, I honestly did not give a shit about Ireland and all the depressing stories about oppression. Mack Murphy did. He did something about it. Aedan and Mack and Fergus and Eamon were luring me, whispering to me. I couldn't help but think, "Where the fuck is all this going?"

"What? Key, are you okay?" Arin looked around the restaurant.

"Yeah, why?"

"You just said, 'Where the fuck is all this going?'" she whispered.

"Did I say that out loud?" I honestly didn't know.

Arin nodded.

A few diners were shooting glances my way. I hunched forward.

"I'm trying to take it all in. Four days ago, I was investigating criminals. Now I'm on medical leave chasing a ghost that you say I look like."

Arin smiled.

"You're not alone. I also wonder where this is all going.

But I'm excited about the possibilities." Her eyes locked on mine. "Now that you're here."

I felt my face warm. "I'm happy too."

The waiter placed a plate of jerk sausage bruschetta in front of each of us. The spice had a kick that put a slight burn on my throat. I loved it and dug in for more fire.

I delighted in watching Arin enjoying the food and wine. Truth was, I delighted in just watching her.

"Do you know that twenty-five percent of all Jamaicans have Irish heritage?" she asked.

"No, I admit I don't know much about Jamaica."

Dean Martin started singing "Baby It's Cold Outside". I snuck a glance at people swimming in the pool then turned my attention back to Arin.

"Black Jamaicans have surnames that are predominately English, Scottish, and Irish. As I said, they were stripped of their African surnames. Most English and Scottish surnames come from adopting the plantation owner's or slave master's name. Most of the Irish surnames come from the intermarriage of Irish and Africans. The Murphy men had traditionally married other Irish women, though. There were a lot of them in Jamaica at one time. My father was the first to marry a Black woman."

"And the results are amazing." I smiled. Arin blushed. I raised my glass again. She followed. "Here's to the Murphys," I toasted, trying to cover my awkwardness. "And here's to you, a woman with one foot in Jamaica and the other in Ireland."

"And this Jamaican woman has a class to teach in the morning. I've arranged for the hotel to bring you to my office at ten. I'll leave a notebook on my desk with some letters from Mack. I'll be there around eleven thirty."

Arin held her glass still, seeming to have disappeared for a moment. "Will you help me find it, Key?"

The gods of tranquility have abandoned me. My head

bobbed in the affirmative. I could feel a grin take hold. My smile disappeared as I pictured Jimmy Downey and recalled my father's words from just this morning: "There are people willing to kill for it."

Her glass reached mine, and the ping of glass against glass rang out. So did the Jamaican accent of Dreadlock Man, peering into my future, just weeks ago, his gun aimed at my head. His words: "I'm coming for yuh, bwoy. One day."

CHAPTER 14

November 22, 2019
The University of the West Indies

The University sat in the valley, the Blue Mountains ranging upward from the foothills, the grass browned, the sun pounding it with its hot fists. The driver explained that this had been a sugar plantation and that some of the plantations' slaves' skeletal remains had recently been uncovered. I wondered if this was where Fergus Murphy and the other Irish were brought to work the fields.

The driver took a short detour to point out the track where Usain Bolt trained. He proudly boasted that they were cousins. I wondered if Jamaicans had the same definition of cousins as the Irish, where a cousin was actually just a friend of a friend of your real cousin.

Arin's was a typical professor's office. Books, photos, diplomas on the wall. Bachelors from Yale, Masters from Cork, Doctorate from Georgetown. Impressive and expensive.

Photos were scattered around bookshelves and on the walls. Arin with a group of young people in front of Big Ben. A photo with Arin and another woman standing with Bishop

Tutu and Nelson Mandela. The real surprise: Arin, and I assume her parents and brother, standing with President Obama. A gold plate below read: *President Barack Obama, Jamaica, April 2015.*

I sat at her desk and opened the binder. Her grandfather had written a foreword not so different from my own father's.

I, Kevin Murphy, attest that everything you find in these pages is my experience as best I can relate it. Here you will find the direct testimony of my grandfather, Mack Murphy.

I write this to document his life for future generations of our kin. I grew up knowing that my ancestors before me had "the gift". Although I did not have it, I learned in Mack's letters that he met a man in Ireland from the distant family tree who also had it. His name was Eamon Murphy.

I wish I possessed this gift. It is maddening to read Mack's letters and to realize that he was unique among men. It gave him a purpose that traveled through time and touched me as it did my father. We are of mind and purpose to find the *Book* and fulfill his legacy. Until then, may future generations of our family hold true to this vision. If you have the gift, learn from it and use it for the good of our family, our country, and humanity.

The Irish are a superstitious people and lovers of fables. Even those of us separated from Ireland for over one hundred years still talk of fairies and Druids and magical trees. The Jamaican Africans are even more magically inclined. It would be easy to dismiss what you read here as Irish imagination, but if you do, then you short-change the significance of your true family history.

I never met my grandfather, Mack Murphy. He left when he was eighteen, seeking passage through America to Ireland. He promised to return to his wife, my grandmother, though that was not to be. He had to get to Ireland, for there, hidden for a thousand years, was something left by our ancestors.

I looked up from the page to the photo with Arin and Obama and was overwhelmed by the fact that Mack's progeny was standing with the first black president.

This was his first letter from the U.S.

My Sweetest Moira,

I was never so happy to feel the earth beneath my feet. The journey north was not for the meek; the waters were often troubled and dangerous, but also mesmerizing and beautiful. New York is indescribable. Kingston is but a quiet village in comparison. The energy and life here is intoxicating. How I wish you were with me to feel this young country, still in its infancy, growing and expanding. Even with the war raging, it feels as if only optimism and opportunity abound here.

In the two days that I have been here, I have met so many Irish. They marvel at my accent, and when they learn about us Irish in Jamaica, they all wipe a tear, for the story of what they call the "lost ones" is well known. To a man and a woman, all of them curse Cromwell. Little do they know that had I not grown up in Jamaica, I would not have known my Moira, and for that I am the happiest man I know.

I must keep this short as the ship that will carry this letter to you leaves in a few hours. I am well. I miss you every moment of every day. As soon as I have a way for you to write to me, I will let you know speedily.

Your loving husband,
Mack

I scanned several pages. They were typed but with handwritten notes in the margins. Most were initialed A.M.; I assumed meaning Arin Murphy.

I focused on the note that said Pennsylvania, and read Mack's letter.

To My Moira,

Not a moment goes by, my love, that I do not think about holding you in my arms. You are the light that guides me, and I pray to our Father in Heaven that this journey is short and that he returns me to you soon.

My eyes glided over his poetic words, searching for some insight.

I am in a place called Pennsylvania. Our camp is among rolling hills and streams, and I can imagine us together here with a brood of six children and a peaceful life on our own terms. As a soldier, I may become a citizen one day.

Every week or so I am seized by the memories. I am learning to control their effect on me, but some are so jarring that I fear it happening when I am in battle and need my wits about me. The images are becoming clearer, and I believe that Deaglan will lead me to the hiding place one day. I have seen The Book in his hands and am filled with awe that I will recover it and return it to its rightful place. Till now, I have not seen the clues that Conall and Deaglan discuss. Or, if I am seeing them, it's not clear.

I stop reading. My hands are shaking. "This is crazy," I say to Jerome Pinter's jersey. "Mack had the memories of Deaglan. Dad has the memories from his brother Conall."

I finished reading the rest of the letter.

It is painful how much I miss you. I miss the smells and beauty of Jamaica. I long for our swims in the cool streams, and the fruit that God must have created just for Jamaica, for none here have the flavors of home.

I picture myself holding you, loving you, and kissing your divine lips.

>*You are forever in my heart.*
>*Your husband, Mack*

"Holy crap," I say to no one as I walk around the desk.

Eighteen freaking years old, I think to myself. What kind of fire must have burned in him to do this? What stuff was he made of? I felt inferior in the presence of his letters, but he had lit a spark. Was I capable of chasing his dream? I needed to find out.

I contemplated what new memories I might experience and what they might reveal. I wished I could make them happen by will, but I could only wait for them to expose themselves.

I sat, ready to read some more. Arin entered. I looked up, hoping to see her smile, but she didn't. Her jaw was tight, her shoulders slightly bunched. In place of a T-shirt, she wore an elegant white blouse with gray pants. A colorful humming-bird necklace dangled between the separation in her blouse, accenting her brown skin. Her curls were pulled back into a short ponytail, a few strays lying on her cheek.

"Good morning," I offered.

"Hi. We're having lunch with my mother. She will fill in a lot of information for you. She's leaving for a meeting in Ocho Rios in a few hours, so we need to go quickly. Bring the folder. We won't be coming back here."

"One minute; I need you to read something." I pointed to the paragraph with Mack writing about Deaglan and Conall. She skimmed it.

"My father sees through the eyes of Conall."

She looked down at the page again, her body wobbling a moment, a smile beginning, her green eyes widening.

"We're going to find it," she said, turning to me. "Right?"

I lifted the folder from the desk, pursed my lips, took a deep, reassuring breath.

"Hell yeah."

———

I followed Arin to a different parking lot than I was in yesterday. We passed a beautiful modern building close to completion. Unlike the other buildings made of concrete, this one was all glass, steel, and aluminum mesh. As we drew closer, I noted that the columns at the entrance were in the form of DNA strands. The sign outside read:

THE JAMES AND JOYCE MURPHY BIOTECH CENTER FOR ADVANCED RESEARCH.

And I was about to meet Joyce.

I was unsure what kind of car I expected, but I was surprised to get into a crappy Camry. It didn't fit the sense of royalty that I observed last night. I guess she noticed my confusion.

"Kingston still suffers a fair amount of crime. I don't like to draw attention to myself, especially when I'm alone. Better to blend in."

"Makes sense," I said. "Tell me about your mom."

"My mother is one of the most powerful people in Jamaica." She pulled her seatbelt on and headed for the exit. Students were walking out of buildings. I assumed, like me, hungry for lunch.

I turned back to Arin.

"She and my father started a commercial bakery business almost thirty-five years ago, selling to the resorts, hotels, and grocers. They started buying some smaller hotels before the boutique concept even had a name. They leveraged that into buying several large resorts and eventually banks, telecom, and IT companies."

"From buns to banks." I knew Arin had probably heard that a million times, but I couldn't help myself.

Her smile caused another charge of electricity.

"She's still very involved, but it's my brother Joseph that runs the businesses. My interest wasn't business, which is good because my parents had other hopes for me."

"Which are?" I shifted in the seat and turned to her.

"My parents are fanatics about education, my mother in particular. We are a small country with a poor education system, and too many Jamaicans still live in poverty. Wealthier families send their kids to private schools and then to the U.S., Canada, and England for their degrees. Most educated Jamaicans remain in one of those countries. We want them back here contributing, building the country, creating a tax base that can financially support education for poor kids and help break the cycle of poverty." Arin stopped at a traffic light and started laughing.

"What?"

"I sound like a politician."

"You sound passionate." I nodded to her. "So, what's their hope for you?"

Arin made a turn and continued, "My mother advises the Prime Minister and the Minister of Education, a role she hopes I'll one day fill."

"Do you mean that you will one day advise them?"

"No."

"That you'll be the Prime Minister or—?"

"Both."

"What do you mean both?"

"She wants—I should say, she plans—for me to be the Minister of Education first, and then Prime Minister."

"Wow, Arin. That's thinking big."

We drove past street markets and strip malls that you might see anywhere in the U.S., then up winding roads of mansions and mini-mansions with gardens that looked like they were from magazines.

Arin stopped the car in front of a security gate. A guard leaned out from the booth and waved as the gates opened.

We wended up a drive as a gleaming white mansion came into view, like something you'd see in Beverly Hills. I was viewing an estate owned by the descendent of a teenager who was torn from Ireland and sent to Jamaica to live a brutal life. And a descendant of an African slave, her history erased and her name replaced with her owner's. Just to think those words, "her owner", made my skin crawl. And sitting next to me was a beautiful and intelligent woman they dreamed would one day be Prime Minister.

Two of the security guards were so old they looked like they couldn't guard a Red Stripe from being sipped, but the third had serious muscle and was packing. This Murphy clan seemed to take care of the people who had been with them. The groundskeepers were also mostly old and slow. They'd probably been with Arin's family since she was in diapers. Arin rolled down the window and waved to one woman in the garden.

"The doctor say?" Arin asked.

The woman smiled, her floral dress falling below her knees, holding a kerchief to wipe her brow. "Everyting irie, darlin. Lickle tired is all."

"Get some rest, ya hear?" Arin said sternly but with a smile. "Christmas coming soon, and your family want to make you cook and dance and have fun."

When we exited the car and approached the beautiful three-story mansion, the door opened. A regal woman stepped onto the patio. Arin's mom must have been in her sixties but didn't look a day over fifty. Stylish black jeans, gunmetal gray blouse, pearl necklace, short gray braids. As I climbed the steps to the landing, she reached out her hand.

"Welcome, Key. I'm Joyce," she said, her eyes never leaving my face. "Arin's right. You look like him."

She walked into the house, and we followed. She stopped in front of a wall of paintings and portraits, and I saw why Arin had been surprised. Mack and I looked like brothers—his hair wavier than mine.

"This is weird," I said quietly to her.

I followed Arin while taking in the details—marble winding staircase, twelve-foot-high ceilings, hand-carved wooden furniture, and what I guessed was African and Caribbean paintings on the walls. I stopped for a moment, my eyes caught by a family portrait. I could see the Mack family resemblance in her father.

"How old are you in this?" I asked.

"Sixteen."

"It's a beautiful painting."

Arin opened the doors to a patio the size of a basketball court where an infinity pool was beckoning, with a knockout view of Kingston and the Caribbean gleaming on the edges.

A maid served lemonade and lunch: curried chicken on a bed of lettuces, slices of mango and papaya on the circumference. Once again, the smell of spices awakened my appetite.

"Key, I must leave soon, so forgive me for jumping right in," Joyce started. "Arin has told me a little of your story. She has told you some of ours. I've also done some research on you and your family. Your mother is quite the Indiana Jones of music. Your father is very connected in Ireland and runs a successful business, one that you might take over."

Joyce regarded me casually. Like Buck does when interrogating a suspect—relaxing them, drawing them in. I'm curious where she's going with this.

"You've made quite a name for yourself as an investigator." Joyce sipped her lemonade. "It's not surprising. You spoke, what, two, three languages by the time you were five. Won championships in math and science before you were in your teens. You were considered a chess prodigy, at least for a time."

Much of my story had been put online years ago by curious media. My rises to glory, my falls from grace. But this, Aedan, the memories. This was different. So was Arin.

"The question is, what do you want from this?"

"I forgot to mention that she's very direct," Arin interjected.

Looking squarely at Joyce, I answered. "It's okay. I have the same question of you. What do *you* want, and can we work together to get it?"

"Good," Joyce replied. "Straight to the point."

"My world went upside down in the last seventy-two hours." I had worked with people like Joyce before. She was used to ruling the world. If I wanted to make an impression, I needed to cut through the bullshit. I looked her straight in the eyes. "I learned two days ago that I was witnessing the memories of an ancestor. Aedan. He was charged by his uncle, the king, with protecting what we know as the *Book of Kells*. I also learned that my father sees through the eyes of

Conall. He and his brother Deaglan are also descendants of Aedan, and they stole the cover and nine pages from the *Book*."

I nudged my chair to the right, facing Arin.

"Your grandfather, three times removed, is Mack Murphy. Mack was a wanted man by the British. He sought out my great-grandfather, Eamon, for help to return to the States and made him pledge that if something happened to him, Eamon must retrieve the *Book* and return it to its rightful owner, Ireland. Mack saw through the eyes of Deaglan."

I held a copy of the letter from Eamon Murphy. "My great-grandfather wrote this as a memoir." I slid it to Joyce. "Please read this."

Joyce began to read out loud, then paused.

"This is from his meeting with Mack?"

"Yes."

"This is Mack talking at first," Joyce said to Arin. "'It seems that we have more in common than our surname. Is it true you have experienced day visions, memories from someone long ago?'"

I waited while she read the remainder in silence.

I fixed my eyes on Joyce. "You asked me what I want. I want, my family wants, to bring the *Book* and any treasure back to Ireland. What do you want?"

Joyce sat silently, her fingers tapping on the letter, glancing at me, then turning away. She did this several times. Finally, she slid a new binder in front of me. She opened it and put her finger at the top of the page. "This is a photocopy of the envelope, postmarked Philadelphia. The date is January 3, 1916.

"A few months before the Easter Uprising," I added.

"Read."

To Moira, my best friend and wife,

Can you ever forgive me for not coming back to you years ago? Can I forgive myself? I have given everything for the cause of a free Ireland. What I have done is not fair to you, but it seems that time and God made me and my forefathers a vessel for this cause. I have now left Ireland to safeguard a tremendous secret. One day soon, Ireland will be free, and I will return the sacred artefact. The Book at Trinity will be whole again, a symbol of Ireland rising, throwing off the yoke of colonialism. And I, as a son of Jamaica, will let the world know the strength of the Jamaican people and how we kept the torch lit for Ireland, Jamaica, and for Fergus.

I have made the artefact safe for now. I have sent word to a trusted relative in Ireland, telling him where to find it in the event of my demise. I do not know if my letters are read before they arrive to you, but I provide these clues. If he fails, then someone in the Murphy clan must step forward.

I visit the grave of my general, with whom we won the great battle for Lincoln and our cause. I pray to him and my brothers from the brigade who dot the earth around me, intercede with the saints to keep the Book safe until I can retrieve it and go back to a free and safe Ireland. I look down at the river after paying my respects, and I travel to the other river:

> *By the church of two ships*
> *Where lay at rest two soldiers*
> *One fought beside me brave and strong*
> *The other a captain from Washington's war*
> *For among these two nobles a secret kept*
> *Safe from the time when Ireland wept*
> *for the future I have made this ploy*
> *to return it home for Ireland's joy.*

May that task be soon, as my aging wish is to be with you, Moira, or at least be buried near you, for Jamaica owns my soul, Ireland owns my spirit, and you have always owned my heart. I walk from the graveyard to the river below. Water, the giver of life, soon deliver me to Ireland and then home to Jamaica.

I love you forever,
Your husband, Mack

"Why haven't you searched for it until now?" I asked.

"Mack made it very clear that only someone from the Murphy clan may be trusted," Joyce replied. "I wanted to hire experts, but my husband forbade it, so we tried it ourselves. There is not much trace of Mack in the U.S. He didn't want to be found, and he didn't want anyone outside of the family tree to have access. His clues are extremely vague. There are hundreds of cemeteries in America with Irish Brigade soldiers. We tried," nodding to Arin. "Perhaps we were supposed to wait for you."

I read the clues once again, took my phone from my pocket, and dialed my mother. She picked up on the first ring.

"Key, how is everything?"

"All good. Do you have your notes handy?"

"Yes."

"Read me the part where Eamon agrees to help Mack."

She did, and I asked, "Do you think he was referring to County Cork?"

"I assume so. The city of Cork is frequently referred to as Cork Town. Why?"

"Eamon was arranging Mack's transport to the U.S. He tells Mack that his friends are in Cork Town. Wasn't Corktown the Irish section in West Philly? It's called Mantua now."

"Yes, your grandfather lived there for a time."

I thanked my mom and disconnected.

"I have a hunch. Probably wrong." I connected to the

browser on my phone. "I believe Eamon sent Mack to Philadelphia. There is only one cemetery that overlooks a river, as far as I know. It's called Laurel Hill. General Meade is buried there. He won the battle at Gettysburg. Several Irish brigades fought under him." I looked back at Mack's letter. "It overlooks the Schuylkill River. But I don't understand the reference to the Church of Two Ships. Everything else fits."

"Is that the cemetery over Kelly Drive?" Arin asked.

"Yes." I nodded to her, remembering her time in my hometown. "Joyce, my flight is tomorrow. I'll be back before the cemetery closes. I can text you and Arin what I find."

"No need. Arin is going with you," Joyce answered, arms folded. As if I was about to argue.

I pivoted to Arin.

"I've made the arrangements." She sat up straighter, her eyes alive and mischievous. "My classes are covered."

"I don't know what we're getting ourselves into. We're talking about a major find that's worth a lot of money." My tone was intentionally serious. "Might be dangerous."

"My daughter can handle herself," added Joyce, a bit gruffly. "This damn thing has been haunting our family for generations. I married into this craziness, and Arin and I are the only ones who can see it through from this side of the family tree. There is no way this happens without us. Are we clear on that?"

"I'm happy to have Arin with me."

Joyce pushed the notebook to me. "Arin can help you understand the context." She said to Arin, "I'll have my office book your hotel in Philly."

"Arin can stay with my parents. There is no way my mom would let her stay at a hotel. I live a few minutes away." I turned to Arin. "Are you good with this?"

"Cris," she responded.

I guessed that was Jamaican for yes.

I turned back to Joyce.

"You never answered my question. What do you want?"

Joyce smiled for the first time.

"The same thing your family wants. I want to honor my husband and his ancestors, Arin's ancestors. I want to complete Mack's journey and reunite the missing pages with the *Book of Kells*." I heard her draw a sharp breath, her eyes intent, her words starting with a quiver. "What I want, what I demand, is that if we succeed, no, when we succeed, the story of the Irish indentured and the Jamaican slaves be told. And that the world looks at Jamaica with new eyes. That it sees beyond the resorts and the rum and reggae—all the stereotypes—to a beautiful people who are honoring the past and creating a profound future. I want them to see an Arin Murphy, a child of both worlds, and understand the motto of Jamaica, Out of Many, One People."

Joyce paused, closed her eyes briefly then opened them to me. "I want them to know that we were the children of bondage and that we have freed ourselves. And maybe, for a brief moment, the world will feel hope, and Jamaicans will feel respect."

I look past Joyce to the horizon, imagining the slave ships heading to the shore and marvel at the endurance of her people. I can't help but think that Joyce has also calculated that our venture would be a perfect platform for Arin's climb into politics.

The patio door opened. A man in a suit entered and addressed Joyce.

"The team is ready."

He turned and backed out.

Joyce stood. I joined her. She took my hands in hers.

"Over one hundred and fifty years, that's how long this family has been waiting to fulfill Mack Murphy's dream. That's how long we have been waiting for you. Let your ancestor speak to you. Indigenous people worldwide have practices where they awaken their ancestors through peyote, ganja, and ritual dance. All in an attempt to hear the ages speak. Let your ancestors lead you. This is your destiny. Own it."

She turned to leave then looked back.

"Take care of my daughter, or I'll have to come to Philly and kick your ass."

I waited for a smile, but none came.

CHAPTER 15

5 MONTHS AGO

PHILADELPHIA

The Irish American Chamber of Commerce Annual Awards Ceremony was held in Philadelphia this year. The Honoree was Padraig Collins. In the introduction to Collins, the Chamber President, Kathleen O'Riordan, spoke of Collins's climb out of poverty, his patient investment in real estate, the IT empire that was now global, his philanthropy, and passion for Ireland. There was no mention of the IRA or the fact that he'd been a commander. No one knew that but a few, mostly deceased, former IRA members. He was, for the rest of the world, the self-made man, the Irish Sir Richard Branson.

Collins assumed the role. He put away his feral demeanor and gave them what they wanted, the smooth business leader and philanthropist. The audience hung on his every word. He had invited Dr. Garcia to meet with him while he was in her city and now noted to himself that she was seated in the back of the hall.

As he was bringing his speech to a close, he gestured to her.

"Today we are graced by the presence of a genius, a woman whose discoveries are collapsing the walls that constrain how we think about evolution and memory. She's on the doorstep of medical breakthroughs, expanding our consciousness. She is revealing, through science, what geneticists, philosophers, and spiritual teachers have been urging humanity to understand."

Collins's eyes swept over the crowd. He counted to five in his head.

"Although we joyfully embrace our cultures and celebrate our diversity," he continued, "the reality is that we are all one. There is no Irish or English, Korean or Chinese. We all migrated from Africa millennia ago. We founded cultures and knowledge, which are great things, but, as we race toward an uncertain world of climate disaster, of world leaders pitting one group against another for their own narrow gain, with hatred on the rise, it's the work of people like my friend and colleague that will remind us of our better nature. Please recognize a true friend of Ireland and humanity, Dr. Sylvia Garcia."

As the applause died down, cameras and reporters turned to her. Collins watched her wave to the audience. He saw daggers in her eyes, and it pleased him.

Collins took the wireless microphone from the podium, stepped off the stage, and walked among the tables of his well-dressed American cousins, young and old. Like the seanchaí, the storytellers of old, he spun his tale in campfire whisper.

"My patron saint, Columba, caused division and war among Irish tribes. Many died. Horrified by his actions, he exiled himself to the Isle of Iona in Scotland. There he founded a monastery; it was to be one of many. He traveled inland to the Pict tribes, who were warring with the Scotti. There he taught peace and unity."

Again he paused, as if in search of the proper words.

"The penance for his sins, my friends, was to unite different peoples." His voice rose. "There has never been a better time for us to do the same. Ireland is on the brink of historic change, and we must seize this opportunity to gain a united Ireland, an Ireland that respects all. Although I do not yet know how, I believe that Dr. Garcia will play a role, as Saint Columba did, to help create peace and unity. No bullets, no bombs, no borders. That is the Irish future."

———

As arranged, Collins went into a small private room, away from the Chamber event's prying eyes. Dr. Garcia awaited him.

"I have found someone who has the mutation, right here in Philadelphia," she told Collins. "His name is Shaun Murphy. He is a DNA match to Joseph's family in Jamaica. I made contact immediately. He has the memory of someone who stole the *Book of Kells* from the monastery."

Collins's face beamed at this news.

"This is a miracle. Tell me more."

"I don't have much more to tell. I'll bring Joseph's family and Shaun together at some point, but, and it is extremely important that you understand this, it will take time."

"How much time?"

"There's no way to know," the petite scientist answered.

"Why not?"

The room was the hotel's version of a backstage green room: a table, chair, mirror, two plush chairs, and an ice bucket with small bottles of sparkling water.

Dr. Garcia twisted the cap off a bottle of Perrier.

"I've interviewed a few hundred people who have experienced the memories. Many of them are psychologically damaged. They believe they're crazy, hearing voices, seeing visions, and their friends and family tend to agree. In fact, many of them were diagnosed as bipolar or schizophrenic."

Collins replied, "Aye, that makes sense."

"In many cases, it takes months to gain their trust. Some of them believe they're guarding a secret that's meant only for them." Garcia sipped the Perrier. "I—along with my team of psychiatrists and psychologists—have come to understand that over time some individuals can no longer distinguish between their own memories and the ones they are witnessing. Neurologically, the brain, the nervous system, can't separate them."

Collins leaned against the table and ran his thumb over his chin.

"It doesn't mean that they don't live normal lives. Most do," Garcia continued, "but in this area they tend to be fragile. Luckily, Shaun Murphy seems genuinely enthusiastic about his experience. He claims that his great-grandfather also had the gene."

"His great-grandfather? Did you get his name?"

"Eamon Murphy."

Collins blessed himself and dropped to one knee. "Do you pray, Doctor?"

"I don't," Garcia replied emphatically, surprised to see Collins kneeling.

"Then I'll pray on behalf of both of us. Eamon met Mack Murphy before he left Ireland with the Book." Collins closed his eyes, bent his head, and prayed silently. Then he rose and took his notes from the table. "The clock is now ticking. Do everything you can to speed this up. The saint I pray to preached patience, something I never quite got the knack of."

CHAPTER 16

Arin had switched from her more formal clothes into a T-shirt and beige capris. The shirt read – DON'T MAKE ME REPEAT MYSELF, *HISTORY*.

"It's a thing," she said, pointing to the shirt as she started the car. "Friends and students started giving me these. I must have the largest collection of goofy academic T-shirts in the world."

"I like it," I said while glancing back at the mansion. "Do you live here?" I asked as we exited the property.

"Yes. It's just my mother and me and a few live-in staff. She splits her time between here and Ocho Rios, where we have a home and offices."

I looked at my watch. One forty-seven.

"Didn't I read somewhere that as a proud Jamaican you are duty-bound to make sure a guest doesn't leave without trying some jerk chicken?"

She glanced at me, a conspiratorial look in her eyes. "So,

you want a Jamaican experience?" She had her left-turn signal on, paused a moment, and then made a right turn. "I'm taking you for the Kingston special."

I pried my eyes from her smile to watch as the area transformed from upscale to ghetto. Arin had talked about poverty. It was right in front of me. Kingston was a city of contrasts. We passed dilapidated homes with corrugated rusting roofs. Goats roamed freely. People walked lazily in the heat. Vendors hoped for a passing car to stop and buy something, anything, so that a meal could be had that night.

"Sucks, right?" Arin recognized the look on my face with a nod. "Now you can understand where our passion comes from."

She slowed the car. "Look to the left. That's Tuff Gong, Bob Marley's studio. This was his area, Trench Town."

I glance at the yellow building with a large mural of Bob Marley on the wall. Just after we passed Tuff Gong, I saw cement mixers, men pushing wheelbarrows, shirts sweat-stained, and pylons with rebar reaching upward. Arin explained that the Chinese government ran infrastructure projects all over Jamaica.

I didn't see anyone Chinese, though, only a mass of black humanity, and I felt like I stuck out like a white dot in the dark sea. I realized for the first time what it must have been like to be a black dot in a sea of white. White people, at least in America, rarely got to feel what it was like to be a minority. I thought about Buck and how some white people reacted to him with fear. It pissed me off.

My thoughts were interrupted when Arin pulled under an archway on a dirt lane. A sign said "Welcome to Hellshire Beach".

Colorfully painted wood and corrugated shacks were everywhere. At the sound of the car, at least a dozen men waved us down, trying to direct us to their place. Arin aimed for one shack in particular, parked and got out of the car. A guy with hair down to his waist, wearing only shorts, ran over, lifted and twirled her.

"Mi miss ya, cuz. Ya be hiding?" Before Arin answered, he looked at me with a broad smile and said, "Who da white boy?"

"Key, this is my cousin Jacob. Jacob, this is Key."

I extend my hand for a shake, but Jacob threw a bear hug around me.

"Welcome to Jamaica, cuz."

As he embraced me, I saw a white guy entering a shack a few over from us. Jimmy Downey. What the hell?

Arin and her cousin caught up in thick patois. I heard words like "auntie" and "brudder" and "yardie". They may as well have been speaking French, for all I could follow. We were under his roof, one wall absent and opened to the ocean, with a wooden patio of benches and tables—the smell of cooking oil mixed with the scent of grilled fish and barbecue. The place looked like a junkyard nailed together, painted by someone during a ganja-induced decorating moment.

Arin turned to me. "Let's walk the beach while Jacob is preparing some gastronomic surprises for us. By the way, don't let the rustic look fool you. Jacob has a degree in economics, but this is him, rat race be damned."

We walked out of the shack, past the parking area, onto a small beach. I glanced around to see if I could spot Downey. It was a little overcast, which kept the sun from completely melting me. The water felt cool on my feet. Arin brushed against me, and my heart raced. I had wanted to kiss her the first moment I laid eyes on her. I had wondered if we were cousins; but too many generations separated us, so I let my imagination run free.

"Arin, you've grown up hoping for a chance at finding the book. I'm ready, but you're way ahead of me."

"You're the one with the memories. It's me following you."

I thought about this as the sun bathed my skin and the gulls swooped and cried out. I stared toward the horizon and the calm turquoise Caribbean became the murky rougher waters of another place. The palm trees morphed to scrubby pines. The sounds of waves rustled a stony beach.

"Aedan, you mustn't bring her. Our uncle will be most unhappy." Tomás nervously pushed sand around with his foot. He gazed downward, refusing to look me in the eye.

"You are wrong, Tomás. Our King knows my heart. He knows why he put me here."

"I fear for your soul. You have become one of us. You cannot forego your vows."

Tomás is blood, my closest friend. I've met no one with a bigger heart. "My vow was to our King, to protect the Book and the church treasures. You know that I never took your vows. The Abbot knows it. Tomás, I love you." I placed my hand on the back of his neck, just as we have done since we were young men. "And I know that you love me. But I am not like you. You pray for the souls of the Norsemen, and I want my sword to send their souls to hell. If God has spared Siobhán, she will go with us to safety. I will find a home for her, and when our King decides it's time, I will join her."

I gave a playful punch to Tomás.

"When we reach Ireland, we will travel up the Boyne. The King has ordered me to secure the treasure in a safe place of my choosing. Siobhán will go with you to Kells. Her brothers will remain with me. You will bring the Book to the Abbot, and you will keep Siobhán in safety."

A nod from Tomás was all that I needed.

He reached a hand to my shoulder.

· · ·

"What did you see?" Arin asked as my eyes opened. My hand was on her shoulder and her hand on top of mine.

"What's it like?"

I told her, the moments still so vivid in my mind, then asked, "What do you see? You said you get images?"

Arin pointed to the sea.

"It's like these tiny waves. An image washes into my brain then quickly rolls back out. I see rifles. I see a dead man on a hill, boats at sea. From what we know of Mack, I'm pretty sure that they emanate from him, but I'm not certain about that."

Arin's eyes searched mine.

"Have you seen him? Do you know what Aedan looks like?"

"No, I hadn't thought about that. Maybe I'll catch a reflection of him in one of the memories."

"I'll bet he was handsome." Arin smiled.

"Why do you say that?"

"Because all the Murphy men are."

My stomach tightened at the compliment. I rolled my pant legs up and walked into the calm and inviting water, cool against the tropical heat. Arin followed. The water was up to my knees.

"Give me your shirt." Arin put her hands out.

"What?"

"You can't be in Jamaica and not get a little sun. Give it to me," she said, smiling.

I pulled my polo shirt over my head.

"Know what comes next?" she said, taking my shirt.

"What?' I said, trying to sound calm.

"The Hellshire Baptism." She took me by surprise and pushed me over. As I fell, I grabbed her wrist. She splashed in the water next to me.

Arin scooped some water and poured it on my head.

"I baptize you as a Jamaican Murphy. It's official. Now you will definitely find Mack."

I needed the laugh. It was hard to take my eyes off of her, her scoop-neck shirt clinging to her athletic body, her eyes playful as we stood in the gently rolling waves. I noticed a woman standing on the beach, casually taking photos on her phone. It seemed that Arin and I were her favorite subject.

We walked back to Jacob's hut, baptized and hungry. Plates of lobster and jerk chicken were served along with a fried bread called Festival and a spinach-like vegetable called callaloo, all tasting amazing, me channeling Anthony Bourdain. The Red Stripe was freezing cold, which made it perfect, cooling the hot spices threatening my tongue. Arin wouldn't drink since she was driving, so I drank hers. Jacob played Marley, and I wished I could stay a few more days.

"It'd be nice to come back when this is over, see more of the country." I surveyed the landscape then landed my eyes on the empty plate. "And come back for more of your cousin's delicacies."

"It's a beautiful country, especially in the mountains. I'd love to show you around," Arin answered enthusiastically, seeming to have inched a bit closer while she gestured around the beach area. "This is cramped and a bit polluted, but Negril, Port Antonio, you'll love it."

I finished the last bite of fish, chewing slowly, trying to extend the day. My clothes were almost dry in the Jamaican heat. The laid-back vibe here felt good.

Jacob stuck his head around the corner. I offered a thumbs-up.

"Thanks, this was great," I said to Arin.

"Ya mon," she started, with an exaggerated accent. "Every little ting gonna be all right." She dropped the accent. "At least, I hope so."

"Are you worried?" I asked.

"Not in the least. I've been waiting all of my life for this to happen." She looked out to the sea. "And then one day, you arrive." She tilted her head, a sheen of sweat on her cheeks. "When I first heard your name, I knew the gods were answering my prayer."

I pulled my head back a few inches, my heart skipped a beat.

"What do you mean?"

"Cián means 'ancient one'. Murphy means 'from the sea'. We're going to find it, Key."

I too scanned the calm waters, but I sensed a powerful undertow tugging at me. "There are a few things that you need to know."

She turned her full attention to me. "Your mother mentioned that several times in my life I have had temporary …" I paused, trying to find the right words. Arin added them for me.

"You've been a genius several times."

"God no, not genius," I laughed, "but I've had these amazing skills or talents. The problem is that they come and go. Dr. Garcia said that it results from the genetic mutation. Arin, that means the memories could disappear at any time."

"So, what, we do nothing?" She rubbed the top of my head, like a teammate might, trying to get your mind back in the game.

"No, I just want you to be aware." I gave her my most grim look.

"What?"

"There are dangerous people looking for the treasure." I told her what my parents had said about the Holy Grail. "They believe that there are people willing to kill for it. You might want to reconsider."

She calmly reached for her purse, opened it and took out her car keys. "I don't think you understand. Without you, they don't stand a chance of finding it. Trust me, my father spent a fortune trying."

We said goodbye to Jacob and walked back to the car. Two shacks over, Downey sat with his back to me, talking to three bikini-clad Jamaicans.

"I'm not loving it," I said under my breath.

CHAPTER 17

November 23, 2019
Norman Manley Airport

I sat in the back of the Mercedes, Arin next to me, my eyes searching for anyone following. The driver was taking back streets to avoid the morning traffic. He hit the brakes and I jolted forward, no apparent cause.

"Dem goats." He blasts the horn. Two goats walk away from the front of the car. One stares up at me with a look that says, "Eff off."

"Now you know why we eat a lot of goat here," Arin laughed.

We made it to the causeway and joined the bumper-to-bumper traffic. I glanced at my watch, certain that we'd miss the flight. Arin was relaxed, watching the turquoise waters of the Caribbean, humming what I thought was an Alicia Keys song. As we approached the departures area, the driver turned right and stopped at a security gate, which lifted at our arrival. The security guard waved familiarly to our driver. A woman in a tailored uniform greeted us as we exited the

Mercedes. What the hell was going on here? She held open a door for us.

"Arin, what about our luggage?" I asked.

The woman in the uniform answered.

"No worries, sir. The porter will bring it to you." She moved behind a desk with a computer. "May I have your passport?" She gave it a cursory glance, lifted her eyes to my face, and returned the passport. Arin had already produced hers.

When the woman finished, she turned and walked, with Arin right behind her. She opened a door revealing the tarmac and a sleek jet, as a well-dressed man waved from the bottom of the steps.

"Dr. Murphy, how are you this morning?"

"Cut the 'Doctor' crap, Noel." Arin kissed his cheek.

"Noel, this is Key. Key, this is Noel King. Noel went to school with my brother. He's been working for the family for a dozen years, but he's more like part of the family. Don't let his leading-man good looks fool you. He's a badass. He spent six years with British Special Forces and heads company security."

I shook his hand. We were of similar height and build, but he had a few years on me. His relaxed smile didn't hide the cold and calculating fix of his eyes.

"It seems Noel drew the short straw and is babysitting us today. Why are you here? Where's Stewart?" Arin clarified to me, "Stewart is normally the flight attendant."

"I'm meeting your brother in New York. Stewart was scheduled off. The Queen Mother asked me to drop you in Philly, so here I am, princess, at your service." King's Jamaican accent was flavored by his years in England.

We climbed the stairs, and Noel locked the cabin door behind us. I'd been on a private jet once in my life; I'd seen a bunch in magazines and movies; but this was over-the-top luxurious. We sat on side-by-side leather recliners. A burnished wood table with a colorful wooden inlay of a hummingbird served as our desk.

"I guess I'm not getting on the American flight. This is a surprise."

"Good surprise or bad surprise?" asked Arin.

"Good, just wondering why you didn't give me a heads-up?" I waited for an answer, watching Arin's jaw tighten slightly.

"It's weird. What do I say? 'Key, we are wealthy, and I have a private jet'? Most people have no idea who I am. They just assume that, as a professor in Jamaica, making about forty thousand a year, that I'm just like them; and I prefer it that way." Arin's eyelids fluttered. "Besides, I wanted to surprise you. I hope you aren't put off."

"Hell no. And yeah, I'm pretty surprised and delighted to be on the Murphy family jet." I cocked my head and let a question form in my brain. "Is that why you're not sure about the Prime Minister thing?"

Arin took a deep breath and peered out the window for a moment, her face taking on a more serious look.

"It's more complicated than that. Politics in Jamaica can be a dangerous and dirty business. I guess like anywhere, but here, in this small country, you're under a microscope if you come from money. I prefer the shadows. I want to make changes in Jamaica, but for now, from behind the scenes." Arin stared past me for a moment. "You can see that my mother is very strong-willed." She leaned forward. "All I want right now is to find whatever Mack left behind and let it take us wherever it leads."

"What if it leads nowhere?"

"It's not going to lead nowhere," Arin answered, with an edge that assured me I just got a word-slap. "That letter from Mack has been around for a hundred and four years. You read it and began putting the pieces together."

The image of Tomás flashed in front of my eyes as he

descended into the tunnel. The image faded as Noel peeked out from the cockpit.

"Time to buckle up. I'll bring food as soon as Captain here gives me the okay."

After I attached my seatbelt, I took the binder containing Mack's letters and handed it to Arin. "I'd like to read more, see if anything jumps out. Any suggestions?"

She looked through the binder and settled on a page.

"Mack believed that finding the *Book of Kells'* cover would be a powerful symbol of Irish history and dignity. He found it and hid it …" Arin placed the binder in front of me. "And he's handed the rest of its journey to you."

Her jaw was resolute, her brow arched, her lips a thin line.

"I think you mean us," I said.

Her eyes smiled. She stole a glance out the window, the sun playing magic with the clouds.

"Us." She tapped her right hand on the page. "Read this."

Hello, my love.

I must tell you the most fantastic story straight off. We received word that a division of soldiers from Massachusetts would march past us and make camp a mile away. Our boys gathered to greet the soldiers on their march. As the troops drew close, it became clear that they were all Negros, save the white officers. Our commander told us that this was the first infantry raised of all black freemen in the Union. My spirit soared as I witnessed these fine soldiers on proud march, uniforms and rifles, their Massachusetts standard held high.

I was not sure how my fellow soldiers would respond. At first, they were mute, perhaps slack-jawed, and then a wave of applause rang out. Our commander ordered us to attention in full salute to our fellow Union soldiers. The Irish were the dirt of America. The trod-upon. Many spoke only Irish. They knew a plough but not a pen, a gun but not a page to read. Rough men that saw themselves in the Negro dispossessed that marched before them, heads held high, as the Irish had tried to do. And I felt proud of both.

But this, my dearest Moira, was not the biggest surprise.

I was ordered to the tent of our commander, a lad from Kildare, where a mulatto man was introduced to me. He wore civilian clothes, but I was told he was a high-ranking officer. My commander took leave, and the officer, light of skin tone, reached out and shook my hand. He said he had heard of the Irish soldier from Jamaica and inquired about meeting me.

My curiosity as to his purpose was soon satisfied. He told me that he was a spy for the Union. He had traveled throughout the South, his mostly white features allowing him easy passage. His father was an Italian immigrant, his mother a mulatto free-woman. He spoke fluent Italian. He also could speak with the accents of the South. He has reported on troop strengths, fortifi-cations, and other wartime intelligence on his many trips there.

He made a proposition. He would train me in espionage and prepare me for the battles soon to come in Ireland. I would be his white accomplice for his trips to the Deep South, one whose anti-slavery fervor was as strong as his.

My heart soared. To strike a blow against the slavers and their army and prepare myself for Ireland is a gift from God. When I agreed, he informed me that I was already cleared for this duty. I was to pack and move to a secret facility. I asked his name. He told me that he had several names, all Italian, depending on his mission and his cover story, but he is known by his assets in the South as The River. Intrigued, I asked him why. He answered, "I cut through enemy territory with the ease of a river, twisting and turning, swiftly, like rapids, creating tribu-taries of allies throughout the land, all aiming to crush this evil *and return the South to the Union. I will teach you to do the same."*

My love, you have received this through a trusted courier. I do not know by what means I'll send you letters, but I will write to you and send them as I am permitted.

As always, I pray for the end of this war and to face our commitments in Ireland so that I can make a swift return and hold you in my arms and kiss your beautiful face.

> *Longingly,*
> *Mack*

With my eyes closed, I tried to picture Mack in his uniform, but it was my face that I saw. Where did you put it, Mack? ... Aedan is sending me to bring it home.

CHAPTER 18

5 MONTHS AGO

CLONTARF, DUBLIN

In the affluent Clontarf district of Dublin, the Clontarf Castle had been converted into a luxury hotel. Padraig Collins motored his Mercedes-AMG GT Black Series up the drive, slowly passing topiaries, sculptures, and spires. The nineteenth-century castle stood like a monument to time travel, but Collins was traveling to meet a twenty-first-century dilemma. His plans were falling behind schedule. Having returned from the award ceremony in Philadelphia armed with new information, now was the time to accelerate the plan.

Turning left into the car park, Collins continued to the rear of the converted castle. He parked in front of a tall hedgerow and entered under a carved arch in the hedge. Three feet into the arch, not visible from the car park, a metal door blocked his passage. He took his smartphone in hand, tapped in a code and listened for the door to release. Collins entered the courtyard of a large carriage house, one that long ago served the needs of the castle owners. It looked warm and inviting, like a large-scale version of a hobbit house. The motion detector cameras followed his every move. He put his eye to the sign reading "Welcome", a retina scanner. The door opened.

His Chief Information Officer, Catherine Norris, nodded to him. Catherine was a Belfast misfit. A Catholic father, Protestant mother, neither political. The extremist Protestants had murdered her mom for marrying a Catholic, and the Catholic extremists had matched them, leaving Catherine parentless at twelve, to be raised by an aunt.

Collins needed information in every corner of Ireland. When he found Catherine, she was eighteen and brilliant on the computer. Now, prosperous and happily married at thirty-two, she was fiercely loyal to Collins and he to her.

Collins had arranged for her to be hired at Stormont, the Parliament building in Northern Ireland, and paid for her degrees at Queen's University in Belfast. As a young and ordinary-looking girl working in the secretarial pool, she was all but invisible. The information she had provided was revelatory. One of the many results was that he became a major landowner in the north for pennies. He let it sit for years, and now he was preparing to build two large projects, bringing over one hundred and fifty million dollars' worth of jobs to the Northern Ireland economy.

Padraig Collins looked at the three hackers, all of them brilliant misfits. Like himself.

Most companies believed their finance team was the center of the universe. For Collins, it was hackers. He who controlled the information was he who knew where money was going. His job was to get there first and collect most of it.

Collins greeted each one in turn. He allowed an edge into his voice, just enough for them to want to make him happy.

Lihua meant "beautiful and elegant" in Chinese, but she was neither of those. Scrawny and unattractive, she was most often mistaken for a teenage boy. Her parents had left Hong

Kong for Canada before she was born. They were dissidents. The Chinese government hackers had wiped out their bank accounts as punishment. They were left destitute but built their way back to a middle-class life. Lihua hated the Chinese government. Ten years ago, at fourteen, she had hacked a Chinese enterprise that banked at Barclays in London. Her parents were now millionaires.

The Edge came from a family of Pakistani asylum seekers. His mother was a programmer, his father a lawyer and member of the opposition party. The government did not take kindly to his father. When Catherine found The Edge, his fame had been growing in hacker circles. He had laid bare the corruption of the Pakistani military and politicians, exposing their bloated bank accounts, and the details were leaked to social media. Catherine recruited him and brought his family to safety in Ireland. A U2 fanatic, he adopted his handle from the famous guitar player.

Collins's favorite, though, was Anwulika from Nigeria. Her name meant "my joy is great". She was the leader of the Clontarf team and reported to Catherine. Stifled by sexism in Nigeria's paternalistic corporate world, she became a self-taught hacker. She'd been harassed and gang-raped for being a lesbian. She famously said in hacker circles, "They stole my body. I won't let them steal my joy, but I, on the other hand, will steal their money and secrets. While they raped me, I chanted an Igbo proverb."

Personally recruited by Collins, she confessed to him that she found her rapists and, one by one, over a six-month period, slit their throats while repeating that same proverb. Collins offered her a new life in Ireland.

None of them had a saint to intercede for them. He had Saint Columba.

They had him.

His principal offices were in the nearby Docklands district. "Clontarf Team" did not exist anywhere in his corporate filings. If you could penetrate the trail of shell companies surrounding Clontarf, you would reach a dead-end in the Maldives.

"Lihua, I want you to find out everything you can about Shaun Murphy." He handed her a paper. "Here's some details." Turning to Catherine, he continued, "Have the fire-walls been tested on Futuro?"

She nodded.

"They've been repaired. The Edge is about to try to breach them."

Addressing The Edge, Collins said, "You've left a back door as we discussed?"

The awkward Pakistani raised his eyebrows, thick and dark as a black shag carpet.

"It's a work of art," he answered.

The three hackers sat at their consoles, like a NASA control center, with large screens on the wall to project onto if they needed to share data or get assistance.

Collins turned to Anwulika. She was in charge of pene-trating the secret lives of Northern Ireland's Unionist politi-cians. She rolled her head back and forth, widened her eyes, and started to dance in her seat, arms gyrating.

"Got some good ones for you today, but boss man got to pay. It's Saturday. We need some time to play." She sang it as a rap in her singsong Nigerian accent. She stopped and rubbed her fingers together, signifying cash as only Anwulika could get away with.

Collins always got a laugh from her antics. She handed him her report.

None of them knew of his sins. He knew all of theirs; he held them tightly in his heart. Like him, they were of troubled souls.

"Get to work," he said, "then go play." He pointed to Catherine. "Boss lady will take care of the bill."

CHAPTER 19

J olted awake by the plane's landing, I was momentarily disoriented by where I was. Arin stirred beside me.

"Sorry, I didn't mean to sleep the whole time."

"I slept too. Guess we both needed it."

I turned on my phone. A text from Buck came in: *Your mom told me where you're landing. I'm picking you up.*

"Arin, my friend Buck is meeting us at the flight office. He's also my boss. I want to go straight to Laurel Hill."

Noel dropped the steps and waited for us to go down before joining us. He said to Arin, "We're heading right out. Anything you need?"

"Thanks, Noel." She gave him another kiss on the cheek. "I'll text you or Mom if I need anything."

I shook his hand, still trying to wake up.

"Thanks for the ride."

Buck was already in the lounge, talking to someone. He saw us.

"You didn't tell me you were bringing Miss Jamaica with you."

"And he didn't tell me that Buck McCoy was a handsome black man. I thought, with a name like that, you were another Mick. Guess we are both surprised." Arin's devilish smile flashed again. "Hi, Buck. I'm Arin."

"You must be a saint, putting up with him for a few days. It's a pleasure to meet you."

Buck moved away from the desk so that we could process immigration. Then we grabbed our bags and headed to the car. Arin turned and waved to Noel, who was talking to the pilot outside while the plane was being refueled.

Buck turned to us as we arrived at his car and held up his hand, looked up at the sky as a plane went over, and waited for the noise to die. "I visited your mom today. When the hell were you planning on telling me about this memory thing?"

Hands on his hips, face pulled tight; no one does the "I'm pissed" look better than Buck. I tried for my contrite look with my shoulders tightened, palms faced upwards in a "Please forgive me" posture. "Honestly, I never gave you a thought. I was too busy having dinner and hanging out at the beach with Arin."

"You're my witness," Buck pointed at Arin. "He's such a …" He let the rest hang in the air.

Arin looked horrified until Buck laughed and threw his arm over my shoulder. "It helps explain why you are so weird."

"We need to go to Laurel Hill Cemetery." I explained why as we headed up I-95 and into the city. Arin gave Buck a short version of the Mack Murphy story.

We exited the Vine Street Expressway at the art museum and followed the Benjamin Franklin Parkway. The museum had the usual crowds running up the famous Rocky Steps, people dancing around at the top like Sylvester Stallone in the movie. This scene was re-enacted hundreds of times a day, every day of the year. We passed the Azalea Gardens and Boat House Row as we merged onto Kelly Drive, following the contours of the Schuylkill River.

It was that time of year when the few remaining yellows and golds resisted dropping to the ground, trying to hang on for dear life; the inevitable process of nature soon to win, the river carrying them to the sea, the earth mulching them to itself to make new life. I wondered where I was in this natural cycle. I was clearly a freak, a slight tweak of a gene, a moment of genetic substance gone wrong or gone right. Was I being carried in that river, or was I the river?

"I forgot how beautiful Philly is in the fall," said Arin. "I can't believe they're still sculling this time of year. I'd freeze."

I viewed the boats in the water, the sculptures decorating the river landscape, content in my reverie as I traveled the same bends in the road that Mack had assuredly traveled. I was back in the comforting familiarity of Philly, but seeing it anew, Mack and Aedan and Arin my guides.

Arin was in the passenger seat next to Buck. She pointed to the right.

"There it is."

I looked up to see elaborately decorated mausoleums, angels reaching into the sky, and crosses guarding the hillside graves.

We would soon stand where Mack once stood.

Buck turned onto Ridge Avenue, and within minutes we passed between the stone walls that led into the cemetery. We followed the winding drive to the right; thirty-foot-tall obelisks, twenty-foot-tall angels, metal sculptures of loved ones, and mausoleums the size of a small house greeted us. Littered throughout the grounds were smaller headstones, American flags keeping them company.

We maneuvered toward our location. I had General

Meade's grave on GPS and directed Buck where to park. A security vehicle pulled up next to us. The guard lowered her window. "Sorry, folks, we're closing in fifteen minutes for a special event. We'll re-open at six if you want to come back." She pulled out in front of us, her car idling.

"This place is amazing," Arin said while getting out of the car. "I've never seen a cemetery this beautiful."

Buck scanned the statues and the running paths fifty yards below on Kelly Drive.

"Man, I've lived here all my life and I've never been here. Which is crazy since some of my people fought under General Meade."

"We should have a quick look," I said as we walked on the recently mowed field, the pungent smell of wet grass in the air. We passed several graves before I spotted Meade's. Buck and Arin joined me.

"That's it? That little headstone? He's responsible for winning the Battle of Gettysburg, and all he gets is this?" Buck shook his head.

"There are monuments to him in Gettysburg and D.C., but this is surprising," I added. "I read up on him last night. His parents lived in Philly, but they were transferred to Spain. His father was a naval delegate. General Meade was born in Spain, but the family eventually moved back to Philly. His grandparents were from Kilkenny, Ireland."

The Meade Society had planted a wreath at his grave. Meade Society markers, signifying Civil War veterans that fought under him, were all around the immediate area.

"Key, what are your thoughts?" asked Buck. "If it's even here, how would we find it? We can't just start digging."

"That's exactly what we need to do," I answered.

"We need to get permission."

"We can't. It would take months to get permission, and it would become public. We would lose all control."

"Key's right," Arin added. "But let's not worry about that yet. First, we need to decide where we think it is."

I opened my photos app and found the picture I took of Mack's clues. I read aloud.

"I visit the grave of my general, with whom we won the great battle for Lincoln and our cause. I pray to him and my brothers from the brigade who dot the earth around me."

"There are Meade Society markers all around," Buck added. "Let's find out if any of them were Irish Brigade. I'll go up the hill. Key, there's a bunch over that way. Arin, you walk the other side."

We split up, and only a minute later Arin called us over to her. A fading plaque lay beside a Meade Society marker, proudly displaying a flag. The plaque read, "Garrett Nowlen, Irish Brigade".

I turned to the sound of a horn. The security guard leaned out of the window and pointed to the watch on her left wrist.

"I'll tell her we need more time." Buck started to walk to the guard, pulling out his badge.

"Buck, don't. We don't want her getting curious and being able to ID us." I pulled out my phone and took photos of the marker. "Let's go. Aedan and I can come back later."

Buck and Arin stopped cold, staring at me.

"What?"

"You just said, 'Aedan and I can come back later'," Arin responded.

I stared blankly for a moment, then shook my head. "Maybe I meant it—but don't worry, Arin. You can join us."

CHAPTER 20

November 23, 2019
Delancey Place

B uck pulled up in front of the house on Delancey. Most of the three- and four-story homes were historically certi-fied and retained an old-world elegance—deep blue shutters, flower boxes, white marble sills, and cement arches framing the doorway with cornice work at the top and *Architectural Digest* amazing on the inside.

"I need to go to the office. I'll see you later," said Buck, popping the trunk.

I grabbed the luggage and headed up the steps, Arin behind me. I had texted ahead; the door opened before I could get my keys, and my mom stepped back to let us in. I put down the luggage.

"Arin, this is my mother, Megan. Mom, this is Arin Murphy."

"Fáilte romhat chuig ár dteach Arin, is deas bualadh leat." My mom reached forward to shake her hand.

"Go raibh maith agat, tá sé an-cineálta duit," Arin responded.

I looked at Arin.

"You didn't tell me you speak Irish."

"You didn't ask."

"Ní dóigh liom go bhfuil a fhios ag mo bhleachtaire mac conas an t-idirlíon a úsáid," my mom continued.

Arin laughed. I was oblivious. Despite my mother's attempts, I didn't speak Irish.

"I told Arin that I don't think you know how to use the internet." My mom took Arin by the arm and led her into the house. "Arin speaks five languages. She's an expert on the Irish and the West Africa diaspora. You should search her name sometime."

"I guess we know who the real detective is around here," I said to Arin. "Where's Dad?"

"He'll be back in about thirty minutes. Arin, I have tea brewing, coffee as well. Dinner in about an hour. In the meantime, may I show you your room? Key, my laptop is open and ready. We'll be down in a minute."

Arin grabbed her suitcase and followed Mom up the steps.

"Mrs. Murphy, your home is beautiful," I heard Arin say.

"Megan or Meg, please, no Mrs. Murphy around here."

As I sat at the kitchen counter, I pictured General Meade's grave. I concentrated on the surroundings. On each side of his gravestone was a Meade Society marker, his initials interlaced, and a small American flag inserted at the top. Something was different about the flag. I saw the thirteen stripes and then tried to visualize the stars. I replayed the entire visit, from driving through the gate to walking the grounds. American flags were everywhere. Each of the Meade markers held a flag. I compared them in my mind to the others—fewer stars. Not the fifty that I knew, but whatever number of states there were at the time of the Civil War. I opened the photo I took at the cemetery. Thirty-six stars. The colonial flag had thirteen stripes and thirteen stars in a circle. There was not a single colonial flag in sight.

I opened Wikipedia on the laptop and entered "Laurel Hill Cemetery". There it was in the first line. Obvious. *Laurel Hill Cemetery is a historic cemetery in Philadelphia. Founded in 1836.*

Mack's clue said there was a captain from Washington's war. Somewhere else maybe, but not at Laurel Hill.

Mom and Arin entered the kitchen. Mom poured tea, and Arin stood behind me. I entered "Church of Two Ships" into search. Nothing.

"Something's wrong," I said.

Mom handed Arin her tea and put a coffee in front of me. They looked at me expectantly.

"I don't think Laurel Hill is the right place," I explained. "I'm missing something." My dad came in. I made introductions to Arin and gave him an update. "Can either of you picture a cemetery next to a river in Philly?" My parents shook their heads.

"Arin, you probably know this, but there are two rivers in Philly. The Schuylkill, with West Philly on one side, and the Delaware, which separates Pennsylvania from New Jersey. I've searched online but can't find any cemeteries along either river aside from Laurel Hill." To my folks, I asked, "What about the Church of Two Ships? Does that mean anything to you?"

Again, met with a no.

I thought of Christ Church in Old City and typed it in. It was old enough. Ben Franklin was buried there, but it was too far from the river. There was a subheading on the search results page: "Old Church Cemeteries". I clicked, and a Google map opened with a sidebar of church names and the corresponding pins on the map. One sat at the river's edge. I clicked on "Gloria Dei Old Swedes Church". A photo of the church, surrounded by old graves, stared back at us. I became aware of the breathing of my folks, and Arin watching from behind.

I directed the mouse and clicked on the "Images" tab. Most of the photos were external. Church and graveyard. I examined the thumbnails and opened the images from inside the church. Nothing jumped out until the eleventh image. Mom gasped. Arin said, "Oh my God."

Suspended from the ceiling were two large schooners. The Church of Two Ships.

"Let's go."

CHAPTER 21

I headed down Pine Street, watching Arin take in the city. Pine was just a few blocks south of the skyscrapers but a world away in feel. The farther east we headed, the further we went back to colonial time. The buildings that housed the numerous shops and restaurants had been around for at least two hundred years, built on the bones of structures older than that. Revolutionary War soldiers walked this street, as did Washington and Jefferson. Civil War generals had lived in these homes, now occupied by doctors and interns, tech entrepreneurs and med students. History was etched into the dust and fabric of this city, so it was no surprise as I turned onto Christian Street to see the redbrick colonial church, its white spire reaching toward the heavens, a beacon for the Swedish settlers.

"I've driven by here a million times and never gone in," I told Arin as I grabbed a flashlight from the trunk. The sun was fading fast.

We entered the small alleyway to the churchyard and

stumbled forward as if ejected from a time machine into the colonial era. This humble graveyard was the opposite of the grandeur of Laurel Hill. Many of the markers were flat to the ground, some tall, all old. The first gravestone I saw was dated 1678.

I took a moment to get my sense of direction. "The website said it's to the east, in section five."

It was a small cemetery. We easily located the grave marker.

Captain John Douglas
Patriot and
Revolutionary Soldier

"We need to see if there's a Civil War soldier close by." I played the flashlight over gravestones, then let light stay on one.

It read:

John C. Hunterson
Medal of Honor
PVT CO B 3rd PA CAV
Civil War
Aug 4, 1841. Nov 6, 1927

"Hunterson died in 1927. Mack's letter to his wife is post-marked 1916," I added.

Another flashlight flickered. I turned to the source. A rotund man in a tie-dye shirt and jeans approached. I assumed he was the caretaker.

"Sorry, folks. The grounds are closed now," he said in a surprisingly high-pitched voice.

Arin took over. "Good evening, sir." Her accent, though not exaggerated, was pronounced. "I am so sorry for the inconvenience. My flight from Jamaica was delayed. I'm doing a lecture at Temple tomorrow and was hoping to include some history from here. We just need a few more minutes. I have a question for you. Would you know if there are any other Civil War veterans buried here from 1916 or earlier?"

It took a long moment for him to shake the Arin spell.

"Right behind you, by the wall facing the Delaware River."

He walked past the captain's grave and stopped at the wall, turning west and shining his flashlight on a tombstone that read:

Mack Murphy
Irish Brigade – Gettysburg
April 22, 1843 to December 5, 1865

Arin began to shake. Her arms crossed as she hugged herself tight. I needed to get her out of here. She looked faint. Instead, I looked across the wide expanse of Columbus Boulevard to the Delaware River, around three hundred yards away.

"This would have all been fields back then."

The caretaker pointed to the river.

"Everything you see out there is landfill. The riverbank was about twenty yards from the church. The merchant ships docked straight ahead."

"Thanks for the info." I started walking next to him

toward the exit. "One last favor. Can we have a look in the church?"

He looked up at me with his very round face and pointed goatee, unlocked the door, and turned lights on. Arin held my arm as we stared at the two sailing ships and an angel suspended from the ceiling.

"I'm here to bring you home, Grandpa Mack," she whispered.

———

Arin directed her gaze toward the river as I turned the car onto Columbus Boulevard. Glancing at her, my heart skipped a beat. She noticed my attention with a slight grin.

"Tired?" I asked.

"Stunned is more like it," she responded. "I just stood where Mack stood.

I'm walking in his tracks." Arin brushed a tear away. "I've dreamed about this since I was a pickney—sorry, a kid. I'm not tired. I'm determined. And I wonder who's in that grave. It certainly isn't Mack."

As tired as I felt, I didn't want to leave Arin until she was ready for sleep. When we arrived back at my parents' house, she and my mom chatted, and I stayed to do more research. Finally, she said it was time to say goodnight. She stood next to me and kissed me on the cheek.

"Thank you."

"For what?" I asked.

"Yesterday, I was teaching. Today, we found Mack's hiding place. Thanks for an adventurous day and putting the puzzle pieces together."

"Might be nothing there."

She seemed to consider that for a quiet moment. "True, but at least we're on the hunt."

I watched as she slowly climbed the stairs, her vibrant

energy replaced by a thoughtful melancholy. She turned at the top to see me looking, staring back at me for several seconds. I gave her a slight nod as she disappeared down the hall, feeling confident that she was having a quiet conversation with her father.

My parents looked at me. Nothing needed to be said.

CHAPTER 22

The kiss, the warmth of her breath as Arin had leaned in, the current that ran through me at her soft touch against my cheek. I replayed it, despite my aching need for sleep. I rolled over onto my right side, scrunching the pillow for better comfort. She leaned in one more time, and, in the sleepy soup of my imagination, Aedan crowded her out.

I entered the room and a small group of monks quietly acknowledged me. Perched over the book was an older monk, examining the pages closely. Daylight streaming in from the windows illuminated the illustrated pages, the vivid colors seeming to dance around the words. This was not the work of mere mortals but of holy men who were but the channel of God's imagination.

The older monk turned stiffly in his chair and waved me to his side.

"It's in perfect condition," he said. "Young Aedan, you have served us well."

All eyes fell upon me in response to this rare praise.

The older man continued, "Kells is not yet fortified. Your work is not done. You must keep this place secure until the monastery is completed and the defenses are in place."

The image of Siobhán and the child growing in her surrounded and delighted me. My freedom must come soon.

"As my King has charged me, so it will be."

I stood behind the monk, the master painter of the book, mystified by the detail, the colors, the sheer passion of this tedious work. I had observed them working in Iona, preparing the pages, drying the skins, mixing the inks, but somehow, in the tedium of the long days, I had missed the majesty of what they had created. Now, here, in the stillness of this room, I fell to my knees.

"Brother, God is in your brush. He has worked through you. I will do everything to make certain that this book lives forever."

CHAPTER 23

"Siobhán is pregnant," I announced to my folks. They reacted excitedly, as if I had told them that I was having a child.

"What are you going to do, decorate a nursery?" I asked. My mom swatted my arm in response.

I told them about my experience of Aedan in Kells, his witness of the book being examined by the Abbot. As I finished, Arin came down the stairs wearing a black Temple University T-shirt. I just wanted to stare, but instead I offered coffee.

"Your mom made me a great breakfast. I'm ready." She grabbed her jacket. "Anything below seventy is chilly for me," she said while putting it on.

I downed my coffee, took a slice of bread and cheese, and headed for the car.

. . .

We pulled into the parking lot at Old Swede Church. I needed to study the approach to getting in and out of the graveyard unseen in the dark. I discussed this with Arin on the ride over. Luckily, there were already a few tourists there, roaming around the historic cemetery, taking photos of the graves. We blended in.

The grounds were beautiful, peaceful even, nestled by a picture-perfect colonial brick wall. The west end held a daycare center and the church offices, pumpkins and corn stalks decorating the façade. Someone was baking, the smell of chocolate drifting in the air. I-95 screamed overhead. Southwest was open land, clearly the neighborhood dog park, given the fifteen or so people milling about with coffee cups in one hand, leashes in the other. We exited through the park gate under I-95. Across the street was a block of modern row homes. I could walk through there that evening, and it was likely no one would pay me any attention, but it wasn't worth the risk.

We followed the wall south then turned left on Washington Avenue toward Columbus Boulevard. A strip mall was across the street, a Dunkin Donuts in the parking lot, making this entry too exposed. We turned left on Columbus, its morning traffic still heavy and fast. I spotted an embankment that met the wall. It narrowed to less than three feet high, unlike the rest of the perimeter at five feet tall. I walked up and saw an easy two-foot drop to the ground. Twenty-five yards away was my target.

I went back to Arin. "I'll go in through here."

"There are so many cars going by." She gestured to the road. The traffic was stopped for the light as far back as to where we stood.

"On a road like this, a pedestrian barely exists for these cars. I'll be a blur when they're doing fifty." I looked back at the wall. "I'll only go over when the traffic is moving. Let's go back to the cemetery. We need to take measurements."

. . .

Children were coming out of the daycare center, kicking soccer balls half as tall as them as we entered the grounds and made our way to the grave. "It's just as shocking to see his name as it was last night." Arin knelt in front of the gravestone and ran her hand over Mack's name, then joined me by the wall.

I took photos from the wall to the headstone, then stepped behind the headstone and took them from there to the captain's grave. I opened the measurement app on my phone and got the rough square footage of both sides of the small headstone, then another measurement from the grave to the wall where I would enter. Twenty-six yards.

"What are you doing?" She sounded more like a teacher than a treasure hunter.

"Getting the layout and measurements."

"You don't need that." Arin pointed to the gravestone. "Mack buried it here. He put his name on it. I'm coming in here with you tonight."

As I started to argue, she held her hand up sternly. "As an anthropologist, I have been on dozens of digs to help interpret the finds. How many have you been on?"

She read my silence as an answer.

"I know what tools we need. Dial your mom on speaker."

I complied.

"Hi Megan. Do you have a GPR?"

"It's already packed, along with a turf blade, four-inch trowel, and foldable spade," I heard my mom answer. "Anything else you'll need?"

"That's perfect." Arin handed me my phone. "I'm excited, are you?"

"I'm worried. If something goes wrong and we're caught grave-digging, you could be thrown out of the country and have your visa revoked."

"It's you I'm worried about; a police consultant grave robber. They'll think you've lost it. The U.S. Ambassador to Jamaica is a very close friend of my mom's. Take a wild guess as to who his best friend is."

"No clue."

"The Secretary of State. I'd be free and clear in sixty minutes—so I should come here alone. You're the one who could be in trouble."

All I could do was laugh and shake my head. I surveyed the grounds one more time. Getting in and out would be easy. I took my time, scanning the area to see if anyone was observing us.

I looked at my watch. "Have you ever been to the Reading Terminal Market?"

"Always meant to, never made it."

"Let's go. I'm starving."

CHAPTER 24

November 24, 2019
Reading Terminal Market

"Welcome to organized chaos." I held the door open for Arin and entered behind her. "Lunchtime here is an insane slice of Philly, pretty much any cuisine you want, but the longest lines will be for cheesesteaks. Especially if there's a convention in town."

I walked her up and down a few crowded aisles for the experience, past the counters serviced by the Amish, the Italian pulled pork sandwich shops, Peking duck stalls, Thai, Mexican. It was all here—the smells of dozens of different lands and the astonished faces of tourists who felt lucky to encounter a Mecca of global food under a roof six blocks from where the Declaration of Independence was written.

We stopped in front of Murphy's Pub. Arin saw the sign and laughed.

"Murphys are everywhere," she said.

"Trouble's here." Arin turned to the woman who spoke. "Whattya doin with this ugly excuse of an Irishman?"

I stifled a laugh, but Arin didn't miss a beat.

"I found himself beggin' on the sidewalk so figured a wee pint and a meal would do him no harm," she answered in a perfect Irish accent.

They both looked at me. I was still laughing, but I managed to speak.

"Arin, this is my cousin, Noreen, and this is Arin, from Jamaica."

"Damn girl, you sound Irish, but give me a little Jamaican and I'll make sure the kitchen takes care of you. Not him." She nodded to me. "Just you." Noreen gave me a hug. "Aunt Meg told me you had company. Grab a seat. I'll visit in a bit." Noreen put her hand on Arin's forearm. "Nice to meet you, honey, but it's rush hour here. We'll catch up."

Noreen hurried off to manage her lunchtime empire. In five minutes, there wouldn't be any seats in the place.

I grabbed a high-top table with a reserved placard. Arin didn't know I had texted Noreen. I had also told her what we wanted to eat. Arin ordered for the two of us in Kingston, so I thought I would return the favor.

Arin hung her jacket on the back of the stool, folded her arms on the table and leaned forward. "I asked your mom about Buck this morning. She told me a little, that you and his sister were very close. She died. I'm so sorry."

My chest tightened. My breathing changed. I knew we would get to this; I just didn't know how.

"I'm sorry, Key. I didn't mean to upset you," Arin offered.

"Did she tell you about our families?"

"It's an amazing story, the little she told me." She leaned in a little closer. "Please, I want to hear more."

I closed my eyes and rubbed them, picturing Buck, Tanya, and me as kids.

"Buck's dad was my father's commanding officer in Vietnam. Dad was on a reconnaissance patrol and ended up cornered by two Vietcong soldiers. He'd already been hit by shrapnel and was hurt badly. He was maybe three seconds from a bullet when Buck's dad shot them. The bond was sealed. They were brothers. Not commanding officer to an underling, but raw humanity, I-got-your-back humanity, no questions asked."

Arin nodded for me to continue.

"I grew up in awe of that. My father tried to repay the debt when Tanya and Buck's mom was dying of cancer. Dad was doing well financially, but the McCoys were on hard times. There were no medical bills, there was no funeral bill; Dad took care of that. From what I know, no words were said. It was just family taking care of family. So Buck is my brother, forged by fire if not blood."

"And Buck's sister, Tanya?" Arin asked.

I sat silently, not knowing how to let Tanya out of the box that I'd put her in since she died. I started to say something but faltered, feeling a familiar well of anger and tears. I rapped my knuckles on the table, like I was knocking on a door. "We grew up together. Tanya was a year younger than me. Buck about six years older. As kids, he was off in his own life, like an older brother, a protector, and a pain-in-the-ass tormentor. As we got older, Tanya and I became soul mates. Black girl, white guy, in a world still confused about all that."

"Were you lovers?" Arin asked tenderly.

I pushed a sugar packet around the table. The chatter of the lunch crowd filled the pub. Arin put her hand on my forearm.

"Spiritually, yes. Physically, no," I finally answered. "Everyone thought we were lovers. We were in love, but not that way. We held hands. We snuggled. We bared our souls."

"What happened to her?"

"She slowly slipped away from me. From Buck, from her dad, from everyone that loved her. Something changed in her.

She was diagnosed with bipolar disorder. That gave Buck and his dad something to work with, you know, therapy, pharmaceuticals." I looked at Arin for affirmation. She squeezed my arm, like Tanya used to do.

"She'd started using drugs, opioids. That's when she distanced me. And one day, she ceased to exist. An overdose, fentanyl. I still have no idea why she went down that path."

I could feel tears forming and, for a moment, I thought it looked unseemly in front of Arin, but I had the sense that she didn't care about that. She put her hand on mine.

"Is that what made you decide to work with the police?"

"Buck was destroyed. Big fucking badass Buck." I realized my language. "Sorry on the cursing front."

"Shit, Key, never heard any of those words before," Arin responded with a smile.

I smiled in return.

"Buck *is* a badass. Decorated military. Decorated cop. He felt like his life ended when he couldn't protect his little sister."

"I have a feeling you fit in here," said Arin.

I told Arin how I found the dealers and about the arrests. A waitress hurriedly dropped some drinks and two cheesesteaks and a salad at the table.

"But you got her dealers," Arin said. "That's good."

"Arin, the drug bosses operated out of Queens, New York. Most were Jamaicans. I helped put them in jail."

"Jamaicans? I'm so sorry." Arin drew in a deep breath and pulled her hand from my forearm.

"Why? Irish, Russians, Chinese, everyone has gangs. But all I need to know is that a few other Tanyas got saved."

"What is it with us Murphys, always trying to save the world?" She picked up her sandwich, took a bite, rocked forward, letting out a dramatic hmmm. "It still sucks that Jamaicans had anything to do with Tanya."

My cousin Noreen sped by, giving us a wave.

"Did you always want to be a cop?"

I put my hands up and shrugged my shoulders.

"I never wanted to be a cop. I just wanted to put the people in jail that hurt Tanya. It turns out I'm pretty good at it. But that might change."

"What?" Arin tilted her head, and her eyes narrowed, "I don't understand."

I put my sandwich down.

"As you know, I've had other times in my life where I've been able to discern patterns, make connections that seem obvious to me but not to other people. It's disconcerting in a way, feeling different, and at some point that talent disappears. I was the state chess champion in grade school. I could see the proverbial ten moves ahead and then some. But by my freshman year in high school I lost most matches. It happened to me in college around football. I was the man. People wanted to be around me. It was addictive. I was a good athlete, not spectacular, but I had an ability to read plays and see what was about to happen."

I turned away from her gaze, my left hand tapping my leg.

"I was invited to work with the coaches, to review the scouting films. I could discern the strengths and weaknesses of the other teams' strategies. The quarterbacks, all of them had little tells. Micro-movements that happened so fast no one else could see them. But for me, I saw the play. I knew where the ball was going. I was interviewed on ESPN. I was written about multiple times in *Sports Illustrated*. I was being scouted for the pros. And then it disappeared. Not gradually, but like a light switch. Gone."

"And?" Arin leaned a little closer.

"I was at Penn State, where football reigns supreme. Articles were written about my demise. I went from football god to nobody. Everyone wanted to be around me, and then overnight no one wanted to be around me. I was twenty-one, and it kicked my ass. I crawled into a corner and sank into depression."

Arin's eyes searched my face.

"Tanya saved me. I was back in Philly, away from the Penn State spotlight, and Tanya set me straight. She let me know that whatever that talent was, it would come back in some other form. She believed in me far more than I believed in myself. The more time I spent with her, the less I wanted to be with anyone else. When she pushed me away, when she left the earth, my heart went with her."

"You two were fortunate to be so close. Most people never get to have that."

Arin's quiet calm, the kindness in her eyes, reminded me of Tanya.

"Tanya was right, too. That talent returned when I started to solve her murder. She technically overdosed, but as far as Buck and I are concerned she was murdered. I started seeing patterns and connections again. Buck nurtured, pushed, and mentored me. We have put some truly nasty people behind bars, and I wanted to add more. But I live in fear of the lights going out again. When I started having the ancestral memories, I thought I was losing it." I took a deep breath. "Arin, my parents are counting on me."

"We both have a lot of pressure on that front. You met my mom." Arin speared some salad. "How do your parents feel about you being a cop?"

"I'm not actually a cop, not yet. Maybe not ever." I inhaled deeply, noisily, the image of the giant falling back on me as two bullets hit his body, the gun leveled to my head. I could feel myself recoil at the memory.

"What's going on. Are you having a memory?" Arin looked alarmed.

"Yes, but not one of Aedan's," I whispered. I closed my

eyes and recounted the night I almost died, barely three weeks ago. When I opened them, I witnessed a tear running down her face.

"I would never have known you," she said, a tremble on her lips. "You and Mack would have been lost forever."

CHAPTER 25

The Clontarf Team office was empty on that Saturday afternoon, except for Anwulika and Catherine, who sipped tea while waiting for Padraig Collins to finish reading the report. Anwulika had invaded the privacy of seven of the most influential Unionist politicians in Northern Ireland. Collins needed them to support open borders and press for a special status for Northern Ireland to stay in the European Union. As part of the United Kingdom, Brexit would take Northern Ireland out of the E.U. along with England, Scotland, and Wales.

Collins cleared his throat, glanced at Anwulika, then back down at the report. He whistled, smirked, and drummed his fingers on the desk. Anwulika had written the report. Catherine had proofed it. They knew the bottom line. All seven of the politicians had more deposits in their bank accounts than their government positions paid. One had way more. And the cherry on top: this mother of three, a gospel-spouting paragon of conservative Protestant values, was having an affair. With another woman. The trade minister from London.

Collins laid the report on the desk. Anwulika looked at him expectantly. His face betrayed nothing. He stood, placed his hands on her face, then kissed both cheeks. Her smile spread. Collins reached into his pocket and withdrew a set of keys which he placed in her hand. Collins had promised her a bonus if she delivered.

"It's red, just like you told me you dreamed of having one day."

Anwulika opened her hands. The key-chain read: Corvette.

Collins stood back to watch the inevitable. Anwulika started laughing, threw her arms up and danced in a circle. "Chai! Bossman don dash me gift ooo," she said in her Nigerian pidgin.

Catherine gave her a high-five and a hug.

Collins nodded toward the door. "Let's have a look."

She took Collins by the arm, as no other employee would dare, and danced her way out the door. He shook his head and smiled, her brashness welcome in his ordered life.

CHAPTER 26

November 24, 2019
Old Swede's Church, Philadelphia

Mom had the photo of Mack's grave on her computer screen. Arin and I hovered over it, Dad viewing from the side.

Mom pointed to Mack's headstone and ran her finger forward.

"Arin, concentrate the radar here. Start at the headstone and set the grid at three feet by sixteen inches. It will stream directly to me. The GPR tablet is programmed to read the images, but it will throw light, so I suggest that you only use it as a back-up."

Arin nodded. "What depth would you expect?"

"Educated guess is three feet maximum. Graves were normally shallower, being that close to the river. We better hope Mack packed it in metal. Given that he spent much of his life on islands, he likely understood the problems with water tables."

"Assuming that it's there at all," Dad observed. We all turned to him. "Fifty-fifty at best," he added.

"Probably less than that," I answered, "but I'm good with those odds."

Buck texted: *Pick you up at 9:15.*

"Buck is going to pick us up. He's going to play back-up."

The four of us passed the time with dinner and reviewing plans. Mom told a few archeology stories. Dad shared a little about Conall and his memories. Arin enthralled them with some legends of Mack Murphy.

I enjoyed observing Arin as she spoke with my parents. Her image began to blur, to jump, to fade. I reached over to Tomás.

She is with child, cousin. I braced for the lecture, but none came. Tomás beamed, taking my arm in his.

"There is no more fortunate child than of your loin. Tell him to call me uncle. I am happy for you, cousin. The time for you to leave the monastery is coming soon. Have you told our uncle?"

I am jolted back by the sound of my phone pinging. "Let's go. Buck is here."

———

Buck pulled into the strip mall and turned toward the Dunkin parking area. We were surrounded by asphalt and neon, and I was struck by the sheer ugliness of this place. Across the street lies the Church of Two Ships, nestling the sailors and seamstresses, soldiers, and the children of the men and women who settled this area. There, behind the colonial brick wall, cuddled by trees and flags, they rest in peace. We were there to disturb one of them.

153

. . .

"I'm parking here. There will be cars here until at least midnight. We'll blend in," said Buck. "I'll wait on the corner until I see you go over the wall, then I'll enter through the dog park to keep watch. Make sure your phones are silenced. Text only if needed."

Arin and I took our packs with the equipment from the trunk and started walking north on Columbus. The traffic was heavy and fast, making us as unnoticeable as fire hydrants or bushes. We were about nine yards from the wall when the traffic slowed for the red light. I put my hand on Arin's shoulder.

"Let's appear to be talking until the traffic moves." My eyes wandered over the cars to see if anyone paid attention to us. Not a single glance our way. They were all staring at their phones.

Forty-five seconds later, the cars buzzed by at fifty in a thirty-five-mile-per-hour zone. Arin's eyes darted around. "There's too much light here. We should go in through the dog park."

"Trust me on this." I ran up the embankment and over the wall, leaving no time for discussion. I reached back to give her a hand, but she buzzed past me and dropped low against the wall. I met her at the grave.

With our backs against the brick wall, I looked out across the church grounds, the ambient light casting gray shadows of trees and tombstones. The cars behind us slowed for the stoplight, and the faint sound of someone on a speakerphone reached us from the dog park.

The grass was moist with dew, the ground harder than I would have liked. Arin's breath puffed out in the cold. Her hands shook slightly as she prepared the equipment.

Arin had the ground-penetrating radar device ready in less than a minute. It was surprisingly small, like a three-inch-thick smart tablet on wheels, a joystick protruding from its neck. The neck contained a wireless device, pre-programmed to feed to Mom's iPad at home.

I prepared the topsoil remover, a twelve-inch serrated blade. Arin had instructed me to cut twelve square inches at a time, two inches deep. They were to be laid on the tarp in the exact order in which they were removed.

I took the collapsible spade from my pack and placed it on the tarp while Arin moved the GPR next to the headstone. A police siren blasted, its flashing lights hitting the church wall a few feet from us. I spun around in reaction and slammed my elbow into the wall. Gritting my teeth, I forced myself to be silent. Arin's chest heaved. The car sped off, the siren fading into the distance.

Arin turned her attention back to the task. She was connected to my mom by my headset and phone. They had explained to me that the GPR would read unusual variations in the soil. We were searching for what wasn't there: rock, dirt, sediment. Their absence meant something else was in their place.

Arin whispered, "Megan sees the coffin. I wonder who's in there."

She continued to move the device in a left-to-right grid, very slowly, listening for comments. I watched her stop approximately two feet from the wall and hold the device still. Thirty seconds later, she began moving it east, west, north and south, clearly by my mom's directions.

She stopped, placed the device on the ground, and whispered, "She's enhancing the images; three to five minutes."

We both sat with our backs against the wall, Arin handing me one of the earbuds so I could listen. The only sound was a few keyboard strokes. I imagined Mack descending the gangway of a schooner just twenty yards away, perhaps finding a nearby pub for a shot of rum or a spill of Irish whiskey.

"There is a fourteen-square-inch variation a few inches above the coffin. Best I can tell, it's around two feet deep. It's in the bottom grid where you just scanned."

I gave the earbud back to Arin as she moved into position. I arranged the tools, then knelt next to her as she ran her finger horizontally over the starting point. "Remove two twelve-square-inch pieces to start."

I lifted the Dig Master blade and removed it from its sheath. Serrated on both sides, this was one nasty tool. If you stabbed someone with this, it would tear everything it touched on the way in and double that on the way out. The inch markers on the blade gave precise measurement. I visually checked for the two-inch setting and forced the blade into the turf where Arin had run her finger, followed the horizontal edge for around twelve inches, then both sides, followed by the bottom of the square. I stuck the blade in on the top corner, then ran it vertically all twelve inches until I met the horizontal line, and repeated my actions on the opposite side. I felt a sense of accomplishment as I laid the first square on the tarp. Four squares in total. Arin put her hand on my shoulder. I moved out of the way.

She operated the GPR.

"Dig eight inches with the shovel."

I checked the eight-inch marker on the shovel then made quick work of it.

Arin held the GPR over the exposed dirt, now twenty inches deep, and paused.

"Got it," she said into the microphone.

"Switch." She handed me the GPR and took the small spade. She pushed directly down around three inches and whispered, "Yes." She smiled at me expectantly. "Use the Dig Master at two inches to break up the soil, and then I'll take over."

I cleared it in a few minutes, then Arin began a careful removal of the top layer. Rusted metal came into view. She dug a perimeter around the object and pushed the tool under it to pry it loose. Arin removed a thick plastic bag from her backpack and placed the dull metal container, appearing to weigh only a few pounds, inside. I crouched beside her as we both stared at it and put my arm around her shoulder for a quick victory hug. After we let go of each other, she slid the package into a padded section of the backpack.

While I'd been digging, Arin had collected stones from around the wall. She dropped them into the cavity as I pulled the tarp to the edge and spread the dirt in the hole. Arin placed a topsoil square over the soil then joined the other pieces to it. Then she began to press the edges against their grassy neighbors with the trough until no separation was visible to the casual eye.

I repacked all the tools and texted a thumbs-up to Buck.

Arin crouched in front of the headstone and ran her fingers over Mack's name. I knelt beside her as she offered a silent high-five. She lifted out of the crouch so that her mouth was next to my ear.

"We did it."

We stayed close to the wall, leaning below the top of it, and moved quickly, parallel to the road.

About five yards before we reached our exit, a voice startled us.

"Don't turn around, and we won't shoot. Remove the packs and lay them on the ground."

Arin and I froze in place while my mind raced to assess the situation.

The voice continued, "Lay on the ground, face down, fingers laced over your head."

Arin turned toward the voice.

"Do what he said," I whispered.

Footsteps crunched across the ground. The backpacks scraped the gravel as someone took possession of them.

"My colleague is leaving. I'll follow in two minutes." The voice came from behind us now. "Keep your face down."

Arin started to say something.

"Don't," I warned her.

"You will stay as you are. A shooter with a night scope will leave five minutes from now. You are then free to go."

I could hear Arin's fingers scraping the ground next to me. It seemed as if I could feel her pulse banging against her skin. Perhaps it was my own, the smell of dirt and grass and dog piss adding to the mix as I tried to concentrate on the minutes passing.

The man began to move. His steps came from behind, stopping inches from my face. Small pebbles and dirt stirred beneath his feet, landing against my cheek.

"Three minutes to go. Move and you're dead."

I jolted at a new voice. "On your knees, asshole."

Buck held a gun to the back of the head of whoever this was, his ski mask still in place.

"You might still find the other guy," Buck said to me. "Take my keys. I'll deal with this."

"What happened to the shooter?" I asked, my eyes darting over the grounds.

"I used my night scope. There is no shooter. It was bull-shit. Get going."

Arin started to move toward the guy, seeming ready to tear his head off. I grabbed her by the shoulder.

"Get the hell out of here," Buck demanded.

We hurried over the wall and down the embankment, surprising three wiry, unkempt men walking toward us,: two white, one black, all clearly high.

"What the hell is going on, Key?" Arin pointed to our backpacks, both of them lying unopened on the side of the embankment.

Before I could get to the packs, the three guys stopped with a look of surprise and delight, as if an unexpected meal had been delivered to the hungry. All three hadn't seen a bar of soap in a while. They also stank of whisky, which they likely used to wash down some pills.

"Looks like you two been havin' some fun." The white guy on the right looked at Arin. "Got some left for me, sugar?" He looked forty but probably wasn't a day over twenty-nine.

Streetlights and cars lit the scene. It would be easy for a passerby to have a good look at Arin and me. There was no time for this bullshit. We needed to get the packs and get the hell out of there.

"It's time to move on, boys," I said. They looked at me as if they didn't know I was there. It had the effect I expected. Testosterone mixed with adrenaline mixed with drugs, some odd caveman reaction in the back of the brain that created the fight reaction, but not the flight. The drugs interfered with discernment. The black guy took two steps forward to Arin.

"Perfect cup a mocha here." He leered at her, again as if I didn't exist. "Think I need me a little."

He stood in the middle of the three of them, bobbing and weaving with excitement and anticipation, not a single brain cell warning him of danger. He reached for Arin. My right hand caught his right hand, and I bent it toward me. My left palm smashed into his elbow. Maximum pain, minimal damage. He howled. The other two woke up to danger.

The white boy on his right yelled, "Mother fucker," and leaped forward, all stupid rage. I punched him in the solar plexus, driving the air out of his lungs. Shock, temporary paralysis. He would be down for at least five minutes.

The opioids must have numbed the black guy's pain, though. He took a swing. The punch had power and form. It caught me on the shoulder. I rocked back a nanosecond then landed a kick to his knee, trying to go easy with this drugged fool. He came in even harder, faster. Another left, a right. An uppercut caught me on the chin trapping my tongue between my teeth. I tasted blood. Reaching in fast, I grabbed his shirt, pulled him toward me, and elbowed him in the side of his head. He dropped.

I was about four feet away from the remaining guy.

"This ain't your lucky night," he said. "Me and my boys want a little, we get a little." His right hand came from behind his back with a ten-inch blade. He was a foot away from Arin but talking to me. He'd dropped his knife hand to his side, blade resting on his thigh. Ten inches of steel making him feel like Superman.

"Get lost, asshole," Arin said.

Shit, I needed her to stay out of this.

He did a slow burn tilt of his head toward Arin and showed a hungry grin, two teeth missing, not a care in the world, before he turned back toward me.

Arin stepped in and trapped his knife hand to his leg with her left hand and delivered a palm strike to his chin with her right. His neck snapped back. He landed hard on his back.

"Nanny Raas bitch, teach you to fuck wid a Jamaican woman." Arin turned to look at me.

Damn, that was fast.

"Dr. Murphy, you are full of surprises," I said, then spit out some blood.

"Traffic is stopping. Let's go," said the Queen of Cool.

I stepped over two of the guys lying on the ground, grabbed the pack with Mack's box in it, and felt it to make sure it was there. Arin was already halfway down the street before I caught up, both packs in hand.

"Ain't nothing good about this. What the hell is going on, Key?"

CHAPTER 27

1979
DERRY, NORTHERN IRELAND

Padraig Collins laid prostrate at the altar. It was two in the morning. He was a patron of St. Columba church in Derry; he had his own key.

This time it was worse than when he killed Jimmy Riley.

This time it was an IRA test. Of his manhood. His commitment. His strength to lead. A lad he had never met was informing the Brits on bombing missions being prepared by the IRA in London. The war was intensifying, and a message had to be sent. No mercy to traitors. Collins was chosen as the messenger.

At 11:45 p.m., he had entered the house. Collins knew the man wasn't home but in London. His wife was alone. The fireplace was covered in soot, the smell of mossy peat, pungent in the nose. Pieces of wallpaper were flopping toward the floor. What little furniture they had were pieces handed down ten times before arriving here. The life of Catholics in the North was summed up in this shithole, yet they chose to be traitors. One bullet, all that was necessary. He pulled back the blanket to check for her pulse. No one had told him she was pregnant. He felt his soul enter another dimension. He feared he might not ever find it again.

Lying on the altar, he begged Saint Columba for help. He waited patiently for his heavenly voice. The smell of incense and spilled wine rose from the floor and filled his nostrils. He tasted it in his mouth. The pain of the parishioners who spoke their confessions, their unholiness, in this holy place, sifted from the confessional and found entry into his pores, his every breath contained them. Collins dared not move, no matter the hours that passed. His desperation grew. And then his blessed saint arrived, this time not just in voice but in vision.

'Padraig, my son, I sowed death and division. In my shame and penance, I exiled myself to Iona and dedicated my life to healing and unity in the name of our Lord. You, too, must heal and unite. You will face many more trials. You will sin again, and like me, you will pray for forgiveness. God has wrapped you in a bigger purpose for himself. Unite your people in peace. It is your only path to save your soul. I will send you a sign when the time comes.'

Collins lay there in rapture when a thought came to him: "Have I gone mad?"

Yet he dismissed it and contemplated his mission. For any reconciliation between the Catholics and Protestants to happen, the Protestants needed to feel economic pain. Only then would they demand change.

CHAPTER 28

B uck called as I turned onto Walnut Street. "Where are you?"

"Second and Walnut," I responded.

"Pull over by the movie theatre. I want to see if you're being followed. Troy just picked me up. I'll text you when I'm in place."

I pulled over and turned my attention to Arin. "Don't worry about me," she exhaled deeply. "Keep your mind on the mission."

She's tough but unconvincing, her fingers tapping rapidly on her knee, staring out the window and avoiding eye contact.

My phone buzzed. "Go."

I continued straight up Walnut Street and made my way to Delancey.

Buck arrived as we parked. We climbed the steps and opened the door as my mother rushed into the foyer and put her hand out for the pack.

"Meg, Shaun, please sit down," Buck announced. "We have a problem. And Shaun, yes, I'll have a shot of that good Irish whiskey. We all need one."

My dad looked at Buck.

"I'll pour the whiskey, but the rest of it will have to wait. Nothing will keep her from that," dad said, acknowledging the pack with Mack's treasure.

Mom took Arin's hand.

"Come on, honey. You've been waiting a long time for this."

Arin looked back at me, her smile so big I wanted to stand there and memorize it in case I needed it for another time.

Buck nudged me, and we both looked at Dad.

"Go, I'll bring the whiskey." Dad waved us off.

We followed Mom down the basement steps. Mom and Arin chatted in front of a wall that was decorated with an Irish Claddagh ring, a hand on each side of a heart, a crown on top. My father arrived and pushed buttons on a remote control. The wall opened, revealing a glass-enclosed room, approximately eight feet wide, twelve feet deep.

Arin took my mother's hand.

"This is fantastic."

"What the …" Buck left it unfinished. "Meg, I didn't know this was here."

I was only in it once. As a music archeologist, she dealt with delicate materials, most of which were hundreds of years old.

"A woman must have a few secrets." She winked at us. "It's an archeology lab modified for old manuscripts, temperature- and humidity-controlled. Arin will recognize most of the components."

I took in my mother's private world: framed manuscripts hung on the wall, an ancient Irish harp was on display, microscopes and an array of electronic equipment lay at the ready. I had been in the police forensics labs, a place to be reminded that, no matter how good a detective you might be, these are the places where things the size of a grain of sand deliver a universe of clues.

As she stepped into her lab, her movements were swifter, lighter; her eyes widened and beamed.

Arin leaned into me. I was pleased to see her put her arm into Buck's, and Buck put his arm over Dad's shoulder.

Mom lifted an industrial mask over her nose and mouth. She placed the pack on the lab table. With lab gloves on she retrieved the rusted case and took a deep breath, her chest expanding. It seemed as if she was exhaling the years of waiting, the moment of truth finally having arrived. For me, the story only started a few days ago. For Mom, Dad and Arin, it had been most of a lifetime. We watched her as she raised a metal snip. The old, rusted lock dropped to the lab table.

My mother's face betrayed her shock when she opened the box. Instead of the Kells artefacts, she held a roll of leather tied by a cord. We looked on as she unrolled it, revealing a single sheet of aged paper. She held it for us to read through the glass.

Find The River
He rests among his USCT comrades
From Camp William Penn
His father an immigrant from Rome

Mom let the reflexes of the aged leather roll back to the shape it had held for more than one hundred years, then stepped out of her domain. Her eyes lost their thrill. Her shoulders visibly sagged.

Arin beamed a smile at my mom while pointing to the leather scroll, bouncing onto tiptoes in excitement.

"This is amazing Meg, Think about it. We found Mack's clue when there could have been nothing. Now we need to figure out what he means. I know what the USCT is. Buck, your folk would have served with them. It means United States Colored Troops."

"How do you know this?" asked Buck.

"My specialty is the Irish and African diaspora, in particular how they converged in the U.S. The government didn't allow blacks to serve until 1863, but they comprised ten percent of the Union Army. And they kicked butt."

I joined in. "In the last letter I read, Mack was introduced to someone known as The River."

"Good work, detective," Arin responded.

"What are you talking about?" asked my father.

"Mack described being recruited to spy on the South by a mixed-race spymaster of the time. He went by the alias 'The River'. He arrived near the Irish Brigade encampment with a division of USCT infantry, according to the letter," Arin finished.

"He knew of Mack's plans to go to Ireland to fight the Brits," I added. "He promised to train him in all matters of spying, tools that would serve him later in Ireland."

"That's incredible." We turned to my mom; her Irish accent more pronounced in her excitement. She removed her gloves and absently brushed her bangs away from her eyes. "My wild guess: something spooked him. He returned to move the book and replaced it with this new clue."

"Hold on. We have a huge problem," Buck intruded with his commanding voice. "I don't mean to be the downer, Meg, but you all need to know what happened tonight. Mack's little treasure chest has caught the attention of someone who wants to take it from you."

Mom's hands went to her face as she took a step or two backward. Dad almost dropped the bottle, steadied himself, and nodded to Buck. Buck looked at the whiskey and Dad poured, waited a moment, and gave Buck a refill.

Buck recapped the story to the point where Arin and I left the cemetery. "The one with the gun on you was Officer Felipe Ramirez."

"A cop, a freaking cop?" I felt like someone had slapped me, hard. I started pacing back and forth, stopping to look at the rolled-up leather and the metal case sitting on the lab table.

"Who hired him?"

"He said it was a cutout, a middleman. He always works through a cutout, he told me. The guy is dirty. You hear rumors." Buck points to the pack with the tools in it. "How did you get the packs?"

"They were on the embankment, just over the wall," Arin answered, "but why would his accomplice leave them there?"

"Because ..." I nodded to the whiskey bottle. My father added some to a glass and handed it to me. I swallowed, one shot. "Someone made him." I looked at Buck and tapped the empty glass on the table next to me. "Whoever Ramirez is working for wants to take it from us, but a different group forced them to leave it behind."

I peered into the lab, the leather roll sitting in Mack's metal box. "We were meant to have it."

The truth of my statement settled in. Mom just stood quietly, her hands in the pockets of her jeans. I knew that look, her archeologist brain in search of answers.

"'Without you, they don't stand a chance of finding it.' That's what Arin told me in Jamaica. You guys have told me that the only way to find it is if I can see the clues in Aedan's memories," I said to my parents.

Dad fidgeted with the whiskey bottle, his eyes on Mom. "What do we do now?"

"There's only one thing we can do." Arin eyed all of us. "Key finds the book."

"We—you mean we find it. Right? By the way," I said to Arin, "where did you learn to fight like that?"

"Like what?" Dad asked.

I recounted the sidewalk bedlam. "She took out the guy holding a knife in seconds."

"Much respect," Buck said.

"Do you think there was a connection between those three and Mack's box?" Dad asked.

"No way." I shook my head. "I don't put much stock in coincidence, but these guys were stoners." I spread my hands to Arin. "They had no interest in the packs, only in you."

"What if you're wrong," Arin replied. "What if someone sent them?"

"I'm with Key on this," Buck answered. "If they were stoners, no way."

I let out a sound akin to *pffffffffh*, then leaned on the glass wall of the lab, looking in. I sensed everyone eyeing me. "Ramirez's accomplice takes the packs and goes over the wall. Three minutes later, Arin and I go over the wall, and the packs are sitting there on the embankment."

I turn to the four of them. "We all agree someone forced him to leave the packs, presumably at gunpoint. The only people we see are the three stoners. The packs would not have been left unprotected. If the stoners got there before us, someone was nearby to stop them from taking them."

Arin pursed her lips and scrunched her eyes. Something I've seen her do. "Mi no happy bout dis." She paused. "Sorry, when I get excited the patois comes out."

"I love it, but I think you were about to make a point," Mom added.

"Yes, Key's right. Someone had to be waiting to make

THE KEY TO KELLS

certain that it was us who took the packs." Arin shook her head. "Happened so fast. I don't remember seeing anyone."

We remained quiet, thinking. I broke the silence. "You didn't say where you learned to fight."

"I was a judo champion in high school, studied jiu-jitsu when I was at Georgetown." Arin stole a look at the lab. "And now let's get to work finding The River."

"I'm leaving this part for you guys," Buck said, "I need to get a few hours' sleep."

Arin gave him a big hug.

"Thanks for saving our butts."

We all nodded to Buck.

"They weren't going to hurt you, not if they needed you," Buck said.

"Not yet. They wouldn't hurt us, yet." I could feel my cortisol, my stress hormones, jump through the roof as the realization hits me. "Sonofabitch. We don't even know what the clue means." I pointed my thumb back toward the lab. "Ramirez's people would have been back for us in no time once they realized that this was not the Kells book. And they likely will be back. And whoever stopped them, they're waiting to see our next move."

"To summarize," Buck said, "this is getting intense fast. I apologize, but I have to go. Make sure the security alarm is on." Buck held up his phone. "24 7."

I watched Buck take the steps. "Arin, can you and Mom see what you can find about Camp William Penn. I'll see if I can find anything on The River."

"I can tell you," Arin responded, "Penn was the largest training camp for USCT soldiers. It was in Cheltenham, what, maybe thirty to forty minutes from here? The question is, where are the USCT soldiers buried?"

Arin spoke some voice commands into her phone, my mom by her side. I joined them.

"Look at this." She zoomed in over the words La Mott. "Camp William Penn was right here, near Elkins Park in Cheltenham." She widened the map. "One mile away is Philadelphia National Cemetery. It's a veterans' cemetery, and there is a section for the United States Colored Troops."

"Google the cemetery," I suggested. "I want to see the photos."

Arin clicked on the images tab and dozens of photos appeared. The cemetery looked like a small version of Arlington, and seconds later we found the USCT commemorative marker. Prominent in the display was a photo of around twenty black troops in long white coats and leggings with blue cavalry hats, holding their rifles in military display. Next to them was their commanding officer, dressed in Union Army Blue, the only white man in the photo.

"That sucks." I pointed to the officer.

"There weren't any Black officers, if that's what you mean," answered Arin.

"Still sucks."

I examined the camera angles.

"The cemetery sits in the middle of a neighborhood now, houses on every side. No place to hide." I looked to Arin. "We need to check it out in the morning. It says it opens at nine. I want to be there at eight thirty."

"I'll go with you in the morning," Mom interjected.

"Mom, if my hunch is right, we'll need you here. If the opportunity presents itself, we will act on the spot. And we'll need you on the computer, just like tonight. Besides that, you and Dad might have to bail us out."

CHAPTER 29

"This is worse than I expected," I said to Arin as I took the first pass of the cemetery. "Every house has a direct view."

We drove around the entire perimeter of the cemetery. It sat in the center of a square, wall-to-wall redbrick row homes standing guard over this quiet slice of American history. School buses stopped at every corner. Neighbors chatted on porches, some keeping their eyes on the kids waiting for the bus and the cars pulling out to head to work. A working-class neighborhood, keeping company with the spirits of long-ago soldiers.

"It's strange having a cemetery in the middle of a neighborhood," Arin commented. "I guess the locals hardly notice it. They're so used to it."

"I'm counting on that."

"Yeah, like a tall, redheaded white guy in a Black neighborhood won't stick out." Arin laughed. "Luckily, you have me with you."

"I am very lucky." I glanced at Arin in time to note a slight blush.

I found a parking space near the entry. I looked at my watch, eight forty-five. But less than a minute went by before a Jeep Wrangler pulled up to the gate. Someone hopped out, opened the gate, got back in the car, and left.

"I read on the website that it's unattended, but I thought they would at least go in."

I drove through the entrance and followed the road toward a work shed at the top of a hill. I parked and got out. It was a brisk morning, invigorating to me but obviously chilly for Arin as she rubbed her hands to ward off the cold. We could view the entire cemetery. A few tall, sculptured memorials dotted the field, but it was mainly row after row of white gravestones, flags swirling, offering quiet dignity to those who had fought to save the Union, save for a small section that I read about online.

"There's a burial area here for Confederate soldiers."

"Strange. Why are Confederate soldiers buried here?" Arin asked.

"The irony being that the Black soldiers here might have been the ones who killed them."

"Or the other way around."

We got back in the car and followed the road in its southerly direction before it curved east.

"There it is." I pointed ahead, pulled over, and got out.

My pulse quickened to see it. I wondered how Arin would feel. She put both hands on the marker then rested her fingers over the soldiers carrying the American flag. A tear dropped from her face onto the display. She rested her cheek over the image.

"Mack came to America for this. He might have met some of these men." She scanned the headstones in front of us.

" We're looking for any reference to a river. Also, there

might be a reference to Rome. Why else would he mention that River's father is from Rome?"

We began the laborious process of searching each head-stone, some words barely visible, time and weather-beaten. My eyes constantly scanned the streets for cops and observers. They were mostly empty, except for a jogger and a woman pushing a baby carriage. A sudden cold breeze ran a chill through my body, waking me a little. After crouching at one hundred graves, my focus was starting to falter.

"Key, look at this," Arin called out.

I knelt in front of a small headstone and read the name Umberto Tiber.

"That's an Italian name, what do you think?" asked Arin.

"There's no reference to The River."

Arin started a search on her cell phone. "Oh my god. Oh my god, Key." Her hands shook as she handed me the phone. "Umberto Tiber is called Ponte Umberto Tiber. It's a bridge over the River Tiber in Rome."

I looked at the screen.

"Amazing."

Arin leaned into my arms for a fleeting hug.

"We found it."

She was trembling. I looked down to see her face. I brushed her hair back. She met my eyes and held them for a moment, then jumped up and kissed my cheek like the other night. "Call your mom."

I hustled back to the car and grabbed the equipment.

"Are we out of our minds doing this in broad daylight?" Arin asked while preparing the tools.

"If we were spotted at night, the police would be here in no time. No one is going to give us much thought in the daylight." I scanned the houses again. "But let's move fast. We are on Federal property."

A curtain moved at one of the homes, about eighty feet away.

I kept an eye on the gate. In the daylight, the GPR looked like a toy truck. Arin was on her knees, moving the device slowly, one hand on the joystick, the other on the cold ground as she shifted it forward inch by inch, listening for my mother's response in her ear.

"We've got something," Arin said without taking her focus off the device.

"Yeah, company," I said as a police car slowed on Limekiln Pike and put on the turn signal. "I got this. Don't pay any attention to us. Just keep moving that thing around."

I walked to the police car, my police ID in my right hand, facing forward and extended, impossible to miss.

"Got a call, sir," he responded. "Do you mind if I ask what's going on?"

My stomach is in knots, wondering if he knows Officer Ramirez. I took a good look at him and lit up.

"You're Malcolm's brother."

His eyes narrowed.

"I work with Buck McCoy. We met at a Sixers game a few months ago, had a few beers together." I took a quick glance at his name tag. "Rashid, right?"

He was the one to light up. I reached my hand through the window.

"Key Murphy."

"Oh man, that's right. I remember you."

"Rashid, maybe you can do me a favor?"

"Sir?"

"Please, lose the 'sir' thing. Just Key."

He relaxed at this. Twenty-three-year-old newly minted cop, nice guy, as I remembered.

"We think some drugs were hidden here. My partner is running some scans. I think we spooked the neighbors. Could you sit here, fifteen, twenty minutes, unless you get a call."

"No problem, sir."

"Key," I reminded him. He laughed.

Arin had laid out the tools and scored the ground for the dig. She looked up at me as I returned, seeing the cop car still sitting there and nodding toward it. The car was at an angle and distance that Rashid couldn't see what we were doing.

"He thinks we're searching for drugs. I asked him to stay, so no one else will call the cops. And his brother is a good friend of Buck."

Arin turned back to her work.

"It's only one foot deep this time. I set the spade for eight inches. You are going to cut the topsoil out, same as before, and lay it on the tarp. When you clear the eight inches, that will put us down at ten total. We'll scan it again and then use the hand trowel."

I cleared the turf and then spaded the dirt onto the tarp. "You're trembling," I noted to Arin.

"What?"

"You're trembling," I repeated.

She looked at her shaky hands and took hold of the GPR and scanned as my mother directed her. In less than five minutes she'd cleared the object, lifted it out, placed it in a protective cover, and slipped it into her backpack. "I have it, Meg."

Arin started to stand but then just dropped back to the ground.

"We need to get out of here. What are you doing?"

She pulled the metal chest out of the pack, urgently broke the rusted hasp with the trowel, and opened it, just enough to see inside.

Arin sobbed. She said, in the softest, most angelic voice I've ever heard, "I found it, Daddy. I found Mack. I found his secret."

I knelt to replace the sod, as I had seen Arin do last night. Kneeling next to me, she cupped my cheek.

"Thank you."

Despite the fact that we had just desecrated a grave on

Federal property, had a cop sitting twenty-five yards from us, and a nosey neighbor looking to make trouble, I wanted to prolong the feel of her hands on my face. Instead, I repaired the ground and hurried to the car.

Rashid waved and made a U-turn, then a left onto Limekiln. I watched him head up the road when my eyes landed on an unmarked police car—just sitting there, all nice and cozy. I wondered where Officer Ramirez was this morning.

———

I had texted Buck, asking if he could join us at the house.

My father met us at the front door and walked, the three of us in tow, to the basement. My mother had prepared the lab. Without a word, she took the case and closed the door behind her. She froze, not a breath taken, it seemed, then opened the door to the lab, held out a mask and gloves to Arin and invited her in.

We three men held vigil as Mom opened the case. She put her hand on Arin's arm and stepped back. Arin peered over her shoulder; Mom nodded. A sacred moment was unfolding as Arin reached in. It seemed we were all aware of it.

Arin held it so that we could see a bundle wrapped in leather, leather cords tied around it, dry, like it could fall apart at a touch. She removed the cords and the leather blanket to reveal a frail but thick book cover with at least fifteen jewels in the form of a cross. The jewels were dull and tarnished. The memory of the escape from Iona rushed into my brain, so vivid that I bent over in panic. The claustrophobic tunnel threatened to trap me. I straighten at the touch of Buck's hand on my shoulder and nodded that I was fine.

Arin held it in both hands, lifting it as might a priest or rabbi, an offer to the gods. She turned so that we could see the cover.

In Latin was written, "In cujus S. Columbae uenire." *In Celebration of St. Columba.*

My mother slid her hands under Arin's.

"I promised my father." Arin's voice shook, but her face was alive with excitement. "Megan, I promised. I promised him."

Arin opened the lab door, pulled her mask off, and fell into my arms, trembling, tears rolling down her face. My mom exited behind her.

Mom also had tears that she wiped away with her sleeve. She threw her arms around Dad. "I touched history. I touched your ancestors." Then to Buck. "And in some ways, yours. The man who brought this to us fought against slavery, maybe on the same battlefields as your great-great-grandfather."

Buck rocked back and forth on his heels. He drew in two loud sniffles, clearing his nose. He hugged Mom and kissed her on the cheek.

She took me by the hands.

"Let's hope that Aedan's memories continue to guide you. Like it or not, you are the key. Yes, pun intended."

We all turned at the sound of champagne being uncorked. Dad had quietly arranged five glasses. When we all had one, he raised his toward the lab, the *Book* in view.

"To Mack Murphy."

We raised our glasses to The Ghost.

We sipped, clinked glasses, and I wondered what would come next.

Arin put her glass down.

"I want to call my mother and give her an update."

"I'm not sure that's a good idea," Buck said to Arin. "You have at least one powerful adversary out there. Somehow, they knew where you were going to be last night. Until we know that nothing is bugged or tapped, I suggest holding off on divulging any information."

"How do we do that?" Arin asked.

"I'll bring a scanner when I come back a little later," Buck answered. "I need to go to the office for a few hours." He started for the basement steps but turned back. "You sure are one weird-ass family." An immense smile covered his face. "And I thank God I'm part of it."

"I need a few hours to take care of the book and protect it. Without distraction." My Mom flicked her hand for us to leave. "Let's meet in a few hours."

"I'm taking a nap," Arin announced.

"Whoever wanted us to find the book likely knows we found it," I said when we reached the kitchen. "They have a plan. We need a plan."

"I'll be back in a few hours. We can discuss it then," Buck said.

"See you then," Arin said as she started up the stairs.

"Walk with me," Buck quietly said as he stepped out of the house.

We stood on the street, no one around.

"You really didn't know you had this thing, this memory thing?" Buck asked.

"Do you think I would have kept it from you?" There was nothing Buck and I kept from each other.

"I'm jealous, little brother," Buck said, giving me a sly look.

"Why?"

"Stupid question. What I wouldn't give to be able to see through an ancestor, to see where I come from. And who are you doing it with, only Miss Freaking Jamaica. I see how you look at her. I'll trade places."

"I don't know what to do about her." The words flew out of my mouth, along with a deep exhale.

Buck's eyes widened.

"What do you mean?"

"You know what I mean."

Buck stared at me for an uncomfortably long moment. He shook his head. "You gotta get over this shit."

He got right up in my face, like he does when the big brother thing kicks in. I love him for it.

"Not everyone you love is going to die, not everything you touch is going to turn to crap. Some things will last, some won't. Arin might, Arin might not."

Buck clicked the remote to unlock his car and got in. His window came down. "You are in the middle of some deep shit that we don't understand. Good thing I'm here."

"Except for the fact that you're about to drive off."

Buck gave me the finger. I offered one back. It's a good thing he's here. It's always been a good thing.

CHAPTER 30

I showered and threw on some gym shorts and a T-shirt. As tired as I was, I had a feeling sleep was going to be hard to come by. There was a knock on my door.

"Come in." I assumed it was my father but was thrilled to see Arin. Her hair was wet from the shower, even more curly and sexy, dripping a little on her PJ top, a v-neck showing a little cleavage. I tried not to stare.

"I'm too jangled up, can't sleep," Arin whispered, walking in. "Do you mind if I hang out here for a while?"

I gestured to the bed.

"It's my old bedroom from when I lived here. There aren't any chairs, but we can lean against the pillows."

She bounced onto my bed like a teen at a sleepover.

"We're both jangled. Having a gun pointed at you can do that. How are you doing?" I asked.

Her shoulders sagged momentarily and then straightened. "A little freaked out about last night and thrilled for what happened today."

I followed her eyes as she quietly looked around. On the wall closest to her were three large photos of me on the football field. One from Roman Catholic High, in my junior year, two at Penn State. I don't know why I kept them. A bit of masochism must be in my veins. Arin looked across me to a photo on the opposite wall. Tanya, Buck, and I stood with our fathers in front of the Vietnam Veterans Memorial.

"I was in eighth grade. That was the day that I first learned what happened in 'Nam. Dad told us that had it not been for Uncle Brian, Buck's dad, his name would have been on that wall. He just stood there and cried. It was confusing and embarrassing as a kid, watching my father cry in public. I'll never forget what happened next."

Arin stayed quiet. Full attention on me.

"Strangers, other vets, who were witnessing this whole thing, walked up and shook his hand, or hugged him, or saluted him and Uncle Brian. No one said a word. They just offered respect."

I turned to Arin so I could better see her.

"Then my father took Buck and Tanya by the hand and told them that their father was a hero, and that the Murphy family would always be there for them. Then Buck's dad put his hand on my shoulder and said, 'What your father did that night saved ten other men. He's *my* hero.'"

She surprised me by moving closer.

"It's strange. I feel like I've known you forever."

"I do look like Mack."

"I know, but that's not why. It's something else." She stared into me for a moment, her light green eyes mesmerizing, then laid her head on my shoulder.

I couldn't help myself. I kissed her cheek. She moved her mouth to mine, soft and exploring, tentative at first, then vital. It was as if could feel every cell awake. My erection brushed her leg, and she responded, moving closer, urgent, needy. And I said perhaps the stupidest thing ever to leave my lips.

"Arin, I want this more than I can express. But not while we're in this super-charged moment. If you give me another chance at this, I want to wake up looking in your eyes as if it was supposed to be this way. I don't want to take a chance that it was because of a momentary emotion."

All I wanted to do was make love to this amazing woman, and I just told her no. What the hell was I thinking?

"I should leave." She started to get up, but I held her back. "I want to hold you," I confessed. "Let's just get some sleep. I have a feeling a wild ride lies ahead."

Arin's mouth drew down. Maybe she felt like me: a moment lost and unfulfilled. She brushed her hand across my cheek then left the room.

I wanted to punch myself in the head. Instead, I lay there, replaying her breathing, imagining my hand resting on her shoulder, certain that sleep would evade me as I played her kiss over and over in my mind. But soon I was drifting between thoughts of her lips and the embrace of Siobhán, the netherworld coaxing me to that other realm.

My heart beat loudly in my chest. It was time for Siobhán and her brothers to arrive. My brother monks waited restively. We had to leave before daylight and gain distance in the dark.

The call of a crossbill reached me. I returned the sound as planned. My blood raced at the slight rustle of leaves and the crunch of boots meeting the earth.

Siobhán and her two brothers emerged from the woods. We embraced and made for the boat, but a war cry broke the silence. We turned to see two Norsemen rush toward us, their swords at the ready. They were large and muscular, their braided hair bouncing against their necks, eyes bulging.

I stepped toward them and raised my hand, ordering in their language, "Stop. I bring a message to you."

In confusion, they paused. Siobhán's brothers, warriors, took a knee and readied their arrows.

"My king commands you to bow before us and send yourself to Valhalla with your own blade."

The Norsemen shook off their confusion and began to charge us. Arrows took them by the throat, and I plunged my sword into their hearts, first one, then the other, wishing that there were dozens more, so I might even the score of my sixty-eight brothers slaughtered by these heathens.

I raced back to the boat as Siobhán's brothers helped her climb in. The monks had their oars ready. I did a final inventory, and my eyes landed on the chest containing the relics of St. Columba. We would take them to our new home in Kells.

I was lost, the rolling of the ocean waves vivid in my dreamlike state, mixed with the light breathing of Arin, her head still resting gently on my chest. I wanted to record this memory of Aedan on paper, but I could do nothing but lie still. Arin's sleep could not be disturbed. I was enjoying it too much. I reached my hand to caress her hair, and was surprised to find myself alone.

I slipped downstairs and made some lunch, Arin soon joining me. It was two in the afternoon and I was famished. I poured Arin some more coffee, her eyes not meeting mine. I stood awkwardly with the pot in my hand, trying to think of something enlightening to say. The basement door opened. Dad entered the kitchen, a big smile on his face, energy in his eyes.

"We need you downstairs."

Arin put down her spoon. I grabbed the coffee cups, feeling more alert from Dad's excitement than from the caffeine.

"There are references to the other relics, but they're vague," Dad added, the stairs creaking under his weight. "We're guessing Aedan left very few clues because he assumed he would go back for it, or, if something happened to him, Siobhán's brothers or Tomás would bring it to the monastery."

Mom met us at the bottom of the steps.

"Maybe he did go back for it. It's possible this is all for nothing," Mom offered, "but he wrote something that you need to see."

The Claddagh doors to the lab were closed. Her computer desk, with two large monitors, was now the center of our universe. Mom gestured for me to stand next to her. "It's in Irish, so I translated."

'If trouble finds us and the treasures remain hidden, God has shown me in a dream that an ancient one from the sea will one day unite this treasure with the Church. To him may all blessings be passed'.

"Okay, what am I supposed to take from this?"

Arin leaned in to study it.

"Oh my God."

"What am I missing?" I asked.

Mom emboldened the words '**ancient one from the sea**'.

"Do you think he's referring to me?"

All three stared at me with knowing grins, inferring the possibility.

Arin put her hand on my arm.

"'Murchadh' is Gaelic for 'Murphy'. It literally translates to 'from the sea' or 'sea warrior', and Cián means 'ancient one'."

"Are you all nuts? Sorry, guys. This is from what, 806? It's clearly just coincidental."

"You are right. Maybe." She gave her devilish Arin smile. "But as my mother said, let the ancient ones call to you. That's what Aedan is doing."

I shook my head and rolled my eyes.

"Let's look at what appears to be the map and clues." Mom scrolled down the page and read out loud:

'The evangelist holds quill in one hand, the *Bible* in the other. The *Book* points to the place of the eight stars where St. Columba's treasure lives. The Cross of Kells is above him. Go to the eight stars and then to the fire. The right hand will point the way."

"This is the page that he's referring to," she said, bringing up a photo reproduction from the *Book of Kells*. "That's John the Evangelist."

I looked closely at the enlarged image on the screen. The vibrant colors were shocking, the detail breathtaking. The bearded saint is seated on a blue chair. He wears a red cloak. In his left hand is a decorated *Bible*, in the right a long red quill. His head is framed by two concentric circles, each circle decorated in Celtic art. On each side of the largest circle is an eight-pointed star highlighted in blue, silver, and gold.

"It's interesting that all four crosses have a different Celtic knot motif," Arin said, referring to the crosses atop and below the saint and on each side of him.

Mom put her finger on the cross above the saint. "He states that the cross above him is Kells. It's an educated guess that the cross to his right is the Hill of Tara. This was the ceremonial site of the High Kings of Ireland. I have highlighted this map."

Mom brought up a screenshot from Google maps.

"There were four roads out of Kells back then. These two to the east are the same ones used today, with asphalt in place of a forest floor. One runs to Tara; the other to the Hill of

Slane. The legend is that St. Patrick lit the Easter Fire there. The Pagan King could see it from Tara. If I'm right about this, the eight-pointed star he's referring to is a Druidic symbol. There are two druid stones at Slane."

Mom brought up a photo of the ruins. It appeared to be nothing but rocks strewn over the ground, with a few standing upright, in the shape of obelisks. "This one is said to have an eight-pointed star, barely visible. Is this ringing any bells from the memories?" she asked me.

"No, nothing." I said to Arin, "Maybe Aedan will call my cell phone and let me know where he put it." She didn't look pleased with my attempt at humor and punched me lightly on my shoulder.

"Go back to the map." I pointed to Slane. "Aedan said they would go up the River Boyne to get to Kells. The river runs through Slane. It makes sense."

Mom looked at the map. She placed her forefinger on Slane and her thumb on Tara. "They are right across from each other," said Arin.

"Both were major religious and cultural ceremonial sites for hundreds of years before Aedan was born. Aedan would have known them well," Mom added.

"Why is there a pagan symbol in the *Book of Kells*?" I asked.

"The church co-opted many pagan symbols and rituals. To convert masses of people, they simply gave the existing symbols new meaning. It made Christianity more appealing. The eight-pointed star is found in many ancient religions, all over the globe. Druids believed that it was a symbol of the four seasons and the four elements of the earth. So, the church adopted the eight-pointed star as a symbol of renewal. That's why most baptismal fonts have an octagonal base," Arin answered.

"More specifically, Columba was the John the Baptist of the Celtic Christian world. His message was one of renewal through Christ. Therefore, the eight-pointed star," Mom added.

My breath drew in sharply. Arin and Mom turned to me.

"I just remembered: I had another episode this afternoon. After Siobhán got in the boat, Aedan made sure everything was accounted for. He looked at the chest. An eight-pointed star decorated the top, the same as we see here."

Arin and Mom looked at the screen, then back at me, then back to the screen.

"The starting point is Slane. Your father's searching for flights."

"For when?"

"Today," Mom answered.

I shook my head, "It feels like we're shooting with a blind-fold on. We need to plan."

"Key, the treasure is in Ireland. Sitting around here does us no good." She mumbled something indecipherable in Irish, then caught herself. "We can make a plan there."

"I agree," Arin added. "We have some urgency. You're supposed to be back at work in about eight days, right?"

Her words hit me like a bucket of ice-cold water; there was a timestamp with Arin, an endpoint measured in days. "True—but that's not the problem. Someone is a step ahead of us." I reached my hand to the computer. "Buck's going to run a scan on the house and our devices. But it's more likely that your computer has been hacked. If so, everything that you just showed us …"

I paused to let that sink in. It also sank into my brain that I was the one our opposition needed. Arin and my parents were collateral assets.

Or collateral damage.

CHAPTER 31

B uck had a key to the house. It was his house to come and go, just as it was mine. But he always pushed the bell out of politeness before walking in. Mom frequently jested with him that he didn't need to do that, but that was part of their banter. I was an only child, and since Tanya died, so was Buck. He was parentless for a year now too, and I think Mister Tough-Ass was happy to have my parents as his. I had Buck's parents as a little kid, but his mom died when we were pretty young. Cancer sucks.

I met Buck at the door and followed him as he used a hand-held device that detected bugs and hidden cameras. We concentrated on the basement, living room, and kitchen. Nothing. He used a different scanner on our devices.

"Clean. That doesn't mean they aren't hacked." Buck disabused us of any sense of privacy. "Nothing we can do about it except turn everything off and stick them in a drawer for now. Guessing that's not going to happen."

As usual, we had gathered in the kitchen, Mom, Dad and Arin on the stools at the island.

"Buckle up, everybody. I have some information," Buck said. He remained standing.

"I had a little visit with Ramirez. His accomplice was Officer Colasanti. Twenty years in. You know him?" he asked me.

"No."

"According to Ramirez, the moment Colasanti hit the sidewalk last night, he was stopped by a man with a gun, very discreet, all calm and whispers. Colasanti handed over his gun and dropped the packs. He was told to run to Packer Avenue and not look back."

Buck tapped his fingers on the counter. Something was forming in his mind.

"What would Blade do?" I said to Buck.

"What would Ronald McDonald do?" Buck responded.

Arin lifted her palms. "What are you talking about?"

"They always do this when working out a problem," Dad said to Arin.

I looked at my parents.

"When I took a walk the other night, I went to Rittenhouse Square. Buck had got a call from some plain-clothes detectives who thought I had two guys tailing me. I also had a very suspicious encounter in Jamaica," I added.

"You didn't tell us any of this," Dad responded.

"It was inconclusive—but those guys were following Key. They weren't doing anything illegal, but we diverted them from following Key home," Buck added. "Who else knows about your search besides us?"

"My team in Dublin. Kate, Ben, and Patty. They know the general outline and will assist us there," Dad offered.

"Arin," Buck looked at her. "Your mother, brother, and Dr. Garcia, correct?"

"Yes."

Buck stood, hands resting on the marble counter.

"I want to scare the shit out of you right now. Arin, Key,

you had a gun aimed at you last night. All of you are in danger. There are at least two parties that want what you have. We don't know who they are, but they're powerful enough to have shown up last night."

"Okay, Buck, but it has nothing to do with Dr. Garcia or my family," Arin added.

"Arin, we have in our possession something worth thirty to forty million dollars that could lead you to something worth more than one hundred million. For that kind of money, I don't trust you. I don't trust your family. I don't trust Dr. Garcia. I don't trust Shaun's team in Dublin, and you shouldn't trust me."

Buck walked over to my mother; Arin seated beside her.

"I have seen crazier things happen as a cop—betrayals between the most trusted of family and friends, blown to pieces in momentary decisions. So, I want you all to be paranoid and make no assumptions about who you can and can't trust. I want you to be safe, Arin, and I want my Murphy family to come home in one piece."

Buck drummed his fingers against his leg.

"Someone has an investment in the outcome. Keep your radar up. Shaun, do you have guns over there?"

Dad nodded.

"What? Are you serious?" Arin sounded incredulous. "You think we'll need guns?"

"Arin, I can't go with you," Buck continued. "I'm due in court the next few days, and I'm down a man." Buck pointed his thumb my way. "I'll get there if I need to, but I'm going to feel a lot better if the Indiana Jones family has some protection."

"I'm sure we won't need guns," Mom said to Arin. "What we'll need is a permit. It's illegal to use metal detectors or underground scanners in protected areas like Slane. I started the request, and it's being fast-tracked. I have the equipment for digs at our house in Ireland." She turned to my dad. "Any luck on the tickets?"

"I'm still waiting to hear back from my contact at Aer Lingus."

Arin lifted her cell phone. "Let me check if the company jet is available."

She left the room. Buck poured a coffee, and Mom pushed a slice of her Bailey's-infused pound cake to him.

"Aunt Meg, you're going to kill me with this stuff. You know I have no discipline around it," Buck said, biting into it.

Buck only called her Aunt Meg when she served him food. He called her that growing up, but she preferred that he call her Meg as an adult.

"Good news," Arin announced. "The plane is in New York. The pilots are cleared to fly after seven. They'll file a flight plan direct to Dublin from Philly. We board at eight." She turned to Buck. "Forget Dr. Garcia. I'm like the daughter she never had. She would do anything for me."

"I've said my piece," Buck replied. "Now, let me get this straight. This treasure is maybe worth a hundred million or more, and you're just going to give it away?"

"It's not ours," Dad answered. "Our ancestor hid it to protect it. We're just trying to complete the mission."

Buck broke off a piece of the pound cake, aimed it for his mouth, and paused. "Still, that's a lot of money."

"Buck," Dad interjected, "there is something I need to tell you now that you know this strange part of our family history. Until this happened with Key, the only other person who knew about it was your dad."

Buck returned the pound cake to the plate.

"What do you mean?"

"I was in a private room in the infirmary in 'Nam, just out

of surgery from the shrapnel wound. He visited and found me crying. He assumed it was from the shock of almost dying, but it wasn't. It was the shock that the last thread was almost torn from this story. If I died, the memories died with me. I told your dad. I was expecting him to tell me that I was delirious due to the trauma."

Buck took a dry swallow, his eyes never leaving Dad's.

"You know what he told me, when anyone else would have pronounced me crazy? He said, 'You are a lucky man. You know where you come from. I envy you.'" Dad wiped his eyes. "'All I know is that my story began on a slave ship, and we have fought, inch by inch, to make a history for our family,' he said. 'Get better, soldier. You have a story to complete.'"

Arin's fingers bit into my bicep. She was entirely focused on Buck and my dad. I assumed that the enormity of this revelation affected her as it did me. If Buck had not saved me, the story would end. The McCoys, it seemed, were the guardians of this dream.

My father got off his stool and went to Buck.

"Your father was the best man I have ever known. When I look at you, I see the story continue. He was so proud of you. If we succeed, there will be a ceremony in Ireland. In the declaration that we'll prepare, your father will be honored. If he hadn't saved me, then this would not be happening."

Buck remained silent for a moment, lost in this revelation I assumed, his father's spirit brought to life.

"Thanks, Shaun," Buck said. "Your family has already honored Dad. If Key hadn't found the dealers that killed Tanya, my father could never have rested in peace. And the hospital bills that magically never came after Mom died. I am a detective, guys. That was not hard to figure out."

Buck turned away for a moment, his right arm wiped across his eyes. Turning back, he put his hands on Dad's shoulders. They looked into each other's eyes; no words necessary. Buck turned to my mom and kissed her forehead. She kissed his cheek.

I kept an eye on Arin, wondering how she was handling this. She covered her face with her hands. I could hear her crying. She reached for a tissue, wiped her nose, shook her head, and said quietly, "I'm really missing my dad."

"Arin," Buck said, "I wish I could go with you tonight, but you're in good hands." Nodding to me, he added, "It's on you, little brother. I'll play back-up from here, but if it gets dicey I'll get on a plane. So don't screw up."

"Great, I'm not feeling any pressure. Just a few hundred million at stake, people with guns. What could go wrong?" I tried to laugh. It came out as a grunt.

Mom got off the stool, retrieved her laptop from the table, and laid it on the island countertop in front of us. "I want to show you something."

She stood a little to the side so everyone could see.

"We showed Key this first part the other day. It's from his fifth birthday party." She replayed my fifth birthday party video.

"Oh my God, you were just a baby." Arin stared at the screen.

"This next one is almost a year later." She then fast-forwarded to a new video. We were in a playground. "Buck, you were twelve. Tanya was five. Key was almost six."

Buck was tossing a ball to me while my mom filmed. I dropped the ball, looking sad.

Twelve-year-old Buck said, "What's up, little guy?"

"Why won't Tomás play with me anymore?" I answered. "I don't think he likes me. How come, Buck? Do you like Tomás?"

Buck looked like he had no idea what was going on. We hear mom on the video.

"Tomás's parents moved, honey. He'll always be your friend, but he had to go with his mommy and daddy."

Buck tried to distract me.

"Throw me the ball, Key."

I brightened and picked up the ball.

Mom stopped the video. "Key never said another word about Tomás after that. Twenty-four years later, here we are."

Mom clapped her hands together. "It's showtime, boys and girls. Are you all in, Arin?"

Arin looked at each of us in turn. A tiny smile formed her lips. She stood quiet, in respect to a moment from the past, I imagined.

"My mother thinks she prepared me for this moment. She's wrong. It was my father. We would walk the beaches and play in the surf, and he would look north, misty-eyed, I assume toward Ireland, and tell me stories of Fergus and Mack and how maybe one day his smart little girl might unlock the mystery. I can't wait."

CHAPTER 32

October 4, 2019.
Scotland

Padraig Collins sat in front of the monitors. Lihua and The Edge controlled the cameras. They had been following every move of both women for the past two weeks, monitoring their texts, emails, bookings, and all manner of detail that led to this moment.

Madelynn Wilson had settled into her room. She was sipping Bombay gin with elderflower and tonic, reviewing her notes from the trade talks that ended a few hours earlier in Glasgow. With Brexit looming, Collins knew that the Under-Secretary of Trade was under a great deal of pressure. One of those in attendance at the talks was Theresa Campbell, the leader of the Unionist Party in Belfast. By agreement, Madelynn arrived first and had checked in to her own room at the quiet hotel on Loch Lomond, an hour north of Glasgow. Theresa's room was joined to it by a shared doorway. Collins found it difficult to look away from her, her raven pixie cut enhancing her fashion-model features, the sheer fabric leaving little to his imagination.

Madelynn cocked her head toward the door as she heard some bustling in the hall, followed by a door opening in Theresa's room. Collins watched her go to the fridge for a bottle of white wine. She poured a glass, then stood in front of the mirror and smiled. She seemed to listen intently for Theresa, watching for the door separating them to open, smooshing her lips together in anticipation.

"Mads, can you believe the shit John tried to pull today?" Theresa said, walking through the door. She looked across the room and came to a halt, her eyes dancing over Madelynn. Her lover held the white wine forward, while Theresa still took her in, a sheer robe hung loosely on Mads's shoulders. Her only other clothing was a red thong.

Collins noted that The Edge kept diverting his eyes from the screen as the two women made love. Collins understood his discomfort: he himself was getting aroused and pushed himself to calm his reactions. Lihua had a look of curiosity then tilted her head to better see. After fifteen minutes, Collins nodded to Lihua, who lifted her phone and sent a text. Five minutes later, Anwulika walked through the shared door from Theresa's room. She winked at the camera that she had placed in the ceiling chandelier and said, "Good evening, ladies."

Collins watched intently as the two women sat up, startled by the six-foot-tall black woman who entered their room. Their flushed faces grew angry before finally dissolving into fear. He had coached Anwulika as to what to say.

"I'll be leaving in a moment. I need you to listen very carefully." She held her smartphone so that the women could see it. They were on the screen, live, the sheets barely covering them, captured from the chandelier above. Collins watched as their eyes swept to the ceiling and then back to the phone. "Everything has been recorded. No one need ever see it. Ms. Campbell, you have 230,000 pounds in a secret account. Let's just say that being the party leader has had some side benefits that the public is unaware of. And they will never know as long as you follow my instructions."

The two women leaned protectively into each other, as if that would hide them from the intruder. Anwulika stared them down until Theresa Campbell nodded her assent.

"Your opinion is going to evolve over the next few weeks. You will support open borders and special E.U. status for Northern Ireland," Anwulika stated. "You have six colleagues who have been stealing—I'm sorry, shall we say 'skimming'—the public funds like you. You will find they will be most supportive of your evolution in thinking. Boris Johnson will win the election, but he will lose the North."

Collins had told Anwulika that it was the trade minister who would revolt. He watched as Anwulika took the desk chair and placed it at the foot of the bed, under the light fixture. He saw Wilson's jaw tighten and her hands clench the sheets.

"You bitch, who the hell do you think you're dealing with?" she let out in her BBC London accent.

Anwulika stood on the chair, reached into the chandelier, and removed the recording device. Collins could still see everything from her smartphone, positioned strategically in her front jeans pocket. She heard the movement on the bed, stepped down, and looked kindly at the minister.

"I'm sorry, dear. I didn't mean to leave you out. Your private account has double that of Ms. Campbell. You've been a busy woman. And of course, what I told your lover goes for you. Northern Ireland gets a special exception with the E.U."

Wilson folded back into the sheets.

Anwulika smiled and held the device for them to see. "You have your privacy back. Have fun, ladies." She walked to the door and turned back. "Don't even think of fucking with me. If you do, your accounts will be emptied and the video sent to the press. Do what I instructed, and you'll never hear from me again."

Collins stood. "Keep monitoring their texts and emails," he told Lihua.

Turning to the Pakistani, "Stay on her colleagues. I want a summary every three days as to their texts and emails to each other."

"Lihua, let me have your report on Shaun Murphy," Collins said, extending his hand.

CHAPTER 33

November 26, 2019

Ireland

We cleared immigration in minutes and were on our way. I wanted to use the time to think, but Ireland grabbed me right away. The cool morning air felt clean, and the grass shone with silvery dew as the sun climbed the eastern sky. The sky of Aedan, of my mother's birthplace, of Conall and Deaglan, and my great grandfather Eamon. I felt that I would meet them, not in the flesh, but on an ethereal plane, void of space and time. My mystical meanderings were interrupted by the remembrance that someone wanted what we had come for, and might be willing to kill to get it.

"Arin, when was the last time you were here?" my mom asked.

"Around two years ago. I assisted on a diaspora project at the National Museum, and I gave lectures at Trinity and Cork. I spent a year on my Master's at Cork, but it was a hectic time. I haven't played tourist much."

"When we finish with all of this, I'd love to show you around and celebrate."

"And may the Ghost of Mack Murphy lead the way," responded Arin.

Rush hour on the M50 felt like rush hour anywhere, cars jockeying, horns honking. The driver exited for the small inland lanes and coastal towns at my father's request. The legendary green of Ireland was all around, lawns and lanes with all manner of trees. Georgian-style homes, some white stone, some redbrick, sharing the street with quaint, colorful cottages and the glass and steel of contemporary Ireland. There was little feel of morning rush; people stopped to talk, cafés doled out coffee, newspapers being read. I hadn't been here in almost three years. At thirty, perhaps I was finally ready to discover my ancestral land.

"Arin," Mom started, "we settled on the house about three months ago, but we haven't lived in it yet. We had planned on coming here next month, but obviously our time frame got moved up. Shaun's team took care of getting it ready."

"I'm privileged to help break it in." Arin looked at my father, his head beginning to fall forward, sleep overtaking him. "Tell me again what Shaun's business is," she asked my mom.

"He helps Irish companies get established in the U.S. and Europe. They handle all the legalities, logistics, and real estate. He also brings brands and finds licensing partners in the market. It's a small team, but they're very good at it. Now that Ireland is booming again, he brings U.S. and European companies into Ireland also, providing the same kinds of services."

The ocean came in and out of view. My father's head was bopping up and down. He always seemed young and vibrant, but for the first time I was aware that he was aging. I didn't like the thought of it. Maybe it had been like that for a while and I hadn't noticed.

I wondered if the brothers, Deaglan and Conall, would ever visit him again. It had been a long time since he'd experienced memories. I could tell he missed them. There was a quality to the experience that could be addictive. I'd only had them for a week, but I was starting to crave the next chapter. I replayed them over and over in my mind, trying to see if there was anything I'd missed, any detail that would give me new insight. I always came back to the same thing, though: Aedan's love for Siobhán. I looked at Arin and wondered.

The rolling and swaying of the limo lulled me, images playing in my mind, horses racing along the beach, the two of us, Tomás and me, laughing as the wind blew back our hair.

A guard ushered me into the King's chambers.

"Uncle, Mother sends her greetings."

We embraced. I had become taller than him, his body seeming frail, but his force had not diminished, his eyes a storm of nature. A monk sat beside him and rose for a moment to take my hands.

"Aedan, this is Abbot Ó Maolomhnaigh." I bowed slightly in acknowledgment.

The room was cold. The servant handed me heated wine. After taking a sip, its warmth entered my body.

"You have a great mission ahead of you, nephew." The King raised his goblet to mine. "You will accompany the Abbot to Iona. He is overseeing the most glorious project, the epitome of art and gospel. It will be a beacon for the world and a tribute to our patron, St. Columba, in celebration of his anniversary."

"Aedan will live among you, dress like you, pray with you, but he will not take your vow," he said to the Abbot. "He is a warrior and will be your protector. When you have finished the Book, he will return here to further serve his King." He waited for the Abbot's acknowledgement.

"This is a list of provisions the Abbot has requested. See to it, nephew," he said, handing me the list. He then steadied his hand on my shoulder. "Tomás is already there and is yours to command. The Abbot will follow your directions for securing the monastery and

protecting the work. Understand, young Aedan, this is not just a book. It is the living word of our Lord and a testimony of the love of his Celtic people. Protect it with your life. It must reach into the future and remind our descendants of our culture, of our patron saint, and of our love for the Almighty."

My uncle kneeled before the Abbot. I joined him.

"Father, bless us and our enterprise, and bless the Book at Iona, *that it might inspire future generations."*

I came out of this dreamlike state at the sound of gates opening. A beautiful stone-hewed house sat on the edge of a cliff, high above the Irish Sea. Tall hedges offered privacy and green, while autumnal plants of gold and orange held court, sunflowers rising toward the Dublin-gray sky. It was truly breathtaking.

My parents had told me that they wanted to keep it in the family, that I would inherit it and hopefully pass it down. I thought it was their way of anchoring me in Ireland. Now that I was here, it felt more like home than anywhere I'd been.

Arin got out and walked swiftly to the cliff, her hands on her hips as her head scanned the horizon. "It's beautiful."

"Céad míle fáilte, Arin." Mom put her arm around Arin as they started to the door. "I'm so happy to welcome you here."

Before they get to the door, it opened, and three people spilled out. They all worked for my father. Good, salt-of-the-earth people, smart as hell and not to be messed with. All three came out of the military. They made their way to me first. I knew I was going to get some crazy Irish greetings.

Kate Kelly Goldstein, Dad's sales manager, was the first up.

"I thought you would get better looking with age. Can't always be right. How are you, sweetheart?" She practically jumped into my arms and planted a big kiss on my cheek.

Her husband, Ben, a former captain in the Israeli military intelligence unit. Ben had a scholarly air as always. He could put a man twice his size in the hospital in fifteen seconds. He'd been my martial arts teacher, and we were very close.

"Hey, Ben. I missed you, brother."

Ben smiled. No hug, no handshake. None required. With Ben, it was always like I just saw him yesterday.

The head of IT, Patty McCarthy, was a childhood friend of my mom's and around the same age. He'd been with Dad since he started the business and had done very well for himself. Patty was counting on me, as was my father, to take over the company. He was one of the kindest people I had ever met. He was also my godfather. I didn't realize how much I missed him until that moment. His arm draped my shoulder.

"You're looking good, if a wee tired, Cián."

In Ireland, my name was Cián. No one called me Key.

Kate hugged my mom, and my mom motioned to Arin.

"Everyone, this is our special guest, Arin Murphy. Arin is part of the Murphy clan that ended up in Jamaica a long, long time ago."

Greetings made, Kate stopped everyone from entering the house.

"Shaun, Meg, I know that you haven't been here for a time. First, it's beautiful, but I need to tell you something. I hope you won't be upset."

"Get on with it," Mom said.

"We weren't expecting you for another month. Ben's sister got kicked off the kibbutz. She had no place for herself and her seven children. We didn't think you'd mind. It's just for a few weeks," Kate said in all seriousness.

Mom paused for a moment, trying not to look horrified. But my father started laughing.

"Still full of shite, are you, Kate?"

"Welcome home." Kate smiled.

. . .

Before I entered, I asked my father to stay behind.

"How much does the team know about what's going on?"

"I told them yesterday. They knew nothing about my memories, the *Book of Kells*, nothing. They weren't happy that I kept it from them all of these years," he responded. "They don't know what happened in the cemetery." He let out a deep, labored breath. "Have you heard from Buck?"

"I texted him just before we arrived. It's four in the morning in Philly. I'll hear from him in a few hours. We need to tell everyone about the cemetery. I need Ben's help in thinking this through."

We went into the house and found everyone gathered around food. As I told them what happened, a look of alarm was clear on Kate's and Patty's faces.

Ben was stoical, his mind at work on the problem.

"I agree with Cián," he finally said. "If they knew you were in the cemetery, they know you're here. Cián, you and I are the only ones licensed to carry guns. I'll get them ready. Kate, Patty, I know it's been a while since you've had to think like a soldier, but you need to start right now."

CHAPTER 34

P atty took me aside before Arin and I left to have a look at Slane.

"Your gun license expires in eighteen days. I'll make arrangements to renew it," Patty told me. "I'd feel better if you take a rifle."

"Please put it in the back, out of sight. I don't want to worry Arin."

He handed me my permit.

"Ben can go with you."

"Nothing will happen yet. They won't make a move until they're certain that we found something."

"Cián, assume that someone is watching you."

"I'm counting on it." My hands flexed. Fists formed. I relaxed them.

With Patty's eyes on me, I climbed into the passenger seat, Arin at the wheel.

I hadn't driven on the left in three years. Jamaicans and Irish drove on the left, so Arin motored Dad's company

Mercedes SUV. I punched "Hill of Slane" into the GPS. My parents stayed behind with the team, waiting for the archeology permit and readying the surveying equipment. Arin and I were doing initial reconnaissance. I watched the mirrors for any sign of being followed.

"Key," Arin broke into my thoughts. "You seem a little distant."

"I'm just thinking about what lies ahead." I didn't want to tell Arin about my conversation with Patty.

"Turn right in two hundred meters," the smooth female voice of the GPS announced.

"Go left instead. There's something I want to see," I told Arin.

Arin took a left and started down the hill. Before long, there were numerous cars and trucks backed up at a stoplight, and no cars were coming the other way.

"What's going on here?" Arin asked.

"There's a one-lane bridge at the bottom. The oncoming traffic will pass us in a moment. It's the River Boyne, where we think Aedan and Siobhán's brothers unloaded the treasure. I want to get a feel for how far it is from the Hill."

The oncoming traffic passed, and soon the green light announced our turn.

"When we cross over the bridge, we'll look for a place to make a U-turn."

As we descended the steep hill and began making our way across the bridge, I noted a parking area to the right.

"Pull in there." I pointed.

We sat quietly for a moment, taking in the rolling river and imagining the currach making its way toward Kells, the seven refugees scanning the riverbanks, safe from the open sea. I stepped out of the car and Arin followed. At least a dozen trucks crossed the bridge to Slane. When they passed, I noted a series of buildings on the Slane side of the river.

"I wonder if that area is the footprint of an old village."

"Makes sense. Building on an original site happens all over the world," Arin responded. She interlaced my arm with hers and bounced on the balls of her feet. "I can't believe we're here. Is this where you think they arrived?"

"Somewhere near here. The GPS says it's an eighteen-minute walk to Hill of Slane," I said, eyes on my phone. "It was all forest then, but of course there were roads to and from the river. They were carrying the chest, weapons, likely some food and tools. Let's call it an hour's walk."

"It's very steep, not an easy walk with all that," Arin added.

"If they had horses, they could have been there in fifteen to twenty minutes." I pictured it in my mind. "Imagine that area with the buildings diagonally across the water. There would have been a dock of sorts for boat traffic. Probably a barn for livestock, maybe even an inn for beds and food. This is the closest place on the river to The Hill of Slane."

We got in the car and joined the traffic heading back to the Hill. Three minutes later, we turned left, passed a play-ground, then a residential area, and soon we entered a car park. Arin pulled up to a stone wall, the ruins of the church and monastery some two hundred yards in the distance.

"This is it?" Arin asked. "I was expecting it to be like a museum with an entry area to pay to get in. It looks like you can go in and out any time of the day or night."

"Welcome to Ireland," I answered.

Homes bordered both ends of the car park, their sightlines giving them a view of the grounds. A sign promised twenty-four-hour video surveillance of the parking area, but there wasn't a camera in sight. We made our way through the gate and up a hill. The ruins lay ahead, an ancient church domi-nating the scene, dotted by Irish crosses and gravestones.

Ireland was full of such places, but this one was special. A statue of St. Patrick stood out as the one thing not in ruins, blazing white against the gray- and moss-colored stones. A wrought-iron fence surrounded the figure.

I read the sign on the fence out loud: "Long established tradition tells that Saint Patrick lit the Easter Fire on this Hill of Slane in 433. In doing so, he unwittingly disobeyed King Laoghaire at nearby Tara."

I turned to look in the direction the statue was facing and pointed across the valley.

"I think that's Tara."

The Hill of Slane rolled down to the River Boyne and climbed again on the other side, where there was open land, grazing fields, sheep dotting the landscape in patches of white. The Emerald Isle, aptly named from what I could see, the greenest of green.

"I feel at home here," Arin said as she again laced her arm through mine.

"Saint Patrick walked these grounds. So did Aedan, four hundred years after him."

"It's amazing to me that people have been on this little island for over eight thousand years," said Arin.

"I wonder how they got here," I mused.

"We know with a great degree of certainty how every ethnic group on the planet got to where they are. We all came from the same place, Africa, yet we still kill and hate each other because of differences. Do you know that there is just one gene that determines color?"

I looked at this beautiful, smart woman.

"It shouldn't matter. We are what we are. We look like what we look like. We don't have a say in any of that. It just matters if we answer the call."

"What call? Arin asked.

I tilted my face to see the statue of St. Patrick.

"Do you know what Aedan told me?"

Arin's head pulled back, her mouth dropped open, silent for a moment.

"What do you mean, 'Aedan told you'? Does Aedan tell you things?"

"What?"

"Does Aedan talk to you?" Arin asks.

"Obviously. I have his memories."

"But you just said he *told* you something."

"Did I say that?" I closed my eyes, rubbed them. "Oh my God, Arin. It was a dream, on the plane. I didn't think about it when we landed. I don't know if it was a memory or just a dream."

"What did he say, Key?"

"He told me that it was my turn to be a warrior, to be strong and complete the mission. He told me he would be my guide."

Arin stared into my eyes and inched upward like a ballerina on pointe, her hands balancing on my shoulders.

"Do you think it was just a dream?"

"I hope not."

Siobhán flashed in front of me. She leaned back in the currach to rest in Aedan's arms. I shook off the image as my chest heaved in desire for Arin.

She must have sensed this. She reached her hand to my cheek.

"There will be time to figure us out. Now, listen for Aedan, and let's find the Druid stones."

There had been no one on the hill but us. However, that changed as a school bus emptied with what looked to be around twenty high school kids, with teachers trying to keep up. Behind them was a young couple, holding hands, the girl with a camera over her shoulder. Probably just tourists, I thought, but it was worth keeping my eye on them.

"Here's the photo. My mom said it was never geotagged." I shifted my gaze southeast, about thirty yards from where we stood. "There's a lot of stone. This photo isn't much help."

I followed Arin's stare, trusting her archeological instincts. She squatted, lifted a small rock, turned her back to the direction I thought the Druid stones might be. With the rock in her right hand, she heaved it over her shoulder and spun to see where it landed. "Follow me."

My eyes widened. "You're joking?"

"Sometimes it works," she answered, laughing. "Let's have a look."

"There are so many stones that fit the description. Where do we start?" I asked.

"Filter out everything that is less than a foot tall. She pulled out her smartphone. "I have an app on my camera that makes hi-def contrasts. The markings in the stone are likely so eroded that the eye can't see them. If you think that there are markings, a photo should bring them out."

Arin started, and I followed. About eight feet down the hill there was a jumble of stones that initially fit the description. Grays, whites, grayish-whites, all looked untouched by a chisel. The obelisks we sought were of carved stone and, though carved millennia ago, would stand out with a human touch.

I headed down the hill then glanced back to the wall. The top half of the Saint Patrick statue was visible.

"Arin, I want to have a look at something over this way. I think the statue of Patrick is pointed toward Tara. Both Slane and Tara were Druid pagan sites. I have a hunch."

We went in the direction of Tara, headstones and rocks crowding the hillside. A stone jutted out of the ground, maybe three feet tall by ten inches, and a slightly smaller one was four feet to the left of it, surrounded by rocks.

"It would make sense that they might point the stones to Tara," I told Arin.

Arin went to the tallest one and pointed and clicked her camera on all sides.

"Nothing I can see. The erosion might be so great that time has worn it away."

She made her way to the smaller one, getting purchase between the rocks surrounding it. She clicked the camera … nothing. She pointed the camera to the side of the obelisk facing Tara.

"Come here."

She stood up so I could get a view. I examined the photo. "There's nothing there."

"Exactly, that's why I wish I could time travel," Arin reached down to caress the stone, "and see where the Druids put it."

I had a hard time not staring at this adventuress.

"What?"

"I don't know. You look like a goddess."

"You're funny." Arin gestured to herself. "I'm wearing the same clothes I had on in Philly; I haven't showered, my breath stinks even to me, but thanks. It's the first time I've been called a goddess."

"You are a Druid goddess." I was feeling the jetlag. "Missing teeth, ragged clothing, but really hot to the Druid men."

"I'll take that as a compliment." Arin twirled around, her arms out, gesturing to the ancient site. "We still don't know much about the Druids. Hollywood makes them out to be this scary, demon-like cult, but in fact they were educated philosophers, doctors, and overseers of community rituals, much like priests and rabbis today. Mack was a Druid in a sense. So was my father."

"Then that makes you a Druid goddess." With whatever flight of imagination I was in, everything about her was addictive: her voice, her beauty, but mostly her energy of being. "Or maybe you're just an amazing woman from Jamaica on a mission. Either way …"

Arin took her eyes off me and stood and waved as Mom

and Ben came into view. We ran over to greet them, Arin telling them about our failed search. Mom removed her small backpack and took out her notebook.

Opening to a two-page spread, she said, "This is a lidar of Slane."

"I'm guessing I'm the only one who doesn't know what a 'lidar' is," I said.

"It's a scanning tool that creates a 3-D model, in this case, of the terrain," Ben answered. "Israel uses lidar to search for bunkers and tunnels."

"These photos are from a drone," Mom added. "I have ground-based lidar equipment in the van. I don't see any markers for underground objects here in the photo, but the ground has so much stone that it would be difficult to get any definition from the air. Let's go get the equipment."

As we walk back to the car park, I thought about the Druid stone and where the treasure might be buried, when a sword slashed inches from my face. I felt myself falling back and screamed, "Roidh, Tearlach—to me. Hurry."

We were just outside of the Kells Monastery eastern wall, examining the defenses. I released my sword from its sheath and beat back the first attacker. There were three of them. They heard the brothers rushing to me. The advance stopped. The men were slovenly, undisciplined fighters. Drunken brigands. All three pointed their swords at me. One stepped closer.

"You took a chest from the boat in Slane. We have been searching for it. You will bring it to us, or we will leave no one standing at this monastery. Bring it to where you took it off the boat. You have three days."

They quickly mounted their horses and raced off as Roidh and Tearlach reach me.

"Aedan, are you hurt?"

"No. They saw us moving the treasure. We must go tonight in

the dark and move it to another location. They will have scouts in the area. I know another road to the Hill. Sleep for an hour now, if you may. There will be no chance of rest tonight."

I opened my eyes and found myself kneeling on the ground, my breathing heavy, Arin squatting next to me. I stood and read the concern on my mother's face, Ben next to her.

"You were screaming names and slashing around." Arin put her arms around me. "You good?"

I stood, wobbly, my eyes searching the area for danger.

"Instead of seeing the story, I was *in* the story." My heart pounded. I bent over my knees, breathing fast and deep. I looked to my mother and said breathlessly, "No need for the equipment. They moved the treasure."

CHAPTER 35

D ad and Kate had prepared a light meal on our return from Slane. Mom was a Spanish wine lover and poured her best Tempranillo quite liberally. We were exhausted and excited, not a good mix for sleep. The wine would come in handy. We toasted their new house, and Arin and I recounted our time at Slane and my all-too-realistic episode with Aedan. Kate reminded us that this all sounded like a crock of shit, and if it wasn't us telling the tale she'd have to call social services. No one argued the point.

It didn't take long for the wine to kick in. Patty, Kate, and Ben said goodnight, all agreeing to an 8.30 breakfast meeting. Arin headed to the shower. My parents went off to bed, jetlag calling.

But I was too restless for sleep. I grabbed a few pillows, a blanket, another bottle of wine, and a glass and went out to the patio, four hundred feet above the Irish Sea. I lit the propane fire pit and stared out to the gray clouds and the white-capped waves, letting the images of the day swirl in my head.

I hoped the wine might help conjure Aedan and have him tell me where he took the treasure, but I was not alone in my thoughts for long. Arin came out to the patio; though unusually warm for November, her pajamas were not much protection.

"What time is it?" she asked, leaning over the fire pit.

I looked at my watch.

"Ten after four. The sun is about to give us a show as it goes to bed." I recalled the sunsets in Ireland as a kid. I remember thinking that here it seemed to fall off the earth and explode into a million colors.

"If you told me it was midnight, I'd believe you." She walked ten feet to the low stone wall at the edge of the cliff. I joined her. "It's so beautiful and peaceful here." She looked around at the hedgerows and flowers. "And completely private."

Down toward Howth Harbor, lights were coming on. Sailboats, fishing boats, and restaurants dotted the marina. Long cement piers protected the harbor. A cool breeze blew up the cliff from the ocean. Arin shivered.

"Perfect temperature for a white boy with genes from the North Atlantic." Arin smiled. "Bloody cold for a brown girl from Jamaica."

I walked back to the couch, pulled it closer to the fire pit, then gestured to Arin with the blanket. She sat on the couch and I laid the blanket over her. When I sat, she turned to me. We had talked on the drive back about my experiences today. She asked me questions, drawing more information and detail to the surface.

"How are you?" She pulled the blanket over her left shoulder.

"This one is hard to shake. It still feels like it actually happened."

I picked up my wineglass, took a sip, offered it to her, and enjoyed watching her lips play over the flavors.

"You know what's crazy?" Arin ran her tongue over her lips. "I've only known you for what, six or seven days? In that time, we've found what Mack hid, we've been in three countries, you've experienced several memories, we've kissed once, and you've never asked if there is a man in my life."

I looked away from her, then forced my eyes back. It felt like someone was doing jumping jacks in my stomach. "Maybe I'm afraid of the answer."

The golds and reds of the Dublin sky danced on the clouds above us, the last gasps of the sun highlighting her curls with dabs of gold.

"*Is* there a man in your life?"

"I hope so."

Arin moved her hand from under the blanket and put it on my chest. "My life is too complicated for a relationship. But there is this man I've been seeing. He's amazing. He lost his best friend to drugs and then chased down the people responsible. He passionately pursues others who harm people. A few weeks ago, he was living his normal life, and then all hell broke loose in his head. What would have immobilized most people propelled him. I am in Ireland, fulfilling my father's dream, with him at my side."

I could feel my voice starting to crack, so I blew into my hands then rubbed them together. "I'm afraid of you, Arin."

I could hardly believe I just said that.

Her eyes pierced mine and stayed there, unrelentingly focused.

"My parents told me this place was mine, written into their will. Same with the Philly house, same with the business, if I want it. I didn't earn it. I inherited it. I made none of this happen. Who the hell am I but some lucky kid? I think about this genetic situation. Even these memories are inherited."

Arin caressed my arm as I continued.

"I'm afraid of you because we're in this incredible moment, but eventually it will fade. I'm afraid you'll see that I'm not the man you think I am." I looked at her with more longing than I had ever felt. "And I'm afraid that I could easily get lost in you."

She slid her body, her knees coming to press against my leg. Her fingers rested softly on my thigh.

"And I'm afraid that you will see me as the woman following my mother's plan for my life. Like you, I'm a lucky kid who inherited a lot. So what? Let's use it to do some good."

Arin began unbuttoning her pajama top. She took my hand and moved it to her naked breast.

"Maybe we are just lost in the moment. Who knows? Maybe we can get lost forever."

I started to speak.

"Do you ever shut up?" She put her hand over my mouth and guided my lips to hers, my fingers gently exploring her breasts while my mouth learned hers, her breath, her tongue. There was no hurry. Aedan could wait. I was lost in her. Simply, beautifully, lost.

———

Arin fell asleep on the couch. The fire pit was still going but the air was cool. I went inside, collected a few blankets, and gently laid them over her. I stared into the night sky, startled at the vastness of stars and the feeling that I could touch them. I knew they were always there, but in the light of a big city like Philly they were barely visible. And so I forgot—we all forget—to look in wonder. But here, on the edge of the sea, in the far north of the globe, I looked toward Scotland and pictured Aedan crossing in a ramshackle boat, twelve hundred years ago. The *Book*, Saint Columba's treasure, the monks, and most of all, his love, Siobhán, all in his keep as he sailed to Ireland by the stars.

Something had changed in my body, my mind. Some piece of me had altered. Something was rising. It felt good. I welcomed it; I was ready. I looked at Arin. I'd had plenty of sex in my life, but tonight was the first time that I had made love.

I was surprised at how much my happiness scared me.

————

The patio door opened. I had slept peacefully in the chair next to Arin, my feet sharing an unused part of the couch. Mom walked out with two coffee cups and a plate of bread, jam, and butter. Arin stirred, looked up, and then scanned everything, clearly disoriented. Her eyes landed on Mom.

"Good morning, Megan," she said, her eyes darting away.

Mom sat next to Arin and put her arm around her.

"You've had an adventurous week. How are you doing?"

"Honestly?" Arin answered.

"Of course," replied my mother.

"I really have to pee, honestly."

They both laughed. Arin went into the house, the blanket wrapped around her.

My mother looked at me with that kind of Mom smile.

"She's special, Key."

"No shit, Mom." My cry for motherly wisdom.

"She needs to figure you out." I had seen this look on my mom a thousand times. It meant to take her seriously.

"Figure me out?" I raised my hands.

"Exactly. She's been waiting all of her life to fulfill her father's dream. You enter and are the path to fulfill that dream. But she's not expecting you. You, Key Murphy. And you sure as hell were not expecting her. I could see it in both of you the minute you entered the house the other night. You two are sparks and flints and fire. Don't you dare let her go."

Arin returned in my baggy Eagles sweatshirt and stood awkwardly next to me. I put my arm around her and drew her close.

"Seems Mom figured us out before I did."

Arin slid her arms comfortably around me. My mother looked pleased. My father came onto the patio with his coffee, saw Arin and I embracing, smiled, and said, "It's about time, you two. We better get on with it. We have a treasure to find."

CHAPTER 36

"Goddamnit, it's beyond time to speed this thing up." Collins paced in front of Dr. Garcia. "We have to do something."

Joseph Murphy, Dr. Garcia, and Padraig Collins had finished meetings with their attorneys and bankers, finalizing the Collins investment.

"What do you think, Joseph?" Collins asked.

"She has a plan," he answered, nodding toward his partner. "If it succeeds, you get what you're looking for, and the company will be the talk of the town for a long time to come. Revenues will spike."

"Mr. Collins," Dr. Garcia said in a very measured tone. "Listen to me carefully. We do this my way or not at all. I am the scientist here. We do not rush this. It's dangerous." Dr. Sylvia Garcia stared down the man who was investing an outrageous amount of money in her company.

Garcia's disrespect no longer amused Collins, but she was somewhat of his own making. His media team had lined up the *Time Magazine* article, TV interviews, and more. When it landed in a few weeks, she would be the center of the media and scientific universe. She needed him; he needed her. Collins softened his approach.

"Dr. Garcia, please tell me your plan." In his days during the Troubles, the men were the muscle but the brains were the women. The best intel on the Brits came from the women. "I have a short moment in time to prevent a return to violence in Ireland. I need your help."

Dr. Garcia regarded him. "You won't get much from Shaun Murphy. His memories are limited and haven't recurred for many years. But he has a son named Key. I've tested him for the gene. He has it, but he hasn't yet experienced memories. We must be cautious with him. He consults for the police in Philadelphia and is very intuitive."

Collins stopped at this, his heart racing, hoping for more. "What are you trying to tell me?"

Dr. Garcia closed her eyes and rubbed her forehead. "I am telling you that I have violated my scientific oath and FDA regulations. In the DNA swab for Key's ancestry test, I coated it with a formula that could stimulate the memory gene. We have tested several subjects outside of the U.S., in compliance with their local laws, with a very favorable response."

Collins looked at Garcia with deepening respect.

"What happens next?" he asked.

"We wait to see if it has any effect. We'll know in two to four weeks. If there's no response, I'll find a way to apply it again. But you need to understand: he might experience nothing. He might experience the memory of a seamstress in Galway, for all we know. But there is a small chance that he could see something that helps you."

"Padraig, we're as anxious to find the relics as you," Joseph added.

"I sure as hell hope so. I've offered plenty of incentive,"

Collins responded sharply. "The people you've tested with this formula, what were the results?"

"It's varied. Some have had no response. Some have had minor increases, and some fifty percent have had substantial increases," Dr. Garcia responded.

Collins stopped pacing. He placed both hands on the conference table directly across from Dr. Garcia and leaned toward her. "There's much more to it, am I correct?"

"What do you mean?"

"I have a small team, hand-picked by me, that's made your firewalls all but impenetrable. They report their progress in protecting your data, but they also report every bit of research that is top secret inside the company. Now that I'm a major investor, there can be no more secrets. Do you fully understand the potential of what you are working on from a commercial point of view?" Collins looked at Joseph. "Joseph, do you?"

Joseph started to respond, but Dr. Garcia held her hand up.

"Elaborate."

"I've read the files, Sylvia." Collins observed her eyes narrowing and her jaw tightening at the use of her first name. "The formula that you used, what other results have you seen?" Collins turned to Joseph, then back to Dr. Garcia. He put his hand on a stack of files. "You are sitting on a gold-mine, and I'm concerned that you don't understand it. In your research, you state that this same formula turns back the biological clock in humans. Explain."

Dr. Garcia became unusually quiet. She gazed at Collins. He still leaned on the table, only inches from her face.

" It's very early in the research. Do you know what the thymus gland is?"

"Assume I don't," Collins stood straight, stepping back from the conference table a few inches.

"I'll keep it simple. The thymus is essential for the

immune system to function. Once you pass puberty, the gland itself shrinks until, by the time you're middle-aged, it's stopped functioning."

"So, as we age, we have reduced immunity and therefore are more prone to illness," Joseph added.

Collins nodded to them and began pacing.

"Likewise, for the pituitary gland. It's responsible for growth hormones and regulates the development of every tissue in your body. It too declines with age." Dr. Garcia took a long breath. "I have been able to gene edit the materials responsible for the activity in both and create a gene sequence that, added into a carrier, can be absorbed into the body and affect the mutant gene."

Dr. Garcia went quiet again. Collins turned to her. "And?" twirling his finger in the *hurry up* motion.

"You know the term 'chronological age', your birthday age. Are you aware of the term '*bio*logical age'?" asked Dr. Garcia.

"I've searched it. Some good info but mostly hocus-pocus promises for the Fountain of Youth if you buy this or that product," Collins answered.

"It's a real thing, Mr. Collins. The research on how to reverse the biological clock through pharmaceutical intervention, diet, nutrition, and exercise has proved dramatic. What we've done has affected the DNA markers for biological aging. We have turned back the clock by five to fifteen years. No one will live forever, at least not yet, but it is a fountain of temporary youth. The fact is, your body has no idea how old you are. It only knows your biological age and operates accordingly."

Collins turned to Joseph, who was looking through one of the files.

"Futuro has an Ancestry DNA testing division. What is the net profit on your one-hundred-and-twenty-dollar kit?"

Joseph closed the file. "Ten percent."

Collins put his hands on his hips, turned away, and walked a few paces. He turned back directly to Joseph.

"Where's the real money in commercial ancestry testing?" He didn't wait for a response. "Selling and managing the ancestry data. That can add a twenty to thirty percent margin. Look at the big players. The ancestry test is a loss leader. Selling the data is where the value lies. I want to expand the ancestry side dramatically. As you'll see in a moment, it will all tie together."

"Dr. Garcia," said Collins, "How many people in the world do you estimate have the mutant gene?"

"You've read the data."

"True. But that doesn't mean I remember the detail. Humor me, please." Collins waited.

"Two to four percent. Approximately one hundred and fifty to three hundred million people." Garcia added nothing else.

"Joseph, how much do you sell the memory gene kit for?"

"Six hundred and ninety," said Murphy. He anticipated the next question, "We earn about sixty percent gross on that, twenty-five percent net, but we want to get it down to three hundred and ninety at some point as more of a mass-market product. With more automation on the testing, we can retain the margins but on much greater volume. We expect to sell millions of kits. Everyone will want to know if they have the gene."

"And, Dr. Garcia, is the formula we spoke of a pharmaceutical or an over-the-counter dietary supplement?"

She cocked her head. "Good question, Mr. Collins. It's possible to pursue either direction. Or both."

Collins returned to the table and leaned in toward both of his new partners.

"And now, the big question. How many people would like to reverse their biological clock by what, five years, ten years, or more? Millions, would you agree?" Collins didn't wait for an answer. "If we surround everything with intellectual property protection, data mining, and marketing, I just described to you a multi-billion-dollar company."

Dr. Garcia took a deep breath and then exhaled.

"I told you I would help build your company to be one of the top biotech companies in the world," Collins added. "And now I have a request."

"Which is?" asked Garcia.

"The first part is not a request, it's part of our arrangement, but I want your active participation. We will build a world-class facility in Ireland at the location of my choosing. The DNA testing facility will be headquartered there, along with IT and marketing. It's in the documents. But it means nothing unless you and your team are enthusiastically engaged."

"That's not a difficult request. Of course, I will," Dr. Garcia answered. "The second part?"

"From now on, I'm Padraig, and you are Sylvia. The animosity needs to end."

Dr. Garcia joined the tips of her fingers together, then placed her palms on the table, taking her time. "I know that I'm supposed to be afraid of you, but I'm not. The more I get to know you, the more good I see in you."

"I don't want you to be afraid of me," Collins replied. "I want us to make amazing things happen in the world."

She absently rubbed her traditional Galician silver pendant, known as a St. James' Cross, the bottom of the cross shaped like a dagger. "In the land of wolves you must howl like them." Her Galician-Spanish accent was strong. "It's an old Galician proverb," she said to no one. Her eyes then focused on the Irishman. "Let's do great things, Padraig."

CHAPTER 37

Night had descended, the thrill of Halloween evident around the city shops, revelers dressed for pre-Halloween parties. Likely few of the partygoers knew that Halloween originated in Ireland as Samhain, a Celtic harvest festival. The occupant in the rear of the limousine paid no attention to the happenings on the street; his mind focused on the meeting he was about to have. The gates to the secure private parking area at Government House opened and his driver came to a stop by the door. Two guards awaited Collins and led him to the Office of An Taoiseach, the Office of the Prime Minister.

Padraig Collins had been in this office many times. Occupants changed. The people with the money that got them there didn't. The Prime Minister stepped away from his desk as Collins entered.

"Padraig, good to see you," offered the PM, his hand extended.

"Likewise, Leo. Thanks for seeing me on short notice. It's

been an eventful day," returned Collins. "This won't take long, and as always I depend on this conversation being confidential."

"And as always you have my word."

"Now that the British parliament is dissolved and new elections are called for December twelfth, my data shows that Johnson will win. Brexit will be in full force at that point."

"Our data leads in that direction, but what's your point?" asked the PM.

"Brexit is the best thing that can happen to Ireland, Leo."

He sat on the edge of his desk and crossed his arms. "It seems to be the best thing for you, Padraig, but people in the Republic and the North are scared shitless."

Collins strode to a leather-cushioned chair and sat under the portrait of his namesake, Michael Collins. Padraig was christened Padraig Michael Collins in honor of the Irish Revolutionary. He wished they were family, but they were not.

"Boris Johnson will not push for a hard Brexit. He'll have a year to negotiate. I know the two of you have spoken about ensuring no borders. I plan on making a major announcement that will add pressure."

"And what would that be?" The PM pushed off the desk and took the chair opposite Collins.

"In the North, it's not just fears of the border. It's the lack of opportunity for young people. We both know that's a recipe for disaster. In a few weeks, I'll announce my plan to build an IT and a biomedical research center, one close to Derry, one close to Belfast. We project it will put over one hundred-fifty million into the local economy and produce close to fifteen hundred jobs."

"How does that help the Republic?"

Collins grinned.

"I won't do it if the North leaves the European Union and if there are borders."

"That gets my attention."

"Let me get your attention even further." Collins paused, letting his words settle in.

"You'll take credit for it, along with me. I'll announce that you had expressed your concern about the economy in Northern Ireland and pressed me to help develop business there. After all, I am a child of Derry. I'll tell the press that you look toward the day when there's even greater unification and that, as neighbors that are moving closer together in the face of Brexit, it's time for both countries to look after each other."

The PM stepped back toward his desk.

"That's way too generous, Padraig. What do you want from this?"

"I want you and the rest of the politicians to get off your asses and start planning for unification. No more talk. It's coming, with or without you. It's time for you to lead the way." Collins moved to the door but turned back. "And Leo, Sinn Fein is coming on strong. They want this office. The clock is ticking."

CHAPTER 38

November 27, 2019

Howth, Ireland

I played our lovemaking over and over in my head and longed for the next time. It's a strange brew, the mix of my reality with Arin, twisting and blending with visits from Aedan and Siobhán. When the memories came, it was not a one-time visit. They left fragments behind, moments, pieces of now and the past intertwining. I wrote them down as Dr. Garcia instructed so that I could keep them separate, keep my nervous system protected from them. But they didn't seem to obey the rules. The flashes of memory claimed me. I pictured kissing Arin last night and a sliver, a small but jarring nano-flash, of Siobhán entered and claimed my lips.

I stepped into the shower, put my hands against the wall, and made the water as cold as I could stand it, letting it jar and refresh, while I forced my thoughts to our task:

Aedan moved the treasure. Where? Who the hell knows.

Siobhán caressed my neck. Arin moved my hand to her firm and ample breast. My lips slid in ecstasy over her body. *The currach glides to the roughhewn dock, Slane not far.*

I turned to Roidh and Tearlach. We were tired and muddy from the long night but satisfied that we had hidden the treasure well.

"If something happens to me, you must tell the King where to find the treasure. He will instruct you."

"And if something happens to all of us?" asked Roidh.

"I added a clue in the book last night. Pray it doesn't come to that. Dawn will break soon. We must stay to the forest trail. Hopefully, the brigands are on the other side of the river. We will take our revenge another time."

We mounted our horses and began the descent down the steep hill to meet the trail leading us home to Kells. We advanced slowly to avoid the stinging nettle all around us. My horse snorted in relief from my restraint and made a good trot as the rising sun showed him the wide path.

We entered the outskirts of the village, plumes of smoke rising from homes as the peat warmed them and cooked their morning meal. Hens scattered from our path, but the sheep paid us no mind and grazed, forcing us to go around them or swear them out of our way. We entered the main road to the monastery gate. I pulled up, my heart quickening. Brown-cassocked men that should have been at their morning chores had gathered on the other side of the gate. Their backs were to me, and the low murmur of prayer reached my ears.

We raced through the opened gate and dismounted.

The monks turned to our arrival, and the Abbot stepped forward, his face ashen.

"The brigands delivered a warning," the Abbot said simply. He nodded toward the men in front of me.

The human wall parted to reveal a monk lying on a gurney, throat sliced, eyes closed, arms folded. I dropped to my knees, screaming. Tomás. Tomás. Tomás!

I sat naked in the shower, screaming his name. The curtain parted. The water stopped. Someone climbed in next to me.

"Key, what's wrong?"

I looked at her, remembering where I was, who I was.

"Something's happening to me, Arin. I was Aedan. They killed Tomás. I was there. I touched him. They slit the throat of my cousin."

———

When Arin and I walked into the kitchen, the entire crew turned and looked at me.

"Fuck's sake, Cián. Ya scared the shite out of us, hollering like a banshee. What was that about?" Kate waited for an answer.

I told them.

Ben spoke first, in his usually quiet demeanor.

"I'm concerned. Your father said that the experience was more like watching a movie. You are moving way past that."

I glanced over to see my mom and dad leaning against each other, Dad's arm over her shoulder, Mom's left hand covering her mouth.

Arin said, "Key, when you first experienced the memories, they were disconcerting, but within a few episodes you were managing them, right?"

"Yes," I answered, my right hand tapping my leg.

"Dr. Garcia said to write down everything, not only as a record, but mostly to remind yourself that it's outside of you, no matter how intense the experience. And that's what you've been doing."

Arin surveyed the room, then put her hands on the back of an empty chair. "I've witnessed shaman rituals in Africa. Frequently the shaman enters a trance-like state. When they come out of it, they're usually disoriented. The community welcomes them back and asks them what they saw. This centers them and allows them to relay the experience back to the tribe. We are Key's tribe."

My father handed me a cup of coffee.

"Makes sense to me, Arin," he said. "Are you good with that, son?"

Aedan was still within me, his pain at losing Tomás running through my veins. I nodded my head to everyone.

"I'm starving. Let's eat and then figure this damn thing out," was all I could think to say.

CHAPTER 39

November 27, 2019

arriage House

"This is a Google map of Kells, Slane, and Tara," my mom said as Kate and Ben laid down a tray of fresh homemade scones, jams, and butter. Patty set down the coffee. "As you can see, they form a triangle of sorts. Kells forms the top of the triangle, Slane forms the left point at the northeast corner, and Tara forms the right point at the south-east corner." The computer was linked to a large wall-mounted TV.

She directed the mouse to a smaller, thumbnail image and clicked on it. "This is a map from the year 800, six years before the *Book* arrived at Kells." She superimposed the two maps. "You can see that the roads are almost the same. As the towns grew, the roads were deforested and became wider, but the footprint remains the same."

"Key, just to verify, Aedan said that he knew another route to Slane?" she asked.

"Yes."

"He also said that he hoped the thieves were on the other

side of the river, which we can assume means the Slane, or north, side?"

I nodded.

"I rode my horses on those roads as a kid. In fact, I rode in the Kells to Slane Bike Race for Breast Cancer fundraiser two years ago on that same road," Patty added.

Mom placed her cursor over Kells.

"If they took the north road here and then turned east past Rathkenny," she said, tracing the route with her cursor, "they would have taken this road south, straight up the back of Slane. You can see from the overlay: it's the same road."

"Leave it to the Irish," Kate added, "why bother building a new road when you can use the same one for 1,300 years. Conservationists is what we are."

"Then what?" asked Ben.

"I was going to ask you that question. You are military. So was Aedan. What would you have done?" my mother asked.

Ben studied the map for a moment.

"It depends on where they're going."

I stood up and walked to the screen.

"They're going to Tara. Mom, bring up the slide with the *Book* and the clues."

She did, and we all stared at the now familiar words:

The evangelist held his quill in one hand, the bible in the other. The book pointed to the place of the eight stars where St. Columba's treasure lived. The Cross of Kells is above him. Go to the eight stars and then to the fire. The right hand will point the way.

"In my episode this morning, he said he added a clue, which must be 'The right hand will point the way.' That was bothering me. The quill in his right hand didn't make any sense.

It's the hand by the cross on the right side. Mom, you said that cross likely represents Tara. Slane and Tara were, still are, two of the most important religious and historical sites in Ireland."

I reached for a scone, not hungry, just slowing down my thinking.

"He buries the treasure at Slane, Saint Patrick's original place for converting people. He has easy access from the river. You can see ..." I took a bite of the scone then slapped my hand on the table, putting down the confection. "Mom, you asked Ben to think like a soldier because Aedan was a soldier. A soldier would never have traveled with just two men. There were armed thieves in wait. The treasure was too valuable. He would have taken at least ten to fifteen of the King's men. Patty, how long was the bike ride to Slane from Kells?"

"Around an hour and a half," answered Patty.

"It's nighttime." I walked to the TV and pointed. "They take the north road, which would add time. He would have a front guard and a rear guard. The horses would move slowly in the dark. There was a moment of danger as they approached the Hill of Slane." I rested my finger over the map. "But the thieves have no idea where Aedan buried the treasure. The thief told Aedan that he was seen with the treasure and to bring it to the river where they first landed."

I walked over to Ben. "No one followed them to the Hill. Someone saw them on the riverbank and told the thieves. They would have also told the thieves that it was a group of monks in the boat. That's what led them to Kells. They would most likely be scouting the area around the River Boyne, not up on the Hill."

I looked at everyone. All eyes were on me.

"He retrieved the treasure and headed back to the north road, connecting east toward Drogheda." I touched the screen again. "They reached Tullyallen. There must have been a bridge or a shallow crossing around there. Then they took the south road, which you can see bends west to Carlow Cross, just outside of Tara."

My mother was nodding.

"Siobhán's brothers would have accompanied Aedan when they reached Tara," she added. "Only the three of them would be allowed to know exactly where it was buried. The soldiers would have stood guard. After it was buried, they would have joined the soldiers and ridden back to Kells."

"It's all theory—good theory, but still," said my father.

"Right, then, now all you have to do is find the fecking thing," said Kate. "Just how will you do that?"

Arin smiled my way.

"I have a feeling that Aedan will tell us. In the meantime, Meg, we may as well put our archeologists' hats on and have a look at Tara."

———

My mom pulled a chair to the desk and motioned for Arin to sit. Once again, I marveled at how comfortable they were together, and then it finally occurred to me: this was a moment my mother had been longing for, for me to have a love in my life.

I'd been one second from a bullet to my head. I saw Tomás dead. I felt Aedan's grief and sorrow. It's simultaneously horrifying and liberating to realize that I, we, have zero control as to how and when we die, only how we lived. And by some miracle, Eamon and Mack had brought Arin into my life. I'd take it. For an hour. For eternity. Whatever was given.

"A wee moment, everyone. This is going to get technical," Mom announced. "If you want to leave, no problem. Ben, I need you to stay since you have experience with lidar."

The screen woke up in a gray moonscape.

"Arin, Ben, this is the lidar of Tara. These are the publicly available ones on Google images. Arin, I'm on the board of the Royal Society of Antiquaries. They are going to send more detailed images."

Everyone stayed fixed on the images of the rolling hillscape of Tara. The ancient ceremonial areas sat in stark contrast to the open fields that surrounded them. I felt a hand on my shoulder. My father nodded to the door and walked to it. I followed. He stopped a few yards from the carriage house.

"We haven't had much chance to talk." He ran his hand through his silvery hair. "I just want to check in. It seems that you have gone way past anything I've experienced. How are you doing with it?"

I was a few inches taller than my father. He put his hand on my shoulder, and, as he fixed me with his usual warm gaze, I felt something break. Tears formed. I looked at the carriage-house door. He took me by the arm and we walked to a more private area behind the house.

"Tell me," was all he said.

Images crashed together: Aedan, Tomás, me at my fifth birthday, Tanya in her coffin, the escape to Ireland, Siobhán naked and in love, Tomás dead, Arin bringing her lips to mine.

"Dad, I'm scared shitless, and I've never been happier."

Dad smiled. "I'm one of the few people who can truly understand. Yeah, it's pretty weird—and it's very exciting."

"I couldn't comprehend your enthusiasm at first."

We walked together to the wall overlooking Howth and the Irish Sea, around the same place I stood with Arin last night. A misty fog was rolling in. I wanted to tell him I loved him, but I put my arm over his shoulder instead. For Dad and me, it was the same thing. I thought to myself, just as I did a few days ago in Jamaica, where the fuck is all of this going?

"Bring it, Aedan," I said aloud.

My father laughed.

"Let's get back and see what the Murphy women have cooked up."

He said it as if Arin was part of the family.

I was going to mention the potential for danger, but I didn't want to ruin the rare moment. The fact is, my parents' safety was in my hands.

———

No one looked up as we entered. Mom and Arin were reading whatever was on the screen.

"Meg, if I'm adding this correctly, Tara is the size of maybe seventy-six football fields, correct?" asked Arin.

"Much bigger," came the answer. "Which is a problem. The government began construction of the M3 motorway in 2010. For all we know, Aedan might have had reason to bury it in one of the areas now lying under the road."

"Meg," Patty inserted, "the ceremonial sites of the Kings weren't touched. Here's what we know." He paused a moment, his lips tightly pressed. "There are two things in common with both places. Saint Patrick lit the Paschal fire at Slane to attract the attention of the King. This violated the King's edict that no other fire was allowed at the time of the pagan ceremonial fire at Tara."

I recalled that Patty was a history buff.

"Aedan would know this. He would choose a place of honor for the relics of Saint Columba. If he originally buried it near the fire pit at Slane, it makes sense that he would move it near the fire pit at Tara." Patty finished like he rested his case.

"Do we know where on Tara the fire was lit?" asked Arin.

"That's another issue." My mother brought up an image of a large phallic-shaped stone. "The fire was lit adjacent to the Stone of Destiny. The problem is that the stone was moved in 1798. No one bothered to record the original location."

Mom stood and stretched her back for a moment. "I suggest that we go to Tara. Key, you're in a highly sensitive state, it seems. Maybe being there will stimulate something."

"OK."

I had nothing better to offer. Nothing. So much for being the chosen one, the guy who connects the dots, sees ten moves ahead. Just call me Defective Murphy.

CHAPTER 40

I hadn't been to Tara since I was a teen. I remembered it as a bore. As we rolled into the parking lot and saw the gift shop and café, I had to smile. They had great desserts, my fondest memory of Tara.

I followed Ben, my mom, and Arin through the gate and stopped cold. My heart sank at the size of the place. "This isn't like finding a needle in a haystack. This is like finding a needle on a large farm full of haystacks."

The old church and cemetery with the statue of St. Patrick was one of the few reminders of anything recently man-made. As we walked the soft turf, I understood why people experienced the mythical and magical here. We stopped at the passage tomb known as the Mound of Hostages. It was from the Neolithic era, roughly 3200 B.C., my mother reminded us. The mound was a tall, round, earthen structure with an entry built of stone—a ritual site of kings and Druids.

"That's the Stone of Destiny." My mother pointed further up the hill. "The mythology claimed that when the proper king was selected and touched the stone, it would ring out over all of Ireland."

My hand reached out, as if I could touch it, still over one hundred yards away. It sat on a man-made ceremonial hill, inside concentric circles dug out of the earth thousands of years ago. I ran to it, Arin just behind me. I climbed the five feet of the first ring, slowed as I made my way down the hill, and then up the second ring, again slowing to mount the hill, the Stone beckoning me.

Arin stood beside me as I looked out over the west. I didn't see any towns. They were possibly hiding behind hills and trees, as Aedan's treasure likely was.

Mom and Ben arrived.

"Unless I see where Aedan buried it, we don't stand a chance of finding it."

"Even if you do," added Ben, "it might have been recovered soon after he buried it."

Arin hadn't said a word since we arrived. She took me by the hand and led me to stand inches from the Stone. She placed my hand on it.

"This is the Lia Fáil, the Stone of Destiny. Your destiny is to find the treasure. I do not doubt that you will." I wanted to make a logical argument, but Arin was resolute. "Keep your hand there for a few moments and just breathe in the history surrounding you."

"Put your hand on mine," I said. She did, then closed her eyes. I followed, my eyes closing too. A minute later, I sensed she'd opened hers. She looked at me with such a peaceful and loving stare that I felt like I was in the presence of an angel. But a moment later, I shuddered. Tomás lay dead, and a feeling of dread overtook me. I needed to shake out of this. Instead, I dropped to my knees and stared north toward Slane and then to the Mound of Hostages.

I said out loud, "Bhí m'uncail cosúil le fathach, agus é

gléasta i gclócaí móra, chreid mé go mbeadh sé ábalta béar a mharú lena lámha, bhí sé chomh mór sin."

Arin was next to me, translating words as I finished mine: "My uncle seemed a giant, wrapped in great cloaks. I believed he could slay a bear with his hands, such was his immensity."

"Chuaigh Tomás agus mo féin ar ár nglúine os a chomhair, ár Rí, ár n-uncail.'A nianna, beidh siabh cúig bliana déag d'aois gan mhoill, tá sé thar am daoibh tabhairt faoi bhur gcinniúint fhearúil'."

"Tomás and I knelt in front of him, our King, our uncle. 'Nephews, you are soon fifteen, it is time to pursue your manly destiny,'" Arin softly whispered.

"Tomás beidh tú ag freastal orm san eaglais, Aedan traenálfaidh tú le bheith i mo ghaiscíoch agus i mo chosantóir."

"Tomás, you will serve me in the Church. Aedan, you will train to become my warrior and protector."

"Fuair mé an-tógáil croí.D'umhlaigh mé mo cheann agus d'ardaigh mé mo lámh dheas do m'uncail.Chuir sé a lámh ollmhór timpeall mo rosta agus greim ag mo lámhsa ar thaobh amháin dá lámhsan díreach.Aedan is ainm dom, is as sliocht fada gaiscíoch mé."

"My heart soared. I bowed my head and raised my right arm to my uncle. He wrapped his enormous hand around my wrist as my hand grasped but one side of his. My name is Aedan, and I come from a long line of warriors," Arin finished.

"He's been here many times." As I spoke, I became aware that Mom and Ben were also here.

"Did you know that you were speaking in Irish?" my mom asked.

"I wasn't sure what it was. Strange, since all the other times Aedan spoke English."

I stood. I placed my fingers once again on the Stone of Destiny. I pulled back quickly as if from a hot coal. "Ben, I need you to drop us at Trinity."

"Why?" asked my mom.

"When I touched the stone, the book flashed in front of me. I need to see it."

CHAPTER 41

NOVEMBER 27, 2019
THE *BOOK OF KELLS*

The sidewalk in front of Trinity College was one of the busiest in all of Dublin. The entry gate was a trick of the eye. A large wooden archway occupied the middle of a long, stone-hewed building. Six white columns appeared to hold up a portico four stories above. As we approached the wooden doors, it seemed like we were about to enter a building, but instead we emerge onto the courtyard and greens, dominated in the middle by a hundred-foot-tall bell tower.

With three minutes to spare before our tour time, Arin and I hurried past the bell tower and turned right for the library, the home of the *Book of Kells*. As we wended our way through the exhibit to the book, I was amazed by a display showing how they made the vellum, the calfskin that became the pages, along with the inks and dyes used to create the artwork. That it survived is a miracle. One aided by my ancestors. And Arin's. Humbled by that thought, we walked into the gallery containing the *Book*.

"It's surprising how thick it is," I whispered to Arin. "In

the exhibition, it said the monks used one hundred eighty-five calfskins. They stretched the skins over a thin layer of oak. It looks to me to be at least ten inches thick."

I focused on my memory of seeing it in the scriptorium. "Not that easy to carry. I didn't get a real impression of it in my memories."

"Are you trying to find something specific?" asked Arin.

"I don't know what I'm looking for. All I can tell you is that I had a strong urge to see it."

We inched closer as the people in front of us left the area.

As we stepped to the front of the display, my hands began to tremble. Arin looked at me in alarm. I leaned over the glass to have a closer look, then snapped my head back and threw my arms in front of my face from the shovel of dirt being tossed at me.

"Are ye all right, sir?" asked the security guard.

Arin took my arm and walked me away from the case. "What did you see?" she asked.

"It was like one of those GIF videos you see online, short and jerky. Siobhán's brother was digging and tossing dirt." I brushed my clothes as if some had gotten on me. "They were burying the treasure."

"Did you see where?"

"I didn't see much of anything. It was a blur. Let's hope I see more later."

I took Arin by the hand and turned to the exit. "That's it? You don't want to see more?" she asked.

"No." I looked about the crowded gallery, as young and old soaked in the details of the masterpiece. Their accents and languages floated in the air, reverence in their voices as they imagined the long journey the *Book* had taken to sit here, just feet away from me. A framed blow-up of "The Evangelist", the page the clues referred to, hung on the wall. I backed away, feeling as though Saint John might pull me into the painting and transport me, for the rest of time, into the scriptorium.

Arin tugged on my arm, bringing me back to Trinity. "I'm here, Key."

I read the concern in her face. I had to get out of there. I brought up restaurants on my phone and found one just around the corner. "Let's get lunch."

We easily located the bright pink door with a small black-and-white striped awning, "The Pig's Ear" emblazoned on it. As soon as we were seated, I said to Arin, "We haven't had a moment alone. I want to ask you about last night; are you—?"

Arin leaned across the table and kissed me.

"Does that answer your question?"

I took her hand and nodded. I looked at the menu and knew my choice immediately. Arin saw me put the menu down. "That was fast."

"When a man knows what he wants, why look any further."

She peeked over her menu and smiled at that.

I ordered the shepherd's pie. She ordered the salmon then excused herself.

The restaurant was all brown tables and floors, with black leather chairs. Large mirrors lined the walls. The waiter served my Guinness and Arin's Chardonnay, and I found myself staring at the frothy head in my glass.

Arin returned. "You look too serious. Our brains need a rest. Tell me your favorite food or foods, favorite bands or singer, and the favorite place you have ever visited. I'll do the same. You go first."

When I got to my favorite place, Machu Pichu, Arin's face lit up. "I'm jealous. Was it amazing?"

"Completely. Peru is a magical place."

The restaurant had all but emptied. We talked in hushed

tones spiced with laughs and a few slaps of the table. When we spoke of dream destinations and places we'd been, Arin said, "When this is over, I want to go to Iona with you, see where this whole thing began."

"I'm in."

We got back to her questions, and I was stumped when she revealed her favorite singer.

"Perry Como?"

"Oh yeah, the greatest singer of all time." Arin held her ground.

"You're kidding, right? My grandfather listened to Perry Como. What's your favorite Como song?"

Arin burst out laughing.

"I have no idea. I've never ever heard him sing, just know the name Perry Como. Gotcha." She put her hand up for me to give her a high-five. I'm loving her goofiness.

After I paid, Arin said, "You picked the restaurant. I pick what we do next."

"Sounds good. We have no place where we need to be. Unless I get a text from Aedan."

We turned right as we left the restaurant and stopped for a brief moment to watch a woman add Christmas decorations in a bookstore window. We barely turned the corner when Arin started up the steps and stood under the sign for the Kildare Street Hotel. Arin asked me to wait in the lobby as she went to the front desk. I had no idea what was happening, but two minutes later she took my hand and led me to the staircase. We climbed a flight. This was getting interesting. She opened the door to a room and handed me a toothbrush with a mini-Colgate tube. "Courtesy of the front desk."

"I kept hoping that you would come into my shower this morning. It was all I could do not to go to yours. I'm guessing you were thinking the same thing," Arin said. She opened the bathroom door and turned on the shower, then lifted her blouse and threw it toward the bed. She unhooked her bra, let her pants fall to the floor, then stepped into the shower.

If there was ever a moment of clarity in my life, it was happening now. I was falling hard for this woman. I hoped it was a soft landing.

———

After two or so hours of lovemaking, Arin slipped out of bed and went to the bathroom. I had turned my ringer off. When I grabbed the phone from the nightstand and saw that Buck had tried to call me fifteen minutes ago, I hit dial. Buck answered on the first ring.

"Are you by yourself?"

"For the moment. What's up?"

"Ramirez and I had a nice long talk. He told me that his contact called him and asked if he wanted quick money for an easy job. He jumped on it. The contact told him to expect an unlisted call in the next fifteen minutes. The call came, no introductions. They told him to be in position early in the churchyard. He emphasized that no one was to get hurt. Ramirez repeated it a few times; if someone got hurt, he and Colasanti would pay a very big price. They were to take the bags and get out of there."

"It's not much to go on," I said.

"Key, the caller had a Jamaican accent."

I went silent.

"It doesn't necessarily mean anything," Buck continued. "But it might. And why the big emphasis on 'no one gets hurt'?"

The bathroom door opened, a naked Arin smiling, until she saw the look on my face. "Buck, I have to go."

"What's wrong?" Arin sat next to me. I told her, deciding to leave out the part about the caller being Jamaican.

"Why the emphasis on no one getting hurt?" Arin asked. "I mean, they had guns."

"They needed us."

"They need you." Arin pushed her curls off of her forehead. She stood in front of me and placed her hands on the sides of my head. "What are your thoughts?"

"For me to have thoughts, you need to put clothes on."

"Why?" Her eyes widened in surprise.

"To have thoughts, the brain needs blood. I'm afraid my blood is occupied elsewhere."

Arin looked down and laughed. "I can see that. Can't let that go to waste."

My mind raced to the night of the raid, the killer, his Jamaican accent clear when he said, 'I'm coming for yuh bwoy.'

Arin pushed me onto my back and climbed on top of me, guiding me into her. "We can face reality later," she moaned.

———

The two of us got in the shower again, then got dressed. I called my mother and gave her a quick update on the visit to Trinity. She told me the lidar revealed nothing so far, but she'd receive more images by the morning.

"We're going to stay in town for dinner," I let her know.

"I have a better idea. Why don't you spend the night? You need some alone time." My mom, the sex guru. "Dad and I are going to dinner in Howth. Call me in the morning."

"My mother just suggested we get a room and spend the night. Not a bad idea—what do you think?"

Arin took me by the hand. "I think we should get out of here, have some dinner, and come back for a nightcap."

"I'm taking you to one of my favorite places. It's just a few minutes' walk. Mom used to play in the sessions there."

I sat on the edge of the bed, trying to connect the pieces while Arin arranged her hair.

Ramirez reported the caller's Jamaican accent. It might be nothing, and it might be everything.

We arrived at O'Donoghue's a little after seven and got a table close to the musicians setting up. There were wall-to-wall photos of musicians. Even though this was a relatively small pub, some of the most famous musicians from around the world had come to rub shoulders with Irish music royalty here. Banjos and whistles, Irish flutes and bodhráns were mounted on the wall.

"Do you like Guinness?" I asked Arin.

"When in Dublin." She put her hands up as if to say hell yes.

I ordered and grabbed her hand.

"I want to show you something."

I led her to the wall opposite the musicians, my eyes darting over the myriad photos. I pointed to a fiddle player in a group of musicians. They'd been sitting on the same couch that was right behind us.

Arin stared for a moment.

"Oh my God, that's your mom. She's gorgeous."

"I used to sit right there," I said, pointing to an armchair. "I was probably ten years old the first time she brought me here."

"It must have been magical for you."

I looked around the tightly packed room, picturing the scenes from my ten-year-old mind, the musicians and waitresses making a fuss over me. "It was. Very."

Arin took my hand and we headed back to our waiting Guinness.

One of the musicians, the fiddle player, kept stealing

glances at Arin. I could hear their banter well enough to know they were speaking Irish. Arin was listening intently.

"Watch this. It'll be fun," she whispered.

She walked over to the group. When she spoke in Irish, the shock on their faces was priceless, particularly the glance-stealer. Arin said something directly to him and the rest of the band laughed hard. Next thing, they were shaking hands with her and waving to me.

"Fill me in," I said as she sat down.

"I heard him say, 'That one looks like a good bit of fun.' I went over and told him not to talk about my man like that. You saw their faces. They never expected a black girl to speak Irish. I mean, why would they? Very few *Irish* speak Irish. When they found out that I'm a Murphy from Jamaica, they were amazed."

A moment later, a waitress placed two whiskeys on the table.

"From the boys," she said, nodding to the band.

The band did an array of traditional music, protest songs, and popular sing-alongs. They were in the middle of a rousing version of "The Fields Of Athenry", a mandatory ballad when Irish American tourists were in the bar. It is the repetitive bane of most Irish bands, but it seemed everyone, including Arin, had joined the chorus. I was trying to enjoy it all, but Buck's phone call kept playing in my head. As I was about to ask Arin a question, a man sat down across from us.

"Hello, Key. Hello, Arin."

"Who the hell are you?" Arin answered before I had a chance to say a word.

Something bad was about to happen. Jimmy Downey, the guy from the Pegasus Hotel in Jamaica, sat across from us.

"While you two were fucking your brains out and enjoying a night on the town, we decided to have a little private time with your parents, Key."

I exploded from my chair, fists already clenched.

"You don't want to do that," Downey said, as if he had just mused on the weather. "Sit down. I'll tell you what's going to happen."

My pulse beat in my neck. My legs tightened like a wildcat about to leap.

"Right now, you want to tell me how you are going to kill me, how you will track me to the ends of the earth if we hurt your parents. I've heard that many times in my life, and yet here I am." Downey lifted Arin's empty shot glass and held up three fingers when a large man, the bouncer, began moving swiftly toward our table. He backed off to the bar, an eye still on Downey.

Downey crossed his legs and leaned back like he was considering a nap.

"Let me assure you that we have no intention of hurting your parents or anyone else. This is a simple business deal. You're going to find what you are looking for and then you're going to give it to me. Then life goes back to normal. You become the heroes for reuniting the cover with the *Book of Kells*. Your parents enjoy their new house. Everyone is happy."

I forced every ounce of emotion out of my brain and looked Downey dead cold in the eyes.

"You've mistaken me for someone who won't hurt you." I leaned forward, my arms on my legs, my lips next to his ear. "There is no place that you can hide that I won't find you. And you are going to put my parents on the phone right now."

The waitress placed the three glasses of whiskey and moved on fast.

Downey laid two cell phones on the table.

"The black one is for you to call your mother. You'll need her help. It's on speed dial. She'll have access to her computer. You can talk to her all you want, starting tomorrow. They will be fine unless you involve the police. Then all bets are off. The gray one is for you and me. I'll call you as necessary. Leave it on twenty-four seven.." Downey picked up his whiskey. "I trust you had a good visit at Tara today. Yesterday at Slane seemed to go a little weird for you, Key." He raised his glass, "Sláinte."

"It got a little weird for you too, Arin." He got up and reached his hand to her face.

Arin slapped his hand away and shot to her feet.

"What do you have when you mix an angry Irishwoman and an enraged Jamaican woman?" asked Arin.

Downey smiled. "A good fuck, obviously—right, Key?"

"Wrong, battyhole. You get fucked." Arin shoved him backward.

Downey recovered and showed no emotion. He casually turned to me, rubbing his hands together.

"I'd love to tame this bitch, Key. Maybe another time."

Downey walked to the musicians, casually removed twenty euros from his wallet, placed it in the tip cup, and then slow walked through the exit.

I picked up my phone and dialed.

"Ben, my parents have been taken hostage. I'll meet you at the house in thirty minutes."

CHAPTER 42

November 27, 2019
Northern Ireland

Shaun and Megan were cuffed to their chairs. One of the armed men pulled their hoods off. They adjusted their eyes to the harsh light. Megan started right in.

"Someone better tell me what the hell is going on, you morons. Speak up."

"Shut up," said one of the two ski-masked men. "I'll put the duct tape over your mouth again. The boss will be here in a minute. Not a word from you till then."

Shaun leaned in and whispered, "It's not going to do any good. Save your energy until we see what's going on."

Megan didn't have to say a word. A blind man could have felt her anger and worry. If she and Shaun were kidnapped, then Key and Arin were in danger. She heard the door open. A third masked man entered. He stopped cold in his tracks staring directly at Megan.

"For feck's sake, they kidnapped my cousin." He pulled his ski mask off.

Megan tried to jump from her chair, caught off guard by the restraints.

"Gerry, you stupid shit. Why did you do this?"

"I didn't. A different team took you. We were told to be here. I had no idea it was you and Shaun."

"Get these damned cuffs off of us."

Gerry, a thin man that looked worn down by the world on the best of days, nodded to his men to remove the cuffs.

Megan walked briskly to her cousin and slapped him in the face.

"I thought you got out of this shite," she said in Irish.

"I'm trying, Meggie. It's good money. Now what the hell do I do?" Shaun joined them. Gerry switched to English. "Shaun, I'm so sorry."

"Do you trust these two goons?" Meg said in Irish, nodding to the still masked men.

"With my life," Gerry answered.

"Do they speak Irish?"

"No."

"Tell them to take those masks off," Meg demanded.

Gerry complied.

"Give me your phone. I need to check in with Key." Meg held out her hand.

"Where is he?" Gerry asked.

"Dublin."

"Holy hell." Gerry looked like he was going to vomit. "Why does someone want you and Shaun here?"

"It's a long story," answered Shaun, rubbing his eyes, "but it could involve a lot of money. Maybe Meg will tell you privately, away from other ears."

"Is Cián involved?"

"Aye, give me the phone." Again, Meg put her hand out.

"Not a good idea, Meggie." Gerry fished a cell phone from his pocket. "I was told to give it to you tomorrow and to set you up with your laptop, which they took from the house.

You need to play the role of prisoner. You can't do anything that a prisoner wouldn't do."

"I agree," voiced Shaun.

"Who's behind this?" Meg demanded.

"We never know. It's always someone who has enough money and wants no one to know it's them. I never know who, and I never ask." Gerry shook his head. "I'm in a world of hurt here. If they find out I'm protecting you, I don't know what will happen. We'd all be in the shitter." Gerry frowned. "One other problem," he continued. "My boys expect to get paid. If this goes south, they disappear. They can't go empty-handed."

"How much are they paying you?" asked Shaun.

"One thousand euro per day, guaranteed five thousand each," came Gerry's answer. "You need to guarantee them that much. It'll cost you ten."

"You mean fifteen," said Shaun.

"Na, I ain't taking your money."

"Yes, you are," injected Meg. "And you are going to swear to me that you are out of this shite once and for all. Tell your boys we'll pay double, but they work for us now. And where are we?"

"Newry, on Bernish Road, near the A1."

"Why in the North?" Meg asked.

"You know why."

Meg glanced around the room, still getting her bearings. "It's a Republican town and your friends in the police won't ask questions." Meg thought for a moment. "We need to talk alone. The idiots who took us did so before we had dinner. Send your boys to Blue Print Pizza. I want the Blue Print Special and the Four Seasons. We can share, add what you want. Rocket salad?" she asked Shaun.

"Make it three," answered Shaun. "Do you have beer?"

"Of course."

"They took our phones, but not our wallets." Shaun handed Gerry two hundred euros.

"While they're waiting for the pizza, tell them to run into Wine Flair next to Dunne's and get four bottles of Rioja. Shouldn't be more than fifteen pounds each. Get whatever you guys want. If we are going to play this game, we may as well have some comfort," added Meg. "And Gerry, if any harm has come to Key, you are going to help me find whoever did this."

"There's something else you should know," Gerry added. "We were given the firm order that no harm comes to you, under any circumstances. We can restrain you, but if we hurt you then a world of shite will come tumbling down on us and we won't see a penny. It's a strange order, don't you think?"

CHAPTER 43

B en stood in the doorway when we arrived.

"I have Buck on a video call in the den," Ben said. "Kate was visiting her mother. She'll be here soon."

Arin took my hand as we sat at the desk. Buck's face was on the laptop screen.

"Let's get on the same page," Buck said. "Ben, have you had a look around?"

Ben and Buck knew each other from Ben's many visits to Philly with my father.

"Their car is here. They were going to dinner in town. Whoever took them was watching and waiting for Patty, Kate, and I to leave," Ben reported. "Key, tell us exactly what this guy Downey did and said. Arin, I want to hear from you as well. No short-cuts: everything."

After we recounted the story, Buck jumped in right away.

"He gave you a phone and said you could talk to your parents at any time starting tomorrow. That's a unique hostage situation. I'm trying to understand it. This Downey guy, if he was in Jamaica then he had to know you were going there even before you did."

I slammed my hand on the table.

"Damnit, I didn't even think about that."

"Of course you didn't. You won't think clearly until you've talked with your parents tomorrow," said Ben.

"Arin, when did you learn that Key was coming to Jamaica?" Buck asked, his face and voice as clear as if he were sitting in the room with us.

"The day before you arrived," Arin said to me.

"I only found out two hours before I got on the flight." I ran my hand down my face. "The night at the cemetery, we know there were two parties, Ramirez and whoever forced his partner to drop the bag."

"Ramirez is an idiot," Buck added, "not sophisticated. The other group, that's who took your parents. They've been playing this all along."

Buck was rubbing his chin, his head rocking slightly. Ben sat quietly, his hands in his lap. Arin paced behind me.

"What do they gain by doing this?" Buck prodded.

"I'm really afraid of the answer," I said. "There is no way to find the treasure using traditional archeology methods. It could take months for us to narrow it down. They're counting on me having a memory. That's why they needed me to find the *Book*'s cover and see the clues. They're after the treasure. Downey made that clear, but I can't just close my eyes and ask Aedan where he put it."

"Why not?" asked Arin. "Have you tried?"

"No." I sounded irritated, even to myself.

"Nothing to lose," said Ben.

I shook my head, not in the mood for this bullshit.

"I'm going to have another visit with Ramirez. We need to know who his contact is, to see who was behind him being there," Buck said, then added, "Ben, keep an eye on these two for me. Key will give you my number. I'll keep it on around the clock. You do the same."

"Count on it," answered Ben

"Arin, Key, I know this is going to be hard, but you need to get some sleep. Might not be much after today." Buck disconnected.

Ben poured two glasses of Young Dubs Irish Whiskey and put them in front of Arin and me.

"The Irish answer to all of life's conundrums."

"I don't like whiskey," Arin said.

"This is aged in a rum barrel. It's smooth, Arin, and I'm hoping one or two will knock you out."

"Kate and I will spend the night," Ben stated.

"No need," I answered.

"I wasn't asking," Ben replied. "I want you to make the call to your mother at five a.m. No one will expect that. We don't have much offense to play, so we play what we have."

I was happy to have an experienced military intelligence officer with me. I wasn't thinking straight. Downey was right: all I could think about was tracking him to the ends of the earth and hurting him. I knew I had to drag myself away from emotion. I drank the whiskey in one gulp, then one more. Arin copied me.

Ben was Mr. Stoic, but I could see the pain and tension behind the veneer.

"Thanks, Ben. I'll be down at 4.45."

———

I opened the bedroom door, trying to calm myself. I paced while punching my fist into my palm. Arin stopped me in my tracks.

"Stop it, right now. You don't have time for a pity party. You are Cián Murphy. Act like it."

She put her hand on my face. I turned away.

"What, you think I'm leaving you alone just because you are scared?" She slapped her hands on my chest. I stumbled a step. "Not going to happen."

I slowed my breathing and tried to calm my mind.

"This might sound crazy," she whispered, "but I want you to ask Aedan where he buried the treasure."

"How am I supposed to do that, mental telepathy?"

"I want you to think like the person who found Tanya's killers." Arin's chest was pushed forward, her face tilted up at mine.

I stepped away from her, hoping to hide. I hadn't given Tanya a thought in the last few days. Arin was right, but the pain of Tanya not being there to console me sharpened the ache.

"I'm sorry to bring her name into it, but she loved you. And you need to do this for your parents. Like you did for Tanya. No one else can. I'm here, totally with you." She took my hand in both of hers and caressed it. "Your mom asked if I'm all in. Do you believe I'm all in?"

I stared at her for what might have been days or years or twenty seconds.

My heart swelled in sheer, unbridled happiness. Siobhán held my hand as our children ran before us to the stream. The twins were entering puberty. They remained each other's best friends, but that would change soon, for a short time. She was growing breasts. The village boys would circle. Her brother would be awkward but protective as he began the early days of pubic hair and boyish confusion.

My wife, as usual, reacted to my thoughts, kissed my hand, and ran off after the children.

The King refused to send me for the treasure. I gave him my vow. I would not return it until he commanded me to do so. But he sagged with age. The battles against the Norsemen had increased. He told me that it was not yet safe. But what if I died at the hand of these savages? I instructed my children as to where to find the clues and the treasure. I made them vow to me that they would tell their children and their children and down through any measure of time to honor the family vow.

I stood at the edge of the stream, watching them skip stones and laugh with delight. Images of them played in my memory, their beautiful faces changing with age as they grew. Yet I worried that the treasure might never come home, my mission lost, unfinished, forgotten.

My eyes opened. Arin was fixed on my gaze.

"How long was I gone?"

"An hour, I think."

"An hour? I thought it was a minute or two. You stood here for an hour?"

"An hour is nothing, Key. Nothing. Tell me what you saw, and then let's get some sleep."

I recounted the experience with Siobhán and the twins. When I finished, Arin kissed me so fully that I felt I had transcended time and place, and then she led me to the pillows to continue my journey in the hope of finding Aedan.

"Don't forget to ask him where he buried the treasure."

There was no way I was going to sleep, but I closed my eyes, thought about my folks, and asked Aedan to help me find the treasure. And then, when my parents were safe, to help me find Downey and make him suffer.

CHAPTER 44

Ben poured the coffee while Arin and I sat the designated phone on the desk. Ben said nothing, just tilted his head to the phone. I dialed and tapped the speakerphone icon.

"Key, are you okay?" The worry in her voice chilled me.

"I'm fine, Mom. Are you and Dad okay?"

"Yes. Just pissed off, frightened, and worried sick about you and Arin; but we're being treated fine."

"Did they hurt you?"

"Not really. It happened so fast. They put hoods on us, cuffed our hands. I cursed so much that I need a month of confessions. They put duct tape over my mouth," Mom answered.

"Mom, they have been watching us all along—in Philly, Jamaica, here. They're professionals."

"Key." My dad had taken the phone.

"Hi, Dad. Are you okay?"

He didn't answer the question.

"I want to get your mother home safely. That's all I care about now. Don't worry about us. Focus on doing what they want. Understand?" I could hear the strain and imagined him wiping a tear.

"I got this, Dad."

"Key: no cops, no heroics. I am sorry I got you into this, but now you need to get us out."

"I will, Dad. I'll figure it out. I love you," I answered, as I imagined crushing Downey's face with my fist.

"I love you, son. Here's Mom."

"I'll get the computer going, but I won't likely see the new lidars until mid-morning. Maybe we can all get a little more sleep," Mom said.

"Mom, how did you book my ticket to Jamaica? And how far in advance did you do it?"

"The night you told us that you had the memories. I called Dr. Garcia that night, and she made the arrangements with Arin and her mother."

"Mom, I love you. I'll call back in a few hours."

Ben sat next to me, eyes closed, listening.

"Meg's phone must have been tapped, or her computer hacked, but that's not the big question," Ben said.

I looked over my shoulder at Arin. "The big question is how did they know to look at me in the first place. The only answer is Dr. Garcia." Arin's jaw tightened as she turned away from me. "We have to ask the uncomfortable questions. You know this."

She put her hands on the back of her chair and leaned forward. A sigh escaped her.

"You're right. I pray to God that there is an innocent explanation."

"Your brother is her chairman," I said. "Should you call him?"

Arin sat. Actually, it was more like she was pulled into the chair by an outer force. She was fighting tears, but a few of them won. Light from the lamp danced on her green eyes, but there was no shine, no mirth, no Arin. Just troubling shadows.

"Buck said not to trust anyone. Right now, I trust Dr. Garcia more than I trust my brother."

I glanced at Ben then back to Arin, her jaw tight as hell.

"Explain, please."

"He's become obsessed this past year with finding the *Book*. He's been pushing my mother to hire professionals. He's seemed frantic. When I ask him why now, he said he wants to find it before the fourth anniversary of my father's death."

"Do you believe him?" asked Ben.

Arin froze. Not a sound, not a move. "No. I'm obsessed. My mother's obsessed. Joseph always thought it was a waste of –"

Ben jumped in. "Do you think he would do something like this?"

"Like what? Kidnap Shaun and Meg? No." She dropped her head into her hands. Without looking up, she added, "He knew I was in Philly, and he knew why I was in Philly. I can't believe I'm even saying any of this."

"Arin." I took her hand. "It doesn't make any sense. If he knew you were with me and we found the treasure, then it's a success for both families. The vow to your father fulfilled."

"You don't know Joseph. It was probably driving him crazy that I might be the one to find it, not him. It always has to be him. I pray I'm wrong, but I have a bad feeling."

Kate came down the steps to join us and took a look at Arin.

"You look like you could use a cup of tea and a few moments to think. Come with me, darlin."

Kate reached out her hand. Arin took it.

After they left the room, I turned to Ben.

"Buck told me that Ramirez took his instructions from a caller with a Jamaican accent."

My right foot tapped nervously on the floor, my eyes falling on a photo that I hadn't seen in years. It was the year that Buck and Tanya and Uncle Brian came to Ireland with us. I think I was ten. We were horseback riding on the beach, not far from here. I lingered on Tanya, her nine-year-old tiny head resting on the neck of the horse, her arms draped around it, her smile happy and content. Ben waited patiently for my response. "I hope you're keeping a clear head. Mine is screaming right now. If Arin's brother is responsible for Ramirez, then how does Jimmy Downey know I'm going to Jamaica, and who does he work for?"

Ben is around five-nine with a slightly olive complexion. He once told me that he could blend in anywhere, Jerusalem or the Gaza Strip, Egypt or Ukraine, and that calm awareness was the key to survival. I was counting on that now.

"Downey told you that you could have the *Book of Kells*. He made certain that Ramirez didn't get it. Interesting, no? According to Meg, it is priceless and could easily command tens of millions of dollars." Ben looked at me. "Tell me his words again."

I pushed my eyes tight. "'You become the heroes for reuniting the cover with the *Book of Kells*. Your parents enjoy their new house. Everyone is happy,'" I recited.

"It's not money they're after. There is something in that treasure of even greater value, and they are willing to kidnap for it," Ben said, matter-of-fact. All obvious to him.

"Dr. Garcia and Arin's brother are the only two that make sense. They know I'm the link."

"You left out two people." Ben waited until I faced him. "Arin and her mother."

"Don't do that to me." My shoulders bunched, and bile burned my throat.

"Honeytraps are the oldest form of infiltration. You told Arin that the tough questions needed to be asked." Ben stood and looked me in the eyes. "Ask the tough questions, Cián. That's all they are, just questions, not conclusions."

"Ben's right." Arin had quietly entered the room, Kate behind her, throwing up her arms. "If it were reversed, I'd be asking the same questions. So, let me give you the answer. I have no idea what's going on. As much as it pains me to say it, I have to consider my mother and Dr. Garcia."

Arin walked across the room, Kate following. I stood, concentrating on her words.

"Ben," she continued, "I don't care if you believe me. I only care if Key does." Arin stopped in front of Ben. "My father invested his hopes and dreams in me. I am the most obsessed, even more than my mother. His was a beautiful dream. He wanted to fulfill this mission that started more than a thousand years ago, but in a million years he wouldn't hurt anyone to do it, and neither would ..."

Those were the last words I heard as I collapsed onto the couch. I was screaming something.

I lay in my bed and watched as Tomás's friend Aedan tried to fight the bad men. He tried to fight them with his sword, but there were too many. Mommy, they killed him. They killed him. I tried to stop them, Mommy, but Tomás couldn't help me. Tomás was already dead. I pulled pillows over my head and cried like I had many other nights until Mommy came into my room and ran her fingers through my hair and sang me the happy songs.

My eyes opened, my body was shaking. I felt as if someone was squeezing my throat. I finally recognized Arin, kneeling beside the couch, stroking my hair, calming me. I lay there for a few minutes. No one said a word, knowing I needed time. But I bolted upright.

"Where's the phone to call my parents?"

Arin reached into her pocket and hit the speed dial. My father answered on the second ring.

"Is Mom with you?"

"Yes."

"I need you both to listen. I just had an episode unlike anything else. I wasn't seeing through Aedan's memory. It was my memory as a kid. I saw Aedan being killed. Did I ever say anything about it?"

Arin, Ben, and Kate had their eyes on me, stunned looks on their faces. My mother answered.

"No, but you had many months of nightmares, around the same year that you talked about Tomás. Most kids have nightmares. I wondered at the time if there was a connection, but you never said a word."

"Mom, as I was coming out of it, Aedan said, as clear as I am talking to you, 'Follow the right hand of God. He was pointing to Adamnan.'"

My mother gasped.

"I'll call you back."

I handed the phone to Arin.

"There's something else I recalled as I was coming out of the episode. When I met Dr. Garcia, she told me she was testing a formula that could enhance and speed up the memories. I've been swabbed two times. The first time when I took the DNA test." I shook my head, trying to ward off the slight feeling of vertigo, unable to focus on anything in the room. Ben. Kate. Arin. The walls were threatening to spin. I forced my eyes shut. "Dr. Garcia did the second swab herself, in person. She came to my parents' house for it. Why?"

CHAPTER 45

November 28, 2019
Adamnan

M eg raced to her laptop, Shaun in tow.
"Saint Adamnan wrote the biography of Saint Columba. I don't remember much detail."

Meg logged into the Royal Society of Antiquaries website. She entered Adamnan into the search bar. "He became the ninth Abbot of Iona in 679," she read to Shaun.

She scanned the article but didn't find what she'd hoped for. Opening a new search, she typed "Adamnan Hill of Tara."

"Oh my God, Shaun. He held a church synod on Tara around 697. The Cross of Adamnan stands in what is now the churchyard, near a smaller standing stone. If you face north toward Slane, the churchyard is on the right. The right hand of God is Jesus, represented by the cross. Aedan would have known about Adamnan. It's perfect. He buried it at the site honoring Columba's biographer and follower." She turned to her husband.

"Dial Key."

. . .

I answered immediately.

"Put me on speaker," Mom said, before relaying what she learned.

"I'll study the lidars that show the churchyard. Ben, go to Tara with the equipment. Arin, I listed you on the permit. Make sure you have it with you. Remember, no digging at all, at least in the daylight. Just run the above-ground scans. Key, call me when you get there."

Ben wrote on a piece of paper and held it for us to see: *Leave both phones on the table and go to the kitchen.*

Once in the kitchen, we gathered around him.

"There's probably a listening device in the phones that Downey gave Key," he whispered. I'm going to open them and see what I can find. I'll signal you if I find anything. I can't remove it at this point, or they'll know. We need to make a plan. We can discuss this on the way. If I find a microphone, we will need to keep the conversation real but vague."

We followed him back to the living room.

"Arin and Key," Ben said, "check the equipment in the car. Let me know if there's anything else you need. Patty will be here in a few minutes. He's going to want to go with us."

Ben gathered the four of us beside Patty's van. The company Mercedes sat beside it.

"The phones are clean: no listening, no tracking. That means they are confident and watching us closely."

"What if they're listening through Meg's phone? Didn't we just tell them what we're doing?" Kate asked.

"They told Key that they'd watched him at Slane and Tara. They are a step ahead and in charge. But, Key, what is the central tenet of Krav Maga?"

Ben had been my teacher in the deadly Israeli martial art. I answered without hesitation.

"Every defense should include a simultaneous counter-attack."

We arrived at Tara around eight a.m. and the parking area was full—joggers, dogs getting their walks, friends sipping coffee, having a chat before heading off to work. It hit me for the first time: much of Ireland was a living museum, with ordinary life all around it. How very Irish: a love of the history and lore mixed with a fuck-off disregard, taking dogs for a piss on the grounds where the Irish kings were crowned. And here I was, trying to find a little box left here twelve hundred years ago. The futility of it left me feeling like an idiot, but for the profound sense that I was being led here.

"It's here," I announced as if I was the Irish-American mystic, the divining rod of Celtic treasures.

Ben, Kate, and Patty looked at me skeptically. I called my parents and learned that the aerial scans my mom received revealed nothing.

Arin opened the trunk of the van.

"He says it's here, so let's go. Help me with the GPR."

This GPR was the real deal. Instead of the toy-truck version in Philly, this was more like a lawnmower, with a tall steering column and a smart tablet built into it to display the radar.

I let the three of them get the equipment, and I raced up the path to the churchyard. The standing stones commanded a space behind the church separate from the graves. The taller one was Adamnan's Cross, alone but for a tree that seemed to guard it. I recalled the tales of trees and fairies and magic from my mother, wondering now if they were tales or truths. I walked to the small space between the two stones and dropped to my knees. The palms of my hands felt the ground. I glanced up the hill to the Stone of Destiny in the far distance and expected the earth to shake. Nothing happened.

I heard their footsteps crunch the ground while I lay prostrate. I looked up and started to say something when Kate grabbed me.

"Get up. Arin needs to get the sensors in here."

So much for being treated as the seer of truths, the guide to the past.

———

Twenty minutes later, Arin came to me.

"You nailed it. Where your knees were, that's exactly where the radar picked up a disruption in the ground. It doesn't mean that it's the treasure, just that something inorganic was detected."

"We can't dig in the daylight, and people are up here until around ten or eleven, though it's getting colder at night," Patty said. "Likely no one here past ten."

"Midnight. Just to be safe. You should call your parents," Ben added.

"They might be listening," Arin objected.

"It doesn't matter. They probably have someone watching us right now." I hit the speed dial, and my dad answered immediately. "We found something. We'll be back tonight."

CHAPTER 46

I t was just Arin, Ben and me. To our collective relief, there were no cars in the parking area.

"They are watching us from somewhere," said Ben, "or, since they know where we will be digging, they might have a camera feed installed."

There was enough ambient light from the glowing moon that flashlights were unnecessary. Ben and I followed Arin's instructions for preparing the site.

The night was eerily beautiful. The silhouette of St. Patrick's statue sat thirty yards away while the moon cast shadows from the gravestones. Druids and kings, saints and sinners, millennia of history and change, and the mind-boggling possibility that we'd find a treasure left behind by my ancestor. I'm not often found in prayer, but I looked to St. Patrick and silently asked his help to get my parents back. He had walked these very hills. Perhaps his spirit was listening.

Arin interrupted my thoughts.

"I need another ten inches."

Ben and I cleared the ten, moving slower and with more care as we neared the object.

"Key, concentrate in this area." She drew lines in the dirt. "Two inches at a time and go easy. We're getting close."

It wasn't long before the spade made contact. Arin leaned over the hole and began gently clearing the earth. "Ben, I need a little light here."

She used a small broom to brush the dirt away from the object. A shape emerged—an eight-pointed star.

"Holy shit." My poetic pronouncement.

"Save it for later," Arin said. "I need eight inches on all four sides."

Ben lifted his spade, but I waved him off.

"I need to do this."

I excavated the first side, my mind drifting to Hellshire Beach in Jamaica, being baptized a Jamaican Murphy by Arin, seeing Aedan and Tomás, and hearing the plan to travel the River Boyne. I felt a hand lay gently on mine and looked to see who it was. Ben and Arin saw me look up, but they were a few feet away. The gentle hand guided me. I sensed Aedan's presence.

As I almost finished clearing the final dirt, soft fingers joined my hand.

"Almost there," Arin whispered, her skin translucent in the moonlight, her green eyes alluring and beautiful. "You did it, Key," she said as we removed the final scoops of dirt. "Aedan has been waiting for you for over twelve hundred years. Ready?"

We gently lifted the box out of the ground. God, I wished my parents were here to see this.

The three of us hugged after we laid it on the tarp. Arin wrapped it while Ben and I quickly replaced the earth and then the grassy squares, attempting to erase our disturbance of this sacred ground.

• • •

I stood at the rear of the car, looking down at the tarp and its treasure. I didn't want to close the trunk. I knew the moment I did, that unknown forces would begin to reveal themselves. Ben nodded to me. It was time to let it play out. I got in the driver's seat and took the middle road. It was a small, one-vehicle lane with trees densely lining both sides. No lights anywhere. I put on my high beams and carefully made my way down the hill. Thirty yards before I got to the crossroads, the phone rang, the gray one. Jimmy Downey. My heart started pounding.

"Yes?"

"Well done, Key. Now stop the car. Arin and the Israeli will get out. You go to the house. I'll call you when you get there." Downey disconnected.

"What?" Arin looked frightened.

"He wants you and Ben to get out here. I'm to go to the house." Ben opened the back door. The cargo light came on.

I put my hand on Arin's.

"You are of Mack Murphy. You are a child of The Ghost." I kissed her. "I promise that I will see you soon."

She put her hand on my face then joined Ben. Thank God Ben was with her. I couldn't have handled this otherwise. I directed the GPS to Howth.

———

Ben and Arin stood there on the dark lane.

"They're going to separate us. Do your best to stay calm."

"How do you know that?" Arin asked, her voice quivering.

"After years in Israeli intelligence, you learn how to think like the enemy."

He made his voice as soothing as he could. "They know that I'm ex-military, therefore a threat. They will leave me here to isolate me. But you give them leverage over Key. I need you to trust me. Key and I will come for you."

One minute later, a car rolled up, window down, a man aiming a gun.

The hooded man commanded, "The girl gets in."

Ben nodded to Arin, and Arin forced a smile as she pulled the rear door closed.

———

Ben stood silently until he heard the soft crunch of tires on gravel, moving slow, no headlights. It stopped in front of him. He got in.

"They just took Arin."

"I know." Buck lifted his night-vision goggles. "I arrived this morning as promised. I've had eyes on you this morning and tonight."

"I know," answered Ben.

"Of course you do. Where to?" asked Buck.

———

At just after two in the morning, the sedan turned onto the dock in Howth and crawled past the long-closed restaurants on the left and the fishing trawlers on the right. The car stopped in front of a pier, a large pleasure craft waiting for them. A cuffed Arin and a hooded man with a gun walked to the boat as a figure emerged on the deck.

"I've been looking forward to seeing you again, Arin," said Jimmy Downey.

Arin stiffened, but the hooded man pushed her forward. Downey opened the cabin door.

"Perhaps the time for taming has arrived."

———

I had just pulled into the driveway when the gray phone rang.

"What?"

"Listen to me carefully."

"Who is this?" I asked. The voice was not Downey.

"Secure the box in the house and come to the dock in Howth. Go to the end. You'll see a large motorboat by the pier. Stay in your car unless told otherwise. If you want to see your parents again, then do as I say and be quick about it."

I removed the treasure from the trunk, unlocked the front door, and urgently moved it to the den. I flicked the light on and was frozen in place by the photo not twelve inches from my face. My parents' wedding photo. I was mesmerized for a brief moment—they looked like the two happiest people in the world—and then my rage began, and I swore I would find Jimmy Downey and cause him pain.

I hurried to the car, threw the trunk open, and removed my rifle. It sat next to me on the passenger seat, where Arin should be sitting. As I rolled into Howth Village, I spotted the turn and drove slowly toward the end of the pier.

A black Mercedes pulled up beside my car. A man stepped out of the back seat. I started to open my door, but he lifted a gun, a silencer attached, and waved me off. I put my window down and raised my voice so he could hear me.

"Where are my parents?"

He put a finger up, dialed his phone, and put it on speaker.

"Jimmy, where's the girl?"

"She's about to be tamed, just like I promised her."

I recognized Downey's voice and grabbed the rifle. The man with the silencer raised his gun and shook his head.

"Put it on pause," he said into the phone. "I'm on the dock. I need you out here now."

I lifted the rifle. He didn't even glance at me.

"If you want her alive, put the gun down and let me handle this."

I lay the rifle on the seat.

The cabin door opened, and Downey emerged. He stopped, looked around, and began walking toward the pier.

As Downey got close, he yelled at the man, "I always take a prize when I do a good job. What's the rush?"

"Did you hurt her?"

"No; in fact, I'm about to show her a good time. Want to watch?" Downey smiled.

The man swiftly aimed his gun, silencer attached, and put two bullets into Downey.

The man nodded to his driver. "Clean up the mess."

The hooded man who had brought Arin onto the boat watched the scene unfold and saw the man with the gun nod to him. A minute later, an un-cuffed Arin ran up the ramp, shirt torn, her fists flexing, seeming more pissed off than terrified.

I exploded out of the car, the man with the gun nodding, my mother's voice echoing in my head: *"Never let her go."*

I stepped over Downey's body and lifted her into my arms.

As I passed the man on the way to the car, he said, "Meet me at the house. Your parents will be there."

CHAPTER 47

November 29, 2019
Eight-Pointed Star

Arin sat quietly on the short drive from the pier to the house, seething. Mount Vesuvius, erupting any moment. I just wanted to get there so I could attend to her. As I arrived at the house, headlights shone behind me, and a white van parked. Arin and I stepped out of the SUV, but my rifle was still in my hand, obscured inside the vehicle.

The side door of the van slid open. Mom and Dad stepped out, throwing their arms around me. Then Mom spotted Arin and pulled her in.

The driver's door opened.

"Cián."

"Gerry?"

"Yer mam and I will explain over a pint another day." Gerry turned to my mom. "Ye need to go inside."

I took the rifle from the car.

"Ya need to leave that, Cián."

I looked at my mom. She nodded. I left the rifle on the seat and took Arin by the arm as I locked the car door.

When we entered the house, a figure sat at the dining-room table, a silenced gun rested in front of him.

"What the hell is going on, Padraig?" my mom said to the man. "What are you doing in my house?"

"You know him?"

"Padraig Collins. Everyone knows him. He's one of the richest men in Ireland, and among other things, he's an antiquities collector who's purchased several of my finds." She walked to the dining-room table where he was sitting. "Answer my question."

But I answered first.

"I just watched him kill the guy who had you kidnapped, Jimmy Downey. Downey took Arin back at Tara. He had her on a boat at Howth pier."

"The rules were strict." Collins unzipped his leather jacket. "He broke them. He knew the consequences were severe. No one was to get hurt. He was about to rape Arin. He had to pay the price."

"You were behind this? You sonofabitch." Mom moved quickly to slap him in the face, but he grabbed her wrist mid-air with lightning speed.

Sensing my move toward him, he raised the gun with the silencer pointed at me.

He looked me in the eye for a good ten seconds and then took the gun by the barrel and stretched the stock out toward me.

"It's your turn to hold this thing." He spread his arms toward us. "Now it's your choice. Have me arrested or help me avoid the coming bloodshed between the extremists."

I took it from him and looked at the silencer's smooth metal, the gun surprisingly light. Kate and Patty had entered the room, standing quietly at the edge.

"You sent Downey to Jamaica?"

"Aye."

"You made sure that we recovered the book in Philly so I'd have the clues?"

Collins tapped his fingers on the oak table.

"And you didn't disappoint."

I glanced at Mom and Dad standing a few feet away.

"You kidnapped my parents?"

"I'm sorry, Meg. I'll explain in a few minutes." He put his hands together, prayer-like, and tilted them toward my mother. "They were never in danger, Cián. I made sure your cousin Gerry was in charge of them. And before you ask, Megan, Gerry had no idea it was you until he got there, and he didn't know it was me making it happen."

"You had Downey take Arin on that boat. You said yourself what he planned to do to her."

Arin had my jacket over her, unzipped, her torn shirt still visible. I aimed the gun at Collins's head, adjusted it four inches to his right, and pulled the trigger. I heard the empty click of the gun above the screams in the room. Collins looked at me, his face blank. There was no explosion of wood or wall or glass.

"Just as I thought: blanks. It's all bullshit. You didn't kill Downey." I shook my head and turned to my folks. "It was all a show. You are playing us."

Collins reached into the pocket of his leather jacket and pulled out a gun clip.

"I thought there was a small chance that you might use the gun. He tossed me the clip. "Try again with that."

I examined the clip. Two bullets missing.

"You still haven't asked the right question." He motioned to the dining-room chairs. "Please sit. We have a lot of decisions to make."

Kate's face was red, like she'd been hit with pepper spray.

"Where the hell is my husband?"

"They separated us a quarter-mile from Tara," answered Arin. "For all I know, they left him out there."

"I repeat, no one was to get hurt," Collins said. "I'm sure he's fine."

"Start talking," I said to Collins. I exchanged the clip of blanks for the real bullets and laid the gun in my lap. "No more bullshit."

"If I'm right, the contents of the chest have the potential to help unite Ireland. The clock is ticking. Brexit will either tear Ireland apart once again, or, if managed correctly, bring us together."

Collins folded his hands and spoke directly to my mother. " I've known about Mack Murphy, Eamon, and Fergus for about two years. I became one of the major investors in Dr. Garcia's company. I only learned about your connection to Eamon and Mack a few weeks ago."

Collins turned to me. "Cián, I'm sorry. I had to put you under stress. Dr. Garcia believed it might accelerate your response."

"What are you talking about? Dr. Garcia is involved in this?" Arin's voice rasped as she laid her head in her hands.

"Maybe Cián would have put the puzzle together in weeks, or months, or perhaps never, but I needed you to find the treasure now. Lives depend on it. Dr. Garcia knew that. I asked her a simple question: could trauma accelerate Cián's response? Her answer was yes."

Collins closed his eyes; his lips moved, a barely perceptible murmur—Latin, I think. He patted his heart three times, then opened his eyes, his face both excited and serene.

"The Murphy families have dreamed of this moment. So please, bring the treasure here. Let's see if the ages have played tricks or if my patron, Saint Columba, has saved my soul."

My head spun. I didn't know if this guy was totally nuts or if he was about to reveal the truth. Dad sat ramrod straight in anticipation. Finally, Arin put her hand on my shoulder, "It's time," she whispered.

. . .

The tarp was stained with dirt, bits of earth and time clinging to it. I brushed it with my fingers, expecting Aedan to appear at any moment. I recalled what he wrote in the *Book*, that "an ancient one from the sea will one day unite this treasure with the Church". I wondered if I should pray, but I had to laugh instead as the lyrics from my favorite Grateful Dead song popped into my head: 'What a long, strange trip it's been.' My life in seven words.

I lay the treasure on the table and unfolded the tarp. My mother gasped at the sight of the eight-pointed star, and I watched as she brushed away a tear.

I placed my hand in Arin's.

"Let's open it together."

We reached for the lid. Suddenly, loud, violent voices shouted, a blur flew by the window. Three men burst through the door. One had a gun aimed at him, blood dripping from his mouth.

"Buck, what the hell are you doing here?"

Buck held his gun steady.

"Ben had a plan. I flew in this morning," Buck answered. "We found this guy hiding outside."

Ben, behind him, held a handgun. "It's a Sig P226. A favorite of U.K. special forces," he said, pointing to the newcomer.

The bloodied man lifted his head. The steward from Arin's jet scowled right at me.

"Noel, what's happening? Why are you here?" Arin steadied herself, her hand on the back of a chair.

Noel King looked at the treasure.

"Oh my God, Joseph sent you. Tell me I'm wrong!" Arin screamed at him. Noel King said nothing.

"I'm going to kill him. Look at me, Noel."

With no response from King, Arin leaped at him, all sinew and violence. She slapped his chest so hard he gulped for air.

Padraig Collins stood.

"It's not completely your brother's fault, Arin."

Arin turned to Collins like a fighter, hands ready, as if she would vent her rage on him.

Collins put his hands up in reaction.

"When I invested in Futuro, I made an arrangement with him. If he found the treasure and gave it to me, I would reduce my shares in the company by half. But he proved incompetent and greedy. So he sent those men to take the book from you in Philadelphia. And now your friend here, Noel, has been sent to retrieve the treasure, it seems."

Collins approached King. In a soft, almost friendly voice, he started: "The rules were simple, Noel. No one was to get hurt. Jimmy Downey violated that rule. At this very moment, he's being dropped to the bottom of the Irish Sea. He'd been with me for twenty years. You," Collins's voice took on an ice-cold edge, "I don't know you, but if I ever see you again, you will join him."

King looked down, avoiding Collins's glare. Collins reached over and lifted his head.

"Show some respect when I'm talking to you. My men are going to take you to the airport. Go home, wherever that is, and never come back to Ireland." Collins paused to send a text from his phone. Thirty seconds later two men entered the foyer. One put flex cuffs on King and led him out, Arin looking on, slack-jawed.

"Now what?" I asked Collins. "I have the gun. I have the treasure."

"It doesn't belong to you, or me, or any of us. It belongs to Ireland."

Mom held Dad's hand. They had the same goal as Collins.

"What's in this for you?" I asked him.

"Forgiveness, Cián. Saving my soul. To accomplish that, Saint Columba told me that I must unite our country. You think I sound like a madman. I assure you, I'm anything but.

Yes, Columba has visited me in visions. Likewise, Aedan has visited you in memory. So, which of us is crazy?"

Buck was leaning against the wall, his eyes roaming over the room. Ben stood with Kate, her rubbing his back. Patty stood behind Mom and Dad, Arin next to me, quiet, spent. The chest with the eight-pointed star sat on the dining room table, a chandelier lighting it from above. It had traveled over twelve hundred years to arrive at this moment. All because Aedan made a promise.

"If this is what I pray it is," Collins continued, "it will be used to bring the people of Northern Ireland together. Megan, you're the resident expert on antiquities. Please show us whatever is in there."

My mother went into the den and returned wearing latex gloves and handed Arin and me a pair. The chest was beautiful. Oxidation had produced colorful patinas in the metal.

Arin and I lifted the lid and stole a glance. There was only one item. My mother reached in and lifted out a chalice with a bluish patina and two bands of gold relief, one rimming the top, the other the middle. Jewels formed a cross, tarnished, but otherwise in good shape.

"This was Columba's Chalice?" my mother asked reverentially.

"Yes, and yet far more powerful. I have a diary from one of Mack Murphy's closest friends in Ireland. Mack had discovered an ancient document while in search of the treasure himself. It spoke of the chalice, of how Columba was its caretaker, using it to say mass in Iona and to convert the Scots and the Picts. It was the Holy Chalice of Saint Patrick himself. Megan, look under the base. Tell me if you see any words."

My mother turned the chalice over and angled it for good light. She began to wobble on her feet.

"Oh my God, Shaun. Etched into the metal is the word 'Patricius' … *Patrick*." She rested it on the table.

No one dared speak. Religious or not, everyone in the

room understood the magnitude of the object. It had been held in the hands of two beloved saints. It was worth a fortune in gold but a greater fortune in spirit.

Collins opened his cell phone and handed it to my mother. I got closer to get a view. A photo was enlarged on the screen, an illustration of a man drinking from a chalice.

"That's from the *Book of Kells*," Collins stated. "Scholars believe that the figure represents Saint Peter drinking from the Last Supper Chalice, The Holy Grail. He sits atop Abraham's name, representing his figurative lineage with Jesus. He is the leader of Christ's mission on earth. 'Upon this Rock I will build my church.' Megan, examine the jewels. At the bottom of the cross should be the only emerald."

Mom and I looked closely. She nodded.

"Are you saying that this is Saint Peter's Chalice?"

Collins laced his fingers together, his gaze firmly on the chalice.

"Not his chalice, but an emerald from his chalice. Emeralds are native to Israel. They come from a rock. Peter is the Rock. The Vatican has documented that there were twelve emeralds on Peter's Chalice, representing the twelve apostles and the twelve tribes of Israel. The twelve emeralds were dispersed among early missionaries, this one making its way to Saint Patrick's Chalice."

Arin joined me for a closer look.

"Megan, what you hold in your hands is a direct line from Jesus to Peter, to Patrick, to Columba. You hold the spiritual thread of Ireland. You hold peace." Collins finished and made the sign of the cross.

My mother bowed her head, brought the cup to her lips, and breathed deeply from it. She kissed it lightly then handed it to me. Arin rested her fingers along the rim. If what Collins said was true, we held one of the most important historical finds in human history.

Arin asked Collins, "What do you want to do with it?"

Collins stood and approached the chest, his fingertips

almost brushing the star.

"I want the Archbishop of Armagh, the Anglican bishop, and the head of the Presbyterian Church in Ireland to be its caretakers as a symbol of unity, each in turn for three-month periods. Displayed at the Catholic and Protestant Saint Patrick's Cathedrals in Armagh and Dublin."

Collins squatted eye level to the chalice, looking, not touching.

"I'm arranging for a Papal Mass here in Dublin at which the Pope and the leaders of all denominations in Ireland will pledge unity. No more boundaries between us, no borders to divide us."

He turned to my mom. "Megan, Brexit is about to divide the country once again. We must act fast to heal it. And I want the combined Murphy families to tell the story of how it came to be that the Sacred Chalice and the *Book* have been handed to you by your ancestors."

My father slapped his hands on the table, and all eyes turned to him.

"Key, you witnessed him kill a man. We can't ignore that," my father said.

"That's completely up to you." Collins looked as calm as if someone asked him to pass the salt. "I could have done it quietly, but I wanted Key to witness it. Now you have something on me, just as I have on Arin's brother and Dr. Garcia. We all go down, or we complete the mission of unifying Ireland. It won't be both."

"Dad, the truth is, I might have shot Downey myself." I pointed to Collins. "You saved me the trouble and the consequences that would follow." I brushed my gloved finger along the barrel of the gun that killed Downey. "That doesn't mean there won't be a price in the future."

"Exactly the point, Cián. It's why I gave you the gun. All of us are now conspirators in fulfilling Aedan and Mack's mission," Collins said. "Shaun," he gestured to my father, then at the rest of us, "let he who is without sin cast the first stone."

My father crossed his arms on the table and leaned slightly forward. "Someone will inevitably lift the stone and throw it, telling themselves that the sin they committed was justified." Dad looked around the table. "Then one by one, not wanting to be seen as a sinner, all will cast their stones."

Kate shook her fists in the air, her cheeks red.

"All this pontificating, Shaun. Downey woulda put a bullet in any of you and not thought a bit about it. Saint Patrick's chalice is sitting there, and Boris feckin Johnson doesn't give two shits about Ireland or you, or the dead piece of crap that you, Mister Collins, brought into our lives."

I had a glimpse at Buck. I thought he was going to burst out laughing.

"If you had hurt my Ben, I would have chased your rich arse up the Boyne and buried a bullet in your ugly face." Turning to me, Kate said, "I'm glad to see you've grown up, pretty boy, and are ready to defend that beautiful woman." She nodded toward Arin. "Now, do you have the balls to finish this?" Kate stole a glance at the chalice and blessed herself.

Collins clapped his hands and said to Ben, "You are a lucky man."

Mom interrupted. "It will take weeks to authenticate the chalice."

"We don't have weeks," Collins answered. "The moment you hand that over to the government, every politician will be clamoring for a piece of it, trying to get themselves in the limelight. We'll hold a press conference and announce that the *Book*'s cover is being given to Trinity College and the chalice will be given to the National Museum."

I surveyed the faces of everyone in the room. Kate, Patty, and my parents were all giving slight nods of the head. Ben, as always, was unreadable. Arin, I'm not sure. Buck looked like he'd eaten something foul.

"Why the hell should we trust you?" I gestured toward Collins. "You put us in danger. Something could have gone wrong."

"And yet it hasn't," Collins retorted, his hand gesturing to the chalice. "I don't expect you to trust me, but I do sincerely hope that you'll trust my plan and vision."

I started to respond, but Mom interrupted. "You believe that this chalice will be enough to bring the North together?"

"No, Meg, not by itself." Collins nodded to her. "As usual, it is fear that will bring people together, just as fear has torn them apart."

Collins and my mother stared at each other for a moment. My mother's slight nod told me she understood.

"There are three pieces to the puzzle: politics, money and religion. I am investing in two new facilities in Northern Ireland. One will headquarter Futuro Biologics' European division. They will bring close to fifteen hundred jobs. Meg, you are a border town girl from the North." He leaned toward her. "You know the fear that everyone has if the borders come back. It will choke both sides. I'll only invest in the North if the North gets a no-border agreement and special European Union status for trade."

Collins surveyed everyone. "You will find that several influential Unionist politicians have had a change of heart and will break from London on having borders. They will insist on a special deal for Northern Ireland and the EU. I've seen to that."

I noticed my mom squeezing my father's shoulder.

"Fear by itself is a Molotov cocktail. It must be mixed with hope. Saints Peter, Patrick, and Columba are revered by Catholics and Protestants. The chalice represents national pride, and most importantly, faith. I have the commitment of the prominent clergy that, if we found it, they would come together around the chalice as a symbol of unity." He spread his hands like Moses beckoning his flock. "Here sits the final piece of the puzzle."

For one of the few times in my life I saw Ben betray emotion. Jesus and Peter were Jews. He never talked about religion, but as he stared at the chalice, I imagined that my Israeli friend grasped the power of this relic to heal.

"Between the pressure from the streets for the economic stimulus and from the Church to unify around this treasure," Collins held both hands toward the chalice, "we have a once-in-a-lifetime chance, but we must move fast. I'll schedule a press conference four days from now. Every media outlet around the world will be there. We control the story. We control the outcome."

I went to the chest and ran my fingers over the star, the symbol of renewal. I pictured it sitting on the beach in Scotland. Aedan, Tomás, and the others kneeling in prayer. And now it sat before us, Aedan's promise fulfilled.

"Why the urgency? Why four days from now?" I asked.

"The U.K. elections are on December 16th, barely two weeks away. Johnson will win. Brexit will move forward." Collins checked the faces before him. "Polling shows that he will lose Northern Ireland. If so, it will be the first time that the Unionists are in the political minority, and unification can move closer to reality."

"The press conference is timed to move the vote?" I asked.

"Exactly." Collins drummed his fingers on the table once again. "That's why I did what I did."

"Fuckin brilliant," Kate hollered out. We all turned to her. "I still don't like him for the dangers he put you in, but you have to admit it's brilliant."

"Mom, Dad?" They both nodded their heads.

I put my left arm around Arin. She nodded also.

Ben stared at me, assessing my moves. It would normally be easier to read *War and Peace* in Russian than his face, but this time I saw his agreement.

"Buck?"

Buck looked everyone in the eyes, one at a time. "This one's on you, little brother, but keep your eyes on him," nodding to Collins. "I don't trust him."

I considered Buck's words and drew in a big breath, exhaled like I was trying to clear an awful smell. I stepped over to Collins so that we were a few inches apart.

"We will work with you under one condition."

"And that is?"

I ran my fingers through my hair as my thoughts formed. "You were going to give up fifty percent of your holdings if Joseph delivered the treasure." I folded my arms and looked down at him. Part of me wanted to plant my fist in his face; the other part was growing in admiration of this bold lunatic. "We delivered the treasure. That fifty percent is ours."

Collins's shoulders pulled back, his jaw set in a scowl, his lips started to move. I held my hand up. "You want salvation? So do I. It's time to bring honor to the dead."

My father's eyes slowly rose to meet mine. He and I had been given a glimpse of the past. It was my time to give form to the future.

"We will create the Tanya McCoy and Mack Murphy Foundation. All of our earnings will fund youth programs in Jamaica, Philly and Ireland."

Buck visibly choked up. Arin squeezed my hand so hard it hurt. I looked back to Collins.

Collins drew a deep breath. "That's a big ask, Cián."

"It's not an ask," I said firmly.

The room was silent, all eyes on Collins. Arin kept squeezing my hands like they were a stress-relief ball. Some two minutes passed.

"We will announce it at the press conference." Collins

tapped both hands on the table. "You and Arin will go on an extensive press tour following the Trinity event. The world will be hungry to hear your story. I'm going to make you stars." Collins gave me his alpha look, his brows knotted, jaw held tight. "That's not an ask."

He turned to Mom. "And now, Megan, there's something you must do. You must go home and bring the book cover to Ireland."

"What makes you think it's not here?"

Collins cocked his head at her as if the answer was that obvious.

"I have my jet on standby."

"When is it cleared to fly?" she asked him.

"Now. I have arranged for a fresh set of pilots for the return. You'll be back here in fifteen to sixteen hours. There are comfortable beds on the plane."

"I'm going with you," my father stated.

"Shaun, I'm going to need your help with some arrangements," Collins responded. "The *Book* and the chalice are in your possession. I'll need you, Arin and Cián, for meetings tomorrow with Trinity and the National Museum."

"I'll go with you." We all turned to Buck. "I'm not letting you get on his plane without me."

"Thank God you're here, Buck. I want you to be part of this," Mom took his hand in hers.

"Arin," said Collins, "please call your mother and have her and your brother here in forty-eight hours. I'll call Dr. Garcia."

"I'll call her," Arin said firmly. "She has some explaining to do." She walked over to him. "Mr. Collins, I owe you an apology."

Collins shrugged his shoulders. His eyes narrowed.

"For what?"

Arin's fist flew hard and fast into his stomach. He doubled over, grabbing the table, gasping.

"For not doing that earlier. You let Downey touch me. And no, we're not even. Not yet."

Collins steadied himself. Drawing in air, he pushed himself up, turned his head to Arin.

"I earned that—fair play." Then, to the rest of us, "Can we just fucking get on with saving Ireland?"

CHAPTER 48

November 29, 2019
Hot Toddies

I was buzzed and felt like I might stay up for days, but I had enough experience with adrenaline to know that, at some point, I'd just fold. Arin looked as jazzed as me. She had earbuds on and was swaying to music. It was going to take her time to get over what happened with Downey. Or maybe it was me. Perhaps it was going to take me time to get over what almost happened with Downey. I didn't protect her.

"Do you have hot toddies in Jamaica?" I said loudly.

She removed her earbuds. "Sorry, what?"

"Hot toddies, do you have them at home?"

"Of course. My mom calls them tea toddies. She uses rum."

"I think we could use one." I opened a few cabinets to find the tea, honey, some cloves, and of course, liquor. "No rum here. Bourbon or whiskey?"

"Bourbon."

I made the drinks and set them down in front of Arin to

cool. She was on the stool at the kitchen island. Her eyes darted around, avoiding mine.

"Tell me."

She gave me a weak smile and blew into the tea to disperse the steam.

"Nothing. Key, I'm elated. Tired but elated. I haven't processed everything. This has been a dream, my connection to my father, like our little conspiracy. It was my private land-bridge to my father's soul. Now, mission accomplished, but he's not here to share it. I'm missing him terribly."

I walked around the counter to sit on the stool next to her. We both sipped the toddy, feeling the heavy pour of bourbon. I put my hand on hers.

"I get that, but I sense something else is bothering you."

"You mean the fact that I want to beat the shit out of my brother, and I'm pissed and confused about Dr. Garcia? And, of course, Downey. I wanted to kick his ass and would have if the punk didn't have a gun pointed at me."

"Yeah, all that, but there's something more."

She locked on to the still rising steam, her breathing was deeper, faster.

"What?" I asked.

She slowly raised her eyes to meet mine.

"In four days, we will be at the press conference. For two to three weeks after that, we'll live in a storm of interviews, TV appearances. Eventually, the media will move on, but then there will be book deals, movie right offers. Do you have any idea how big this story will become?"

"I haven't thought about it," I answered. "But it will be what it will be."

Arin held the cup in both hands and stared into it, as if reading the future in the tea and spices. "My mother will do everything in her power to make sure I go back to Jamaica as if I'd been crowned the Queen."

"Even that will be temporary."

"Maybe not." Arin blew on the steam, the scent of cloves and bourbon in the air.

"What do you mean?"

"Everything has happened so fast. I've had no time to think about Jamaica, the future. Any of it."

"By any of it, you mean us?"

Arin rested the cup on the counter, placed her soft hands against my cheeks. "My whole life was the thrill of the hunt. I've been praying that my father would rest in peace when I found it. Now ..." Arin stopped speaking and stood. She took her cup in hand, kissed my cheek, and started down the hall. She stopped at the bedroom door. "I'm sorry Key, I probably just need some sleep."

I grew aware that dawn's light seeped through the windows and that reds and purples painted the morning sky. I begged my feet to move. I too needed sleep. But my feet abandoned me. All I could see was the bedroom door closing behind her.

CHAPTER 49

Trinity was in a delightful frenzy, more party atmosphere than historic moment. Students in small groups talking fast and loud, some rolling cigarettes, friends in winter jackets sharing blankets on the lawn. Arin and I were escorted onto the campus by the Vice Provost. We picked up snippets of conversation as we walked past groups of students:

"What's going on?"

"I heard it has something to do with the Pope."

"Devlin said she saw Bono coming out of the faculty club."

The Provost told us that security was at its highest in the history of the famous university. Classes were suspended during the press conference. Students and faculty had spread blankets and lawn chairs on the Green to catch a view from the jumbo screens set up across the campus lawns. The day was Dublin cool and cloudy, but no rain was in the forecast. All entry points to the building were secured, and only those with press credentials or on the invitation list were allowed through the metal detectors. The Provost led us past security into the Edmund Burke Lecture Hall.

The TV cameras had been tested in the control booth, as had the microphones on stage. Dignitaries and the press assumed their assigned seats. Already seated in the front row were Buck, Patty, Ben, and Kate. Arin and I greeted them before going backstage.

Arin had been as affectionate as ever, but there was some shadow, some unseen little moat around her, and I didn't know how to breach it. Everything had happened so fast, as Arin had said. Exhilaratingly fast. It was the slow crumbling that I feared. As we found a quiet corner backstage she leaned into me, her arms hugging me tight.

"Are you nervous?"

"No," she barely whispered, "I was born for this. It's what follows that scares me."

A TV monitor showed the jumbotrons that had been erected in Saint Peter's Square in Vatican City. Crowds of the faithful filled the immense plaza, the casual tourist unaware that they had stumbled into a moment of history in the making. When the press learned of the Vatican's involvement, it set off a frenzy of rumors and talking-head chatter world-wide. All one heard about for the past three days was the headline from the press release:

Historic Find Contributes to the Global Unity of Humanity

Padraig Collins's press team had most definitely stirred the pot.

The news conference was scheduled to begin at one p.m., eight in the morning eastern time in the U.S. and Jamaica, designed to be the drive-time discussion of the day. News outlets hoped the hype of the last three days was worth it. Little did they know that Ireland's Archbishop, Michael Fahey, had pulled the strings that set the Vatican bureaucracy into motion.

At one p.m., Arin and her family, my parents and I, stepped onto the stage along with Dr. Garcia and Padraig Collins. Long, narrow conference tables held our nameplates, a microphone, and water in front of us. The press and public had been teased about what was to come, but no one knew the details. The hall was buzzing with conversations, each reporter it seemed, each guest, trying to probe and pry the tiniest fragment of information from the person they were talking to, only to find that the other swam in the same void.

The hall fell quiet as the Taoiseach, the Prime Minister, entered the stage. His blue suit, brown shoes, red tie, and early morning visit with his stylist made him camera-ready.

After welcoming the press and dignitaries, he said in crisp Italian, "Un benvenuto speciale ai nostri amici in Piazza San Pietro." The screens showed the masses cheering in Saint Peter's Square, and looking into the camera, he addressed the global audience.

"The 3rd of December, 2019, will hereafter be remembered as a historic day for Ireland and the world. For some twenty years following the Good Friday Peace Accord, Ireland has been in the process of healing from violence and sectarian division. Great gains have been made, but only a fool would believe that the healing is complete. The threat of borders once again raises the specter of those violent times. No one in Northern Ireland or the Irish Republic wants walls between us. Unionists and Nationalists, Protestants and Catholics have stood together in opposition to borders."

The Prime Minister placed his hands on the rim of the podium; his eyes searched the audience. "However you think of yourself, British, Irish, or European, we stand with you. As you witness the events of today, we invite you to think of yourself, and all on this island, in fact all on this island called Earth, as fellow neighbors and global citizens. Céad míle fáilte, a hundred thousand welcomes."

Collins took to the podium and told of his plan to build the new Futuro facilities in the North, but only if there were no borders and if the North remained in the E.U.

He soon walked to where Dr. Garcia was seated. "Last week, *Time Magazine* featured a brilliant scientist on its cover." He pointed to the screen that had the *Time* cover projected on it. "That story shook the world. Dr. Sylvia Garcia has discovered a genetic mutation that allows the holder to view the memories of an ancestor. She was instrumental in bringing two families together who are responsible for what you will witness today. Please, Dr. Garcia."

Dr. Garcia pulled her microphone forward; her eyes seemed distant, and it felt to me that she was viewing some long-ago moment. She pushed them shut, opened them, and leaned into the microphone.

"Seven years ago, my dear friends, the Jamaican Murphy family told me the amazing story of their ancestors' search for an artefact that had been missing for over twelve hundred years."

She extended her arms to the side as a visual reference to the march of time.

"I was in the early stage of identifying a mutated gene that had evolved over millennia and traveled through Europe as part of the great Celtic migration. Several months ago, I met Shaun and Megan Murphy and learned that Shaun was a genetic match to the Jamaican Murphys."

I glanced at the TV monitors as the cameras tightened the view on Dr. Garcia.

"Some thousand years ago, two brothers from Donegal began families. One was Deaglan, the other Conall. Deaglan's clan, through the rough-and-tumble vagaries of time, hundreds of years later, produced a young man named Fergus, who was sent on a prison ship to Jamaica. Conall's progeny landed relatively recently in Philadelphia. And here they sit, in living color and contrast, about to lift the veil on history."

The audience followed her every move and motion, some in the back straining to see her.

"Before Conall and Deaglan came Aedan, their ancestor." She motioned to me. "Cián Murphy experiences the memories of Aedan. Dr. Arin Murphy is the keeper of the memories from Deaglan's tree. They will tell you their story."

Arin and I told of Aedan and Fergus, Eamon and Mack; of the Church of Two Ships, Slane, and Tara. As Arin unveiled the extraordinary life of Mack Murphy, his love for Jamaica, his dedication to Ireland, and his fierce hatred of slavery, I watched the audience come under her spell. One of the monitors had the feed from the lawns of Trinity and the walls surrounding Vatican City. No one was moving, all eyes on the screens in front of them. My heart pounded, knowing that they had seen nothing yet. I could feel my hands shaking in anticipation as I started the finale.

"I invite to the stage Archbishop Michael Fahey, Bishop Kathleen Wilson, and the Reverend Paul Smythe, along with the President of Trinity College, Mr. Patrick O'Leary," I said, Arin's arm gently resting against mine.

The three men stood side by side while an assistant wheeled a table in front of them with two covered objects. I continued.

"Our ancestor, Aedan, was responsible for protecting the *Book of Kells*. I watched him, through his memories, escape the Viking attack at Iona as he moved the book to the new monastery in Kells."

I had planned what I was going to say, but I don't know where it went. The images of the past few weeks were being stirred into a cauldron right there in front of me. Aedan said to me, as I stood in this lecture hall, not a hundred yards from the *Book of Kells*, *"Tell them the truth."*

What truth? Which truth? The truth I know is that nothing is permanent.

"Things get torn. Things get ripped away. It seems to be the essence of our lives. And in that pruning comes renewal. Your lover dies, but your grandchildren fill the hole in your heart. The tree falls, but the sapling beneath it reaches toward the sun to build new roots. Likewise, the tree of life builds branches that go this way and that, but in its own measure may find a way to bring you back. And here sit the Murphys, separated and renewed."

I stood and turned to the *Book*, hidden, waiting to be greeted by a world in need of joy.

"Ireland was torn. A piece ripped from her but yearning to be whole. In the year 1006, our ancestors Conall and Deaglan stole the holy *Book of Kells*. Not for fortune, but because Aedan had written clues to a treasure that could heal. They returned the book, minus the cover. Torn and now renewed, we bring you the missing cover of the *Book of Kells*."

The President of Trinity College and the clerics lifted the veil that hid the missing cover as the TV camera projected it on the screen. Gasps from the audience filled the room. I examined the people, many of them wiping tears, no one taking their gaze off this miraculous reunion.

I sat as Arin took over.

"We invite the Director of the National Museum of Ireland, Moira Nolan, and the Chief Scientific Officer of the Vatican, Dr. Giorgio Consalvi, to join us."

Arin paused as the new guests stood beside the clerics. All five, side by side, their attention drawn to a still covered object in front of them.

Arin glowed, her face so alive, channeling, I believe, the force of nature that was Mack Murphy. And her father.

"Aedan taught his children to teach their children on

down through the ages, that he had written clues in the book. He intended to return for the treasure himself and bring it to Kells, but that was not to be. Miraculously, it made its way to us." Arin gestured to the Murphy families.

"When Saint Columba was exiled from Ireland to Scotland in the year 563, he was given a powerful relic with which to spread the gospel." Arin nodded to the clerics. They lifted the cover to reveal a metal chest with the eight-pointed star.

The TV cameras focused on Arin as she said. "We bring you the Chalice of Saint Patrick and Saint Columba."

The clerics reached into the chest and raised it for the cameras to project onto screens around the world. There was not a sound from the press or the two hundred guests in the hall as they took in the scene. Then, as if choreographed, everyone stood and applauded. The clerics placed the chalice in front of the treasure chest. Cameras clicked, sending the images to all corners of the world wide web.

The Vatican's Dr. Giorgio Consalvi approached the microphone.

In slightly accented English, he began, "The Chalice of Saint Peter held twelve emeralds on its face. The emeralds were passed to disciples of the emerging Church. Several have been recovered and identified. We conclude that the emerald on this chalice is one of those twelve. Here, in front of the world, sits the Holy Chalice of St. Peter, St. Patrick, and Ireland's St. Columba."

The Prime Minister and all of us at the table rose and walked toward the clerics and dignitaries. We joined hands as the Archbishop asked the audience in the hall, at the Vatican, and around the world, to observe a moment of silence and prayer for peace and unity.

There was rustling in the hall as most of the audience began kneeling in front of their seats. The screens on the stage showed the feed from the Vatican, where thousands knelt, hugged, and cheered. The scene switched to the lawns of

Trinity, as the realization washed over the crowd that they were but footsteps from the history that was unfolding.

Collins walked back to the podium, the Prime Minister at his side.

"The *Book of Kells* will soon be reunited with the cover and will go on display for the world to see right here at Trinity." Collins smiled as he waited for the applause to end, then stepped aside for the P.M.

"The chalice will be consecrated at a Papal Mass in Dublin on March 17th, Saint Patrick's Day, with the assistance of the leaders of each major denomination in Ireland. It will then be placed in the care of a cross-denominational clerical committee, chaired by Reverend Smythe of the Presbyterian Church, Bishop Kathleen Wilson of the Church of Ireland, and the Catholic Archbishop, Michael Fahey. Following the consecration service, it will be on traveling display in each of the St. Patrick cathedrals in Ireland, starting with the Protestant and Catholic cathedrals in Armagh."

The guests on stage shook hands, talked in excited voices. In a few moments, the press portion would begin, eager correspondents vying to get on camera. I closed my eyes and saw through Aedan's as he happily watched Siobhán and the children play in the water. I opened them, stole a look at Arin, and felt a longing that I didn't know existed.

CHAPTER 50

DECEMBER 13, 2019
SHELBOURNE HOTEL, DUBLIN

After three days of an all-Ireland press tour, we continued on, from Belfast to London, Paris to Rome. The highlight was an audience with the Pope. Our families joined us, as did Collins and Dr. Garcia. The press loved it.

We had finally had a night all to ourselves, and it was glorious but short-lived. Our flight to New York would leave in a few hours.

Dr. Garcia and Padraig Collins arrived for breakfast. Collins had a large grin and a friendly handshake.

"You're all smiles. It's not like you," I said.

"Did you hear the news?" Collins asked.

"Johnson won, but you expected that."

"Yes, but that's not why I'm smiling. The Northern Ireland Unionists lost big. For the first time, they aren't a majority. The talk in the North is about the economic future with the Republic. And the Scottish National Party won. Seems they want to stay in the E.U. but say goodbye to England. The future is bright. It worked, Cián, in large part thanks to you."

The bedroom door opened, and Arin stepped into the living room. She wore a gray cashmere sweater that clung to her athletic body, and the tightest black jeans I'd ever seen, more painted on than worn. Her hair had taken on even more curls. I'd seen her every day for the last several weeks, but I was still overwhelmed. Apparently, so was Collins.

Garcia saw us jaw-dropped and said, "Calm down, boys." Turning to Arin, she continued, "Damned genetics. They can't help but drool. But my dear, if I weren't your adopted grandmother but a young stud like Key, I'd be doing the same. You look particularly beautiful today."

"Thanks, I needed to hear that,' Arin said, giving us a model pose. "After a month of muffins and breads, I wasn't sure I would fit in this."

The bell rang again—room service. A cart was rolled in, the food arranged as a small buffet—fried eggs, bacon, bangers, brown bread, fresh butter, a bowl of yogurt beside a bowl of berries. I poured the coffee. We sat, Collins wasting no time on small talk.

"Sylvia and I want you to think about something. You're both now the face of Futuro Biologics. Since the press event, the company has been overwhelmed with orders of the DNA kit. There are going to be hundreds if not thousands of stories like yours that lead to important discoveries and knowledge."

Dr. Garcia took over.

"We would like you to work with the company. You would decide which of the people to follow and guide them into their story, much like Arin helped guide you, Key."

"Sylvia, you know what my mother is hoping for," Arin responded.

"I do, and her dream is vital for Jamaica. I wouldn't want to lead you from it, but I never believed it was your dream for you. You are a gifted anthropologist, Arin. This would give you a front-row seat into one of the biggest sea changes in human evolution. And you, Key, are a gifted detective. You would still be a detective, but you would investigate Aedan-like stories of people from around the world. Who but you two are better suited?"

I put my elbows on the table and leaned in toward our guests.

"There's only one problem." I looked at Dr. Garcia, a woman of greatness. And Collins. Both of colossal will and wonder and flaws. Two people of consequence. "I don't trust either of you."

Dr. Garcia bit her lip and sat back in her chair. Collins slapped me on the shoulder.

"You had me worried, Cián," he said. " I'm happy you don't trust me. It shows you have some balls. In my defense, I've shown you my cards in the hope of earning your trust."

"Trust me or not, you know that a greater good has happened and will continue to happen," Garcia added. "What I am about to say is something that you can trust. I'm an old woman. I've witnessed a great deal of life. And this I can tell you both: I have never seen two people more in love. Maybe you haven't used those words yet, but it's obvious to me. You have been drawn together by the fates. You have made history together. Why stop now?"

Arin squeezed my leg. I returned the squeeze.

"We still have to get through the press trips to New York, Philly, then Jamaica," Arin said. "We'll catch our breath over Christmas and let you know."

Arin put her hand on her mentor's and gave a little tap. Dr. Garcia looked at her and smiled, letting out a small sigh of relief.

Over breakfast, Collins updated us on the political situation in Northern Ireland and on the preparations for the papal event on Saint Patrick's Day. "It's only three months away, a short time for a major event like this. Speaking of events,

Sylvia and I have a meeting with architects for the new Futuro facilities."

As we were saying our farewells, Collins said to Arin, "I want you to know that I enjoyed meeting your mother at the press event. She's an amazing woman. We spent some time talking at the reception. I asked if I could see her again. She agreed."

Arin shrugged her shoulders. I watched a shadow cross her face. I was unable to determine if she was happy or unhappy about this.

"Two adults, not sure what to say." Arin looked at him quizzically.

"I just wanted you to know." Collins opened the door to leave. "Safe travels to New York. I'll be following the news."

Dr. Garcia held the door open as Collins walked through. "Padraig, I need a minute. I'll meet you in the lobby."

She let the door close. Her normal upbeat and confident energy was replaced by a serious demeanor. "I owe you both an explanation," she took Arin's hand, "and an apology."

Arin looked kindly at her mentor.

"Arin, you know I love your family. Padraig has information that could hurt all of you. He offered to forget it if, in exchange, Joseph and I helped him find the treasure. As you know, he invested two hundred million dollars. The good we'll be able to do with that money is ..." She paused, then tilted her head to me. "The good that has already been done by you finding the treasure."

I let her words linger. "Key, I would never have given you anything that would harm you. But I've harmed your trust," turning to Arin, "and yours."

She held Arin's eyes with hers. "Padraig talks about his need for forgiveness. It helped me remember that he's not alone." She reached her hand to Arin's face. Arin leaned toward her, meeting her hand as Garcia gently touched her cheek.

Arin took her hand, kissed it, and held it. "You always taught me that none of us are getting out alive. You said, 'When you go, go empty, leave it all, give nothing to the grave but dust.'"

Those words penetrated. I almost went to my grave but a few weeks ago. I looked longingly at Arin.

"You, Momma Sylvia, when you go, you will go empty. And you will go loved."

I wondered if the same would be said about me.

CHAPTER 51

S eated on the Murphy family jet to Kingston, I opened my
passport out of curiosity. November 21st was the day
that I flew to Jamaica and met Arin. Today was December
20th. If I were told I had met her ten months ago, I would
have believed it. I looked at Arin and put my arm around her.
She leaned against me. I sensed she'd be asleep in a moment,
and I hoped to follow quickly.

Like the first trip, I had no idea what to expect. Our press
team was seated in the front, making notes and preparing for
the initial press conference. It would take place at the airport
shortly after landing. The following day we were booked for
TV interviews, not just for Jamaican TV but also for outlets
from the other islands. On Sunday, there would be a ceremony with the Prime Minister at Emancipation Park,
followed by a reception at the Pegasus Hotel. Joyce had been
working to make this a Murphy family conquest.

I had faded in and out of sleep and enjoyed having Arin
resting in my arms. I was looking forward to a peaceful break

over Christmas. Some snorkeling, boating, time to play out of the spotlight we'd been living in. Time to get to know each other outside of the turbulence that has been the past month. At forty-five minutes to landing, I brushed her hair with my fingers, gently waking her. We took turns in the bathroom to freshen and change.

Our press team kept the conference to a merciful thirty minutes. Arin mingled with the Jamaican reporters, and I found privacy just in time. I could now anticipate when a memory would begin, the swirl of images giving me a few seconds warning. It lasted but a few seconds: *Aedan and his friends knelt before the treasure chest in Scotland before loading it on the boat.*

I could feel their sense of the sacred and profound.

I went back to Arin and a team of public officials, all beaming that they were part of the entourage. They excitedly led us to the arrival hall.

The doors opened and applause filled the airport. Hundreds of people, young and old, waving the Jamaican flag, greeted us. Two schoolchildren with bouquets were ushered to us and handed us the flowers. A stately man walked up to Arin, and I heard her say, "Mr. Governor-General, it's good to see you."

The cameras rolled; the Governor seized the moment to give a speech welcoming home Jamaica's favorite daughter. In the din of the airport, I recalled the memory I'd just experienced. This same one had visited me a dozen times. I sensed it was still trying to tell me something. I concentrated, trying not to skip over any detail.

"Son of a bitch," I said, as softly as I could, though I wanted to scream it.

Arin tugged on my sports coat, trying to be subtle.

"What's wrong?"

"I missed something."

"What?" she whispered.

"When Aedan was praying at the treasure chest, the chest was open. He was staring in as he prayed. There were two objects in there. The Chalice and something else."

"You're certain?"

I dropped my head, my chin nearly resting on my chest, trying to recall the details. I heard the buzz of excited voices around us and forced them out.

"I'm certain that Aedan had seen two objects. It hadn't been open in twelve hundred years until the night that we opened it. It was only at the house for about thirty minutes before we got back from the dock. The only person that was in the house before us was Collins. He couldn't have been there more than a minute before we arrived."

Applause broke out when the Governor called Arin a national hero. She waved to the crowd and said a few words. The Governor walked us to the exit doors, where another crowd waited outside, more press with cameras. A rope line kept everyone on one side or the other, giving us a corridor leading to our awaiting limo, the rear door open.

A large SUV stopped at the far side of our limo. Through the open sunroof, a head emerged. I grabbed Arin and pushed her to the ground a nanosecond before the bullet grazed my shoulder.

All I could do was put my body over Arin and hope like hell that our world wasn't about to end. The first Aedan memory I ever had rushed into my brain: the Viking leaping the wall, the slaughter that ensued in Iona, Aedan running to the escape tunnel. I had to get us out of here.

I stood, lifting Arin with me. The rear door of the limo was still open. She grabbed my hand, and we shoved our way toward it as a phalanx of security guards surrounded us.

Sirens wailed, getting closer. A police escort had lined up, and the limo driver followed them out of the airport.

———

My wound was minor, a flesh wound, but my worry was off the chart. What the hell just happened? We had stepped off the plane into a tropical paradise and exited the airport into a tropical hell.

The doctor assured me there was no damage but that it would hurt for a few days. Joyce entered the room the moment the doctor cleared me. We hadn't seen her since our audience with the Pope.

Arin hugged and kissed her mother.

"Key thinks they were aiming at me."

She stole a glance at me then held Arin by her shoulders.

"Thank you," Joyce said to me, "I saw what you did."

While Joyce and Arin continued talking, I retreated to a quiet corner and called my mom. She answered quickly.

"I'm sitting here in a panic. Are you and Arin safe?"

"We're fine. Freaked out but fine. I'm not going to stay on. The authorities are moving us to the hotel. Just wanted to let you know we're good. I'll call you soon." I ended the call.

"Where is Noel?" Arin asked her mother. Noel King's face flashed before me, bloodied in the struggle with Buck and Ben.

"Good question. He disappeared after that stunt he pulled in Ireland."

"I need you to find him."

"What do you need him for?"

"Unfinished business."

As we exited the exam room a group of heavily armed officers met us in the hallway and escorted us to the limo. One thing the authorities in Jamaica are not is subtle. There were at least ten police cars and seven motorcycles in the entourage, sirens blaring, lights blinking. I had the impression that they were giddy with excitement. Not much international news happened here, and they were putting on a show. Police had secured the driveway into the Pegasus—news vans visible, reporters waiting by the door, the Chief of Police keeping them busy as we arrived.

We were escorted into the lobby by the police, the TV crews moving with us. Staff and guests had gathered, and we were met by applause and kind faces. Joyce said a few words. Arin answered a few questions. A reporter turned to me.

"In light of today's events, will you move the celebration from Emancipation Park indoors?"

"Hell no. Jamaicans don't scare easy." I nodded to Arin and Joyce. "I figure I'm now an honorary Jamaican." The applause was loud and raucous. The people in the lobby tried to press forward to shake hands, and several of the older women made me lean over so they could kiss me on the cheek.

We finally moved on to the elevator and exited on the sixteenth floor.

The hotel manager showed us to the Liguanea Suite, telling us proudly that this was where President Obama once stayed. Elegant florals covered the wallpaper, and dark wood furniture empowered the space. A small round table held a tray of some of the appetizers I had tried weeks ago. An opened bottle of white wine was sweating in an ice bucket, and a bottle of Cabernet sat at the ready. And I was ready.

But as I walked to the food, my phone buzzed with a text.

If we wanted you dead, you'd be dead.

Arin took the phone from my hand. Her face went pale. She ushered the manager out of the room as fast as possible. I noted that two policemen had been stationed in the hall. When she closed the door, Joyce spoke first.

"What is it?"

"Let's get away from the door," I said, and moved us to the dining area of the suite, stopping to pour a Chardonnay for Arin.

Arin handed her mother the phone, and after Joyce read the message aloud she just sat and stared at her hands for a moment. "Any idea who sent this?"

Arin and I both shook our heads. My phone rang. I reached in front of Joyce to retrieve it. It was Buck.

"Little brother, you've become a shit magnet. You and Arin okay?"

"Yeah," I said while walking into the bedroom and closing the door.

"I have Ben on with me. Can you talk?"

"Yes, I'm in the hotel suite with Arin and her mom. I stepped away."

"Cián," said Ben, "Buck and I have been analyzing the video from the news. In conclusion, they were aiming at your arm. They could have easily made a kill shot."

"I know. Three minutes ago I received this text: *If we wanted you dead, you'd be dead.*"

Buck whistled. "Holy shit, you remember the night of the raid, the dreadlocks guy said, 'When we want you dead, you'll be dead.'"

"Yeah, when I saw the text, his words came blazing back." I could feel stress hormones releasing in my body; my stomach fluttered in their presence.

"Hold on. It's the first I'm hearing this," Ben said. "Details."

Buck and I recounted the scene in Philly some six weeks ago when I was captured in the van and almost shot.

"There's a connection between the drug raid and Jamaica. And possibly the people who tried to take the book from you in Philly, yes?

Buck and I made guttural sounds into the phone. "And I thought Padraig Collins was complicated," Buck added.

. . .

"Do we stay in Jamaica, or do we get the hell out of here?" I felt myself taking a deep breath, wiping sweat from my forehead in this air-conditioned room.

"Are you safe there? Good security?" Buck asked.

"We're the biggest thing to happen, news-wise. The authorities know the world is watching, so they are all over it."

"Stay," Ben said. "They are playing a psychological game. You'll hear from them soon. You want me on a plane?"

"No, it's almost Christmas. Let's wait to see if they contact me again." My heart pounded a bit. "But guys, I could change my mind. It would be great if you were on standby."

"Screw that," Buck said. "Your parents will never forgive me if something happens to you and I'm not there. I already took off for Christmas week."

"Buck's right. Kate and I will get there ASAP. Buck, we'll connect Dublin to Philly and get on the same flight."

CHAPTER 52

December 22, 2019
Emancipation Park

Yesterday, Arin, Joyce, and I had walked to the park after the press conference, a police escort surrounding us. A large sculpture of a man and a woman in all of their naked glory stood at the opening, rising from slavery to freedom, shackles broken. Arin told me that some three hundred thousand people had been enslaved in Jamaica. Staring at these bold and beautiful figures, I glanced at Arin and Joyce, then at the people surrounding us—all black but for a few of the foreign press—and I thought of their ancestors and what they had endured creating a country of their own.

From my hotel window, I could see today's police presence was far from subtle, but I suspected that the attendees felt comfort in that. I did.

Arin had spent time this morning with her mother. She entered the suite and joined me at the window, but she seemed disconcerted, her eyes red.

I touched her chin to lift her face to me.

"What's up?"

"Just a little sad."

"Missing your father?"

Arin gave a distracted nod and pointed to the growing crowd below. "You made a challenge to them when you said Jamaicans don't scare easy. You'll see. There will be thousands."

"It's the Sunday before Christmas. I'm surprised."

"Normally, Jamaicans would be drinking sorrel with friends and eating rum cake. But there's nothing normal about this Sunday before Christmas."

She pointed to the newspapers on the side table by the couch.

"You saw the headlines yesterday. Every newspaper and newscaster on the island is urging everyone to show the world that Jamaica supports its own." Arin laughed for a moment. "Trust me, by Friday night every Jamaican around the world was saying, 'Mon, dat white boy okay. See 'im protek dat yardie girl? Much respeck.'"

"It's not over, Arin. We could have been killed." Something flashed on her face. Anger? Fear? I let it go.

"Do you know where Ian Fleming wrote the James Bond books?"

"No idea," I answered.

Arin pointed out the window. "Just over an hour away, on the north coast. A reporter said yesterday that you are the new James Bond and even better looking than all of them. I agree."

"I don't want to be the new James Bond."

"Why not? He always gets the girl." Arin put her arms around my waist.

"But he never keeps her." I placed my hands on Arin's shoulders. "I don't want to lose you. Ever."

Arin said nothing, just looked at me, pulling me into her,

her lips softly caressing my own, not fully kissing, more like breathing into each other. I found the salty taste of tears on her lips and looked at her. She began to tremble slightly.

"The panic I had when you were shot." She brushed my lips with hers again, sensual and mysterious. "I know we need to talk. Let's get past this and catch our breath over the next few days."

Arin's phone buzzed, and we both tensed at the sound. She read it to me.

"Five minutes." She checked herself in a mirror. "My mother is downstairs with the Prime Minister and some other dignitaries."

"Arin, they're going to text me right in the middle of the event."

"How do you know?"

"It's what I would do if I were them."

———

Twelve of us sat on the makeshift stage. Arin told me that her mother culled the list of twenty-three that were vying for a spot. The Prime Minister, Arin, Joyce, and I were at a table, pitchers of water and iced tea in front of us. The Catholic and Anglican archbishops sat across the stage, along with the opposition-party leader and other big shots that I couldn't remember. I tried to listen to the speeches. I caught pieces of the Prime Minister's words, emphasizing the need to understand where we come from and create an inclusive culture.

My mind raced in a thousand directions. Collins's PR team had left for Ireland in time for Christmas. It would soon be my turn to give a speech, but I had no idea what to say. And I was the only white guy. Panic rose. I was aware that

Arin was introduced. I tried to focus, but all I could see was me pushing her to the ground before the bullet struck, followed by her running up the ramp to me after she escaped Jimmy Downey. The loop played over and over. I wanted to get the hell out of there.

Penetrating the fog of my brain came a shout from the audience to Arin.

"Duh yuh luv di white bwoy?"

My stomach churned and tightened. Arin stopped cold, said nothing, turned to look at me, and waved me to her side. As I stood with her, knowing millions were watching from their TVs around the world, I felt like I was going to throw up. Finally, Arin reached her arms around my waist. She said, just loud enough for the microphone, "Yes."

My heart pounded.

The crowd yelled and applauded. Then, a woman near the stage let out loud, "Whatcha waitin for, James Bond? Kiss di girl."

So I kissed her. I felt a million neurons explode in my brain, and a clarity and calm settle over me. In that moment, everything slowed. We had been living our life in public for the past nineteen days. Every private corner of my life had gone on display: the little prodigy kid, the nearly suicidal athlete, Tanya and drugs, and reporters digging into my non-existent love life. But this moment, a declaration of love, I wanted just for us.

I whispered to her, "I'm going to sing you a Perry Como love song tonight."

Arin released our embrace and allowed her devilish smile to make an appearance. She was laughing as she took the microphone. She tried to stop, but failed; the audience was picking up on her contagious laugh. Finally, she managed, "And now, to tell you his story, my James Bond, Key Murphy."

. . .

As the applause receded, I could hear my pulse in my ears, the thumping of blood coursing around my body. I flashed to the moment that I was in Arin's office for the first time, when I was looking at Jerome Pinter's Eagles Jersey. I had turned, seen her, and felt my world change.

I looked out at the crowd, hoping I could find some poetic and inspirational line to drop.

"I keep hearing I'm the new James Bond. But look at me—do I look like James Bond? I look like vanilla ice cream." I pointed to my ginger hair. "With a cherry on top."

Thankfully, people got the joke.

"In a few moments, I'll tell you about Aedan, the ancestor whose memories I see, and about the clues from Mack Murphy and the promise that Fergus Murphy made here in Jamaica. When I first met Joyce Murphy, she told me that when we succeeded in our mission she wanted recognition of the Jamaican people, for the world to see your beauty, your heart, your strength. And now I understand why." I pointed to Joyce and waited for the applause to fade.

Taking Arin's hand, I said, "Before I tell you this amazing story, you and everyone around the world saw what happened Friday. Someone shot at Arin and me. Later that night, they texted my phone with the message: *If we wanted you dead, you'd be dead.*"

The response from the audience was a collective gasp. Then I heard defiant grumbles throughout the crowd.

"I'm not the new James Bond." I nodded my head to Arin. "But she is, and together we are going to find you and kick your ass."

The crowd went wild. Just as I expected, my phone buzzed.

The message read, *Good Luck.*

A moment later, a second text. *You wouldn't want Arin ending up like Tanya.*

Arin saw the text and shot a frightened look toward her mother. Marley sang in my head, "Don't worry about a thing, 'Cause every little thing gonna be alright." And I thought: not this time, Bob. Not this time.

CHAPTER 53

DECEMBER 22, 2019
PEGASUS HOTEL RECEPTION GARDEN

F or Jamaicans, the winter afternoon temperature was a chilly seventy-nine degrees. For me, it felt like summer. The political and business elite had surrounded us, wanting to be regaled by tales of my ancestral memories and our search for the treasures. The reception was in the gardens used for weddings, the broad leaves of fan palms providing some cover from the sun.

Arin leaned into me and led me a few feet from any listener.

"We have to smile our way through the reception, but we need to get away as soon as possible. There are some things I need to tell you."

Palm trees swayed lightly in a gentle breeze. Birds of Paradise showed off their tropical splendor, and my rum punch went down easy. I could read that Arin wanted to get away, fast. But fast, it seemed, was not the Jamaican way.

Arin had instructed me that in a country like Jamaica, where the elite was small in number, competition and envy are the curse of the wealthy. She explained that eighty percent of the elite would hate her for her newfound celebrity. Twenty percent would celebrate it. One hundred percent would try to bask in it, hoping that their photos with her or me would end up in newspapers and magazines.

Finally, Arin separated us into a quiet corner.

"We need to talk."

"How about you talk, and I listen?"

Her eyes welled, face strained.

"I'm afraid if I talk now, I'll lose it. Let's say goodbye and go to the room. We need privacy."

———

I opened the door to our suite. Arin pushed by me, seeming to want to cower in the corner.

"You're scaring me." I put my hands together. "Please."

She tried to take a calming breath.

"I'm afraid that you'll want nothing to do with me or my family." She wiped her eyes.

I noticed that the suite was now full of flowers, I assume sent by well-wishers while we were at the reception. A large centerpiece dominated the dining table. Arin stood in front of it. I gently placed my palm on her face. She rested her hand on mine and forced herself to look me in the eye.

"When I talked to my mother before the rally, she said something, inadvertently, that alarmed me. I confronted her about it."

I kept my hand on her face and felt a few tears fall on my skin.

"She was responsible for you being shot on Friday."

My breath escaped. My hand didn't move away, but my eyes must have clouded and betrayed my confusion.

"It was supposed to be a near miss. She confessed that she did it to make us mythical, that the press would have forgotten about us before the New Year. But being shot at elevates us to near martyrdom."

Arin took my hand. "I'm sorry. I'm so ashamed. Please don't be mad at me."

"Why would I be mad at you?" I stammered. "But your mother is nuts."

"That's not all." She put her head down, unable to look at me. "I believe she was in on it with Joseph in Philly and Ireland. I told them both to come to the room. They should be here any minute."

Viewing my ancestors' memories seemed almost normal in comparison to this news. I couldn't help but wonder if the entire family was mentally ill. I had met Arin one month prior, and we'd been at each other's side almost every moment since. The intensity of our past month made it feel as if we'd been together a year, but at the sound of the door buzzer, the reality hit me hard: we hardly knew each other.

Arin opened the door and Joyce walked in, stern, confident, not an ounce of apology in her. Joseph followed, a tall, handsome man, dark-skinned like his mother, so different from Arin's light brown skin and Irish features like her father.

"I assume that you told him?" Joyce addressed Arin as if I wasn't in the room. She strode to the dining table and laid her purse on it, admiring the floral arrangement as if that was the purpose of her visit.

My eyes bore into Joyce. I held the phone in front of her; the text threatening Arin opened for her to read.

"Explain this," I demanded.

Joyce bridled at my tone, unused to being spoken to like that.

I turned to Joseph, who was leaning against the wall, and held the text message to him.

"You too."

"Who the fuck are you to talk to us like that?"

"I'm the guy you had someone shoot."

"What are you talking about? I had nothing to do with that," he protested. We all focused on Joyce, Joseph speaking first. "That was you?"

Joyce maintained her regal calm, her short gray braids an inch above her shoulders, her dark eyes fixed somewhere in a faraway place.

"No harm was to come. We will use the fame that has followed for good." She moved to the side of the couch and placed her hand on the back of it.

The sadness on Arin's face broke my heart. I brushed her shoulder with my fingertips.

"Do you know who Tanya was?" I asked Joyce, her eyes glassy, trance-like. "I asked you a question." My voice rose. I turned to Joseph. He shook his head. "She was my best friend, my little sister. I put her drug dealers in jail. They killed her."

I wanted to scream at their silence.

"Did you hear me?" I paced between Joseph and Joyce. "They killed her. And now their bosses are threatening Arin. Your daughter, your sister." The remembrance of Aedan commanding Tomás to protect Siobhán flashed before me. "Take a seat. You're going to tell me who they are and where to find them."

Joyce flicked her hand, "Go home, Key. You are out of your element here."

"Sit down, both of you," Arin commanded as she sat on the couch, patting the seat next to her.

Joyce stood over her, rigid, the fingers on her left hand flexing. "Falling in love with a cop was not part of the plan."

"He might want nothing to do with me after seeing what a nightmare of a family I have," Arin's voice strained.

"Arin, I …" Joseph stopped and turned toward the window, shaking his head.

"You sent men to take Mack's treasure from us in Philly. Armed men. Who did you arrange that with?"

Joseph opened a bottle of water that he retrieved from the mahogany credenza.

"I apologized to Arin. I explained what happened to her."

I was in interrogation mode, all bad cop. "I want to hear it from you."

Joseph gestured to Arin to come to his rescue. She regarded him coldly.

"Don't do that, Joseph. I want answers," I said.

Finally, he looked my way, a sideways glance, his back mostly to me. "I have a contact in Queens. When I need something extra, I call him."

I grabbed the edge of the chair next to me and steadied myself. Queens. The memory of the gun rising, the trigger almost squeezed, the words, "I'm coming for yuh, bwoy."

"What's his name?" I demanded.

Joseph took a quick glance at his mother, who stood next to the couch a few feet away.

"He goes by Rabbit. To me, anyway. Guys like him probably have a dozen names. That's all I know."

"Jamaican?"

"Maybe. I don't talk to him directly. His reach is throughout the Caribbean, including the diaspora." Joseph shook his head. "I don't want to know his real name. These are dangerous people."

I moved quickly into his space, feeling his breath on my skin. He stumbled back an inch or two.

"Why did you send Noel King to Dublin?"

"What?"

"You sent him to steal the chalice, trying to salvage your deal with Collins."

Joseph looked at me like I was crazy.

"I have no idea what you are talking about."

"We had nothing to do with Dublin," Joyce added.

I studied Joyce as she sat on the arm of the couch, hovering slightly above Arin. Behind her youthful figure and air of command stood— what? What kind of person would have me shot as a publicity stunt? A mirror on the wall behind the couch displayed our tableau: mother and daughter seated, Joseph pacing behind me. And me, the interloper, colliding with a wealthy and powerful family.

"Joseph, you called Rabbit for Philly?" I confirmed.

"I'm not proud of it," he said to Arin, not to me.

"Joyce, who did you call to shoot me?" She sat silent. "You seem proud of that," I pressed. "Mythical, right? You made us mythical. Now they've threatened to kill your daughter."

Joyce, silent, impenetrable, interlaced her fingers yet betrayed nothing behind her practiced resolve.

Arin's face contorted into an angry scowl.

"Mother, answer him, goddammit."

Joyce brushed the fold of her pants.

"Rabbit," she answered, barely above a whisper. "But he's on the middle rung. The people on top are the dangerous ones. They sent a marksman. That's why Key has only a flesh wound."

Her face jutted forward. "It was never supposed to go this far. But I'm not sorry for what I did." The muscles in her forehead and arms and fingers were taut. "You talk a good game, Arin. The anthropologist who wants to change the world, do big things—but you are weak. Nothing changes because you want it to. It changes because you make it change. I, me ..." She slapped her hand to her chest. "I have given you a platform. You are heroes and near martyrs. Stop whining and do something with it."

Arin stared blankly, her arms folded around her, fingers splayed on each side like the straps of a straitjacket.

Joyce closed the space between us, hands on her hips, the pleasure of triumph in her grin.

"Let's be honest, Key. You were just a do-gooder soon-to-be cop. You helped people. That's commendable. But you would have been chasing your tail all over Philadelphia for the rest of your life."

I started to respond, but she put her hand up.

"Thanks to Dr. Garcia, your memories awakened. Thanks to Collins, you found the treasures. And thanks to me, no one will ever forget you. So man up."

There was too much truth in her words, but I needed to slow this down.

"Excellent deflection. You're quite skilled at it." I stared back at her, hard. "One little problem, Joyce. They've threatened your daughter. And I'm going to find them."

There was a brief moment of warmth in her eyes, but she recovered.

"I had no idea that you had fucked with these people in the past. This is on you, not us. I'll protect Arin." Joyce turned to her daughter. "Let's go. It seems that Key has tired of us."

"I've tired of *you*," I said directly to Joyce, "but I need you back here tomorrow. Buck, Ben, and Kate will be here, and you're going to help us find these people." I walked to the door and held it open.

"I've made you a hero." Joyce tapped me with her purse as she left the room. "Don't waste it."

Joseph seemed wordless but turned to Arin.

"I'm truly sorry."

He put his hand out to me. I didn't take it.

"Be here tomorrow," I said, closing the door behind him.

"I know we need to talk, but I have to collect my thoughts," I said to Arin, brushing past her.

I changed into my swim trunks and grabbed my goggles. When I walked out the door, Arin was still on the couch, her knees up on her chest, arms wrapped around them, seeming somewhere between shocked and dejected. I felt like an asshole leaving her there like that, but if I'd stayed, I probably would have said the wrong thing.

———

The lights on the pool deck had been dimmed, allowing the stars to show off. Eddy, the bartender I remembered from weeks ago, was closing up. He waved a Red Stripe at me, so I walked over to the bar.

"You a hero now, Mr. Key." His smile made me forget the insanity that I just experienced, at least for a moment.

"Thanks, Eddy." I raised my beer to him and then pictured Arin sitting on the pool deck, Abbey Road T-shirt, Converse sneakers, so alive with curiosity about my ancestral memories.

I stood at the far edge of the pool deck where there was less light and looked up at the stars. My mind drifted back to a few weeks earlier, sitting next to Arin at my parents' house in Ireland, a firepit defending us against the cold, stars playing in the North Atlantic sky. Me taking her in, her black curls framing her intoxicating face. She had placed my hand on her breasts, her lips drawing me into an ecstatic moment. Making love. Tender, hungry, passionate love.

Arin had placed her hand on mine at the Lia Fáil, the Stone of Destiny. I recalled the angelic look on her face and felt I could cry from the sheer happiness she brought me. And my mother's words, as emphatic as anything she has ever said to me: 'She's special, Key. Don't you dare let her go.' I feared she was letting me go.

I dialed Arin's cell phone.

"Hi." She had clearly been crying.

"Did you bring a bathing suit?"

"The pool is closed," she answered, more smile in her voice.

"It seems that nothing around here is closed for Arin Murphy. Especially me."

CHAPTER 54

The door to the pool deck opened, and Arin emerged in a white Terry bathrobe. Eddy had gone home. It was just us. Arin rushed to me and began to apologize for her family. I put my finger over her lips and gently folded her into me, standing in a quiet embrace. She began to cry, and I continued to hold her. Tanya had done that for me. When I had fallen into a deep depression after college, people had tried to cheer me up, as if jabbering endlessly was therapy. But Tanya just sat quietly, and I was grateful for her silence.

We stood like that for ten minutes, Arin's tears finally subsiding.

"I've never met a man who hasn't told me not to cry." She reached her hand to my face and brushed away my own tear, then took my hands in hers. "We good?"

"I don't know. Are we?" I answered.

Arin leaned back, creating some separation. "What do you mean?" Her voice pitched higher.

Oh God, please don't let me screw this up. "You seem tentative lately, uncertain." I held her shoulders. "About us."

She buried her face in my chest for a moment, then looked up at me. "I feel like a slow-motion train wreck. I have since Dublin. And now, with you being shot, the insanity from my own mother, the threats." Arin's lip began to tremble, more tears fell, she tried to stifle her sob. "I'm all jumbled inside, Key. But you are the only person I've ever felt safe being jumbled with. So no, I'm not uncertain."

My muscles started to relax, but the thought of the threatening text made me tighten. "Your mother is crazy, but she's not completely wrong. We have a lot to talk about."

"Let's talk in the morning. We need a moment to play." Arin let the bathrobe drop to the ground. A skimpy bright red bikini greeted me. She was as astonishing as the first time I laid eyes on her. Arin took my hand, walked to the pool, jumped in and popped up, her ringlets clinging to her face.

I walked the pool deck to the deep end. Before diving in, my eye caught something. I looked to my right, to the chair that Jimmy Downey had sat in just a few weeks ago. I shook my head to get rid of him and dove, swimming to the shallow end, where Arin stood. I popped up and slapped the surface of the water so hard it hurt my hand. Arin pulled back at my violent gesture.

"Your mother and brother were not lying about Noel King in Dublin."

She pushed her head forward, her mouth open.

"What do you mean?"

I smacked my palm to my head. "Freaking obvious," I muttered. "As head of security, would he be aware of your travels?"

"Generally. What are you getting at?"

"He would have known when I was going to arrive in Kingston. He escorted us to Philly. He knew our flight plan to Dublin."

Arin started to speak, stopped, started again. No words came out.

I turned in the water, recalling the images of the night at Tara, letting them wash over me.

"I'm going to fucking kill him."

Arin's eyes widened. "Who."

"Collins."

I returned my focus to Arin.

"That night in Tara, Downey told me to drop you and Ben and go to the house. When I arrived at the house, I received a call. It wasn't Downey. I was told to secure the treasure in the house and then hurry to the dock." My knuckles tapped against my jaw. "King was at the house, waiting for me to leave. He took the second object. He's been working for Collins."

We both stood quietly for a minute. Arin shivered, the night air chilling her wet skin. I hugged her close.

"The people who sent the text. Do you think they're connected?" she asked.

"Nothing would surprise me, but I don't know. And not knowing can get you killed."

"Then we need to find them and kick their ass." There was no smile in her eyes, no lightness in her voice, no bravado. Just a statement of fact.

CHAPTER 55

The ancient journal of Saint Columba sat on Padraig Collins's desk in a temperature-controlled plexiglass container. The night Noel King removed the journal from the chest, it had been transferred immediately to its caretaker as planned. For Collins, this was the real prize. The Chalice of the Saints was for uniting Ireland. The journal was for him.

Collins hired a Latin scholar to translate the document, paid him generously for his work, and double that for his silence.

Collins studied the translated words, making notes, as he had for the past two days. Over the centuries, scholars and biographers had studied and written about Columba's prophecies. Some prophecies were mundane, some profound; many of them had been documented to have occurred in their time.

St. Columba had come to Collins in his time of need and converted him from a man of violence to a man of power and peace. With Columba's guidance in his dreams and prayers, Collins was close to fulfilling his penance.

In a vivid vision, Columba had told him to find his words, left behind for the world. "They are with St. Patrick's Cup." Now he scoured the journal, searching for hints and prophesies of what was next.

His phone buzzed. His limo was ready to take him to his Christmas party. He regretted the disturbance, but this gathering was part of his plan, a cocktail party with the Who's Who of Irish politics and society. He had arranged for several Unionist movers and shakers to attend from Northern Ireland; he wanted them welcomed as equals, and he made that clear to the Dublin politicians. He was pleased that the Unionist leader, Theresa Campbell, had accepted the invitation, as had the trade minister from London, Madelynn Wilson, their husbands in tow.

Collins chose the Teeling Distillery as the venue. Their logo captured the moment: a phoenix rising from a still, symbolizing the current renaissance of Irish whiskey-making. And, soon, the rise of a united Ireland.

While his employees partied on one floor, which he would visit later, the elite gathered in the gallery, light and dark woods, elegant crystal from Ireland on display, waiters and waitresses in white shirts and bow ties conveying fine food and drink.

Collins was forty minutes into making the rounds when his Chief Information Officer, Catherine Norris, slid beside him. Collins knew from the moment he saw her enter the gallery that something was up. He made a polite separation from his guests and walked to a quiet corner.

"The Clontarf Team has been following some troubling chatter coming out of China. Lihua was able to track a lead. It took her to the Center for Disease Control in the U.S. They issued an intelligence report to their State Department. The

Chinese are covering up a viral outbreak that is potentially bigger than SARS. There are at least fifty dead."

"Where in China?" Collins asked. Scientists and intelligence officers had been warning of a pandemic for years. To them, there was no if, only when. Monitoring outbreaks has been a priority for the Clontarf Team. Collins was keenly aware that a pandemic could scuttle the best-laid plans of men and gods. Resources would move to mitigate it, and a race for vaccines would ensue. There would be disruption everywhere. Collins needed to know where the money was going and get there first.

"A place called Wuhan."

"What else do we know?"

"Our contact in Beijing told us there was an international environmental conference in Wuhan a week ago. There were attendees from all over the world."

Collins sensed what came next.

"Yes, there were three from Ireland," she responded.

As a major shareholder in Futuro Biologics, he knew in his gut that DNA test sales would drop, precipitously, if there were a pandemic. Billions of dollars would shift to mitigation and prevention. He needed to get Futuro ready.

Collins stared off, his thoughts transported to the words in the journal:

"I fear for the future of our generations to come. There will always be trials and tribulations. It is the way of the world and the way of God's reckoning and setting things right. I see a great cleansing, from which no man or woman is safe. It will storm from the East to the West, from the West to the South, from the South to the hidden corners of the world. It will be known as The Crown."

. . .

"Look up the translation of 'crown' to Latin," Collins commanded.

Catherine lifted her phone and entered the search. "In Latin, it's translated as *corona*."

CHAPTER 56

8 Months Ago
Manhattan

Her nails dug into his back. Her moans driving him to thrust harder. The sex, as usual, animalistic and hungry. He wondered for a moment if he could restrain his release, not wanting to stop until she was sated. He found her nipples with his teeth, giving them small bites, playing the edge of pain and passion. Her breathing sharpened and grew more intense, his thrusts, slower, deeper, stronger until she cried out in a primal mix that said ecstasy, that moment when all burden was released, if only for a fragment of time.

He rolled onto his side, his eyes taking in this magnificent woman, her satisfaction obvious as she lay there for several minutes of quiet. Finally, she opened her eyes and smiled.

"Damn, you know how to fuck me."

Joyce Murphy touched her lover on the face. Padraig Collins kissed her hand and glowed from the most addictive compliment a man can get, especially a man about to turn sixty-one. He watched Joyce roll off the bed and head to the shower. Like the other times, they would discuss business over dinner, enjoying the wine and cognac, and slip back into bed for another, less intense, round of lovemaking. It felt good to have sex like a hormone-driven teen. He looked at the clock: 4.30 on a Sunday afternoon, a concession to age. He laughed. They'd probably be asleep before 8.30.

Joyce stood by the window in Padraig's apartment over-looking Central Park, content in his arms, the winter days numbered. Padraig broke away for a moment and returned with a snifter of deep golden cognac, which they shared. He reflected on the fact that he was attracted to women that didn't need him. Joyce was rich; he was richer, but a level playing field, nonetheless. Women that need you were complicated. He preferred strength. Padraig was all about simplicity, economy of motion, the tiger lying in wait for the wounded prey. Joyce was a tigress. This was a woman to love and respect.

She took a sip and then slid his arm over her shoulder. "Any questions about my proposal?"

Collins grew aroused at the gesture.

"I have studied every corner of Dr. Garcia's company and her research. It's completely amazing."

"Padraig, before my husband died, I made a vow to fulfill his dream. I already told you this. If we can find what Mack hid, and it helps you fulfill your dream of uniting Ireland, then we'll have made history."

Squeezing his hand, she added, "Follow my plan, and you and I will own the controlling interest in Futuro. Dr. Garcia is growing old, and we'll take good care of her and her legacy. The key to doing that lies with my son. He needs to be taught a lesson. Joseph will take over the business one day, but he has grown arrogant and petty as he feels his power grow."

Joyce walked to the table where the wines were waiting for her. She poured an elegant and very expensive Bordeaux for both of them.

"Here's how you bend him. When he was eighteen, he

made a mistake. It could have come back to destroy our family. Someone died, and Joseph never paid the price. I made sure of that. From what I understand, my darling, you can relate. You made similar mistakes when you were young. Do you understand, Padraig?"

Joyce kissed his lips with unexpected passion. Collins returned the kiss, the passion. He wrapped his hands around her ass and pulled her tightly in to him.

"I can love you in ways that you can't yet imagine, but never threaten me again. Ever."

"If we control Futuro, then we control the future and the past." She took him by the hand and headed to the bedroom. "I don't make threats, darling. Like you, I make deals."

CHAPTER 57

We talked past midnight, trying to purge the thoughts of her mother's actions and the threatening text, if but for a moment. The lights of Kingston had gone to sleep, while the sound of tree frogs filled the air. Tiny salamanders scurried across the pool deck. The same stars that guided the prison ships from Ireland and the slave ships from Africa stared down on us as we gazed up at them. I tightened my arms around Arin.

"You were number three."

"What?"

I smiled inwardly, recalling my mother's request.

"The day I first flew here and met you, my mother had asked me to do three things. I didn't want to do anything. I was exhausted. For six months, I searched for Tanya's killers without regard for rest. I was seconds from a bullet to my head. Then the memories started." The vision of Siobhán making love to Aedan slipped into view, and I pulled Arin even tighter.

"When my parents told me that I was the only thread to finding the treasure, I felt the crushing weight of their hopes. I told them I couldn't, not yet. I had no energy left in me."

I let my fingers slide between her curls, wet and thick and lovely.

"Mom asked me to do three things and then to decide if I was ready." I recalled the feel of the embossed leather book. "She had me read Eamon's memoir of his meeting with Mack. Then came our time with Dr. Garcia. Finally, Garcia and my mom asked me to meet Arin Murphy." I laughed at the thought of it.

"Don't do that," Arin playfully splashed the water at me. "Tell me the rest."

"I didn't know if Arin Murphy was an eighty-year-old or a ten-year-old."

I splashed her back. "I'm still not sure. I think you're both." She splashed me some more. "That was number three."

I thought I heard a noise over my shoulder. I turned protectively, imagining the ghostly outline of Jimmy Downey and feeling the inexorable pull of Aedan.

"On your mount," I ordered. My men took to their horses.

Tearlach had scouted the brigand camp. He overheard their boasts of killing the monk, my cousin, Tomás. Fifteen of my best trod their horses quietly, one mile to the encampment. My arm raised, and they dismounted. Swords, knives, arrows, and bows ready, we made up the distance on foot. The price, there's always a price when something is torn. Something must be paid before there can be renewal.

I looked up at the Irish sky, yet the outline of the Pegasus Hotel looked back at me. Two spits of land, Ireland and Jamaica, no reason at all that the angels of anything might have joined them.

Arin followed my upward gaze, then returned her eyes to meet mine. A delicate smile crossed her face. As she took a breath, I felt drawn in with the air and entered her spirit, the Druid Goddess dancing with my soul, our hearts commingling with the ancients.

"Is tú an stór, stór m'anama."

Arin pulled away, startled. "What did you say?"

"Is tú an stór, stór m'anama," I repeated. "I just heard Aedan say that to Siobhán. But I sensed he wanted me to say it to you. What does it mean?"

Arin rested her head against my chest, my heart. "You are the treasure, the treasure of my soul."

And someone has threatened to take you from me, you Arin, my spirit guide. Bringing justice to the memory of the dead was my only hope for renewal. I pray, Tanya, that I have done that for you. And now I must do it for the living.

If the barbarians don't kill us first.

––––––

Joyce sat in the Mercedes while her driver navigated the hills of New Kingston. She tried not to think about the confrontation with Arin and Key, if even for an hour, so that she could consider it with fresh thought, unclouded by emotion. She concentrated instead on Padraig. How wonderful it would be for him to surprise her and arrive in Jamaica for Christmas.

Her thoughts were interrupted by the sound of the gate lifting, the security guard nodding to her.

Joyce stepped out of the car and paused, noting the quiet, her eyes climbing the sky and taking in wisps of clouds and the sparkle of starlight. It was just as her eyes found one exceptionally bright star that the bullet struck, grazing her right thigh, collapsing her to the ground. Her cell phone lit up, casting an eerie light on her face. The text read: *If we wanted you dead, you'd be dead.*

The End

THRESHOLD

BOOK 2 IN THE KEY MURPHY THRILLER SERIES

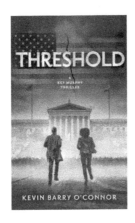

These things I know:

1. The Vice President is coming to Philadelphia.
2. Someone is going to try to kill her.
3. We have four days to stop them.

Key Murphy has been urgently summoned to Philadelphia. There is a threat to the Vice President of The United States.

That's all he knows. It's what he doesn't know that scares him:

Who made the threat? What do they have to gain? Why does someone want him involved? Is the threat real, or is someone just trying to create chaos? What the hell is he supposed to do about it?

"Fans of thrillers like the Bourne series will have a great time with Threshold." –*Readers Favorite*

———

Available for purchase on June 28th 2023!

AUTHORS NOTE

I lived and worked in Kingston, Jamaica, for several years in the 1990s. I was struck by how many of my Jamaican friends had Irish surnames. I expected English and Scottish names; after all, Jamaica had been a British colony. But Irish surnames? Ireland was also a British colony, and the Irish had little to no rights in Ireland until Independence in 1922. Most Irish had nothing: no money, no power. How did they end up in Jamaica?

There is a famous Irish song called "The Fields Of Athenry" (the home of my maternal grandmother). The opening lyrics:

> By a lonely prison wall
> I heard a young girl calling
> Michael, they have taken you away
> For you stole Trevelyan's corn
> So the young might see the morn
> Now a prison ship lies waiting in the bay.

Some of those prison ships were bound for Jamaica, where thousands of Irish worked the land as prisoners or indentured servants. As the Atlantic Slave Trade provided labor for the plantations, the prison ships were replaced by slave ships, and masses of Africans were stolen from their land. From this mix came many stories, many families, and many struggles. Although I stayed true to much of the historical facts, this is a work of fiction, a story of the almost invisible strings that tie us together in the human journey.

Two small Islands, both former colonies of the Empire, separated by oceans and thousands of miles but joined by servitude and slavery. Two people, Key and Arin, heeding the call of ancestors, joined by ancient strands of DNA, find a way to fulfill the promises made long ago by Aedan and Mack. They also know that they are the guides to thousands of people around the world that have the Ancestral Memory gene. What they don't know is where it will take them next—but they do hope that you will join them on the journey.

ACKNOWLEDGMENTS

Writing may be an act of solitude, but it does not occur in a vacuum. My gratitude goes to Catherine Norris, an educator of all things Irish. She introduced me to the Hill of Tara and the Hill of Slane and provided a deeper understanding of the *Book of Kells*. My thanks go to Kris Sispak, who is not only a phenomenal editor, but she pushed and prodded me to dig deeper and write better. Thanks to all my early readers for feedback and support. Hugs to my daughter, Jen, who was thirty at the time of editing. She was my guide to the world and behavior of thirty-year-old's and kept me on track. And big thanks to my very patient and encouraging wife, Lee Tracy, who assumes that our children and I will always strive to achieve our dreams.

ABOUT THE AUTHOR

Kevin Barry O'Connor performed and wrote for the stage for 12 years, built a global marketing business and has traveled to over 90 countries. As the grandson of Irish immigrants, he holds dual American and Irish citizenship. Kevin lives in Philadelphia with Lee Tracy, his traveling companion and spouse of over forty years. The Key to Kells is his debut novel with sequels on the way.

You can visit the website at www.kevinbarryoconnor.com

ALSO BY KEVIN BARRY O'CONNOR

Key Murphy Thriller Series

The Key to Kells

Threshold

Shake the Jar – coming soon!

Printed in the USA
CPSIA information can be obtained
at www.ICGtesting.com
LVHW052225250924
792182LV00029B/337